Evil in Return

A stirring story of intrigue and violence :
Hitler when a young British soldier is
control.

About the author

Now in his mid-fifties and a businessman recently retired from the tyre industry; he originates from North Staffordshire, but has had homes in Glasgow, The Ivory Coast, and France, and has travelled widely through out Europe, West Africa and Asia. He now lives in East Sussex. He has written a number of articles, short stories and radio plays; this is his first full-length novel. Mike enjoyed turning extensive research and imaginative conjecture into a stirring story of intrigue and violence.

This book is also published in e-book format, details of which may be obtained from www.authorsonline.co.uk

An AuthorsOnLine Book

Published by Authors OnLine Ltd 2001

Copyright © Authors OnLine Ltd

Text Copyright © Mike Cartwright

The front cover design of this book is produced by
Terry Frances Coelho, coelho.moore@virgin.net

The moral right of the author has been asserted

All rights reserved. No part of this publication may be reproduced, stored in a retrieval system, or transmitted in any form or by any means, electronic, mechanical, photocopy, recording or otherwise, without prior written permission of the copyright owner. Nor can it be circulated in any form of binding or cover other than that in which it is published and without similar condition including this condition being imposed on a subsequent purchaser.

Printed and bound by Antony Rowe Limited, Eastbourne

ISBN 0 7552 0045 4

Authors OnLine Ltd
15-17 Maidenhead Street
Hertford SG14 1DW
England

Visit us online at **www.authorsonline.co.uk**

... hope you enjoy the read
Mike Cartwright
12.02

for John

with thanks for their assistance and support to:
Alma, Clare, Julia, Linda and Terry

I and the public know
What all school children learn
Those to whom evil is done
Do evil in return.

"September 1, 1939" (1940)

W H Auden. 1907-1973

—:—

As soon as men decide that all means are permitted to fight an evil, then their good becomes indistinguishable from the evil they set out to destroy.

"The Judgement of Nations" (1942)

Christopher Dawson. 1889-1970

authors
OnLine

Evil In Return

By

Mike Cartwright

CHAPTER ONE

STONE TO BRICK

"You will be the Chief of Police, Judge, jury, executioner, tax collector, Mayor, no, unopposed ruler - King of that bloody town, get it?"

Terry nodded at the overly expressive sergeant who was driving the un-sprung two-ton truck south out of Hamburg. It had taken an hour to negotiate six miles of city ruins. Bulldozers had cleared much of the rubble and created a two-lane road but the surface was pot-holed and uneven. Even at that hour of the morning they had to queue to cross the two Bailey bridges over the river Elbe. There were many military vehicles, mostly trucks, and then there were the civilians slowing everything down. The civilians they encountered carried bundles of belongings wrapped in newspaper and tied with string; others pulled small carts piled high with bits of furniture and bedding; one pushed a wheelbarrow that contained an old lady surrounded by boxes. Occasionally there were bicycles being pushed, never ridden - boxes, baskets or metal baths perched on their saddles, wheels buckled and all tyres flat, each wobbled and wove its way round the fallen house bricks that littered the roadway's edge. Both the adults and children wore multi-layers of drab woollen clothes despite the warmth of the June sun. Everyone moved slowly as though in shock and no one spoke. The people stared ahead blankly. Children, clutching an adult's hand and shuffling their brown paper shoes in the dirty brown dust, rarely glanced at the military vehicles that passed; it was too early in the morning for the soldiers to be generous.

Terry was amazed at the number of people entering the bombed out city in search of shelter, or food, or family. He thought the equally large number of sad people leaving having found no roof, or food, or family, could have warned those entering of the waste of time and effort but they didn't. The silent walkers were mostly women and children and older men and women; the young men were all in camps. Terry knew this for he'd spent the last six weeks in Holland guarding some of them.

Terry Hall's eighteenth birthday was on the 1st February 1945 and the following day he'd visited the army recruitment office in Stafford and volunteered to join the Staffordshire Light Infantry Regiment. After twelve weeks basic training as a rifleman and one week of leave he'd been posted to Leeuwarden, Friesland, in northern Holland. He arrived there on the 9th of May to find the German war had ended and that guarding rather than killing Germans was to be his occupation.

He was to stay at an undamaged two-storey school on the edge of the Dutch town. The upper floor was given over to the British soldiers and officers so dormitories and mess rooms had replaced the classrooms. On the ground floor there was an interview room, a rarely used and poorly stocked medical clinic, an office, a washroom, a guardroom and a large kitchen which continually baked bread and smelled warm, cosy and inviting. The large concrete schoolyard was now an open-air transit camp for prisoners of war. Each morning trucks would arrive to collect the four or five hundred bedraggled cold and weary German soldiers and airmen and each evening different trucks would deliver another four or five hundred replacements. During their overnight stay the prisoners would receive something to eat and drink and be assigned a small area of concrete on which to sleep. If it rained during the night the prisoners got wet.

On one side of the schoolyard was a lavatory block with twelve cubicles. Six of these were for the exclusive use of the thirty British troops based at the school. Six Germans, usually officers, were selected from that evening's guests and ordered to clean these toilets. The six remaining toilets were for POW use and were rarely cleaned. Terry was told that the prisoners came from camps in France, Belgium and even England. Most looked tired and unwashed; they rarely spoke. They proceeded the next morning eastwards into Germany, apparently heading for an enormous POW camp near Wilhemshaven. On arrival at the school the prisoners were counted, three times during the night they were counted and on leaving they were counted. The young captain in charge of the transit post always contrived to have all five counts match. He thought that was what his senior officers wanted and what *he* wanted was a minimum of hassle.

Terry, being the newest British soldier, having the rank of private and having had no shooting experience, was assigned the unpopular duties. He spent most nights on a wooden platform fixed to the roof of the lavatory block. Here he sat holding his rifle and surveying the mass of German bodies sleeping fitfully in the dull light of the Kerosene lamps strung along the schoolyard fence. His post was smelly and uncomfortable. During the day, between departure and arrival of prisoners, he would sleep in his dormitory, wash, eat and write letters home. Once each week he would be excused his night time duties and would visit the town with two or three other soldiers from the school and endure getting drunk with them. All of his fellow troops had been in service for over a year and although often only a little older than himself, they looked and acted differently. Terry found it difficult to empathise with them and much of the time he avoided conversation or contact. The other men's main topic of conversation concerned the imminent but elusive receipt of their demob number. Terry had signed on for two years so demobilisation was a long way away for him.

On Thursday 17th June the captain informed Terry that on the following morning he was to board one of the trucks and travel with it as far as Bremen, then find his way to Hamburg. He was to report to Major Connolly, Governor's Office, Hotel Astrid, Hinter der Kirche 26, at 1600hrs on Sunday 20th where he would then be assigned new duties. It took Terry almost three days to travel to Hamburg and when he arrived at the Hotel Astrid at 15hr15 he was tired, unwashed, unshaven and hungry. The corporal at the hotel reception desk scanned his papers, then showed him to a bathroom and told him to be ready in forty minutes. Within a few minutes the corporal returned and gave him a mug of very hot tea and a thick cheese sandwich. While sitting on the lavatory Terry ate and drank with relish.

At five minutes before four o'clock Terry presented himself again to the reception desk corporal who escorted him to a bedroom, now an office, on the first floor. The corporal knocked on the door and opened it slightly.

"Private Terence Hall, sir," he announced as he leant round the door. "D'ya want him now?"

Inside the room Terry was faced with a tall stocky sergeant who stared at him intently and saluted. Terry returned the salute and turned towards a thin wiry major who was sitting behind a small single pedestal desk. Behind the officer was an unmade bed pushed tightly against the un-curtained window. Terry stamped to attention and shouted too loudly. "Private Terence Hall, 986735, Staffordshire Light Infantry, reporting as ordered, sir."

"Sit down dear chap," the major said, indicating the small wooden dining chair in front of the desk. "Thank you for attending so promptly. Sergeant Wilkes and I have been looking through your service folder."

Major Connolly looked meekly towards the sergeant standing, towering, at the side of the desk and holding a sheet of white paper on which were a few lines of typing. Sergeant Wilkes sneered at the officer, then looked at Terry.

"Bin in Europe five weeks, dun some guard duty, know sod all, dun sod all, Private Hall. That's about it son isn't it?" he said.

"Yes sir," Terry stared at the sergeant who was probably four or five years older than him but who seemed much older, wiser, experienced and confident and old.

"There's sod all on this bit of paper about you 'cos you don't happen to have done much wrong, right?"

"Yes, sir."

The major looked kindly at Terry.

"I have a vacancy for a soldier with initiative, integrity, a cool head, the ability to work and be on their own. Are you such a soldier Private Hall?"

Terry thought about the question for a moment. He considered that everyone was bound to reply positively, so was there a catch somewhere? Would 'yes' be taken as volunteering for this unspecified mission? Would 'no' be a simple way of getting back to the roof of the lavatory block and the stench of five hundred leaking Germans?

"Yes, sir, that seems to describe me," he answered.

"Bit of a loner are you? Ever bin in trouble with the police?" asked the sergeant abruptly.

"Sir, yes I get on fine being alone, but I think I get on in groups too." He looked up and into the sergeant's hard unfriendly eyes. "The police, well I was once done for riding my bike on the pavement in Stoke, but that's all".

"Bin screwing the Dutch girls in Holland?"

"No, sir."

"Why not, are you a Nancy-boy?"

Terry hesitated, but continued to stare directly at the bullying sergeant.

"I was too busy guarding Germans, sergeant, sir."

Sergeant Wilkes relaxed and a slight smile reshaped his thin taught lips.

"Shame," he said, "no chance here in the bloody Fatherland, we've got a no fraternisation order, haven't we major, sir?"

"Yes sergeant we have," Major Connolly looked kindly at Terry, "and if that is what Field Marshal Montgomery has ordered that is what we shall do, or not do, as the case may be. Do you know Private Hall that I have a report right here?" The major pointed to a small pile of documents stacked neatly to his right. "One of our Medical Officers estimates that of the seven hundred and sixty female Displaced Persons who appeared in camps in the vicinity of Hamburg in the first week of this month, ninety percent had VD, mostly gonorrhoea, but possibly twenty percent had syphilis - that is females between the age of eleven and seventy - contracted, possibly, through contact with dirty Russian soldiers. We don't want any of that mess to reduce the effectiveness of the British Army, do we?"

"No, sir," both Sergeant Wilkes and Terry replied in unison.

"Now let's get down to business shall we? I'm Major Thomas Connolly, as you probably know, newly assigned here to the Governor's office. You will be reporting to Sergeant Wilkes, who in turn reports directly to me. We appear to have a shortage of junior officers in this department at present. As you know Field Marshal Montgomery has been appointed Governor of the British Zone of Germany. For the moment he governs via his military personnel, you and me. The population we are responsible for contains, we estimate, some twenty million civilians and two million prisoners of war in good health and one million in hospitals".

Terry felt tired and irritable and could not hear the numbers let alone comprehend their meaning. He shuffled on the hard seat, but the major droned on.

"The total population is increasing daily as displaced persons cross from the Russian Zone. Possibly one thousand each day officially - God knows how many unofficially. More prisoners of war are also arriving from Norway and camps in England and North Africa. Our objective is to release twelve thousand POWs every day; I don't think we have reached that number yet though. All released POWs have been interviewed, interrogated, and priority release is given to those who were, in civilian life, farmers, builders, carpenters and those with some medical training. When we find any SS officers, members of the Gestapo or camp guards, we put them into secure prisons to await trial. You've seen the newspapers and newsreels and are aware of what they've been doing?"

The major stared at Terry waiting for a response. As Terry only smiled back the major decided to continue and hope.

"Field Marshal Montgomery's orders to us are to see that our German population are a) fed, b) get some kind of shelter and c) can receive simple medical treatment to keep disease at bay. These orders will be very difficult to achieve this year, but they are to be our only priorities. Later we may consider transport, communications, road building and things like that. Much of the finances and industry of the country is to be sent back to England and some to Russia as reparations. As the Government of Northern Germany we will feed, house and give medicine to the population in an effort to keep them all alive this year. Here is an English language copy of the message we have distributed to the Germans this month. You will be given a number of German language copies to give out to civilians you will meet."

Major Connolly handed a sheet of paper to the sergeant and continued his monologue in a bored, irritated fashion. He was vexed at having to be on duty on a Sunday afternoon.

"As soldiers we are now required to police the population. Eventually, British and German civilians will replace us. The sooner that happens the sooner we can all go home but I fear it will be some time yet. For the time being all German laws are cancelled. We will impose English law which, in practical terms, means we will use our common sense to maintain order. The Nazi Party and its evil organisations are banned. Former Nazi Party members are now criminals. As a result of this we find that we have no government officers, no judges or prisons, no police force or post offices or radio stations. It would be very easy for us to lose control of the situation here. So, no German is to carry any weapon. Today doing so is a capital crime. Nazi leaders, even at the lowest level, must be watched and we must ensure that they can no longer meet and organise and plot against us. Senior Nazi officials should be arrested and imprisoned. War criminals like them and the SS, Gestapo and concentration camp guards will be tried in a court of law and punished for the terrible things they have done."

At this point Sergeant Wilkes interrupted. "I'll explain the problems and rules regarding that matter, sir. Don't confuse our young private too much."

"Yes, that's quite right sergeant," the major went on hurriedly. He had a whole list of other items to cover and he was playing in an Officers Mess bridge tournament that evening. "Field Marshal Montgomery needs to send some of us to face the Japanese in order to finish them off. As you know we need lots of troops to guard the POWs and food stores and military arms dumps. For some reason we have stopped destroying German tanks and guns and have them parked all over the place. We have to guard and organise the German soldiers we're using to repair buildings and roads and bridges; I hear we have over five hundred thousand German soldiers still in uniform working for us. Many of us have been fighting for a long time and want to go home on leave or better still for good. As a result of all this we haven't been assigned many officers to look after the German civilian population in our zone. We in the Governor's Office are very thin on the ground. You are still with me Private Hall, aren't you?"

"Yes, sir, I fully understand but I'm wondering what you want me to do, sir".

"I'm coming to that matter directly. I've been given the area around Luneburg to control - starting about seven miles southeast of Hamburg, to fifteen miles north of Hanover. Look here on this map.

You can see that the eastern boundary is the river Elbe, on the other side of which are the Russians. Although we still have some tanks over there, I understand. Now look carefully". The major's thin, short index finger waved enthusiastically over a pre-war Michelin map. "See this road running from Luneburg, bowing slightly easterly and heading towards Hanover? Yes? Jolly good. Well Sergeant Wilkes patrols that road. He's responsible for the people in each of those little towns and villages and in most of them he's placed one or two of our soldiers to act as his policemen. These policemen enforce law and order and carry out instructions as we receive them. Each week I'm given a number of DPs, displaced persons, and released POWs to distribute across my area. I allocate a proportion of these to Sergeant Wilkes and he shares them among his men. They try to place the people into the towns and farming districts to make best use of any skills they may process. Remember, POWs returning to their hometowns will probably be farm workers and are therefore very useful with regard to our orders to feed the whole population. Sergeant Wilkes tells me that there has been no fighting along his road, so little or no damage is evident. I do not allocate any building workers to him, nor has he any need for German army workers." The major paused, looked stern and leaned towards Terry.

"Now Private Hall we come to the point you've been waiting for, I think. You are to be the representative of the Military Government of the British Zone of Germany and of Field Marshal Montgomery, in the small town of Altewiese, the town furthest south on Sergeant Wilkes's road. For the moment you will act for us as Mayor of the town. If there is already a mayor there when you arrive, he will certainly be a Nazi, so dismiss him. You have your card with the Field Marshal's orders regarding non fraternization with Germans, don't you? You may find the post a little lonely as you will be the only soldier we can spare at the moment. Here's a copy of the message given to the people on 10th June on that subject. Sergeant Wilkes has a batch of copies for you to distribute." Terry was stunned. He wanted to ask what a mayor did all day, but the major ploughed on.

"We are very short of communications equipment. There is no telephone or postal service. I can't issue you with a two-way-radio, as we have no spares just now. The sergeant will visit you twice each week. Sergeant you tell him the strict rules regarding your contact."

"I'll be visiting you in Altewiese at eleven o'clock precisely, every Tuesday and Thursday," the sergeant said with some force. "We'll have a meeting place arranged and you will bloody well be there. If you're sleeping late or you're half way through a wank and don't turn up, we'll assume the locals have shot you. I'll then have to send for a regiment of tanks to find your body and punish the locals. It would be too embarrassing for me to then find you swaning about alive, so I'd probably shoot you myself and say it was a Nazi what did it. So always be there at eleven o'clock. If I didn't show up for whatever reason I'd send one of my men. You'll meet some of 'em soon. You got the message Hall?"

"Yes, sir", Terry replied instantly, although he was starting to feel uncomfortable and beginning to dislike the idea of his new assignment.

"Finally, Private Hall," the major said, "we want you to carry some sign of authority, apart from your rifle, so, with effect from sixteen hundred hours today you have been promoted to the rank of lance-corporal." The major smiled and after a moment continued, "and from six hours tomorrow you are to have the rank of full corporal. The paymaster will adjust your army pay accordingly, but it may take a few weeks to organise. I give you my congratulations on your promotion and I'm certain you will be a splendid NCO."

"Thank you, sir, I'll do my best."

Sergeant Wilkes signalled to Terry that it was time to leave.

"We'll be off to the stores now sir, to get a few stripes for this young man. I've already collected the equipment he'll need. I want to be on the road at zero six hundred hours in the morning so I'll arrange for him to eat early and get a good night's sleep. You'll be sleeping in one of the rooms here so there'll be no chance of getting clap."

Terry rose, went through the standing to attention and saluting routine and wanted desperately to find writing paper. He felt sure his Mum and Dad would be overjoyed with the news of his promotion.

Before dawn the next morning Terry rose, washed, shaved, cleaned his boots and rifle, enjoyed a splendid full English breakfast and was standing on the front step of the Hotel at five minutes to six. He stood in his battle dress uniform, his beret correctly angled on his head, his greatcoat and helmet draped over his green canvas sack of belongings. He wasn't wearing his coat for he found this early Monday morning warm and in any case he liked to check the stitching on the bright white stripes on each arm of his tunic. At one minute to six a small, dumpy, camouflage-painted, two-ton army truck pulled up at the kerb. Sergeant Wilkes emerged from the driving seat, curtly bid Terry good morning and untied some of the ropes holding a black tarpaulin sheet over the hidden load on the rear of the truck.

"Put your coat and kit bag in here, but keep the rifle with you," he said. "You'll be riding shot gun today, I'll do the driving."

Terry swung the bag and coat over the sideboards of the truck and noticed that already loaded were some green metal ammunition cases and small wooden crates. From the shape the tarpaulin was taking nearer to the cab end there were also three ten-gallon oil drums. The sergeant pulled the tarpaulin tight over the sideboards of the truck and then arranged four thin damaged planks of wood across the top of the covered load. He passed ropes over the planks and tied these firmly to the side hooks below the truck's loading bed. The process took some minutes and Terry watched but made no comment.

"Right off we go then," Sergeant Wilkes spoke loudly as he crashed the gears and the truck sluggishly pulled away. "Had a good breakfast? Good. Carrying standard issue in your bag are you? Good. Bin given forty rounds for your rifle? Good. The rifle's bin cleaned this morning, I can smell it. Good. Hold it so as the nice passive civilians can see it shine. Good. We're going to see a lot of poor civilians for the next hour or two and some of them are so desperate, hunger I suppose, that they might try to cut the ropes, remove the planks, cut through the cover and nick some of our precious cargo. But it would take all of thirty seconds for the most desperate to do that, by which time you'll have shot their bloody heads off. Get it? Your rifle and the ropes, planks and covers give us a good chance of getting a full load through to our needy base".

The sergeant was driving expertly and quickly past rows of demolished grey stone buildings. He rarely looked at Terry. He appeared to sense the nodded replies Terry gave to his questions, or perhaps he didn't care what the replies were. He wore a short brown leather coat without stripes or insignia over his uniform. The coat was dusty and had patches at the elbows and cuffs. He held the thin metal steering wheel firmly with both tanned oily hands. There were openings but no glass in the windows of the truck doors, nor behind them overlooking the load. Terry soon came to realise that the debris dust would eventually coat him and his newly sewn stripes.

"What do you think of him, our erstwhile commanding officer? Major Connolly, he of the limp wrist, spine and willie, a toss pot of the first order." The sergeant had begun to speak again. "He was a local government officer in Civy Street and bin in the catering corps till now. What a weak arsed bastard he is, but I must say he has his uses. Signed me a wad of requisition forms blind yesterday, he did."

They were travelling south through the suburbs of the heavily bombed city, using the right hand side of the road. Terry sat in the passenger seat on the left of the truck and the sun was beginning to warm him a little too much. He shuffled his rifle about, trying to find a comfortable position for it.

"Hold tight to that buggering thing," the sergeant instructed. "We don't want one of these refugees snatching it off you. They'd sell it within five minutes, I bet. Right, let's get settled in, it'll be two hours to our first stop, so if you urgently need a piss or shit, hard luck. When we get to my little patch I don't like us to give the civilians any of our last names or numbers. I'm not sure why, it just seems safer. Among ourselves, me and the boys in our section that is, I'll call you Terry. If there are any bloody Germans in earshot, I'll call you Corporal. Among ourselves you can call me Sergeant and in front of Germans you call me Sergeant. Got it? Good. Now, while I negotiate our little darling two-ton Tessy past this damned overturned shitty water tanker, or we'll be here all sodding day, you tell me about Mister Terence Hall and his recent life in Blighty".

The sergeant gently reversed the truck, then steered it through a brick jungle of a railway yard, over the remains of a small shop, down a side street and back on to the main road south. During these manoeuvres Terry told his story.

"My Mum and Dad own and run a fruit and vegetable shop in Stone in Staffordshire."

"I know Stone, bin near there a few times," the sergeant interrupted, but Terry speaking even louder persevered.

"I've been working in the shop since I left school. My Dad wanted for me to get a market stall set up in Stafford or even Hanley, but we can't get any extra produce with the rationing and everything. I felt I needed to get away from my Mum and Dad for a while and when no call up papers came, I just volunteered for two years. You'll think I made a mistake and you'd probably be right. I miss my home life a lot. I've been writing home almost every day. I've taken a few girls to the pictures in Stone, but nothing serious came of it. I'm therefore not married and have few ties. At school, I was pretty average at most things. Since I was nine I worked in the shop, so my reckoning was good, but division and stuff, I found a bit complicated. Strangely the only subject I really liked was art. Not the actual drawing or colouring, but reading books about it - the history and techniques and styles of various artists. I discovered I could understand what it was all about. My classmates gave me a hard time; they thought the subject was sissy. I always worked in the shop on Saturdays and school holidays so didn't go to Stoke or Wolverhampton to watch the football, or play games with other kids at the weekends. That's why I've become a loner as you called me yesterday; I don't mind, I don't know any different so I'm quite happy. I was hoping that a couple of years in the army would show me more of the world and give me some new ideas. There's nothing wrong with being a greengrocer, but what are the alternatives that's what I want to know."

The sergeant laughed loudly and shouted above the engine noise as the truck laboured up a slight gradient.

"Alternatives.... you're going to have some alternatives in Altewiese that's for sure. You will be Chief of Police, Judge, jury, executioner, tax collector, Mayor, no, unopposed ruler, King of that bloody town, get it?"

The truck turned left at the next crossroads heading directly into the bright sun. Both of the men had to squint and occasionally shield their eyes from the glare. At the junction, a roughly painted road sign had indicated that they were now moving towards Luneburg and that it was three miles away. There were fewer military and no civilian vehicles on this stretch of road. The refugees were all facing them; no one was walking in an easterly direction. The city had given way to open countryside with few trees but vast overgrown meadows void of cattle or sheep. Rarely now were there burned out tanks or trucks lying at the roadside. The farmhouses were, with few exceptions, undamaged and looked picturesque and tidy, but empty of farm animals or activities. The malaise seen in the eyes of the pedestrians seemed reflected in the countryside and buildings they passed. The walkers walked and the grass grew, everything else was standing still, nothing was happening, or happy.

"I'll tell you a bit about me if you like," the sergeant spoke again. "I left school without qualifications and started work in a warehouse in Nottingham. You'll know from my accent I'm from Nottingham. Then I got the chance to drive a lorry. I quite liked that although most of the time it was down to London with a load of cigarettes, then back with rolls of newsprint paper. I never knew my parents, they pissed off when I was born. My Aunty Elsie bought me up. It was OK. When we could see the war was going to happen my Uncle Fred got me a job driving a lorry for one of the local coalmines, delivering coal to factories all over Nottinghamshire and Leicester. Uncle Fred had seen action in the first war and the canny old sod knew that working with coal would probably keep me from being conscripted. He always told me to avoid the military. Anyway, the job paid well enough, so I got married to Dorothy, rented a little terraced house and we were talking about starting a family. Early 1942 that was. I was twenty-five. Then what happens? I get the call up papers through the post. We were well and truly pissed off I can tell you.

After basic training, where I made sure I didn't excel at anything, I didn't know where I'd be sent. The dangers of being shot at in

North Africa, or to a posting in the south of England to be shot at by the invading Nazi bastards, Dorothy was rightly worried I can tell you. You know it's a rule of the army to assign you according to your worst skill? Like if you're the best London chef and cross-eyed to boot, they'll send you to be an aimer for an artillery unit; and if you are a gamekeeper and the best bloody shot in training, you'll end up in the catering corps. Well there must have been an almighty cock up, 'cos me being a lorry driver, I was sent to the Royal Corps of Transport as a lorry driver. Now it's an unwritten law of the army to post men as far as possible away from their homes. The Scotsman always ends up in Kent and the Dorset type is sent to Inverness; well there must have been another almighty cock up with me, cos I get posted to Nottingham. So seeing as we must be ever so lucky, Dorothy and I decide we'll have a baby anyway. I'm driving all over the country, but we find time to do the necessary. The sort of journey I get is to Liverpool docks to collect some American wooden crates and deliver them to an army base near Stone in Staffordshire. I did that a few times, that's how I know your hometown. When on that run I'd billet at a pub called the *Labour In Vain* in a little village near the base, you'll probably know it.

So now it's early 1943, Dorothy has this enormous bulge in her stomach and I'm driving a load of very highly explosive, high explosives from Bristol to the frequently bombed barracks in Maidstone and it's cold and wet and I'm feeling tense and uneasy, expecting the bombers to attack my route through South London, and North Kent, which is what they normally do. I'm driving through the night under escort, 'cos the load's special and what happens? I'll tell you what happens, the Gerry bastards decide to drop a few bombs on the coalmines of Nottingham. Mostly they miss but they got Dorothy. I wasn't allowed to see her before the funeral as she was pretty much a mess, I'm told. Bloody ironic isn't it?" Wilkes was silent for as long as it took for him to scan the rear view mirror screwed to the door frame of the truck.

"I spent a bit of time with Uncle Fred and Aunty Elsie, and then went back to driving. Like you, lorry drivers are loners, you know. Spending a lot of time with their own thoughts. It was at those times that I came to terms with the death of Dorothy, with its fatality. To tell the truth I still haven't laid her to rest in my head, but the hurt is almost all gone. I don't carry photographs of her now; it got too morbid. What I did do was ask for a transfer to a fighting unit. I wanted to get a few Gerry bastards to pay for those misdirected bombs they dropped on Nottingham, but nothing happened. The first six months of last year were very busy though. Moving equipment from Liverpool to the south coast. We didn't know then, but it was all for the Normandy invasion, D-Day."

They were entering the outskirts of Luneburg. The truck slowed to wind its way through the busy military market town. There was little damage to the roads and buildings and very few civilians on the dusty dry streets.

"Then I gets this strange consignment and delivery address," the sergeant continued, "six crates of top secret equipment. Collection from Liverpool docks on the 10th July and delivery to C in C, 21st Army Group, Caen, France, no later than 16th July. I'll say it was strange 'cos at that time Caen was still in German hands. Anyway I got my lorry through to Caen by the 15th, just four days after it fell to us. I even saw Montgomery and shook his hand. I still have no idea what was in those crates. Since then I've been driving lorry loads of stuff up to our front lines as we advanced from France to here. It was quite near here that Monty took the surrender on the 5th May. I didn't see it but the bloody party we had that night was something special. I got this assignment only five weeks ago. Rank, you ask? Well I've been up and down like a barmaid's knickers. I was made a sergeant major when I arrived in Caen. Then I got caught transporting some goods that I shouldn't have. I was trying to repatriate a nice volume of Calvados, via the docks in Le Havre, to a colleague in Portsmouth. The supply boats were all travelling back empty, so I thought my bottles would act as ballast. Unfortunately some nosy unbribable shit of a major did not. I got reduced to lance corporal and lost a lot of leave. Our new leader, Master Battor Connolly, gave me two stripes back when I joined him here in Luneburg last month." They were moving slowly down a wide tree lined main street.

"Look, look over there, the next road on the left, that's Ulzener Street, where one of our smart interrogation teams let Himmler kill himself. It was the end of May and a right stink it caused. War criminal number one since Hitler's dead. I think it was some of our transport boys that picked him up from a roadblock not far from here, just down the road a bit. Reich Marshal Heinrich bloody Himmler and those silly intelligence buggers let him die on them. I reckon they were squeezing his bollocks too hard and he snuffed it. Himmler, he was chief of the SS, Gestapo, the camps and all the horror stuff. We're only twenty minutes drive from Bergen-Belsen and some lads were telling me about what they found there. Bloody awful it must have been. Reich Marshal Himmler was probably the richest of the Nazi big wigs having stolen all the money from the Jews. I wonder if one of our intelligence officers was being intelligent and asking old Himmler where he'd hidden all his gold.

Sod it. I'd have squeezed his bollocks to get that information. Which brings me nicely to the matter of our arresting bad Germans."

They were leaving Luneburg and travelling south over a virtually treeless heath. Thorn bushes and scraggy tufts of grass covered the ground as far as they could see. The road was in good condition, only rarely being broken and uneven where tanks had crossed and re-crossed the concrete surface.

"You've heard what the major had to say about bad Germans and you've seen the list of targets we should be looking to arrest and send for trial. Down here, and after this next road block, we will be entering my parish - this is where reality begins. I would guess that ninety percent of the population of Altewiese voted Nazi and seventy percent are full party members. So if you arrest that lot you won't have much of a bloody town left. To make things happen you will need to use some Nazis; the bastards are good organisers and can be hard working. They're no longer arrogant goose-stepping shits, but you won't find many good Germans 'cos there aren't any. Now remember, I like an easy hassle free life, with a minimum of forms to fill in and reports to write. If you find, for example, that one of your flock was a Gestapo policeman with a very nasty record of doing away with POWs, you could arrest him and give him to me. I'd then have to take him to Luneburg and I'd be filling out reports for a week and I would not be happy. He'll be put in a prison for two or three years and when his turn came he would have a fair trial, be found guilty and hung. But, there is another way. You arrest the bugger, you make sure he is guilty, you shoot him. That way you will have saved the taxpayer a lot of expense, save the army a lot of time and he'll be just as dead. Most importantly you will have not caused me to be unhappy. Got it? Good. You can tell me what you've done, but no written reports for God's sake. If his family take the unusual step of complaining to a higher authority, which means me around here, I'll shoot the moaning shites. So you've nothing to worry about. If in doubt ask Tommy Gun, he's always right, 'cos no dead bugger's going to argue. If you find a really top Nazi, like Himmler, that's different, but there's no way that a really big Nazi will bother to visit a quiet backwater like Altewiese."

They had arrived at a red and white barrier pole, shaded within a small and unique copse of trees. A corporal approached the truck and smiled broadly at Sergeant Wilkes. While they chatted Terry glanced to his left and spotted the rear of five Sherman tanks under camouflage netting. There was a tent and men were brewing tea. Terry was sure that there was something wrong with the scene, but couldn't see what. The barrier pole was lifted and Tessy chugged out of the shade and on to the road across the open and featureless heath. Terry glanced back and realised that the tanks were all facing east. Their guns were pointing at miles of short gorse bush. They were not positioned to support and strengthen the check point. Terry wanted to ask Wilkes why this was, but the sergeant had begun to shout again.

"Near Osnabrook, I'm told, there's a warehouse containing two million German rifles, which we're keeping in good working order for some reason. Two million bloody rifles, who the fuck counts that lot every day? If some of those rifles went missing and ended up among the ex-SS soldiers, we would have trouble, it would be dangerous. Today our laws state that Germans cannot carry weapons of any kind. It's a capital offence. If you see a German with a popgun, you shoot the bugger. I mean shoot the bugger dead. You can't afford the time to think about it for the evil bastards will take advantage. You're very young and have had no fighting experience, so it will be hard for you, but Terry, for my sake as well as your own, don't let them bugger about with guns. That is an order. On the other side of the Elbe the Russkies have killed all the men and raped all the women. Over here the Germans are living in comparative paradise and they know it, so you shouldn't have too many problems."

Terry grew even more concerned. Had he actually been ordered to execute war criminals and armed civilians? Would Sergeant Wilkes confirm the unwitnessed order if something went wrong? He was going to be alone in a strange town and he didn't want any trouble or danger. He was no longer looking forward to what he'd thought of as his new adventure.

"You've seen the orders regarding fraternization and you should read Monty's latest letter to the Germans. I have an English copy for you in the file. Don't take the orders too literally. They're meant for the normal service man, but in our case we are more like policemen and we will have to converse with lots of Germans. If you settle in nicely and your conversations lead to the odd fuck, just make sure there are no witnesses and that your dick is still clean. Got it? Good. Monty may be the world's best General but he knows sod all about the real world. He's been an officer since he was a kid and has had no experience of living as a civilian. He's been given this job to do and he's trying to bluff his way through it, but he can't use an armoured division to run a bloody country; a bloody country is shopkeepers and lorry drivers and market traders and babies and death and things. His absolute priorities for food, shelter and medicine.... it's meaningless. Transport and commerce should have been given all the effort and priority. What's the use of farmers growing loads of potatoes for the starving city people if there's no way of moving the potatoes from the farm to the city?

There's tons of cement in store in Denmark but we have allocated no lorries or petrol to move it to Hamburg or Berlin. We are not repairing the railway system fast enough either. Without lorries and spare parts and fuel and lubricating oil and train lines to move things from were they're stored to where they're needed we're wasting our time. And commerce too; we must have active markets full of things to trade, even luxury goods. A farmer will grow enough to feed himself and his immediate family and then he works hard growing extra produce to take to market. There, he can turn that extra produce into value, barter, or cash, so that he can get hold of some luxury he wants for himself or his family. If a farmer's wife demands a pair of silk stockings or she won't let the farmer have a fuck for a month, he'll go out and grow an extra bag of vegetables, so he can secure some happiness. If there are no silk stockings at the market, why should he bother growing the extra vegetables? He's not going to fuck for a month, so why not take it easy and sit in the empty veggie patch and wank. No incentive, see. If the stockings aren't available 'cos we have no civilian transport to move them, or the factory that makes them is closed 'cos we haven't allocated fuel, or material, or labour to it, then the extra food will not be grown. I use silk stockings as an example; it could be metal buckets, dresses, kids' shoes, coffee, anything that is manufactured and can't be grown by him and his neighbours.

You've read about the shortage of coal. There's no coal to be had. I've bin told there are over one hundred and fifty coalmines working today in Northern Germany. So where is all that coal going? What little private transport does exist is moving it from the mines to the ports. It's going to England. Well I agree with that but why not increase the output at the mines and send the extra coal to the factories here? Why not, 'cos there's no way of moving the extra coal to the factories, 'cos we've got no petrol for the lorries or tracks for the trains. Transport again, you see. So, that's where we, our little unit here, can play our part to help rebuild the economy. We can do some haulage and trading on the side, in our off duty hours. We buy some foodstuff, or timber products from the people in my parish. We take it to Luneburg, or as far as Hamburg where it is desperately needed. There we sell it and buy some luxuries, silk stockings, metal buckets, candles or whatever is available. We bring this stuff back to our villagers and townsfolk and exchange it for more food or timber and off we go again. It's a nice little co-operative; our community is happy, the city people are a little happier; it's simple.

Now of course we must be rewarded for all this effort, that's only right. We should make a small, perhaps reasonable, profit at each turn, to cover incidental expenses and salaries. You're a shopkeeper, you know the rules. The profit is useless if it's in Reich Marks, so we must turn it into items we can eventually sell in Blighty to give us good old Pounds Sterling. We acquire gold watches, jewellery, things that will be easy to carry back with us. We never steal from any of these poor bastards. I think all looters should be shot. We are honest traders, buying and selling and moving goods. Looting, you've seen Monty's letters to us all on that subject, we're not allowed to use any German property without written approval from a senior officer. If you are General Horricks and you want to use Goring's old staff car, you'll need Monty's written permission. Jesus bloody wept. So, if we here want to use a German's car or lorry, or use a hotel for a billet, we have to have an officer sign a requisition form. What we may want is for military use otherwise we can't operate properly, and even so we need the damn form signed. Can you imagine how long that would take? Weeks! The lorry would have rusted away by the time we get permission to use it. Monty knows nothing about the real world but luckily I've found that if you shout the obvious, very loudly into the pansy ear of Major Connolly, he understands. I'll be giving you ten signed but blank and undated requisition forms when we reach Altewiese. Ask me when you need more. They have to be filled out in quadruple. When you use one of the forms the top copy is for the German owner of what you want; you keep the second one in case some nosey officer queries anything, and you give me the other two copies. Those I take to Luneburg for filing, where they will be lost forever. What will you need to use them for? Security and comfort, mostly. You choose your billet, say it's someone's house, give the house owner the top copy and he will receive compensation from the Government for the use of his house, or lorry, or whatever. Come on Terry, don't ask me that stupid question, no German is in a position to refuse you anything, you have the gun remember. Have you not been listening to me? We aren't the bloody Russians, kill then ask. We borrow and the German will eventually get some compensation, one day. Which reminds me to tell you about our own compensation arrangements. We get an allowance to help run the towns and villages. It's in German marks, some notes and lots of coins, so it's pretty worthless to us personally. With it and the requisition forms, we should be able to arrange things so that we live in some comfort without needing to use any of our own pay. I suggest you let me tell the Paymaster's Office to bank your corporal's pay which will give you a bit of money when you get home.

I would like you to assist your colleagues and me in doing some honest trading; buying and selling things with the locals. Each month

I'll calculate the net profit we've earned and you'll get your share. I'll be paying you in jewellery, possibly, but it'll be very good stuff. When on leave you take it with you and cash it in; Stafford or Paris, wherever you choose to go. You'll get one week's leave every five or six months and I would expect each leave you could buy with your share a market stall in Hanley, or ten clean Parisian Countesses per night to fuck. You're a sensible lad though and I bet you'll put it into a safe place and save it till the end of your service, am I right?" Terry nodded silently. The sergeant changed gear abruptly and went on, "Another thing I've noticed about you is that you don't smoke".

"When I was ten, I tried two Woodbines in the school bog. I puked for a week and never dared try again, but sergeant I've not seen you with a fag either?"

"I smoked a lot once," Wilkes replied. "Most drivers tend to chain smoke. Dorothy smoked too, but on the day we moved into our own home we both stopped. We couldn't afford the house rent and to buy fags. Neither of us cheated and I've never wanted to start again since. What have you been doing with your allocation of army cigarettes?"

"Selling them to other blokes in my unit," Terry answered.

"You can do the same here, but I'll give you a bit of advice. Keep them with you and use them to buy things from the civilians in Altewiese. There are very few fags available on the civilian market and they are therefore valuable. I learned last weekend that in Hamburg, two fags could buy an all-night fuck in a docklands brothel. Cigarettes are becoming more acceptable than Marks and I think things are going to get worse. Understand? Good. I'll be visiting you on Tuesdays and Thursdays and I'll bring you your post office mail, cigarettes and things you might want. Have a shopping list and your letters to your Mum and Dad ready for me each visit. Newspapers - which do you prefer? Yes, we get the Army newsletters and pamphlets and posters, but you can tell me which newspaper you prefer and I'll see if I can pick up a few copies each week for you. What do you mean you don't read a bloody newspaper, who's talking about bloody reading? At your Dad's shop in Stone which newspaper do you use to wipe your arse?"

They both laughed at his nonsense, but Terry was still feeling uneasy. They were getting closer to his posting but he felt that he knew nothing of what to expect; of what he was really going to have to do. He was beginning to suspect that the sergeant's high volume diatribe, apparently giving advice and instruction, could well be fifty percent bullshit, but which fifty percent, that was Terry's worry. He decided to go onto the offensive and interrupt the sergeant and ask the questions that would help his understanding of the situation he was to face.

"How many bad Germans have you had to shoot in the past five weeks, sir?"

"What, well none myself, but Hardaker's done two of them in. Shot the bastards full of holes, he did. Hard bastard is our Corporal Hardaker." Before the sergeant could expand on this topic, Terry interrupted.

"Have you found many Germans carrying weapons?"

"Only two," he replied. "Those two were the one's Hardaker took care of."

"Are there already some German policemen in your towns and villages?" Terry asked quickly.

"Sure there are and the first thing we had to do was disarm them. All the one's we've had to deal with so far have been very placid, shell shocked by the defeat. You can see it in their faces, white and gaunt, with staring eyes. For the moment it's like herding sheep."

"Do we have any civilian doctors, or any of our Medical Officers available to help with the sick?"

"No," the sergeant said, "and that's going to cause us big problems before too long, I feel. There's a chemist's shop in Altewiese that I've not had the chance to inspect yet. The only other chemist is in Bad Farven, the place we're about to come to. The old people who run it are useless, frightened, or untrained I think. I've already found a contact in Hamburg who says, at a price, he can get us most drugs and medicines but I'm not sure which one's we actually will need. I've asked the local people to tell me where all the doctors disappeared to. They say that they were all taken into the armed forces, even the older ones and none have as yet returned. I reckon there must be ten or a dozen trained nurses around here somewhere, but none of them have volunteered their services so far."

"Do we have a medical problem," Terry interrupted again, "an epidemic?"

"No, not that I'm aware of, but there will be soon I feel sure. The DPs we have received since we've been here - three hundred of them up to last week - are in a dreadful state. They arrive here dirty, starved, lice ridden and raped; before long one of them will bring us Typhus, or some other horrible disease. When that happens Major Connolly says he will request MO assistance for us. It will be too late by then, is what I say. I'm going to give you a box of medicines I picked up, I don't know what they are, but see what you can do with them. It's the refugees that bother me most, the numbers are just too big. Connolly is arranging for us to get another one hundred on

Thursday, plus twenty released prisoners of war. At least that number again next week. We don't have the systems or organisation to handle these numbers. The locals only want to accept the people they know; they fear that there won't be enough food for any more population. They always want the Displaced Persons to be sent to the next town. It's becoming a right pain in the arse."

"How many lads are there in our unit Sergeant?"

"That's another problem Terry, there isn't enough to handle this job properly. Including you and me there are seven of us. Since we got this posting I've been requesting more men, but all Connolly has come up with is you. On this road of mine and including the isolated farms, I estimate we have twenty-six thousand inhabitants. That is twenty-six thousand old enemies who don't like us and are not yet willing to co-operate with us. Shit, they don't even want to talk to us."

"I don't speak any German Sergeant," Terry suddenly realised.

"None of us speak German, but why the hell should we? They lost the war. We've managed to find a few locals who speak English so we employ them to translate and run messages and organise things for us. We use school teachers mostly."

"But, aren't the school teachers needed in the schools?" Terry asked.

"It's really hard to understand the position we find ourselves in. There are school buildings, there are teachers and there are schoolbooks, but there is no education. The schoolbooks are full of Nazi propaganda, I'm told, and so we can't let them be used. In England who pays the school teacher to teach our kids?"

"The government does," answered Terry.

"There is no Government here in Germany today, we cancelled it remember. So the teachers we find are all unemployed. Some teachers have kept on teaching, without pay, but not many. It's the same with the police; we found the constables were in the police stations on duty, but they have no pay and until we arrived they had no superiors. If they arrested someone for pissing in the street what can they do with the pisser? There is no law against pissing in the street, because there is no law, nor judges, nor courts. If you decide, when you reach Altewiese, that you'll give some of your expenses to the police constable as a weekly wage and you tell him you don't want any pissing in the street, there is a good chance there will be no pissing in the street. Why? Because you and only you, have the power to punish the pisser. Tommy Gun, again, get it? Good. The policeman will do as you say because you have the authority of the conqueror, money and the only gun. His old bosses are all sacked, in prison, or dead."

"It seems so unreal. A massive population like this with no laws, or schools. Seven weeks ago they had armies, a Government, systems, strict rules, a police force with the power of the Gestapo, businesses and banks and now nothing."

"That's correct Terry. Now you're seeing the picture. It's our job to replace all of that organisation and control. We've been trained to fire a rifle, drive a truck or whatever; we have little or no experience of politics, the workings of a government, or law and order, but we have been given the job to do just that. It'll be ages before this mess is sorted out and until then it'll be you and me that'll keep these bastards alive. Serious, complicated and impossible is what I think of it, so take my advice, look after number one first. If it all goes wrong in a big way - starvation, disease, revolution, make sure you are safe and comfortable. If the seven of us in this unit stick together, share problems, help each other, we'll be all right. All for one and one for all. Look there, those folk by that farmhouse, they're part of our flock. You can see Bad Farven up ahead, we'll have a break there and you can meet one of your new mates."

They had been travelling through heathland covered thickly with low thorn bushes; recently there was evidence of grazing meadows appearing in patches between the more barren areas but there were no animals to be seen. To the right of the road was a farmhouse with low buildings set in the field behind it. Two old men leaning on a fence rail watched the truck speed by. They did not wave or acknowledge the two dusty British soldiers bouncing in its cab. One mile further on the road led into a large town behind which a tree covered hill rose gently. The tree line stretched along the whole horizon seeming to run in a straight line from east to west. From a distance the town looked colourful, old and very German. Cream and white half-timbered houses were nestling among tall pine and low beech trees. A short stubby church spire pointed out of a group of three storey buildings in the centre of the town.

"As you can see this is quite a big town so we have posted two here, Christine and Tony Lodge," the sergeant said.

"But, I thought no wives were allowed to be with us, sir," questioned Terry. The sergeant looked intently ahead for a moment, then smiled in comprehension. "No, you're right, they aren't. Corporal Tony Lodge is the man I took with me to Hamburg last Friday. The lucky bugger has got a week's leave back home. We managed to wangle a lift to some place in Cambridgeshire, on board a RAF transport plane. Tony is making for Ipswich so that's handy for him. His mate here, who is now on his own for a few days, well, his Mum and Dad must have wanted to take the piss out of their bonny wee lad. You see Mr and Mrs Stein from Glasgow christened their son Christopher. Naturally his Christian name would be shortened to Chris and therefore we now have Chris Stein. Shame for the poor bugger really.

"Anyway when we first got here there were just five of us: me, Christine, Tony Lodge, Arthur Witherspoon and Harold Hardaker. Don Morley arrived a week later for some reason I now can't recall. We were in Two Ton Tessy here and this is the first town we came to. From the German guidebook, we were able to make out that there was a population of over five thousand, but that was in 1930. It was a spa town and attracted a lot of visitors - bird watchers, walkers, that sort of thing. We found four nice hotels. There's a small sanatorium which treated people with TB. When we arrived all of these were empty. The townsfolk were all hiding from us, maybe they thought we were Russians. The whole place was very quiet. At first we considered posting just one soldier here or even none at all as it seemed so peaceful. Then I start to think about it. There are advantages for having two lads working the town, so much so that I even gave them one of two radio sets so they can talk to me any time. Two of them mean we have a chance to have our eyes open all day and night. That way we can check if there's any trouble heading our way from the direction of Luneburg and I'd have some warning and be able to prepare for it. Trouble you ask, well there I mean officers coming to inspect, or pry, nosey bastards and the like. Also, we can spot DPs walking into our parish without permission. The lads here can call me and we can be up here quickly and head them off. Send them back towards Luneburg.

The other reason I felt we needed two blokes here was the number of free bedrooms that were available. Between the hotels, empty houses, unused schoolrooms and the sanatorium, we calculated there must be space to accommodate three hundred guests. The plan was that when I'm allocated a batch of DPs we firstly bring them all here and put them up for a short time, till we know what to do with them. For that we would need two good lads to organise and control what's going on. To assist Christine and Tony we now have six local policemen who we can trust and we manage to have cover for twenty-four hours every day. Tony chose which hotel the two of them would use as a billet and base. It's that one on the right of the town, slightly up the hill; it looks like a Swiss cuckoo clock. It's a nice place, has good views, has proved practical and the lads are very comfortable which is the most important thing. We're going to stop and have a chat with Christine and deliver some stores and post to him."

With his left thumb swinging over his shoulder, the sergeant pointed to the load gently bouncing behind them.

It was just before eight o'clock in the morning when they reached the centre of town. There were a small number of people hurrying along the pavements; shutters were being removed from one or two shop windows. At the crossroads at the edge of the town centre square was a policeman directing traffic. At the moment that Two Ton Tessy drew up to him he had halted six bicycles and seven pedestrians. The policeman saluted the truck and immediately gave it priority and waved it through. He was dressed in a dark brown uniform with cream coloured shoulder and cuff embroidery and wore a small brimless brown hat; he carried no weapons or sticks. Terry thought he looked like the first class platform attendant at Waterloo Railway Station. They had turned right at the crossroads and chugged up a slight gradient passed more closed shops, a hotel and some smart modern houses with overgrown gardens. As they arrived at the front steps of the cuckoo clock hotel, an army corporal emerged from a side door carrying two steaming mugs of tea.

"Bloody brilliant Christine, we made good time and I do need this cuppa," the sergeant said as he took one of the mugs and slurped its contents seemingly oblivious to its just boiled temperature. "This is Terry Hall, our new boy; Terry this is Christine our old boy. You two say hello while I find the lavatory, 'cos I'm dying to have a shit." With that he bounded up the steps and through the large double doors into the hotel reception area. Christine smiled at the back of the disappearing sergeant and turned to Terry.

"Call me Christine, it makes life so much easier. You've been two hours alone with our Sergeant Wilkes, you will need more than a mug of tea to calm your nerves and repair your ear drums."

"Yes, quite a journey so far."

"Come with me, I've organised some burnt toast and jam; it's hidden behind the bar, so it'll give me a chance to add a little whisky to that tea, any problem with that?"

"None at all," beamed Terry.

The toast and whisky bottle were locked in a cupboard beneath and behind the bar. Both men stood like barmen taking a tea break as they looked over the clear counter on to a bar full of dirty and mostly old people. There were more than ten round tables, each surrounded by ten dining chairs, all of which were occupied by elderly men and women. At one table there were ten children aged between five and eleven. A number of middle-aged women scurried in out of the bar bringing large trays filled with cups and glasses of various shapes and sizes, each containing a thick potato soup. As these were placed in front of each sitter, they were greedily lifted and drank.

"Breakfast, second sitting, we didn't receive any bread from the bakery this morning so the poor buggers will have to do without," explained Christine in a sad and weary voice. Terry estimated that Christine was forty years old. Unlike Terry he was dressed in a smart clean uniform, wore no beret and his hair, face, hands and nails were pristine clean. He spoke quietly with a slight but cultured Scottish accent; his lips smiled but his tired eyes seemed close to tears. "In front of you there are one hundred and ten lost souls. At the earlier breakfast sitting we had one hundred and eleven. Let me introduce you to some of them."

Christine spoke as he walked from behind the bar to the first table. There was an old wizened lady in the nearest chair sitting with her back to the two approaching soldiers. She wore a heavy green woollen overcoat and had a bright blue scarf wrapped clumsily around her head of silver grey matted hair. Christine leant over her shoulder and read from a small paper card hanging from a piece of string around her neck.

"This is Anna-Marie Becker, last residence Berlin, last occupation Opera Singer, aged fifty five, looking for family members possibly located in Hamburg. She couldn't have found any, so she got shunted to us for resettlement. She has no money, nor food, nor useful skill. She does have trouble with her bladder you will have noticed, she certainly is lice ridden, is probably in pain, is traumatised and lonely. If I had the right medicine, sufficient hot water and any soap, a larder containing fruit and vegetables, knowledge of her language and the patience to sit and talk to her for a few hours, I feel I might just be able to help her forget her nightmares and to remember an aria and she could sing to me. Having done that I would then move on to the next one of our problems. If I chose to move left it would be to this kind looking old gentleman. Let us suppose that I could help in some way ten of these people today, what am I going to have to do with the fifty more that will arrive tomorrow, or the existing two hundred and twenty-one residents already here? You have heard people say, so what, all Germans are bad Germans; they are getting their just deserts. I would suggest that the only thing that Anna-Marie has ever done bad in her fifty-five years was in 1933 when she put a pencil cross on a ballot paper next to the word Hitler and for that badness she is being disproportionately punished."

They returned to the bar and their mugs of tea. After a few sips Christine calmed down and went on, "Sorry to burden you like this but I wanted to give you a picture of what we are up against that may differ from that given to you by our loving sergeant, who is likely to interrupt and disagree with me when he returns from his ablutions. I'm no longer certain that his bombastic, cavalier attitude is wrong. It's the two ways of looking at the problem we have been lumbered with; I have only one cheese sandwich in the world, do I give it to Anna-Marie and then worry myself silly about the hundreds standing in the row behind her, or do as Wilkes would do - throw the sandwich in to the air and let the best catchers try to survive on it. It's the numbers that are incomprehensible. The field marshals and the generals use a word like 'million' and appreciate that it has seven letters while we at the front line see Anna-Marie, with an endless line of Anna-Maries behind her, and we can help so few of them at the moment.

I find it so frustrating, mind you, you have probably gathered that by now. My mate Tony, he found it frustrating and it made him so angry that he became sick. We'd only been in this mess for three weeks when he starts working twenty-two hours a day and puking if he eats anything. Wilkes did well though; saw the trouble and got him leave in England. I can't see Tony coming back. I think Wilkes would have alerted the medics to Tony's breakdown. Me next you ask? No, I'm frustrated but no longer angry. Two DPs died last night but I never knew them and this nice lady is still here, which is good."

"What are we supposed to do with them?" Terry asked.

"Force the local families to take a lonely one each; put family groups or friends in empty houses and supply them with food, heating, medicine and a chance of employment. Sounds easy doesn't it and I think if the DPs arrived in tens per day our unit could manage, but we are being overrun. There is not enough time, supplies, or local charity to handle the numbers and Wilkes keeps saying it will get worse."

"And you still have the local Nazis to police?"

"After the first week here I realised that their reputation was far greater than they deserved and we've tended to ignore them. The town is running along quite smoothly so what does it matter if the police chief and mayor are ex-Nazi. What I'm now going to do is put some pressure on them to give me a hand with these refugees. I might need to borrow Hardaker to put my point over more forcefully though. We are all guessing, experimenting, in doing this job. The only training I have had to qualify me for this post was at school a long time ago. I was a pencil monitor for one term; forty-four kids in our class, so I was responsible for the forty-four pencils. One morning I counted them and there were only forty-three. I was frantic, crying, kicking doors, shouting at the other pupils; the loss of that pencil meant a lot to me. Here, I have five thousand people, real people, to care for and I keep losing one or two every day and I don't know whether to kick doors or shout."

"Come on you pair," Sergeant Wilkes marched into the bar, "we have to get some of the stuff off the lorry and I want to be on the road again in five minutes. Corporal Hall, visit the lavatory; Corporal Christine come with me and let's get unloading, I have some private words to say to you. Look sharp, both of you."

"Sir," the two shouted in unison. Before leaving the dining bar, Terry took one last look over his shoulder at the urine-scented opera singer and felt depressingly sad.

By the time he rejoined his two comrades at the lorry, they were having a heated argument.

"You cannot do that, sir, no," Christine was shouting.

"We have no bloody choice", the sergeant was shouting back, "Connolly is sending them to you on Thursday whether you like it or not."

"Where am I to put one hundred more DPs and twenty ex-prisoners of war?"

"I'll come up with Arthur and give you a hand. The POWs can be moved straight out to whichever town or village they claim to come from. I can't give Terry here more than twelve DPs to sort out in his first week, but I'll take a further thirty or so for Bachwald on Thursday and thirty for Don on Friday."

"I'm not happy Sergeant and if you haven't remembered the bottle of Scotch I'll be suicidal," Christine shouted.

"Now that's another thing. I searched high and low in Hamburg and couldn't find Scotch anywhere. Rumour has it that it will turn up next week."

"So what alternative did you obtain for me, sir?" Christine asked suspiciously.

"None, I thought you only drank Scotch." Christine saluted smartly, turned, said good luck to Terry and ran through the cuckoo hotel doors into the darkness within.

With Terry as passenger the sergeant drove the truck to the town centre crossroads and turned right, resuming their previous route south. Within a few hundred yards they'd entered a heavily wooded area. As they reached the brow of the hill the sergeant halted the truck, jumped down and lifted the driver's seat, under which were six bottles of Scottish whisky.

"Thank Christ for that. I thought he may have searched through Tessy's drawers while I was having a crap." The sergeant looked over to Terry. "You can have one of these but I've recently discovered it's started making Christine ill again, so it's for his own good to be without it for a bit." He climbed back into the driving seat and set off.

"Christine said that Tony was also ill, sir."

"Yes, I'm not sure whether Christine hitting the bottle again didn't aggravate the problem. Tony always was a worrier though. I met him five months ago; he had been driving lorries too. We palled up for a good weekend in Fecamp in France; eventually we got involved in a bit of private haulage, but he wasn't comfortable doing it, so we dropped him after a few trips. We met up again in Luneburg. By coincidence Connolly had got both of us transferred to his set up at the same time. Funny how these things work out, isn't it? Nice bloke is our Tony, but I doubt if he'll be back here; his nerves are all shot to pieces. He saw action in Belgium; his lorry came under machine gun fire and his co-driver got badly wounded. I think Tony said that he'd lost both eyes. Tony will probably get a medal for what he did; he managed to drag his mate away from the lorry before it blew up.

Did you notice Christine's medal ribbon? I've got some right heroes in this unit. You are too young to have noticed that Christine's ribbon was for an officer's medal. He was a full lieutenant in North Africa before Monty was out there. Saw a lot of action in Libya and captured a load of Italians. He's regular army like you - signed on in 1937, I heard him say once. He did something naughty while in Egypt and did a couple of years in a military prison. He should have been thrown out of the army but his medal and the shortage of experienced men at the time meant he got demoted to private when he got out of clink. Strangely he was happy about that, he wanted to remain in the army. He did something bad in Glasgow when he was younger and his family doesn't speak to him anymore. Keep him away from alcohol and he's the most sensible and intelligent man you'll find. I thought Tony would keep an eye on him, that's why I put the two of them together. I was wrong. I hadn't realised how stressful the job in Bad Farven was going to be. I haven't decided what to do about that particular situation yet; I need to get you settled in first.

The next place, just up ahead there, is only a small village; its called Weyhe. Three hundred and fifty population I would guess - couple of farms, mostly forestry workers, planters, tree fellers, that sort of thing. Each time I pass I slow down and have a good stare at the place. I'll send Hardaker here soon to have a root around. It always seems quiet to me, but it may come in useful before long. I have some ideas brewing."

As they had left Bad Farven the forest had been heavily thinned out but after a mile it had suddenly become dense. It was old forest with tall beech and elm and no evidence of planned planting. As they got near to Weyhe they met conifer trees set in long rows. The village consisted of quite new dark brick houses, with a petrol station, now disused, two shops, now boarded up, and a cafe bar, open and with two customers sitting at a kerbside table. The sergeant pulled the lorry to a stop in front of them and asked them if everything was OK. One of the two answered, unsmilingly, in growling German. He pointed along the road in the direction they were heading. The sergeant asked if they had enough food. The same man spoke more loudly in German and continued pointing. "That's fine then, goodbye," the sergeant said.

"I thought you didn't speak German. What did he say?"

"How the hell should I know, I *don't* speak German. He pointed in this direction so we'll soon find out if there's anything wrong. If he was only complaining about the noise, or some other trivial matter, so what. I'll have one of my local constables ride up here on his bicycle this afternoon, just in case. In another five miles we'll arrive at the town of Bachwald. It's at the southern edge of this forest and it's where we chose to make our base. It's the biggest town by far on this stretch of road. There's still a weekly market and people travel to it from the surrounding farms and villages. The only police inspector in my parish has his office here. There are six or seven churches and chapels and four schools. There was once a big employer here, a timber factory, which before the war made good quality furniture, but lots of it. When we arrived it was closed but you could tell it had been working up to three or four weeks before. It had been mass-producing wooden crates, packing cases, all sizes, from two by two to eight feet high." Terry wondered what a nearly defeated country would want hundreds of packing cases for. What was left to pack and where was it to be packed off to? But there was no chance to ask the loud sergeant.

"You won't have seen many sheep or cattle on our trip today; that's because they've all been rounded up and eaten by the German army over the last six months. When we arrived here the first time we found that some crafty farmers had hidden part of their herds in the forest. I haven't reported this to Connolly because I didn't want our army to take them and ship them back to England, like they've done in other places, I'm told. I believe these cattle, which are mostly dairy cows, could be of great use to us all here during next winter. I've given instructions that no cattle are to be killed unless I say so. We tell the farmers to keep their cows away from this road and hidden as much as possible. The milk is bought into town each morning and distributed in the usual manner by the town's dairies. It's not plentiful, but the price hasn't risen too much. The dairies have to give me twenty percent of all the milk each day. We run some up to Christine for his DP centres and some we give to the local town hall. The town hall officials distribute it to people in most need. I've told the town hall officials that if I catch them stealing any I'll shoot them. You have to be bloody hard on these bastards. A little of the milk we use ourselves and I have one of the dairies make us the odd pound of butter and cheese. We must remember to look after number one, got it? Good. Now here we are at the town and would you bloody believe it, look over there in that field, a bloody cow. If we'd been a nosey officer or civilian from Luneburg or Hanover, we would have found ourselves in the shit. Some bastard will pay for that laxness." Wilkes hit the metal steering wheel hard with his open hand and then slowed Tessy as they entered the town.

"If we were to turn left at the main crossroads, there up in front, we would reach a bridge over the Elbe in about twenty miles. There's nothing on the other side we would want. The Russians have a roadblock on the bridge anyway and won't let us across. Strange that, because I thought all allied troops had free access to all parts of Germany. The problem is that Germans can bribe their way from the other side to ours. Some swim the river at night too. My parish ends seven miles down that road, so any German DPs heading this way, I turn round. The captain in charge of the parish running along side of the river is supposed to handle all new arrivals so we make sure they all stay on his side of our parish boundary. I have the local police man our roadblock twenty-four hours a day. I've put it about five miles down that road. If any unprocessed people turn up in our towns, we ship them back to Luneburg. We can't handle the number we receive officially without having to worry about a load extra. We're turning right here. This road runs to the factory, it's roughly a mile and a half. After that it becomes un-made tracks to three or four cattle farms. There must have been woods all around here once but they've been cut down to feed the factory. That big grey building is the town hall and next to it is the police headquarters. You see there has been no bomb damage at all. It must be a nightmare for the poor buggers in the cities, having to cope with finding shelter as well as food and hospitals."

They drove past terraced houses and a baker's shop with a queue spilling on to the pavement. There were narrow side roads to left and right, each filled with small two storey detached houses. There was washing drying on clothes lines and children playing in the gardens. Pedestrians were walking towards the centre of town carrying shopping bags and often they smiled at the two soldiers as they passed. Eventually the lorry arrived at a high wooden fence with a tall open double gate by which stood a stooped old man holding a short white and red pole. He held it in front of the lorry as it turned through the gate; it was forced to halt. The old man walked slowly to the sergeant's door and demanded in poor, broken English, "What you want? Where your papers?"

"It's me you silly old bugger, let us in," shouted the sergeant. "I told him to check every vehicle coming in or leaving this gate and report the movements of them all," he said quietly to Terry."He's always been the gatekeeper here, probably started before Christ was born, but he is thorough. The big sheds over there to our left are the sawmills and workshops. In front of you is the store. It's a bloody big warehouse as you can see. Over here to the right are the two floors of factory offices. There's Hardaker at the door waiting to greet us; the dopey sod always wears that grin. Our billet is the upper floor and we've boarded up some of the windows for security. There's a canteen on the ground floor which we share with the factory workers. Yes Terry, we've had this place back in production for two weeks. It's not fully in use yet. We have one hundred and twenty working here on a ten-hour shift five days per week. You can just make out the planks stacked inside the warehouse over there. We bring in three or four big trees each day now and they go into the warehouse to dry out; there's a big oven thing they use as well. Eventually, we turn the logs into planks, you know, floor planks. I've managed to find enough fuel to run that red Benz lorry and its trailer up to Hamburg most days; we've made eight trips so far. We have an arrangement with two building merchants to buy them all from us for hard currency and stores. That's jewellery and watches for our bank and general goods which we sell or distribute among our parishioners."

Wilkes pointed to a tall brick chimney. "That's wood smoke you see coming from that boiler house chimney, so nothing's wasted. The steam drives the saws and lathes and other machinery as well as supplying hot water to the office shower block and radiators in cold weather. There used to be eight hundred workers here before 1939 I'm told. We have found ten people in the town who speak good English, but the most important one is the factory manager right here. He's an old guy, but he gets things organised and up and running efficiently in next to no time. He wanted to restart production of furniture next month. I told him there is no demand for that type of thing yet, whereas planks and floorboards are desperately needed in the bombed cities. When I can procure sufficient extra fuel and oil to run a second lorry each day we will double the production of planks and maybe make roof beams. This enterprise is understood by our masters to be strictly civilian; all we do is guard the factory from sabotage, which is not exactly the truth. Jump out and say hello to Hardaker."

The yard floor was concreted and Terry noticed an old lady quietly sweeping a corner of it with a witch's broom. There were people scurrying about and planks being moved and loaded; there was activity and many of the workers were smiling. It was a bright sunny day and Terry felt that this could be a timber yard anywhere in Staffordshire, except that is, for the imposing presence of Hardaker. He was over six feet six inches tall and looked to weigh in excess of twenty stones of solid muscle. He wore battle dress and bright shining black boots which resembled medium sized rowing boats. A small British army issue tin helmet was perched squarely on the top of his enormous round hairless head. By contrast he had thick bushy black eyebrows and despite an obvious close shave he sported a dark shadow on his upper lip and chin. Below his bulbous broken nose his thick lips shone with a wide infectious smile. The features that caught the attention most rapidly were his large hands; here the Tommy gun he carried seemed lost between his long fat fingers. With his empty hand he swallowed Terry's forearm in a welcoming handshake. There had been no sign of a salute to the sergeant, but the sergeant did not object, he simply introduced the two men.

"You call me 'ardaker, I don't like 'arold," he said in a thick Birmingham accent, "you come in 'ere and 'ave a cup of tea, while I unload the truck. It won't take me a minute." Terry had no doubt that Hardaker's hands and arms would handle the heavy load easily, but the sergeant interrupted.

"Some of the stuff is for Don and Terry so let me show you exactly what to take off. Where's Arthur? When you see him tell him I need to speak to him urgently. We want to be on our way in thirty minutes and seeing as you like our new boy Terry so much, you may as well come with us. I don't expect any trouble in Altewiese but you in the back of the truck should frighten any away. Are you listening to me Hardaker?"

"'course I am, Mr Wilkes, Sergeant. A nice little ride in the country would do me fine, so it would."

The three of them removed the ropes, planks and tarpaulin and Wilkes pointed to each item of the newly uncovered load and said to it 'Terry', 'Don' or 'Arthur'. Hardaker began to shuffle each named item into a group and unload all of the 'Arthur's. The sergeant then took Terry into the office block and through to the canteen. There they found Corporal Arthur Witherspoon pouring three mugs of steaming tea.

Arthur was young and untidy. His uniform appeared to be one size too big for him and had creases to indicate that it had been recently slept in; neither of which assumption was correct. He wore no beret or helmet and his hair was greasy and un-brushed, one section sticking straight out resembling a Red Indian's feathers despite the fact that he had washed his hair thoroughly that morning while showering and spent considerable time brushing and combing it. There was a piece of bloody paper sticking to his cheek, ostensibly in witness to his shaving carelessness but actually he had sustained the wound only recently while in the saw mill - the result of a flying splinter of wood being attracted to his general untidiness. He gave Terry a friendly but sad smile.

"Welcome to Wilkes's wonderful wood works," he said. "You look even younger than me. How long have you been in Europe?"

"I arrived on 9th May. I was eighteen in February and you?"

"Four months older than you and I got out here in March. Got a chance to shoot at a German but missed. Mostly doing guard duty until I was transferred to this mob. I'm from Wolverhampton; worked in a tyre factory there before the call up papers arrived. Hoped I might have missed them but my luck ran out. If you need the lavatory there's a block of them over there; that's where the sergeant has rushed off to. He has a problem with his bowels - always shitting. Some of the boys don't like him, but I think he's OK. He is a bull-shitter, but he watches out for his team; we could have had a lot worse. Here he comes now. I've got a bit of good news Sergeant. You know that group of POWs we received on Saturday, well the man at the town hall told me this morning that one of them was a medical orderly in the German air force. I had him taken to the apothecary, chemist shop in Bad Farven, and he says he knows what the drugs are for so I told him to set up a clinic here in the school by the Lutheran chapel. We can use that as a type of hospital. Which reminds me Sergeant, how's Tony?"

"Bad, I can't see him coming back. Well done with the medic, that's fine."

Before the sergeant could continue, Arthur asked Terry what he thought of Hardaker.

"Big lad isn't he, but gentle giant I suppose?"

"Big, yes," Arthur replied, "but gentle, not often. He's been in the army for ten years and nearly killed three of his enemies; unfortunately they were all British officers. He doesn't like rank, does he Sergeant?"

"Not much, but if you treat him right he can be friendly. Although he's spent a number of years in military prisons, he's been in action and received a commendation in North Africa. He has killed a few of our non-English speaking enemies too."

"He doesn't have a family that acknowledge him, but I understand he was born in Dudley," Arthur explained. "His father is rumoured to be a boxer."

"And his mother a Golden Retriever," the sergeant added and then looked sternly at Arthur. "Listen, I want to tell you our plans for the next few days and don't start bleating if you don't like them, I've had enough grief from Christine already. In a couple of minutes I'll drive Terry to Altewiese and we'll say hello to Don on the way. I'll take Hardaker with me. You get one of the constables to cycle up to Weyhe; some old bloke was shouting at us as we drove through a short while ago. Get someone to find out who owns the cow in the field behind the big yellow house and get it moved out of sight of the road. I'll be back by sixteen hundred hours at the latest, unless we have any problems getting Terry bedded in. I know the Benz is loading today and plans to leave early in the morning. Tell the driver and his mate that when they're reloading in Hamburg to leave enough room to pick up fifty DPs from Christine and bring them here. We'll take them to your new clinic and bed them down in the classrooms. Don't tell me fifty is too many for us to handle; we have no bloody choice. Tomorrow morning you and I will pop down to Altewiese and sort things out for Terry, but we will be back in time to meet the Benz and control what happens. On Wednesday Hardaker and I will run up and give a hand to Christine for a couple of hours and then bring back another twenty DPs.

"Shut up and listen. We'll be able to shift twelve of them to Terry on Thursday; he can't take more in his first week. I want the Benz to go to Hamburg again on Thursday and again to collect fifty, yes fifty, more bodies from Christine on its way back. Some of them will be POWs. Next week, on Tuesday and Thursday, Terry, we will run twelve people to you on each day; they will be any released POW's who claim to be from, or have family in, Altewiese and we'll make up the number with DPs. In the weeks after it will be at least that quantity. Arthur, I know we can't handle these numbers; I know it will put pressure on the local food supplies; I know it is a threat to security and health; and I know there is sod all we can do about it. Got it? Good. Now get Terry some fresh milk to take with him and get Hardaker settled on to the lorry. I won't be a moment, I have to visit the shit house again. I reckon it's your rotten tea that's to blame, Arthur."

They drove south out of the town and were soon in pleasant rolling open farmland. Terry spotted a number of cattle grazing in the fields on either side, but made no comment. Hardaker sat with his back against the lorry cab and was humming an unrecognisable tune in a deep throaty drone. After fifteen minutes they passed through a small pretty village with a narrow bridge over a fast running stream; Wilkes said that the village was called Worpswede and that he had spent two full days there ensuring everything was quiet and in order and had managed to spend an hour fishing in the stream; he had caught nothing but he'd enjoyed the relaxation.

Twenty minutes later they crested the brow of a hill and saw the town of Brick laid out in front of them. There was no sign of factory chimneys as in Bachwald, but there were the same number of church steeples - some tall and pointed, but mainly short and dumpy. As they approached the Town Square they passed the garage and the fenced yard of a tractor agent with six or seven tyreless tractors standing on display. They were showing signs of rust and weathering. There was a blacksmith's yard; here there was activity, with two large carthorses standing patiently in the traces of a heavy wooden cart. The town square was large and surrounded by colourful medieval buildings. Many had their windows boarded but others had open shop doors and customers entering and leaving. There was a bakery with a short queue next to a general store which had a meagre display of merchandise; it had both of its doors wide open and people were standing on its step talking.

The lorry crossed the square and stopped in front of an imposing three-storey office building created from thick black wooden beams enclosing bright yellow plaster. A large nameplate had been removed from the façade above the ornate double doors and where it had hung the yellow plasterwork was faded and had become loose. A tall handsome British soldier appeared in the doorway; he wore no jacket but had the sleeves of his army shirt rolled up high on his muscular arms. On his brown leather belt was a black holster from which gleamed the pearl handle of a silver grey revolver. Neither the belt and holster, nor gun, were British army issue. His face showed concern as he smartly saluted the sergeant.

"What's up, I didn't expect a visit from you today, sir?" he said as he leaned in to the driver's door.

"Nothing is up, we have our new recruit here to deliver to Altewiese. Meet Terry Hall - this is young Mr Dandy Don Morley. Don has been settling in here for the last three weeks and done nicely for himself."

"Hello Don," Terry said leaning across the front of the sergeant and shaking Don's manicured hand. "If this is your billet it's quite a place."

"I've moved a couple of times since arriving but this place has turned out to be very convenient. It was the town's Nazi party offices; the swastika took some removing from above the door. It already had two extensive guest bedrooms and a modern kitchen, antique furniture in the dining room, plenty of office space and a large ornate meeting room. I have managed to find a few friendly English speakers to assist me."

"Bloody strange though," said the sergeant to nobody in particular, "the only English speakers here happen all to be females between seventeen and twenty-five and all of them have nice legs and big tits."

"That is not quite correct, sir," said Don seriously, "at least two of the six have small firm bosoms." He smiled broadly at Terry. "You told me to make myself comfortable and I always follow orders, sir, as you know. For example I do not visit them at home and fraternize."

"Don claims his two bedrooms are his offices and the girls his secretaries; they have to work all night sorting out his French letters and I'm bloody jealous."

During this time Hardaker had pulled back the tarpaulin and unloaded an oil drum and two medium size wooden crates. He had taken them into the building and on his final return journey hit Don on the back, winding him badly.

"'ello Don, that's a pretty pistol, where d'ya get it?"

"Found it in one of the cupboards in there," he answered breathlessly. "It is acceptable for me to wear it, sir, and it does impress the locals." Wilkes smiled.

"Make sure you hide it if any officers show up and if you find any more trophies like that remember to share them with your mates. I would hate to have to ask Hardaker to remove that belt off your waist, without unbuckling it, of course. I'll be coming back this way in a couple of hours and I'd like a chat and we need to feed Hardaker, so cook a horse for him. That reminds me, we passed a couple of carthorses; they were parked in the blacksmith's yard. Who claims to own them?" Don looked puzzled.

"I haven't noticed any horses around here. Someone may have been hiding them but more likely they have come up from the estate just north of Altewiese. I'll have one of the girls check that right now. Do you want to come in and wait? Do you need to use the lavatory?"

"No," the sergeant said testily, "it's only four miles to Altewiese, I'll make it that far."

Don looked over to Terry.

"If you have any problems in Altewiese come up here and I'll see what I can suggest," he said in a friendly manner. "We're neighbours now and may need to lean on each other's shoulders, borrow things, like a cup of sugar. I'm sure the sergeant won't mind if we occasionally meet up for a meal or drink. The Nazi Party offices of

Brick have been known to lay on some superb night-time entertainment, but you must remember to bring your own Johnnies."

CHAPTER TWO

ALTEWIESE

With Sergeant Wilkes at the wheel, Terry alongside him still clutching his rifle, and Hardaker joyfully bouncing along on the bed of the truck, they drove from Brick, again heading south. There was farmland to either side of them and a few copses of trees. The road gently rose and fell and weaved between the occasional farmhouse and cottage. After three miles they encountered a thick wood which began sharply at the foot of a steep hill. They crested the hill and almost immediately the wood ended and pasture land began again. They looked down into a shallow valley at the bottom of which they could see a stream running from west to east with a narrow bridge crossing it and to the left of the bridge, and confined to the far bank only, was a small neat town. The downward sloping road they were now on continued over the bridge and then climbed up the gentle gradient of the far valley side, eventually disappearing into another wood at its peak, possibly two miles away. The sergeant put Tessy out of gear and coasted slowly down the hill. He pointed to the distant wood.

"It's nearly thirty more miles in that direction to Hanover; the old Bachwald district council boundary ends six miles south of the town. That is also the end of my parish. I don't know what troops take over after that but their headquarters are in Hanover. The main road between Hamburg and Hanover is way off to the west and must be in good condition because we rarely get through traffic coming this way, which, of course, would involve ten extra miles of driving and almost an hour more in time. The lane on the right, we are coming to it now, leads to that farmhouse and cottage over there. It has an unusually large barn behind it. You may want to check that out when you find time. This is all good grazing land but no cattle to be seen."

"Terry, look behind us," it was Hardaker calling loudly. "See in the wood we just left, over there look; there's three old men chasing cows into the trees."

"I think you'll be able to find your own milk from now on," continued the sergeant, "and this lane to our left now leads firstly to the cottages in front of those rows of glass-houses and then on through that orchard. You can just make out over the top of the orchard trees the roof and corner turrets of a manor house. All the land to the east of the road we are on belongs to the manor estate. The lord of the manor should be rich and influential and could be useful to you. I was here twice before but never met him. It's a nice little market town is Altewiese; welcome to your new home Terry."

They had come to a halt at the middle of the bridge. The stream below was clear, slow flowing and shallow; it was only ten feet wide as it passed under the old stone bridge, but widened out between brown earth banks as it cut its way to their left. After two hundred yards it became even more sluggish and was bordered by thick reed beds. The sergeant watched the water for a moment.

"I doubt there will be many fish in there, pity. Anyway as the road leaves us to climb up the slope you can see houses on the right and on the left, almost in front of us, is a creamery. That faded old sign on its wall reads 'Molkerei Altewiese', which means it once produced butter and cheese, I bet. Looks empty now, but has potential. After it are a few old houses and on the far side of the next turning left, see it about thirty yards up this road, is a garage. There is no petrol or diesel in its pumps but last time I saw some activity in the repair shop. There are three more houses, then a big yard and building that turned out to be an agricultural merchant. That also appears unused but don't be too certain of that."

Just over the bridge there was an un-made road running to the right and a concrete road to their left. The latter ran close to the riverbank for a while and to its right was the village. "This lane," the sergeant said, pointing to the west, "goes up to that farm and then on to another one further up the valley. I believe it stops there; where as the road to our left goes to those factories in the distance. After that it turns into a cart track but I don't know where it ends. The first of those factories is a sawmill and timber yard which might prove interesting, and further on there's an old fertiliser factory; both appear to be silent. We're going to drive into the market square which is in the middle of the town. I saw two hotels there when I came through before and we might find a room available for you for tonight. If we don't, we'll requisition the whole bloody hotel; remember we are not Joseph and Mary, they only had a donkey, we've got Tommy Gun. I'll be back tomorrow with Arthur and we can have a reconnaissance of the whole place and find the most suitable digs for you. I'm very interested in checking out that fertilizer factory. There are people about, see. That bloke on a bicycle heading down the hill towards us stopped pretty sharp when he saw Tessy. He has decided to return home, but that's not suspicious. Remember these poor buggers don't know what to expect from us. When they see Hardaker standing up they will all bloody hide.

I've had a word with one of the town hall officials in Bachwald and asked him to dig out some details about Altewiese. He says he has found out that in 1936 the population was a little over two thousand in the town itself and a further two hundred in the farms and surrounding district. He was very exact but embarrassed when he added that of the two thousand two hundred in total, one thousand one hundred and ten were male and two hundred and forty were Jewish. From my experience in the other towns on this road, I would guess that the population is now fourteen hundred, of whom one thousand are female and none Jewish. You are down as C of E aren't you Terry? Well here you can choose from a catholic church or a Lutheran chapel. I don't suppose the synagogue still remains."

With that the sergeant put the truck into gear and turned left on to the riverside road. After the creamery were two large Victorian houses on either corner of a narrow side street running south. A path ran up the side of the second house and gave access to the rear of many houses and larger buildings. At the next corner the sergeant turned right onto a short narrow road emerging at the northwest corner of the market square. As they reached the square they halted and the sergeant began to describe the scene to Terry.

"Here next to me is the police station and you can see through the window that our arrival is causing a stir. Next to you is a bank which looks closed, and next door to it is the town hall and then a hotel, but you can't see it clearly from where we're parked. Down the right hand side, or west of the square, there's the Party Offices after the police station - see they still have a swastika etched into the stonework above the door. Make a note to get that removed. Then there are a couple of office buildings - lawyers and accountants, that sort of thing, neither being of much use now. The large building facing us at the top right corner of the square is the post office; it's closed. To its left is a road leading out of the square and then a baker's shop and a closed hotel. Hang on a second, there's a woman opening the door and going in. Let's go and check on that place."

The woman had opened one of the double doors at the front of the hotel and entered, closing the door behind her. The hotel had two wide and tall windows on either side of the doors; they had green and brown glass in the lowest frames, with clear glass above. The first floor had five windows, each with closed curtains. In the sloping tiled roof were five small canopied windows also with closed curtains. The building was constructed of thin red bricks and had a small blue board above the double doors on which was neatly printed in gold paint *Hotel Alte Poste*. The truck eased up the slight slope of the cobbled square and swung round to park at the foot of the three wide and shallow steps leading to the hotel doors. There were two empty terracotta urns at either end of the first step. The three soldiers climbed out of the truck and stood on the top step. The sergeant tried the door handles, but finding both locked, he began to tap the door lightly. There being no immediate reply he increased the power of his knocking, at which Hardaker asked, "Do you want me to bash those doors open Mr Wilkes?"

"No thank you, Hardaker and it's Sergeant when we're in enemy territory; remember we did agree that didn't we?"

"Oh, yes, Sergeant Wilkes so we did."

"Corporal Hardaker," the sergeant went on, "you stand by the lorry and make sure those people outside the town hall and that other hotel down there can see you. If this hotel is not suitable we'll try that one and it does no harm to advertise our resources." The sergeant had just begun to kick the bottom of the door when it opened and the woman they had seen enter earlier faced them. She was tall and well built, with a buxom chest and strong legs and arms. She was over fifty years old but had blonde hair tightly tied in a bun at the back of her head. Her face was stern and angry and she spoke in English with a deep, strong accent.

"The hotel is closed, we have no money or food, please go away." The sergeant held the closing door open and stepped passed the woman; Terry followed.

"You speak good English. Who are you?" he asked. The sergeant turned and stared at Terry in surprise, but nodded to him to continue. "I am the manager of the hotel. It has been closed since January. We have dismissed all the staff. I stay here to guard it for the owner. There is nothing here worth stealing and I am old."

"Please be calm," Terry said, "we mean you no harm. We are looking for a place for me to stay tonight and would like to inspect your hotel. We are British soldiers working for the Government of Occupation."

"We have no rooms, or food. It is better that you go to Meyers Gasthof on the other side of the Town Square."

The sergeant had been looking behind the bar, but returned to the middle of the room.

"Where is the lavatory, madam?" She continued to look frightened but closed the front door and walked towards the corridor which ran between the foot of a carpeted staircase and a polished wood reception desk.

"Follow me please," she said, "the lavatories are dark, there is no paper and you must wash your things in the bucket of water provided and then throw the water into the lavatory you have used."

"Madam," the sergeant said, "what you have just described would be thought of as luxury in the rest of Germany today. I'm surprised, for a closed hotel, that you are so well prepared?"

"I sleep in the back room on this floor," she answered cautiously, "it is next to the lavatories and I use them. The water was for me to use, but I can pump some more after you have left." She indicated a door and the sergeant entered warily.

"What is your name please?" Terry asked.

"My name is Paula Rozen-Kranz."

"To satisfy my curiosity would you show me one of the bedrooms on the next floor, one of those facing the square?"

She was about to speak again and momentarily stared into Terry's eyes, then turned with a shrug and led him up the stairs. There was a wall and landing after twelve steps where the staircase turned on itself and from here Terry looked down on to the bar area. He followed Paula up a further twelve steps and reached a long dark corridor on the first floor. It ran the length of the hotel and at one end had a spiral staircase turning its way to the rooms in the roof space. Terry could just make out five doors on each side of the corridor and on each door was a white porcelain number. At the opposite end of the corridor to the spiral staircase was an open door through which Terry could see a bath and toilet. Paula had been carrying a bunch of keys since they first met at the front door and with one of these she opened the bedroom door at the end of the corridor - the one furthest to the left of the hotel and next to the bathroom; it bore the number one. Terry assumed she had started at this one because she expected to show him all of the rooms.

Once inside Paula opened the curtains and a flood of light illuminated the room. The high double bed was neatly made and showed two white pillows above a green patterned quilt. There was a fireplace, which was set, but not alight, a large heavy wooden wardrobe and near to the bedroom door, a low two-drawer chest which Terry tried to lift; it was made of solid heavy brown wood as was all the furniture in the room. On a stand in the corner of the room were a washbasin and an empty water jug. The floor was carpeted and the walls painted in a light cream colour. Terry laid his rifle on the bed and ran a finger along the mantle piece above the fire; there was some dust, but not much. He looked at Paula who was standing against the window.

"For a hotel that has been closed since January, this bedroom is very clean, why?" he asked.

"The owners retained the staff until April and they had nothing to do except keep the place tidy. We have left everything ready for use in the hope that we could return to normality quickly. Before last year many of our guests were salesmen and businessmen and we hoped they would come back but it has remained totally quiet."

"Are no guests staying here tonight?"

"No."

"Do you have wood and coal for the fires?"

"Yes, fire wood."

"What lighting do you use for yourself at night?"

"I use candles if I need to, but I have a little oil for the lamps we used to use."

"Do you have any food and drink?" Terry stared at her intently and she glared back at him confidently.

"I have sufficient food for myself and there are still a few barrels of beer hidden in the cellar."

"Corporal, corporal, where the hell are you?" The sergeant's calls sounded muffled. Terry returned to the top of the staircase.

"Up here sergeant," he shouted. "Come up and have a look at what I've found." The sergeant appeared around the bend in the staircase and followed Terry to bedroom number one.

"You have a couple of visitors downstairs," he said. "I have indicated to them that they can wait. It's nice to be able to shout at a pair of policemen. Now, this is a fine big bedroom. Plenty of room to store your stuff including the extras we have for you on the lorry down there. Hardaker is enjoying himself marching up and down the side of Tessy, he's daydreaming again, most of the time he thinks he is Tom Mix. The view of the square is good and it's north facing which means you never get unsighted and it won't get so hot that you'll need to leave a window open unattended, which would not be too clever."

"Mrs Rozen-Kranz," she had moved to the wall at the head of the bed to avoid being close to either of the soldiers, "are all of the bedrooms in the hotel prepared for use like this one?"

"Yes."

The sergeant looked at her.

"There are two doors next to the lavatory door and before the rear door to the hotel. The first one is locked and the second one is to your bedroom, a single bed sitting room with colourful curtains at the window. Where does the locked door lead to?" he said in a severe voice.

"To the cellar," she replied curtly.

"Mrs Rozen-Kranz, we would like you to assist us with the translation of our forthcoming conversation with the two policemen downstairs."

The sergeant's manner allowed for no argument and he indicated with his arm that she should lead the way from the room. At the head of the stairs, with Paula already out of sight, Wilkes stopped and spoke quietly to Terry.

"Before you make up your mind to stay here for the night, have a good look round the cellar. You feel this place might be safe do you?"

"Yes, sir. Tonight I would lock the bedroom door and shove that chest of drawers behind it. I think I could get some sleep in there."

"I've seen safer but this hotel has potential, particularly if we can persuade Mrs Rozen-Kranz to stay on. I had a shufty at the kitchens. They were spotlessly clean; polished metal ovens and scrubbed table and floors; a polished brass hand water pump and there was a fair supply of food in the cupboards too, which should worry us. Anyway, we are about to meet members of the local constabulary. I like your confident start and it would help if this lot realised that you are in charge here, so this is what I propose; you do all the talking. Get it? Good. The two coppers in the bar reception area have no guns on them as far as I could see but they are bound to have a basic issue at the police station. We need to disarm them. You talk to them, find out what they want, then tell them what you want which is for your sergeant, that's me, to accompany them to the station and relieve them of their guns and ammunition. While I'm away, you check the cellar and if you're happy, get Hardaker to move your kit and stores into that bedroom. One of you must watch the truck all the time. When I return with their guns I'll take over looking after Tessy's virtue. If you change your mind about staying here, that's no problem, we'll find somewhere else easy enough. If it were me, I'd try this place for tonight. Arthur and I will be back again at eleven o'clock tomorrow and we can have a good look round then. It's up to you Terry. And, don't salute them."

With Terry leading, the two soldiers descended the stairs and walked smartly the few steps to stand close to the two policemen who clicked their heels, twitched to attention and placing their right hand to their round caps, gave an unpractised American style salute. Terry placed his rifle on the reception counter and addressed them loudly.

"Do you speak English?" They understood, but shook their heads. Terry turned to Paula, who was standing behind the counter.

"Mrs Rozen-Kranz, please ask these two gentlemen who they are and what they want." Paula glanced at Sergeant Wilkes but he ignored her and continued staring menacingly at the smaller of the two policemen. She did not speak to the policeman, but spoke directly to Terry.

"The shorter of them is the senior constable of Altewiese, equivalent to a sergeant in your country. His name is Ernst

Fromming. He has been a constable here for more than twenty years; I understand that he is sixty years old. The taller one is a constable, he has been here one year and he is thirty years old, you will notice that he limps. That is as a result of a war injury. They are here to ask you what you are doing in Altewiese." Paula smiled stiffly at the two policemen and nodded.

"Tell them," said Terry, trying to sound like his old headmaster, "that I am a corporal in the British army. I am the Government's representative to Altewiese." He paused as Paula translated and at her signal continued. "These two policemen are now under my command. How many policemen are there in Altewiese?" Paula spoke again and translated Ernst's reply.

"He says that the two of them have continued in service since their inspector in Bachwald deserted them; a third constable has chosen to not report for duty." Terry noted that they both looked healthy and fit; their 'station master' uniforms were clean and expertly pressed.

"Ask them what arms and ammunition they have in the police station and at their homes, or anywhere." After some moments of German conversation Paula replied.

"Senior Constable Fromming says that he is aware of the," she hesitated to find the correct word, "the rules regarding the carrying of arms. He has gathered all the police weapons at the station. They consist of four automatic pistols with fifty-three rounds of ammunition and a shotgun with ten cartridges. He also has three ceremonial batons."

Terry thought for a few seconds and in translation bites issued his orders. "Mr Fromming will accompany my sergeant here, to the police station.......He will there hand over all weapons and ammunition, including batons to the sergeant......He will then report back to me...... The constable will stand on the front step of the hotel and ensure that no German people go near to our military lorry.....Should any one do so he is to call me immediately and we will act severely......Thank you Mrs Rozen-Kranz, I wish to continue my inspection of the hotel with you now, so tell them to go."

Terry turned sharply to Wilkes.

"If you need Hardaker to go with you sir, that's fine, otherwise send him in here to cool down, it's hot in the sun out there and his presence has already registered by now," he said in a low voice. The two soldiers then stood rigidly to attention and gave exaggeratedly correct British army salutes to each other. Terry turned to Paula as the others made for the door.

"Quickly show me the kitchen and your room, then find two torches or lights and take me into the cellar and please do not be afraid of us, we mean you no harm." While Paula and he moved about the ground floor of the hotel he questioned her politely.

"Where did you learn to speak English so well?"

"I learned it at university and spent one year in London, it was 1908. It was a beautiful time to be in London. I can recall my vocabulary, but my pronunciation is poor now. I have continued to read English works but rarely had the opportunity to speak your language."

"How long have you been here in the hotel?"

"I came here in 1943. Shortly after my husband was killed. The owner kindly gave me the position as manageress. He was a...." again she paused, "he was a colleague of my husband and was kind to me."

"Who is the owner of the hotel?," Terry asked.

"Helmut von Lutken; he lives in a big house on the estate on the other side of the river."

She unlocked the door to the cellar and, each carrying a large bright hissing oil lamp, they descended the steep wooden steps into the basement. The cellar was in three equal segments. They had arrived in the middle section which had a wide door in each side wall leading to the adjoining segments. In this central one was wooden shelving running almost completely around the four walls. There were many empty spaces on the shelves but Terry saw neat piles of white bed linen, a row of tall leather bound books that resembled account ledgers, on a low shelf a quantity of pottery vessels including five chamber pots, two rolls of carpet, and boxes of cleaning materials - dusters, brushes and jars of polish. In one corner was a round brick funnel running from floor to ceiling. It was joined to the water pump in the kitchen.

Through the door to the right of the room Terry found a coal shoot running steeply up to the yard at the rear of the hotel; it was closed by a stout wooden hatch at yard level and securely bolted on the inside with three strong metal bolts. On the floor at the foot of the shoot was a small amount of coal - enough to fill the scuttle lying next to it, four or five times only. Against the end wall, facing east, were five un-marked ten-gallon drums, one having a tall hand pump fixed to its screw top. Terry tested the smell of the liquid coating the pump and Paula confirmed that it was lamp oil and that there were two full drums, the rest being exhausted. One half of this cellar was empty and swept clean. Near the ceiling and running along both side walls and out under the square were a number of pottery pipes. Terry assumed they ran the waste from the toilets on each floor. There were metal water pipes and in one corner an electricity meter and fuse box with wiring disappearing up into the floor above.

The third section of cellar, to the west, contained food. Two walls had shelving on which were packets and jars; against the other walls were two sacks of potatoes, three crates of cabbage and a medium sized milk churn. There was a twelve bottle high by twenty-four bottle wide extensive wine rack containing approximately twelve bottles of wine. In the corner of the room was a thick-legged table on which rested three metal tapped wooden barrels and with them two large white jugs. Beneath the table were five more barrels. Paula said "Beer". Terry looked at her enquiringly.

"Where did you find all of this produce?"

"It was always the practice of the hotel management to maintain a full larder and fuel store." Paula sighed. "It has been difficult to keep a good variety for the last year. We have had few new supplies since we closed for business. I have traded some things for fresh milk and vegetables. This is all we have left. Few people in Altewiese know that this much remains or they might have been tempted to steal it."

"Does Helmut von Lutken come here and take things?"

"No, I believe he has sufficient stores at the manor. I would have to give this food and fuel to him if he asked for they belong to him, as owner of the hotel."

They returned to the ground floor and Paula locked the cellar door. Back in the reception area there were tables and chairs stacked along one wall, but one chair had been removed and was now in the middle of the room. On it sat Hardaker, cradling his Tommy gun and quietly singing to himself. He looked at Terry.

"Thank you for getting me out of the sun. I know it was your idea. Wilkes 'as no thought for us. It's all quiet out there."

"Hardaker, I've decided to stay here for the night. Would you help me move my gear from the lorry to bedroom number one on the next floor? It's up those stairs."

"Sure, Terry, anything you want doing you just asks 'ardaker." He rose slowly from the chair and made for the door. Terry turned to Paula.

"Mrs Rozen-Kranz, I wish to rent room number one for one night. Tomorrow by two o'clock in the afternoon I will inform you as to whether I will need to stay on any longer than one night. I will require a meal this evening at five o'clock and I would be happy if you were to join me, so that we could have an informal chat. Tomorrow morning I will require breakfast at six hours thirty. I would like now that you would fetch a large jug of beer from the cellar and three glasses. I may call for other refreshments during my stay. Additionally, I wish to employ your services as a translator, at least until two o'clock tomorrow and definitely at two o'clock today.

I am willing to pay for all of the accommodation and services and would like you to calculate the bill based on your last tariff or rates. You should inform the owner of my demands but please understand that there is no choice for you". He stared hard at her and she politely nodded her head in acceptance.

"I will arrange everything now; there will be hot water in your room and if I must, I will eat with you. It would be simpler for me to set the table in the kitchen. I do not propose to bring in any staff, just for one night. I will contact Mr von Lutken and decide with him the room rate and fees".

"Thank you. This afternoon I will give you an advance payment in cash, which may be of help to you. Would you now show this soldier the way to room number one and then return to me with the room key and the beer."

Paula led the heavily laden Hardaker up the staircase. Terry went to the open front doors and stood next to the watchful constable. Sergeant Wilkes and Fromming were loading guns and small boxes of ammunition on to the now almost empty lorry. The sergeant looked at Terry.

"Is everything OK? You're obviously staying here tonight."

"Yes, sir. I've arranged for us to get some beer so we can have a little break and you can tell me what stores you have left me. I also want to send these two coppers on an errand and therefore will set us a table and chairs here on the top step so that we can keep an eye on the lorry and the square at the same time".

Terry indicated to the constable to follow him and, in sign language, managed to have him remove one of the tables from those stacked against the wall of the reception area. He had this and three chairs placed on the top step. It was out of the sun and the open double doors helped funnel a cooling breeze over the table. Hardaker was carrying the last two items from the truck - two heavy metal ammunition boxes, as Paula appeared with a frothing jug and three tall beer glasses. Terry spoke to her.

"Please ask these two policemen to now do something else for me". She nodded and called for the attention of the constables. Terry continued. "Tell them firstly that as employees of the Government of Occupation, they will receive a weekly salary in cash from me.......Now ask them who has been paying them recently". Paula was surprised by the question but seemed even more surprised by the answer she had to give.

"They say that their official pay stopped in February and since that time they have received a small allowance from Mr von Lutken. It was he who refused to give any pay to the third constable, Kurt Muller, and he therefore refused to do his duty."

"I want you to instruct them now," Terry continued, "to search out certain persons from Altewiese and invite them to be here in the hotel reception area at precisely two o'clock this afternoon.........I will address those persons directly and tell them what is happening and what will be happening in the immediate future to them and Altewiese".

While Paula translated his words, Terry glanced at his watch, it was twelve thirty. He looked down at Wilkes who sat next to him drinking from his beer glass. Wilkes simply smiled encouragement at Terry. He went on.

"The persons I want to gather here will then go out into the town and repeat my words to all of the folk and local farmers.........Please invite Mr von Lutken, the most important members of the town council, the priest and pastor, the bank manager, the nearest local builder, the headmaster of the school, Kurt Muller, the owner or manager of that bar guest house over there, and the post master.........These two policemen should also be here at two o'clock and, of course, I will need your assistance also Mrs Rozen-Kranz."

With that he signalled that they could all leave and sat down to an already full beer glass. They watched as the two policemen walked quickly away. The limping constable set off in the direction of the bar and chemist shop near the far right-hand corner of the square and Fromming towards and into the police station. The sergeant turned and having confirmed that Paula had disappeared into the rear of the hotel he spoke quietly to Terry.

"That's odd, why would he need to visit the station? Still we'll see how many of your list can be found in time for your speech". He lent to one side and retrieved a brown leather briefcase from under the table. Terry had not seen this before but suspected that it existed from things the sergeant had said to him during their journey that morning. From the briefcase the sergeant extracted a large number of sheets of typed papers. These he sorted into five neat piles on the table. He then began to speak and pushed each pile towards Terry as he mentioned it.

"This document is your official orders, signed by Monty himself. He won't remember your name as he must sign hundreds of these every day. It's countersigned by our shit Connolly. The order document is useful when dealing with any Teutonic officials; show them the signature of Field Marshal Montgomery and they treat you like you're Hitler's son. Here are the ten requisition forms I promised you. You know when to use them and how to fill them in. If in doubt, do what you think best and tell me afterwards and I'll change anything that may be wrong. Got it? Good.

On this piece of paper is a list of the stores Hardaker has taken to your room. You're supposed to sign for them but don't bother because we always lose pieces of paper like this. Let me explain what you have got and in a minute or two we'll go and have a look at them. I saw Hardaker here - bloody hell the bugger has gone to sleep - still it doesn't matter for the moment. He took up your helmet, coat and kit bag. Behind the bar, in there, he put a five-gallon drum of diesel. You will easily find a car or lorry here you can use but diesel may prove more difficult to find. Keep the drum safe and use it in an emergency to drive up to Don or even me, if you need to. What did you say? You can't bloody drive! Well, bloody learn, but with your friend Tommy Gun to help, you should be able to persuade a local chauffeur to drive for you. Remember that diesel is valuable, so keep it safe.

In your room is a wooden crate in which you will find a Tommy gun. Always keep your rifle handy, but nothing is more impressive and easy to handle than a Tommy gun. All Germans know what it is, they even call us all Tommie's because of it. I have found it the most useful weapon when working with German civilians. The cleaning materials and tools for it are in the box with it. You may want to carry a side arm; if so we'll acquire one from a law breaking local citizen. I bet you we'll find at least one in the next twenty-four hours. In one of the ammo boxes are one hundred rounds of ammunition for the Tommy gun and an extra clip for it. I have included two smoke flares which I'm told can come in handy when faced with a mob. I'd prefer a couple of grenades myself, but Connolly says we should have smoke. That bayonet you are wearing is useful for peeling apples but not much else; like the rifle it's too cumbersome. In the second wooden box you'll find some rations; there's coffee, tinned meat, the cigarettes we talked about, powdered milk, fruit pastilles, but no sugar I'm afraid. There is a bag of tea and a packet of aspirin and three Johnnies. If she gets a bloody headache, give her a cup of tea."

Wilkes chuckled to himself, but Terry kept his eyes fixed on the top sheet of the last of the two piles of pamphlets; he was reading one of these slowly as the sergeant continued.

"Pay attention, corporal, the contents of the other two ammo boxes are of great importance to you. One is full of one-mark coins and fifty pfennig pieces and the other is full of bank notes of various denominations. As the Army has liberated the valuables hidden inside the banks and mints they have been distributed unfairly. The gold is sent to the Bank of England, officers keep the big notes because they're stupid and the rest and the coins are fed to us to distribute into the economy. The contents of any safety deposit boxes have disappeared. The money is your allowance to make the local community work to produce food. As long as the local community believe in the value of the money, they might work. Hitler's head is on the notes and coins, which may help, but before long, some wise politician will mint a new mark and God knows what real value they will have. Spend them how you want to, but get them in to the market as soon as you can. I'll have another two boxes for you soon. You'll be surprised how fast they go, once you have a load of DPs to care for.

Now let's have a squint at Monty's two messages to the German people. The top sheet is the English version and below each is a quantity of German language ones. We delivered the one dated 30th May a couple of weeks ago. We gave them to the town hall clerk and God knows what she did with them. Let us assume both of these messages are new to the town's people. I thought you had read them before, but perhaps not. Well go ahead now and I'll nip to the lavatory for a shit. I'll take a couple of the sheets with me. I know it's too dark to read in there but I can see which side has no ink on, which is much more important".

Wilkes rose and left the sleeping smiling Hardaker and the studious Terry at the table. Pamphlet number one read:

TO THE POPULATION OT THE BRITISH AREA IN GERMANY
30TH MAY 1945

"1. I have been appointed by the British Government to command and control the area occupied by the British Army. This area will be governed for the present by Military Government under my orders.

2. My immediate object is to establish a simple and orderly life for the whole community.

The first step will be to see that the population has:
    a) food
    b) housing
    c) freedom from disease.

The harvest must be gathered in.
The means of transport must be re-established.
The postal services must be restarted.
Certain industries must be got going again.
All this will mean much hard work for everyone.

3. Those who have committed war crimes according to international law will be dealt with in proper fashion.

The German people will work under my orders to provide the necessities of life for the community, and to restore the economic life of the country.

4. There are in the British Area a very large number of German soldiers, sailors and airmen, and all these are now being assembled in certain localities.

The German Wehrmacht, and other armed forces, will be disarmed and disbanded.

All German soldiers, sailors and airmen, are being sorted out by trades and occupations. In a few days they will start to be discharged from the armed forces so that they can get on with the work. The most urgent need is the harvest; therefore workers on the land are going first; men of other occupations and trades will be discharged to work as soon as it can be arranged.

5. I will see to it that all German soldiers and civilians are kept informed by radio and newspaper of how the work is going on. The population will be told what to do. I will expect it to be done willingly and efficiently."

Signed by Field Marshal Montgomery
Governor British Occupied Germany

The second pamphlet read:

TO THE POPULATION OF THE BRITISH AREA IN GERMANY
10TH JUNE 1945

"You have wondered, no doubt, why our soldiers do not smile when you wave your hands, or say 'Good Morning' in the streets, or play with the children. It is because our soldiers are obeying orders. You do not like it. Nor do our soldiers. We are naturally friendly and forgiving people. But the orders are necessary; and I will tell you why.

In the last war of 1914, which your rulers began, your Army was defeated; your generals surrendered; and in the Peace Treaty of Versailles your rulers admitted that the guilt of beginning the war was Germany's. But the surrender was made in France. The war never came to your country; your cities were not damaged, like the cities of France and Belgium; and your armies marched home in good order. Then your rulers began to spread the story (legend) that your armies were never really defeated, and later they denied the war guilt clauses of the Peace Treaty. They told you that Germany was neither guilty nor defeated; and because the war had not come to your country many of you believed it, and you cheered when your rulers began another war.

Again, after years of waste and slaughter and misery, your armies have been defeated. This time the Allies were determined that you should learn your lesson – not only that you have been defeated, which you must know by now, but that you, your nation, were again guilty of beginning the war. For if that is not made clear to you, and your children, you may again allow yourselves to be deceived by your rulers, and led into another war.

During the war your rulers would not let you know what the world was thinking of you. Many of you seemed to think that when our soldiers arrived you could be friends with them at once, as if nothing much had happened. But too much has happened for that. Our soldiers have seen their comrades shot down, their homes in ruin, their wives and children hungry. They have seen terrible things in many countries where your rulers took the war. For those things, you will say you are not responsible – it was your rulers. But they were found by the German nation; every nation is responsible for its rulers, and while they were successful you cheered and laughed. That is why our soldiers do not smile at you. This we have ordered, this we have done, to save yourselves, to save your children, to save the world from another war. It will not always be so. For we are Christian forgiving people, and we like to smile and be friendly. Our object is to destroy the evil of the Nazi system; it is too soon to be sure that this has been done.

You are to read this to your children, if they are old enough, and see that they understand. Tell them why it is that the British soldier does not smile."

Signed Field Marshal Montgomery
Governor British Zone Germany

(Footnote: both items extracted verbatim from 'The Memoirs of Field-Marshal The Viscount Montgomery of Alamein, KG' – 1958)

"No messing with Monty," said Wilkes now standing behind Terry and looking over his shoulder at the pamphlets, "he has relaxed the fraternization orders; I have a copy dated the 12th allowing us to speak to Germans and play with the children. But, remember it does not really apply to us who have to work with the population. Take the key off the table and go up to your room and check your stores and things. Then get tidied up. I told the manageress to put hot water in your room and a clothes brush. Incidentally she is bound to have a spare key to your room so keep an eye on her and your gear. That chest of drawers may well be of some use tonight. I doubt that you'll be inviting her to join you in bed."

Terry collected the papers and left two piles of German language sheets on the reception counter. He went to his room and looked at the high, soft bed and knew he needed to rest a while. It had been a long day; everything had changed in his life; he had gained longed for independence but the size of the task that lay ahead looked daunting; he felt very tired. He removed his uniform and washed thoroughly in cool water, drying on a small towel that had been neatly folded and left at the end of his bed. He placed his rifle and bayonet in the wardrobe alongside the ammunition boxes left there by Hardaker. He loaded one of the Tommy gun clips with bullets and fitted it to the gun. Having brushed his uniform and removed much of the day's road dust, he dressed. From the green painted metal boxes he took a handful of coins and some notes and put them in his tunic side pockets. He placed the copy of his orders in his top breast pocket, leaving the button undone.

Having brushed his hair and polished his beret badge, he put the beret neatly on his head ensuring the badge was correctly aligned. He looked at his reflection in the mirror on the inside of one of the wardrobe doors; he looked clean, smart and alert; he felt tired, nervous and confused. He began to whisper the speech he was about to make. He became more nervous and stuttered and stumbled in his whispering. He imagined he was his school's headmaster at morning assembly, dominant and sure, but wasn't sure. Terry swung the Tommy gun over his shoulder, closed the wardrobe doors and locked them, pocketing the key. He left the room and while locking the bedroom door he stared at the white number fixed to it. He took three long, deep breaths and spoke quietly to himself. "That's me, number one in Altewiese, now act like you are number one, son". He was shocked and proud at how like his father he'd sounded. He turned smartly to face the corridor and saw standing at the head of the stairs, Paula Rozen-Kranz. She stared at him as he marched towards her.

"You look very like my son," she said in a quiet sad voice. " A different colour uniform but the same confident manner. Your mother would be very proud of the way you look."

"And would she be proud of what I'm doing?"

"Yes, it's your duty. My son followed orders, which he was not sure were correct or fair, but he did his duty."

"Where is he now?"

Her lips trembled.

"With his father, buried in the snow of Demyansk."

"I'm sorry".

"Yes you.... you probably are. It is five minutes to two and almost all the people you asked the constables to assemble are here but there is no bank manager at this branch anymore. The post office manager left the town some weeks ago. If we go to the mezzanine landing I will point out to you each of the men who are present. I have come to know them all since being in the town."

Terry nodded agreement to her suggestion and followed her to the turning in the staircase. There he could see Hardaker standing to attention at the front doors. Each man that had entered would have had to pass his threatening size and menacing grin. Wilkes was standing at the foot of the stairs facing the group. He turned his head towards Terry and winked his support.

"The two policemen you already know," Paula said in a low voice, "they are there standing by the reception counter. Their former colleague is on the other side of the room with his elbow on that stacked table. He has noticed us and is now standing to attention. The tall grey haired man just behind him is the schoolmaster, Mr Schrader, and to his left are the two priests, talking together, which is something they rarely do. Behind them, the short fat man, is Mr Kahler who owns the building yard in the next street. Here in the front of us are the three senior town officials. In the middle is Mr Hasch, the mayor; on his left is the town-planning officer and to his right the town financial controller. Mr Meyer from the guesthouse is just coming through the door. I am sorry to tell you that I cannot see Mr von Lutken. He has not yet arrived."

"Perhaps the constables were unable to contact him," said Terry quietly.

"I am certain they would have contacted him before all of these others. Some of them would not have been here now unless von Lutken had given his permission."

Paula's remarks gave Terry an uneasy feeling. The importance of von Lutken was becoming very apparent.

"We will speak from here," he said to her. "You translate as you have done earlier. You may stand on the next step down if you wish. It will indicate that you are not willingly involved with us." She moved down two steps. Terry looked passed Hardaker but could see no one else heading in their direction across the square. He checked his wristwatch; it was exactly two o'clock. He began to speak, halting often to allow Paula to translate his words into German.

"Gentlemen, my name is Corporal Hall. I have been sent to Altewiese as a representative of the new government of Germany.......Mrs Rozen-Kranz is being paid to translate my words to you, she had no choice......" Waving the copy of his orders he went on. "These are my orders, they are signed personally by Field Marshal Montgomery". At these last words he noticed that all of the eager listeners stiffened as he had spoken them and, again, when Paula repeated them. "I will now be responsible for all matters previously handled by your local, regional and national Governments......This includes the police who will now follow my orders and be paid by me. Should they object to this arrangement they can resign and be replaced."

As the words were being translated to them he watched carefully the reaction of the two uniformed policemen. They continued to listen intently and stare pointedly at Paula.

"I will soon interview any local government officials currently carrying out their duty, or willing to resume their duties and decide if they are suitable to remain in their posts."

The three men at the front of the small audience looked at each other questioningly.

"My orders are to ensure that the population of Altewiese has food, shelter and are in good health. There on the reception counter is a message from the Field Marshal on this subject." He pointed to the pile of pamphlets. "The population of Altewiese will soon grow with the arrival of returning prisoners of war and the allocation to this town of displaced persons."

Paula had difficulty with the translation of these last words and turned to Terry with a questioning look.

"Displaced persons are your German neighbours, who, for whatever reason, have chosen to leave the Russian area of Germany, or who have totally lost their homes and are now refugees. They must be found shelter and fed. You will all help me in this task." The priest whispered to the pastor who nodded in agreement. "Until further notice I am the final judge of all matters of law and order……..You are already aware of many of our new laws but I wish to emphasise two of the most important………Membership of the Nazi party is banned and therefore the Nazi party does not exist. Will Mr Kahler the builder please put his hand up."

As the translated words reached him, the tubby builder shyly raised his right hand. "Mr Kahler is instructed that, on leaving this meeting, he will obtain the necessary material, labour and equipment and place cement into the indented swastika on that building over there." Terry pointed at the party offices. "When the cement is dry he will plaster and paint the whole area around the motif, so as to completely obliterate any sign of the swastika." Mr Kahler looked very concerned, but Terry went on. "I will pay Mr Kahler, from Government funds, the sum of fifty marks for carrying out this work. The job will have been completed by eleven o'clock tomorrow morning. He has no choice."

Terry stared menacingly at the builder and Hardaker tapped the barrel of his Tommy gun on the doorjamb. "No German is allowed to carry any weapon of any kind, whether rifle, pistol, knife or bow and arrow". Hardaker smiled broadly at this last remark indicating that he was enjoying Terry's speech even if no one else was. "Any one found in possession of a weapon will be executed." As Paula finished this translation, Terry paused for a moment and the silent atmosphere was charged, and tingling.

"The second pile of pamphlets over there contains Field Marshal Montgomery's message regarding how you are not to talk to British soldiers. I am in a position to vary those rules where I see fit.......When you men leave here today you must all take a few of each of those sheets, read what they say and distribute them around the town........Make sure everyone has read and understood what they say.......Should any member of the community have any serious or important question they can visit me here between seven and eleven o'clock tomorrow morning when I will be available to answer them if I wish to............While you are visiting the people of the town I want you to ask any English speakers to report to me here during the same period......... I wish to appoint official translators and I will offer paid employment to any successful applicant........Also I wish to interview, for paid positions, any doctors, nurses, midwives, or trained medical orderlies........At ten o'clock tomorrow morning I want the mayor, Mr Hasch, to visit me here..........I want you all to carry out my instructions now. You may leave. God save the King."

At this Terry, Wilkes and Hardaker sprang noisily to attention and gave an exaggeratedly long salute. The audience filed passed the reception counter, each collecting a few sheets from both piles of Montgomery's messages and then silently left the hotel. They all avoided eye contact with the towering Hardaker. Paula was already at the foot of the staircase on her way to the rear of the building when Terry called to her.

"Thank you Mrs Rozen-Kranz, I will see you at five o'clock. She nodded without looking up at Terry. He joined Wilkes who slapped him on the shoulder.

"Well done Corporal, that was excellent. By eleven tomorrow I'll be back here eager to know what response you generated. Bloody good show. We can take a walk around the square for a while, then him and I will be getting back to Bachwald."

They were both walking passed Hardaker, who shouted in Terry's ear.

"That was real good Mr 'all." A compliment Terry much appreciated. He now felt relaxed, but still achingly tired.

"From the name of it, the hotel must have once been a post office," the sergeant observed as he walked slowly down the steps and turned right. Terry, now cradling his Tommy gun, followed closely behind.

"It certainly looks older with these small red bricks. The new Post Office back there is more modern and made of concrete blocks. It looks very nice. So on the left of this hotel you have a baker's shop and here on the right a small green grocery. It will make you feel at home this shop, Terry. Next to nothing in the window though."

They had reached the southeast corner of the square and now turned north to look down the slight incline towards Meyers Gasthof. They walked passed two shops that were closed for business; the first appeared to be a hardware or general goods shop. Through the interior's gloom they could make out odd items on the nearly bare shelves; the second shop was a tailor and dress shop and had two naked mannequins posing in its window. Although closed it was freshly painted and had a relatively new shop sign above its window. Alongside this shop stood the tall, imposing façade of a cinema. Gloria Kino, written above the entranceway, three steps up to four doors, now chained and bolted. From a faded advertising poster could be translated the date Wednesday 4th April, presumably that of the last performance. The cinema's neighbour attracted the attention of the two soldiers; its sign read 'Hindenburg Apoteke'. Wilkes pointed to it.

"That's a chemists shop, let's go in and see what we can find."

Inside it was cool and dark, but they made out the figure of an old man standing in the corner of the shop surrounded by shelves lined with dark brown bottles.

"Do you speak English?" demanded Wilkes loudly.

"No," came the strong reply.

"I have a problem with me bowels, I keep needing to go to the lavatory, can you give me anything for it?" the sergeant persisted.

"No," the old man repeated.

"If my friend was to machine gun your shop would you be able to help me?"

Wilkes was now very close to the slightly bent grey-haired man, who again said "No".

"Fuck you then," the sergeant said and turned and walked from the shop. Terry followed, but as he hesitated at the door he was sure that he heard the old man say very quietly, "Fuck you too, you Tommy shit."

The continuous parade of shops, hotel and cinema, starting with the baker's ended at the 'Apoteke'. A narrow service entry ran to the rear of chemist's shop. The two soldiers stood at the corner of the square where a short lane linked it to the riverside road. On the right was a large private house whose front step fell directly on to the lane. Facing the square, joined to the town hall and running down the left hand side of this lane and therefore probably having a side facing the river, was Meyers Gasthof and Café Meyer. There were three men standing at the door of the guesthouse and café but as Terry turned and crossed towards it, they scurried inside. Terry entered and found himself in a bar with heavy wooden tables and benches. To the rear of the room was a counter with one candle illuminating the darkened shelving behind it. Three customers were sitting at a table to the far left next to the window overlooking the town square and Mr Meyer stood behind the bar. Terry recognised him from the meeting but could see no copies of the pamphlets.

"What do you have to drink, please?" asked Terry.

"No English," Meyer replied boldly.

Terry smiled.

"Is that an admission of your ignorance, or a house rule?"

"No English," Meyer said again and then spoke loudly in German and gestured to indicate that he had no stock of any kind available for sale. Wilkes was standing in the doorway watching the three seated customers, one of whom had a small glass of dark red wine in front of him.

"Very typical first reactions, these are Corporal," Wilkes called. "Come on, let's continue our patrol."

Terry joined the sergeant outside the bar and as they passed the window the three customers were smiling broadly. Terry stared at them.

"They're starting to make me angry. We're here to help keep them alive and all they do is sneer at us."

"Remember it's still necessary to say 'sir' to me Corporal Hall. The war ended officially six weeks ago, but these buggers have not yet come to terms with it. They know what the Russians are doing to their countrymen and they know of the destruction and of the hardship being suffered in the cities in our zone, but they have not experienced it, not yet. These people have contact with others further up the road in Brick and Bachwald and even Luneburg and they know exactly how we have been treating them. They don't like it; they are a proud people who, only three years ago, ruled almost all of Europe and today a young eighteen year old Englishman arrives to rule them. Can you see how difficult it is for them to accept the inevitable? They will try sneering, non-cooperation, defiance and maybe worse, but when they are starving and see that you are their only route to food, well then they'll begin to realise their mistake. If you don't want to wait that long then be strong now."

"Should I go back into that bar and spray a few rounds with this gun? Is that what you're saying, sir?" asked Terry anxiously.

"For what they've just done? No, that would be an over reaction. Wait and watch, one of those shits will try something serious soon, they always do. They'll want to test how far they can push you. It's then that you make up your mind to ignore them like Christine has, join them like Don, or kill one or two like Hardaker did for me. In the end it's what makes you happy; it's what you will be comfortable with. Christine is happy worrying about his DPs, when he's sober that is and Don is happy shafting the local girls. We won't be here for ever you know. Me, perhaps six more months, you - a year at most, I would guess. Get comfortable, make a little extra profit while there's still the opportunity and if the Germans want to starve, then that's their choice. If you want to be hard, that's OK by me. You can borrow Hardaker to do the dirty work."

"No, sir," Terry interrupted. "If there has to be any rough stuff, I'd like to see if I'm capable of handling it….. if I'll be too scared and walk away. I got into a couple of fights at school after I started reading the art books but this would be a real test for me, and if I do chicken out, no one will be here to report it. No, I'm feeling more confident now that I've seen the situation. Once or twice on the drive down I was worried shitless."

"Which reminds me," said the sergeant, "I need to visit the lavatory again, so let's get to your hotel pretty quickly. We can have a look at the town hall and bank tomorrow."

They walked across the centre of the stone square and Terry looked at the Party Offices to his right and noticed that the builders had not yet arrived to fill in the swastika.

"Terry, get one of the policemen to find the keys to the bank and those Party Offices, we should see what's inside them both. Don't expect any money to be in the bank. The bank directors cleared them all out before we got anywhere near them but there might be something worth trading."

Hardaker was sitting on a chair on the top step of the Alte Poste Hotel, smiling and conducting an imaginary orchestra; his right hand casually saluted the sergeant, in mid phrase. Wilkes ran passed him and through to the rear of the hotel. Terry came up the steps to Hardaker and stood next to him and looked out on to the square. Hardaker ended his arm waving and quietly muttered.

"Get the lady to give you the keys to the back door. There will be two keys. Have a look at what's out back. See if you can find your way out. Even big boys like me need to retreat sometimes. From your bed you can see the window at the top of that cinema over there. That means that someone in that cinema window can see you in bed. Embarrassing if you're 'aving a wank, but dangerous if they 'ave a good rifle. Keep the right 'and curtain closed all of the time and move the bed slightly. It's 'eavy, but it 'as wheels on its feet. I don't like the schoolmaster, or Muller or the two policemen, and maybe that's because I don't like any schoolmasters or policemen, but keep a good eye on them, they don't smell very kind people to me. You should ask Wilkes to send me down 'ere for a couple of days and we could sort out any really smelly people."

At that moment Wilkes reappeared.

"Mr Wilkes, sergeant, sir," said Hardaker, "are we going now, because I forgot to bring my comics?"

The sergeant smiled and turned to Terry.

"We need to be off. Are you coming with us, or staying here on your own?"

"Staying. I'm responsible for this town now, so I'm staying put."

"And you have a dinner date with a German lady," the sergeant's smile broadened, "which, of course is strictly illegal. She looks the motherly type, so be careful you don't get suffocated between her tits. Arthur and I will be right here at eleven tomorrow eager to find out what happened to her and the rest of these people. Good luck Terry, you'll do alright."

"Good-bye Mr 'all," said Hardaker as he climbed into Terry's recently vacated passenger seat.

The truck slowly rolled down the square and left via the short lane between the house and Meyer's Gasthof. It turned left and Terry lost sight of it and felt thrilled. For the first time in months he felt alone and for the first time ever he felt that he had a purpose, a real responsibility. The combination made him feel confident and happy. Without knowing it before, this was the adventure he had always sort and he tingled with the anticipation of managing this small town with all its dangers and difficulties. The challenge was real and the confidence he had felt at the meeting was increasing. He now knew that he could give orders and demand respect and be obeyed. Now all he believed he needed was a plan of action, a list of objectives and a selection of operatives to carry out his instructions in order to achieve those objectives. He needed paper to write down his plan.

He turned from the hotel step and made for the dark office behind the reception desk. From the door of the office he could see very little of the interior. He found a light switch and tried it, realising too late that there was no electricity being generated other than on British bases. He walked down the corridor towards the rear of he hotel and called out for Mrs Rozen-Kranz. There was no answer. He turned left into the lavatory. There were two cubicles on the far wall which backed on to the grocer's shop but that building was obviously much shorter than the hotel, for in the right cubical there was a small window set high up. It was the restricted light from this window that allowed the lavatory to be used without the need for candles or lamps. On the wall to the left, backing on to the office, were three white pedestal sinks with dull brass taps. An empty bucket in front of the taps indicated the lack of mains water and that Wilkes had recently used its contents. There was a crumpled towel in the furthest sink bowl. Terry used the toilet in the right hand cubical to relieve the pressure resulting from the earlier beer.

He crossed to the kitchen but Paula was not there, although the table in the centre of the room had been laid with a cloth and cutlery for two persons. There were two up-side-down wine glasses next to each setting. Opposite the door to the kitchen was the door to the cellar which Terry found locked and the last door on that side was to Paula's bedroom. She was not in her room but he noticed the newly cut flowers lying on a small table facing the window and on the wall opposite were three small framed photographs of a middle-aged man in a black SS officer's uniform.

Through the window Terry saw a figure moving in the yard outside. He tried the door at the end of the corridor - this had two locks both with keys in them; the door opened when he lifted its latch and the bright sunlight momentarily dazzled him. Stepping outside Terry found himself in an open yard that led to a road ten metres beyond. There was a detached house set in a small garden on the other side of the road. Close to his right was a tall wooden fence running from the hotel wall behind the door, down to the road. To his left was a spacious yard that served as a rear or delivery access to the grocery and around the corner as far as the tailor's shop. He walked in this direction, passed Paula's window, to the end of the hotel building. He found her sitting on a dining chair with a basin between her knees, peeling potatoes. She looked up startled and dropped her knife into the basin. Terry smiled.

"Sorry Mrs Rozen-Kranz, I didn't mean to startle you but I would like to have a look around the office and need an oil lamp. Can you get one for me?"

She laid the basin on her chair and led the way back into the hotel.

"How many sets of keys are there to this door?" Terry asked as they passed through the back door.

She looked at the locks.

"Those two and I have a set on my master key ring."

"I'll take these two," stated Terry. Paula shrugged her shoulders and continued into the kitchen where she opened an eye-level cupboard and took out an oil lamp with a tall thin glass bowl on top. She took a match from the same cupboard and lit the lamp. Terry took it and thanked her. Paula said nothing but returned through the back door to her peeling.

The sparse furniture in the office was placed tightly against the walls. Behind the door was a red wood desk with a roller shutter cover. He opened it and placed the lamp on to the blotting paper. He found that many of the little drawers and cubbyholes were empty. Only two contained pieces of six-month-old correspondence. Terry wondered if this meant that the electricity had failed six months ago. The wall opposite the office door and backing on to the grocery had a small fireplace on either side of which, set into the alcoves, were rows of shelving. Above the fireplace was a short narrow ledge on which stood an ornate carriage clock and hanging above this was a small white-bordered photograph of Adolf Hitler. Terry went close to it and noted that it bore a short written inscription and a signature. The shelves were almost totally full of filing boxes; one of these contained approximately fifty picture-postcards. The black and white picture on the front was of the town square of Altewiese, taken from the hotel, on a busy market day. Terry took one of the cards and slipped it into a tunic pocket. He discovered that most of the other boxes held copies of old invoices. The one he had chosen at random was a carbon copy of a bill addressed to a man with an army rank that Terry could not understand, but what did attract his attention was his unit. He read 'SS', some more German words, and then 'Bergen-Belsen'.

Terry suddenly felt cold. He had read in the newspapers and heard on the radio about the horrors of the death camps, but this dusty invoice seemed to make the whole thing real. He pushed the invoice back into the box and looked around the rest of the room. Against each sidewall was a leather armchair and on the floor in the centre of the room was a round carpet patterned in red, browns and greens. There was no chair near the desk and he had found no writing paper or envelopes. The only window in the room was a thin quarter light above the door which could be angled to allow for ventilation.

Terry walked up to his bedroom taking the oil lamp with him. He unlocked his door and placed the lamp on the chest of drawers. He pulled the right hand curtain across half of the window and pushed the bed, with difficulty, nearer to the wardrobe. From his kit bag he extracted a sheet of paper and found a pencil in one of his tunic pockets. He sat on the bed and tried to compile a list of priorities and action but his mind could conjure no list for him. He knew he was dreadfully tired and decided to delay the compilation until after a good night's sleep. Rather than waste the paper he wrote a short note to his parents. He would later find an envelope and give the letter to Sergeant Wilkes tomorrow. Terry wrote:

Monday June 21st, 1945

CORPORAL T. HALL (Altewiese)
C/O Sgt Wilkes (Bachwald)
Governors Office
Government of Occupation
Luneburg,
British Zone Germany

Dear Mum and Dad,

   You should use the address I have written above to send your letters to me now. If the censor lets this letter through un-marked you will know I am now in Altewiese. This is a town almost as big as Stone 47 miles south of Luneburg. You can find Luneburg in the atlas in my room. I am on my own here. I am responsible for all the people of the town. It is an important job. The people are defeated and not friendly. This is okay because I have to be firm and strict with them. I hope you are both well. I am very well and have a nice hotel room. The bed is very clean. Next door is a fruit shop but not as good as ours.

Love to you both
Terry (Corporal)

   He reread the letter and folded it. As he placed it next to the lamp he smelt the sweet sickly oil fumes, but could detect another more pleasant aroma. He opened the bedroom door and caught the scent of cooking and immediately felt hungry. He checked his wristwatch; it was thirty minutes to his dinner appointment with Paula. He stripped and washed thoroughly, chose the cleanest of his two vests and long johns, both of which were soiled and smelly and put on a shirt and trousers. He was disappointed he did not have time to stitch stripes on to the shirt sleeves. He selected the least worn socks, polished his boots, and folded his beret and laid it beneath the epaulette on his left shoulder. He looked at himself in the mirror and was happy that his appearance would have pleased his mother. Still having ten minutes, he unpacked his kit placing items in the drawers and wardrobe. From his tunic jacket he took ten, twenty mark notes, the postcard and a handkerchief and put them all in his trouser pockets; the jacket he hung behind the door. He picked up the Tommy gun and left the room.
   Paula was ladling soup into pottery bowls, as he entered the kitchen. She wore a different dress from earlier; it was green with colourful patterns.

"Please sit here," she said pointing to the chair facing the large window overlooking a vegetable garden. At the far end of the garden was a garage, large enough for two cars side by side. Terry sat down, placed the gun under his chair self-consciously and noticed that in the centre of the table was a vase of flowers. He touched them gently.

"My mother has flowers like this on her table every Sunday during summer. Even during the last five years she's managed to find some. Where did you find these?"

"A neighbour grows them. I hope you like onion soup?"

She placed a bowl in front of him and sat down in the chair opposite his. She took a napkin from beside her fork and neatly folded it across her lap. Terry, already blowing a spoon full of soup, quickly took his napkin and laid it on his knees.

"This is very nice soup," he said, now noticing that she was taking a small piece of bread from the little basket between them. He scanned the table to check for any other items that he may have missed. He felt nervous and clumsy but could not explain to himself why. There was no cruet.

"Salt?" he asked.

"No, nor pepper I am afraid. Many items have now disappeared from the larders of the town. Until recently one could ask neighbours and exchange commodities, but now it's very difficult. We have a hotel vegetable garden, you can see it through the window, but on Saturday night someone climbed the fence and stole quite a lot of produce. I believe there are a number of families in the town who are in a critical state. I know that in the cities it's much worse but here in the countryside people should not yet be running short of food. It's those with no work and who have sold all their valuables who must now be desperate."

Terry placed his spoon in his bowl and took the twenty mark notes and postcard from his pocket. He stood and placed the notes on the work surface near to the deep porcelain sink.

"This is an advance payment for the lodging and your translation work. I should have given it to you earlier in case you needed money to buy food or anything."

"I have money," Paula said indignantly, "I did not need to steal to provide this food."

"I'm sorry. I didn't mean to offend you."

Terry felt embarrassed. He looked intently into his soup bowl as he wiped the last drops with a piece of bread. She stood and placed both their bowls in the sink. She offered wine to Terry and poured them both a glass. Terry took a gulp of the cool white wine and was surprised that it didn't taste of vinegar. He had never had wine before but they sold wine vinegar from the barrel at the shop in Stone and he assumed it would be similar.

"This is very nice," he said, looking at the glass. "What make is it?"

"Riesling. It is produced much further south than here - from the other side of Frankfurt. Good health to you Corporal".

She raised her glass and sipped from it. Terry returned the toast.

"I found this postcard in the office. On which days of the week is the market held?"

"Until the end of 1943 it was on a Wednesday and Saturday. After that it was on Saturday only. There has been no market here since the first week in May. A few local farmers have set up stalls on odd occasions since but no traders from Hanover or Luneburg have come with things to sell. At the Wednesday markets there were cattle bought and sold. The fencing for the pens is kept behind the town hall and was erected in the middle of the square. It was smelly and messy afterwards until it rained, but it was very rural."

She placed two plates on the table, the one before Terry having a breast and wing of cooked chicken and hers with a leg; then a dish of steaming potatoes and a dish of cabbage that was finely chopped.

"Help yourself. The cabbage is cooked with vinegar which is normal in Germany but you may find it strange. I hope you like it. We call it Sauer Kraut and it's very popular. That is why you call German people Kraut. We call English men Tommy because of that gun under your chair. Are you frightened of an old woman like me?"

"No. I have been ordered to carry it at all times," Terry protested. "Besides I'm alone here among people who were my enemy six weeks ago. They probably think of me as an enemy even now."

"I cannot believe that anyone in this town would do you harm. You would be replaced and the town's people would be severely punished. We may not like you; we may hate you, but it would be foolish for us to harm you."

"Do you hate me?" Terry asked.

"You personally, no. What you represent, yes. We hate the British and the Americans for defeating our armies. We hate ourselves for allowing them to defeat us."

"And the Russians?"

"We do not hate the Russians, they are beyond hating. The peoples of the East, the Asiatic, are not human, they are evil animals and what they are doing to our people is what a rabid dog would do. If they cross the Elbe then you should be frightened."

Terry considered this an odd thing to say and looked puzzled.

"Why would the Russians attack us, they are our allies?"

"They wish to spread their communism to France and Spain and England. Their army is fit and strong and just twenty miles from here. Your army and the Americans are still fighting the Japanese and that war may go on for many more years. You will be weak and vulnerable and the animals will soon be hungry for more land and women's bodies."

Paula stopped for a moment and took a deep breath and then smiled at Terry.

"Sorry," she said, "my talk is spoiling your meal."

"This cabbage is nice, you must tell my Mum how to make it. I thought the Russians were just Europeans who had been your allies until 1941. Our newspapers say that they suffered terrible things when you... when your armies invaded. I'm confused. Do you personally dislike the Russians?"

Terry helped himself to the remaining potatoes and cabbage and continued eating. Paula had finished her food and placed her knife and fork together on her plate. She poured more wine for them both and then in a more relaxed manner she spoke.

"Let me tell you a little of my life story. You may find it boring but it may help you understand why many Germans, and I, feel as we do. I was born and educated in Munich. I told you that I spent a year in London. I left University in Munich in 1912 with a degree in Chemistry. I had this yearning to find a new chemical and have it bear my name. I found a job in a petroleum company in Regensburg which is a two-hour train journey from Munich. At the next laboratory bench was a charming and shy young man. We fell madly in love with each other and started to live together. My parents were angry and insisted that we get married or live in separate apartments. We chose to get married. Peter was two years younger than I and his parents were never happy about our marriage. We had two wonderful years together. We saved hard and purchased a nice cottage and I gave birth to a daughter in September 1914. Then our luck started to change for the worse. At six months of age my daughter died of a children's disease; I don't know what the name is in English." While she talked she cleared the dishes from the table. She spoke confidently and without emotion.

"Two months later Peter received papers forcing him to join the military service and help win the war. With his education and qualifications he could have been an officer, but we were not rich and his family would not help, so he became a soldier - a rifleman, just like you. Once each year he would return home on leave and we would live twelve months of happiness in two short weeks. For three years he fought in the east, in Poland, against the Russians. When they capitulated he was transferred to the trenches of

Belgium. He rose to the rank of Corporal, just like you. One month before the war ended he was wounded in the chest by a fragment of an artillery shell. Our luck was still not improving; there were to be only four more weeks of shell firing and he had survived for four years until then. I had restarted work at the petroleum factory and was kept very busy as there was a shortage of men. Peter was in hospital in Bremen for six months, but I was unable to visit him because of the job and travel difficulties. He recovered and returned to a convalescent hospital near Munich.

One week after he returned to our cottage, I lost my job. After the war had ended the economy and industry of Germany declined into chaos. I discovered that I was pregnant again. Until our son was born, Peter and I searched for jobs and for four weeks I worked in the kitchen of a hotel near to Munich, which is a coincidence when you see me now, twenty-five years later. Our son was born on 10th April 1921 and we named him Carl Peter. Soon after we had to sell our lovely cottage and rent a room in a poor part of Munich. Peter became ill again, his chest would not be mended properly for three more years. Those were very hard times for people in Germany. We were poor, with no work and little food. We lived by borrowing money from my parents. It was all very sad and degrading. All of our education and knowledge of chemistry and we were having to beg.

Both Peter and I began to read books on the subject of politics. Peter showed a lot of interest in communism, he attended political meetings in and around Munich; we talked endlessly about a better, fairer world, but when we read newspaper stories about Russia and their starvation and pogroms, their style of communism was evidently not working.

In 1924 we had seen a small political party try to win power in Munich by way a putsch, I don't know your word for it, but in French it is a coup d'etat. The party was the National Socialist, or as you say 'Nazi Party'. Peter had once met the new leader of the party when he had been in hospital in 1919 and therefore took great interest in him, Adolf Hitler. Peter began to attend meetings and we would talk of the aims and policies they espoused. In the early days they sounded fanciful, impossible, but they offered an escape from our poverty. Remember Hitler told us he would create full employment and he did; he said he would ensure that all Arian Germans would have food and comfort and he did; he promised that he would make us all proud to be German again and we did. He said communism was not working to improve the life of the poor; it just made every one poorer. Eventually he was to tell us that the Russians were sub-human and have you heard of what they are doing now to the people east of the Elbe, do you believe human beings can act like that? Do the British and Americans do those things to women and children?" Terry made no comment, but stared fixedly at the vegetable garden and listened.

"Hitler said that Germany was in a bad economic state and the Jews were to blame. They controlled the finances of all of Europe and it suited them to hurt Germany at that time. When he eventually removed Jews from industry and banking, do you know what happened? The economy flourished; Germany became the most powerful industrial nation in the world within five years of removing the Jews. Hitler was again proved correct. Hitler gave us work, comfort and pride.

In 1925 Peter was offered a job with the party as long as he became a full member, so he joined. Before his job interview he was asked to supply details about both his and my parents and grand parents. Later we realised that they were checking that neither of our families had any Jewish blood; they did not. The interviewer was Heinrich Himmler, then the Deputy Gauleiter of Upper Bavaria; this was not an important post and was, in English, a regional administrator. Peter took the job; he was to be one of many bodyguards for Adolf Hitler whenever he visited Bavaria, which was often. Peter was to wear a uniform and swear an oath of allegiance; he became a member of the Protection Squad, SS.

At the time I was glad, because the position and uniform made Peter proud and he immediately became healthy again. I supported his involvement and sometimes attended rallies and meetings. Although Peter had been a corporal in the army, he started at the lowest rank in the SS. In 1926 Himmler was moved to a post in Berlin and on the day he left Munich he gave Peter a promotion and told him to be prepared to follow him one day soon. Peter was very enthusiastic and carried out difficult and dangerous tasks and he was attracting the attention of the party leaders, Himmler's bosses, but Peter always had a love for Himmler, despite working for and often being near Hitler. In February 1929 Himmler was made Reichfuhrer SS; he was only twenty-eight years old, and many people in the party were shocked and jealous, but for us this was good luck.

In March we transferred to Berlin and Peter was given the rank equivalent to Captain in your army. We had a nice apartment, a private school for Carl Peter, access to the best doctors and hospitals, a good salary and a mountain of pride. The proudest day of Peter's life came in 1933, when he was chosen as one of the Fuhrer's closest guards at his inauguration ceremony as President and Fuhrer, at the parliament building. In many photographs of that day you will see Peter, there next to Hitler. On that day I joined the National Socialist Party and was proud to do so.

In 1936 Peter was promoted to major and soon after began to work for SS General Theodor Eicke. The work was very secret and important. We moved from Berlin to," Paula paused, staring blankly at Terry and then went on, "to a town not far from here. It was then that we first met von Lutken. Peter met him often and I joined Peter at the big house on the other side of the river for dinner on two or three occasions. There was a severe shortage of labour locally and Peter was able to help supply some labourers for von Lutken and some of the other farmers and factory owners in this area.

In 1940 General Eicke was put in charge of a fighting division, SS 3rd Panzer Division 'Totenkopf'. He asked Peter to join him with the rank of full Colonel and to take control of one of the regiments. Peter accepted, of course. He did not need to drive a tank as most of his troops were motorised infantry and, to begin with, were to handle civilian refugees in the land directly behind the battle line. He joined his regiment in March and trained with them in Poland. Peter told me that he would be travelling continuously for some months and we agreed that I should move back to Munich to be near to my ageing parents. I purchased a fine house on the western side of the city. I was in a prestigious position, being the wife of a Colonel in the Waffen SS. I employed a maid, a cook and a gardener/driver. I invited my parents to the house often and ensured we repaid our debt to them a thousand times over. It was only fifteen years since we had begged for food and now we had comfort, pride and position. Hitler had made the impossible happen.

There was only one darkness in my life and that I will explain to you in one moment. First I will quickly tell you of the actions Peter was involved with. I know of them from his letters and from the things he told me when he returned home on leave. In those two years he was in Munich with me for a total of fifteen days. They were to be our last fifteen days together. In May 1940, he and his regiment transferred to France. He was involved in some fighting near Cambria against British troops, but mostly he and his men worked as policemen behind the lines. He would arrange for prisoners of war to be assembled and transported to camps in Germany; he had to ensure that captured towns and villages transferred to German law immediately; he needed to manage refugees; he had to ensure supplies reached the battle line quickly. The job you are now doing is very similar, Corporal. He was in northeast France until the French capitulated. He then went to the south of France, near the Spanish border. The work was the same, but the fighting had stopped, so I was much happier.

Early in 1941 we became aware of the un-trustworthiness of the Bolsheviks; Peter warned me that they were conspiring with rich

Jews to infiltrate Germany and France and as soon as we were fully occupied in England they would attack us through Poland. To try and prevent this treachery he and his men were rounding up communists and Jews in France and putting them in camps. It was for our own protection. Then in May his regiment was sent to Poland again to do the same thing and to protect the border against a Russian attack. Following much provocation we had to attack the massive Russian armies threatening us. Peter drove through Poland and Lithuania to Russia. His work was the same as in France, but many liberated people in the Bolshevik area volunteered to join our forces to fight the communists and Peter helped to train them.

By October he was in the area of Russia near Demyansk. This is half way between Leningrad and Moscow. The Russians had left many soldiers in the woods and forests behind our armies as we advanced on Moscow and Peter was responsible for capturing them. He wrote to me and told me that it was extremely cold and it had begun to snow and by some error his men had only summer clothes. The situation was so bad that the advance was to stop. I organised the women of my area to knit socks and pullovers and we posted them to our men. We collected old clothes and sent them too." Paula paused and looked concerned and seemed unsure of what to say. Then she smiled broadly and went on.

"Now let me tell you about my beautiful son Carl Peter. To me his life was like one wonderful dream. He grew up in Berlin and went to a very good school. The SS ran it and all of the boys became extremely patriotic. Carl Peter was very intelligent and athletic and strong. His father was immensely proud of him and it was certain that he would one day join his father in the SS service. Carl Peter loved Berlin and in his free time he and his school friends would cycle all over the city, but when he was fifteen we had to move to near here. The new school was in a small village near to a camp where his father worked. He missed Berlin and his long time friends there. He became restless and unhappy but he still had to show the discipline of the son of a SS officer; it was very hard for him. He became moody and argumentative. He visited his father's camp offices quite frequently and I thought that would help him adjust; give him an interest. Carl Peter was very loyal to his father and I and he was still a fanatical German patriot, but one day a dam burst within him, he was seventeen and about to go to a University. Over dinner he had a small argument with his father on some minor subject but then he attacked his father's work. He called it barbaric, evil and a disgrace to the German people. He denigrated the SS and even the Nazi party. He poured scorn on everything we believed in. His father struck him and they both began to fight. I was terrified, my son's eyes shone with insane hatred and I believed that one of them would die. I managed to stop them fighting and Carl Peter left the house. He never spoke to, or saw his father again.

Peter was devastated; he worshiped his son. His whole life had been to ensure he had a secure future within the SS. Carl Peter went to my parents in Munich and told them what had happened and that he was glad. He wrote to me pleading that I should go to his father's work place and see for myself the conditions and treatment under which the inmates had to work. I must admit that I did not ever go and see. Perhaps I feared that I might find that Carl Peter was right and my safe world would collapse. I was torn between my love and devotion to my husband and my love and hopes for my son. It was a very unhappy time for me. Carl Peter was so bitter that he changed his name to my maiden name, the name of his grandparents, Rozen-Kranz. He did not go to University, but worked in a clothes factory.

In September 1939, Britain and France declared war on us. It was a shock. The next day Carl Peter telephoned me to tell me that as a true German patriot he had to help defend his country and he had joined an infantry regiment in the regular army. He did not want anyone to know that his father was a major in the SS and he would now always address his letters to me in my maiden name. When I told these things to Peter he cried bitterly. In all the years together, through the pain and hardship I had never seen Peter cry.

Carl Peter fought in France and won a medal for bravery. He visited me often in Munich, but always checked to be sure that his father was not on leave at the same time. He became my private, secret son. In October 1941 his division, the 290th Infantry Division was sent to the Eastern Front. He wrote to me from near Demyansk. Yes, both my husband and son were in the same district, both were in great danger. I struggled for weeks trying to decide whether to write to them and tell them how physically close they were. I loved them both and they were so near to each other and needed each other. On the morning of the 8th January 1942 I wrote a letter to each of them telling them of their relative positions. Oh, Corporal, the date is etched in my brain, the scar is as clear as a bright light. Fifteen days later my letter to Carl Peter was returned to me unopened, along with a number of other personal belonging. He had been killed early on the morning of the 8th. He had fought bravely in a fierce blizzard against unbelievable odds; his body was in enemy territory and was unlikely to be recovered. I was to receive another medal on his behalf, for his actions that night.

One day after I had the devastating news, I received a letter from Peter dated the 15th, saying how glad he was to be serving alongside his son. He was going to take the first opportunity to visit Carl

Peter's regiment, which was only twenty kilometres away. The snow and fighting made that difficult, but he would try. He had come to feel that his son was much wiser than himself and he wanted desperately to tell him that he loved him. He wanted to tell Carl Peter that he had been right all the time and that he, Peter, had been too blind to see the evil that had torn them apart. I immediately wrote a short letter to Peter telling him of Carl Peter's death. The letter had six lines, I recall; it took me ten hours to write it.

I did not receive any correspondence from Peter for seven months, although I wrote to him every second day for all that time. In the next letter I received from him he did not mention his son. He wrote to tell me of the lice and filth that covered his uniform and of the animal enemy he was dedicated to annihilating. He told me of endless killing; of how the simpleton Russians would run in their hundreds at his guns, so many that they had stopped counting the dead. He said he would soon be in Moscow and then he would empty the city of its population.

In October I heard from Berlin that Peter's bravery in action was now a legend. No Colonel had fought from the trenches along side his men with such courage; it was as though he had a mission. He was awarded an Iron Cross with Oak Leaves, which is a great honour. To me it was obvious what Peter was trying to do and eventually he got his wish. He was killed in November. He had been in Demyansk for almost a year. The battle of Demyansk will go down in history as the greatest battle of all time, I am sure. It will never be forgotten. I cannot forget it for it took away from me my whole life, my reason for living. I am not brave enough to do damage to myself, so I have settled into a routine that will serve until my end comes, however long that may be. Peter is a great hero among National Socialists and as his widow I have been cared for with respect and dignity.

Mr von Lutken begged me to take over the management of this hotel, but I know the party told him he had to do so. Certain people in the town keep asking me if I have sufficient food or supplies and if I said there is no salt, then within a day or two a packet of salt would appear as if by magic. It is the Brotherhood of the SS which reaches everywhere and knows everything and can do anything. Well, that is until May and the death of Hitler. They all disappeared over night. I now wonder if Helmut von Lutken will remain so friendly, now he has no pressure to be nice to me. And, of course, no one wants to be seen associating with an SS widow now that you Allies are in control and are arresting anyone who is brave enough to say they were a member. If you or von Lutken send me from here, I have nowhere to go. Both my parents died last year in the fighting. An American tank shell destroyed the church they were hiding in. If we had won the war that American tank commander would now be a war criminal; he slaughtered twenty innocent civilians in that church but you won and only the defeated can be guilty."

She stood up and cleared the table and started to wash the dishes. Terry sat staring blankly at the empty wine glass in his hand. After some minutes he spoke.

"Mrs Rozen-Kranz, thank you for telling me your story and being so honest, but could I ask you a question, which I find difficult to ask? Did you know of the horrors that were being done by your rulers?"

Paula turned to face him.

"In all wars there are horrors; wars are horrid. Your airmen created horror with their bombs, destroying schools and hospitals full of innocent men, women and children. There can be no fair war".

"But, you starved civilians to death," Terry pleaded.

"There are many lies told in war. Propaganda is a strong weapon. What you have heard is exaggerated, or untrue. We used captives as forced labour, yes that is true, even here in this town. But we fed them. They could not work without sufficient food. It was not the best food and when supplies ran short we fed Germans first and reduced rations for captives, but that was logical. No one was starved to death by us."

"But they were Mrs Rozen-Kranz."

"They were not, you are repeating the lies your government spread. Have you spoken to people that we starved?"

"Yes," Terry said coldly, "when I was in Holland in May. I was in a town in northern Holland and met the Dutch people in the bars and cafes. Last year when their railway workers went on strike your SS blockaded the roads and ports and prevented the supply of food and fuel to all the population under your control. During last winter thousands of women and children starved and froze to death. I spoke to the survivors; I saw the graves, rows of them. The Dutch people I spoke to hate all Germans now. We guarded German prisoners of war, not that they may escape, but to prevent the towns people from killing the un-armed defeated troops."

"No," Paula protested, "they exaggerated. There must have been a reason. We are the most civilised nation on earth; we would not do that. No."

There was a long silence. The summer sun was sinking but it was still light. Terry's fatigue returned and his legs hurt. Paula had her back to him while she washed and dried the dinner things. Eventually she turned round and Terry saw the tears streaming down her face.

"I am so sorry," she said. "I am sorry. We have no desert or tea or coffee. Shall I fetch you a glass of beer?"

"Would you like some tea or coffee?" Terry asked.

She nodded and wiped her eyes on the napkin. Terry walked slowly to his bedroom and returned with an armful of supplies. A kettle was boiling on the wood-burning oven. He placed in front of Paula a packet of tea, a jar of jam, a packet of oatmeal and a tall thin jar of liquefied coffee. He smiled, for it was the same brand he had sold to customers in the shop for many years - Camp Coffee. Paula also smiled.

"We shall have coffee now and tomorrow morning I will bring a wonderful breakfast to your room. And we will be friends. You do remind me of Carl Peter and maybe he would have been your friend too."

CHAPTER THREE

THE NEXT DAY

Terry awoke from a deep dreamless sleep. The strange room was dark but a thin shaft of light peaked through the curtains. He was warm; the soft feather mattress had folded around him as usual but this was not home. Then he heard again the tapping sound that must have woken him. It was the sound of a door being pushed gently against a wooden obstruction. He sat up, now alert and afraid. He could not remember where he had left his Tommy gun. He had left it where he could retrieve it quickly in an emergency and where he would remember where it was, but he couldn't. He peered through the gloom at the chest of drawers that was now at an angle with the bedroom door. The night before he had locked the door and placed the drawers tight against it. The door opened again the few inches it could now achieve and Paula's voice called gently.

"Corporal, corporal, wake up it is six o'clock." Terry recognised the accented voice.

"OK Mrs Rozen-Kranz, I'm awake. I'm coming to open the door. Wait one moment please."

He swung his feet out of the high bed and when they neared the floor they encountered the cold oily metal of his Tommy gun. Wearing his vest and long-John pants he dragged the chest of drawers from behind the door. The door opened and Paula entered carrying a large jug of steaming water and while she placed it on the washstand, Terry bent to pick up his gun and put it in the wardrobe.

"Good morning," he said and turned to face her.

She was smiling shyly and began to speak uncertainly.

"Good morning. I hope you slept well. The water is for washing. In the lavatory next door I have put a bucket of water and a candle is lit. I have put there also some old letters for you to use. In thirty minutes I will return with your breakfast. I hope you don't mind me asking but could I have your underclothes. I noticed that they are dirty. If you could manage without them for two or three hours I think I could have them washed and dried. The sun is already hot. If you gave them to me now I could put them to boil immediately. I will wait outside the door."

Terry's face had turned scarlet and he could not make his mouth work. He took from his kit bag a vest and a soiled pair of long-John pants and also climbed out of those he was wearing. He tried to tie them together using the long legs, but was unable, quickly, to hide all of the stains.

"Please," said Paula from outside the room.

He tossed the un-stable bundle out to her and screwed his eyes tightly shut.

He had looked at his wristwatch seconds before he had fallen asleep and could remember it read twelve minutes before eight o'clock. It was now five minutes past six. He could not recall ever having slept for that length of time. It had been light when he'd looked out onto the deserted town square before closing the curtains. He opened the left hand curtain now and saw three people crossing the square in the direction of the bakery next door. He remembered he had no clothes on and jumped back hastily.

It was again a bright and sunny morning and the sun was high enough already to illuminate the top and higher floors of the building on the left of the square. Terry stepped back towards the window and peered at the Party Office. The swastika was still there, untouched by the builders. He felt an uneasy feeling settle into the pit of his stomach. He would have many meetings this morning, which would certainly take up all of his time before the sergeant and Arthur arrived. After that he and Wilkes were to check on the factory, bank, Party Offices and look around the town for alternative accommodation. Wilkes would be disappointed that the swastika was still there and Terry started to feel angry with the builder. There was still time for Mr Kahler to do the work, but he was leaving it very late.

Terry carried out his ablutions and, wearing his battle dress trousers, opened the bedroom door at six thirty precisely to find Paula walking down the corridor towards him. She carried a large tray covered with a white towel and she bore a friendly smile. She placed the tray on the chest of drawers and lifted the towel to reveal a cup of steaming tea, a small bowl of steaming porridge, a basket of cut bread, a boiled egg in an eggcup, a jug of cool milk and a pat of butter. Terry's eyes widened with delight.

"Where on earth did you find all the things to create this superb breakfast?"

Paula was pleased.

"I was out shopping early this morning," she replied. "The bread is freshly baked and a neighbour's hen presented the egg during the night. Milk and butter from the cellar and the rest from the stores you gave to me last night. Simple really."

"Were there any comments, or rumours flying about at the bakery, you know, about what is happening today?"

Paula shrugged.

"Some, but I think we'll see what happens."

Terry enjoyed his breakfast and began to relish the thought of what he could achieve today. He could have the town organised and under control by tomorrow and be able to offer the sergeant the chance to send extra refugees to Altewiese to relieve the pressure on Christine. He dressed in shirt and tunic, finding that he had begun to itch through the lack of underclothes protection. He polished and checked his rifle and the Tommy gun and took both with him downstairs.

The wide reception and bar area made Terry think of his school assembly hall or even a hospital waiting room. The more he considered this idea, the more it made sense to him. The table and three chairs they had used yesterday lay in the alcove created by the front window and the side of the office. He straightened the table, placed his rifle and Tommy gun on it and placed one chair behind it, with its back to the grocery wall. He sat in the chair and decided to have one chair on the left of the table where Paula could sit and translate and two chairs opposite him for the interviewees. In the bar area on the other side of the front doors he arranged twenty-four chairs in four rows as a type of waiting room.

He un-stacked the tables and shoved them hard against the bar front, the Bakery wall and the front window. He imagined that people could leave their coats or shopping bags on these tables and in any case he found the arrangement looked neat and orderly. There were many extra chairs which he placed facing the tables. He again sat at his lone table and surveyed the room; he was pleased. The flow of people would first sit in the waiting area and, when their turn arrived, would be called forward to sit in front of him.

Terry thought that his two guns were overly threatening. He would leave the Tommy gun on the table, close to his right hand and pointing towards any interviewee, but the rifle would have to go somewhere else. He went to the pitch-dark office and remembering its layout from the previous evening, felt his way to the shelving. He pulled some boxes of copy invoices from the top left-hand shelves and let them fall to the floor replacing them on the shelf with his rifle. He collected a handful of postcards and, closing the office door behind him, returned to his interviewing position. He laid the cards, picture down, in front of himself and took his stubby pencil from his tunic pocket and laid it next to them. His wristwatch read seven o'clock and he called Paula. When she arrived she noted the layout of the tables and chairs and smiled and nodded approval to Terry.

"Mrs Rozen-Kranz, please unlock and open both of the front doors. Show any persons to the waiting area seating and join me here to translate when necessary."

Paula opened the doors, but no one was waiting outside.

"A little too early, perhaps," Terry noted. "Could you ensure that the back door is securely locked and bring six water glasses and a jug of water for my table, please".

Paula left the reception area. From the angle of Terry's chair he could see anyone who entered the front doors and could also watch the foot of the staircase leading to the next floor, but he could not see out of the front doors and therefore anyone who was approaching across the square. Even when standing he could not see out of the brown and green smoked windows. He sat still, but soon became anxious to check if people were crossing the square towards the hotel steps. He rose and went to the door. There were five or six people walking in front of the town hall, otherwise the square was empty. He stood for a while looking around, hoping to see one of the two policemen so that he could call them to assist him with processing the various visitors that would soon arrive. He did not see anyone leave or enter the police station.

Suddenly he realised that he was un-armed, his gun was on his table. He wondered if he was already feeling much safer in this new hostile environment, but returned to his chair quickly. Paula placed the glasses and water jug on the table and went off again only to re-appear moments later pushing a wheeled captain's chair. Its carved arms and dark green leather upholstery were shining brightly. She indicated to him to move his current chair to the side of the table and he sat, regally, in his new throne-like swivel chair. He smiled broadly at Paula.

"It was originally in the office," she said. "I had it in my room recently, but I don't need it and you look very good in it. Very impressive! I'll sit with you for a while shall I and we can talk about the town and the people I know in it."

"Yes, Mrs Rozen-Kranz that would be great, although I feel sure we will be busy shortly. Thank you for the chair, it was a nice thought. Can you tell me something about the fertiliser factory. I was hoping to visit it later."

"You must remember that I have lived here for only two years so may have incomplete knowledge. The factory is owned by von Lutken which would not surprise you I'm sure. It was built I believe in 1928, or 1929. It was designed to produce large quantities of one single fertiliser, a potash based mixture that was for use in wheat, corn and rice production. The company marketed the fertiliser by bagging it for other firms or wholsalers. There were changes and improvements made to the compound over the years and different chemicals were shipped into the factory from various parts of Germany and Italy. I don't know why von Lutken got involved in the project in the first place although I think it did provide much needed work for the townspeople at the time.

By 1939 there was a shortage of local labour because of the thriving economy and military service and it was then that von Lutken asked for help from his SS friends. They arranged for workers from the nearest labour camp to be sent here. The Government used criminals or other bad people who were in prison to work during their imprisonment. Yes, some were Jews, but mostly they were German communists, and eventually Polish peasants. My husband was at the camp and was responsible for the workers here. They did not travel every day to and from the camp, they were housed in the warehouse opposite the factory gates. Camp guards were lodged here at this hotel - the rooms in the roof for the soldiers and two of the rooms like yours for their officers. We would send invoices to the camp for the accommodation and they would invoice von Lutken's factory or estate for the labour.

Sometimes, yes, the workers were used on the farms and even in road and house building. Of course they were treated properly, if they had not been fed they could not have worked. They did not live in comfort, they were prisoners and their conditions here were better than in prison, but not luxurious. I must tell you though, in 1942, some of the production capacity was switched to war material production; they mixed chemicals for firebombs. Please, in your country many factories would have had to make war things, that is normal. This factory stopped all of its production in March. The workers were taken back to the camp near Bergen. Could the factory begin production again? I think not, for I guess that the chemicals for the fertiliser are impossible to obtain and distribution of the finished product may prove difficult. The management, chemists and labour would be easier to find, but that would be von Lutken's choice."

"Helmut von Lutken," Terry said, "seems a very wealthy man. What do you know of him and his family?"

"He is rich, that is for sure. His family has owned all of the land in this valley for almost two hundred and thirty years. They received it from a local Duke as reward for military services during the Napoleonic wars. At that time I would imagine that it was all forest. They cleared the trees and started farming, mostly cattle and pigs. They built the village for their staff and tenant farmers and built the big house about one hundred years ago. Von Lutken is an only child although he must have many cousins. His parents died when he was quite young. How old is he? I would say he is sixty, or sixty-five. He had a military education and training and fought in the 1914 War. He was an officer and won a medal, which he is very proud of, but I don't know where he fought, or if he was wounded.

During the very hard times, between 1920 and 1928, he had problems paying his debts. He was forced to sell the farms to the west of the main road in order to survive. He is very bitter about this. The farmers who borrowed money from banks to buy the land were lucky. Their bankers became insolvent and closed, leaving them with nothing to pay back. Whereas von Lutken's bankers continued in business and demanded that he repay his debts. His bankers were Jewish.

He was married before the 1914 War, but his wife was unable to have children. They are both strong Catholics and support the local church. His wife died in the early 1930's and he has not remarried. In 1928 the ownership of his bank changed and the new owners were very generous to him helping him to finance the fertiliser factory and, when the postal authorities built a new post office, to buy and set up this hotel. He has built a number of new houses on the north west side of the town and he owns the creamery.

Politically he is a.... no.... was a Nazi party member and was the chairman of the local branch. He is a very powerful member of the town council as over half of the voters are his tenants. Personally I find him unattractive; he is overbearing and rude, argumentative and belligerent. When he dies they will have a difficult time finding all of his distant relatives and sharing out his wealth and land."

Terry rose and walked to the door again, but no one was approaching the hotel. He slowly made his way back to the table.

"The postcards here on the table, I have taken them to make notes on. I was wondering whether to send one to my parents but I think the censors would not approve. Incidentally, do you have an envelope for my letter home? No, well never mind. The invoices in the office - you should use them to start your fire and oven - the ink is too smudgy to use in the lavatory. You should burn them soon or hide them in the cellar. The addresses may prove embarrassing. Keep any dated before you became manageress if you wish. The photograph of Hitler, is it yours? I thought so, please remove it; it is better destroyed or very securely hidden. The policemen have not reported for orders and it is almost nine o'clock."

"I will make you a cup of coffee and check to see how dry your underclothes are; I will return shortly."

Terry watched her leave and was once more impressed with her honesty and confidence. He felt he might be able to trust her, particularly, because of her dislike of von Lutken. He was beginning to find her comfortable. He took a postcard and wrote on it:

Sgt Wilkes
SHOPPING LIST
Envelopes
Lice soap
Coffee and tea
More coins and notes
Photograph of King George
Matches
Photograph of F M Montgomery
Paper with letterhead of Government of Occupation
Union Jack and new flag of Germany
Book on fertiliser mixing
Torch and batteries

Paula put two cups of coffee onto the table and a little jug of milk. Terry smiled at her and wrote 'SUGAR' on his postcard list.

"Thank you. Why did von Lutken refuse to pay the policeman Kurt Muller?"

"I don't know," she replied, "Mr Muller is not a local man and like me may have been forced on the town by way of a favour to the Party hierarchy. He arrived last year, in August I seem to remember. At that time he carried one arm in a sling but he discarded the sling quite quickly. He did not arrive here in a uniform but I feel sure he had been an officer. He has a strong personality and is very active, always wanting to be introduced to the people of the town. I would suggest that he had a clash of personalities with von Lutken. Mr Muller is unlikely to have accepted the 'lord of the manor' bullying him, as the other two policemen do."

"Von Lutken lives in the big house which must be almost two miles away. Does he have a house in town also?" Terry asked.

"No. He could have stayed at this hotel if he'd needed to but I think I know what you are asking. How can he have such immediate influence on the town leaders from a distance of two miles? He uses a telephone. Yes, that's correct, there's no telephone service today. Von Lutken had a private line laid under his fields and the river and underground to the police station. It uses the old wind up battery type electricity. It was laid by the imported labour in 1940 or 1941 and therefore would not have cost very much. The senior constable is in constant contact with von Lutken and is always carrying messages for him to the town hall or party offices. Von Lutken rarely visits the town in person, although he has three cars and a butler-driver."

"Was there a Gestapo officer based here?" Terry asked bluntly.

"Not while I have been here. The Party is very strong and the local population is regarded as loyal."

"What happened to the Jewish part of that population?"

Paula hesitated and looked shocked at Terry's knowledge.

"They were sent for resettlement to Poland. That was seven or eight years ago. The cinema over there was their synagogue. The Party office was once a bank owned by Jews, as were many of the shops. I don't know what would happen if they were all to return from Poland. That would be a problem you would have to deal with."

"According to the reports I have read it is unlikely to be a problem I will have to face," Terry said sarcastically.

He went to the door and looked out again. There were no builders removing the swastika. There were a number of men standing at the door of Meyer's bar, all staring in his direction. Terry imagined that they were all smiling.

"The mayor should have reported to me ten minutes ago but I assume he has a more important appointment. The appointment with me was only a matter of his life or death, so I am wondering what it could have been." The mounting anger was beginning to show in Terry's words and gestures.

"What do you know of the right honourable Mayor Hasch?"

"Hasch is a local man. Worked on the estate for von Lutken for many years. He is a strong Nazi. Blond wife, five children; one boy was conscripted in October, he was sixteen and a half. Hasch was delighted, threw a street party to send his son to war. I heard the boy was captured in the Ardennes so may return one day. What are you going to do Corporal?"

"Do? I will have to wait for the arrival of my sergeant who will be very angry with me. He may take me away and send the big soldier and his friends to Altewiese to ensure that Nazism is dead. There will be shooting. Me? I may well be sitting on top of a smelly lavatory for some time."

Paula stared at Terry with a mixture of sympathy and incomprehension.

"Please, it is not your fault Mrs Rozen-Kranz, you have been honest and helped me a lot, but I do not seem to have the personality to influence the people of the town. I must be too young. I will have to write a different letter to my Mum and Dad, too. Would you get a jug of beer from the cellar, that at least may please the sergeant; oh, and ensure there is water and paper in the lavatory."

Five minutes later Paula re-entered the reception carrying a jug of beer and a bundle of washed underwear. Terry took the white clean clothes to the dark office and re-dressed himself. As he walked out of the office he hit the door hard with his clenched fist and splintered the wood. He stared angrily at his reddened knuckles and went back into the office. When he came out again he was carrying his rifle and his jaw was set into a tight grimace. He marched to the doors and placed the gun to his shoulder and aimed at the men outside Meyer's bar; he snarled the words 'bastards' four or five times.

Paula was watching him warily and at the first opportunity slipped away to the kitchen; she stood near to the kitchen door and smiled. Terry lowered his rifle as the men ran, crouching, into the bar; he smiled. He wondered why he had been so naive as to believe that his speech yesterday would have convinced these Nazis to do as he asked. Authority came from power and power should be delivered by violence not the waving of Montgomery's signature. He stood on the top step and surveyed the now deserted square. He felt no fear; he did not consider the consequence of standing in the open, in enemy territory. His gut wrenching anger blinded him to the threat and danger. The audience he had addressed yesterday were all now laughing at him from behind the windows and doors around the square and he wanted to hurt them. He stood in the same position for ten minutes and his temper did not abate.

From the lane next to the police station emerged the noisy, ponderous Tessy. Terry did not smile in relief but reddened in embarrassment and held the rifle in an even tighter grip. The sergeant was driving and pulled up at the foot of the hotel steps. He climbed out of the truck and hurriedly Terry remembered to salute. Arthur carrying a Tommy gun climbed from the passenger seat and walked around Tessy to join them.

"Good morning Corporal, everything nice and quiet," the sergeant smiled, but could see the tension in Terry's face. "How many of the grateful population turned up this morning?"

"None, sir," Terry snapped back.

"Have you worked out why none of them turned up?"

"Von Lutken told them not to, sir. That's my guess."

"Well done Corporal, I'll make an officer of you yet. How does he control them here, when he lives two miles away?"

"Sir," Terry was astounded at the sergeant's obvious grasp of the situation, "he has a phone link to the police station. How did you know that?"

"That is why I'm a sergeant. When von Lutken didn't show up for your little presentation, I knew he would be trouble. When I got back to Bachwald last evening I asked one of our tame police constables what he knew about Altewiese. He told me of the field phone system and that von Lutken was the unopposed ruler of this community. I would have been surprised if any of the people you spoke to yesterday would be brave enough to cross von Lutken. They are much more afraid of him than they are of you. Now, you still look pissed off to me, so what we will do is have a drink of the nice beer you hide here and then you and I will have a visit to God in his manor house."

The three of them walked to the table on which Paula had placed the beer jug and, to which Terry noticed, she had added three glasses. The sergeant looked around the room at the layout designed by Terry and smiled. Arthur put an arm on Terry's shoulder.

"Good try mate. Unfortunately you may need to get a little rough before you get the smooth."

"Arthur you are staying here while Terry and I do the rounds. We'll be back at fourteen thirty, so be ready to go as soon as we arrive."

"Do you want me to get my kit and the stores and the money, sir?" Terry asked.

"You're going to chicken out are you?" sneered the sergeant.

"No sir," shouted Terry, "I assume you don't think I can handle what's happening here and that you are about to replace me, Sergeant Wilkes, sir".

"Are you willing to stay on and sort it out, it might get nasty?"

"If you leave me here on my own it will get sorted out, sergeant, and it will get very nasty. I've had enough of these bastards and would love to have another go at them, sir."

"Good." Wilkes smiled, "by fourteen thirty we will have a better idea of the true situation. If it's looking particularly damn dangerous, you'll come back with us and we'll come down here on Thursday mob handed. You and Hardaker can play Tom Mix and shoot a few Red Indians. I'm going to visit the lavatory; when I come back I'll take your Tommy gun, you bring the rifle and we'll patrol this nice quiet town and have a trip to the manor." He left Terry with Arthur.

"He likes you, he told me on the way down that you'd make a good lorry driver and that's a big compliment from Wilkes. He toyed with the idea of bringing Hardaker instead of me, 'cos he felt there might be trouble. He said that if no one accepted your invitation to attend this morning, he would be angry for you. I reckon old Wilkes is now angry enough to do without Hardaker's trigger finger. If bullets start to fly, remember to duck."

"Thanks for telling me that Arthur," said a relieved Corporal Hall.

Wilkes drove Tessy slowly passed Meyer's bar, Terry peering menacingly through the windows, his rifle pointing in the direction of the bar door. They turned right at the riverside road away from the bridge and towards the factory. Terry told Wilkes what Paula had said about von Lutken and the labour camp inmates.

"That's good. The Nazi bastard used slave labour to earn his profit. War criminal for sure. Guilty."

The first properties on the riverside of the road were six small single storey cottages, followed by two large sheds, all these being opposite a small church and neat churchyard. A road joined them from the right, which switched back over the northern edge of the town to the main road. Terry felt certain that this was the same road that he'd noticed to the rear of the hotel. Next on the left was a timber yard with a workshop building near the road. The gates were locked but the piles of wood looked recently cut and the office windows had been cleaned.

Opposite were some houses and behind these they could just make out a cemetery. They now came to a high mesh fence topped with barbed wire. Behind the fence to the right was a tall wooden warehouse. There was a pair of locked gates and two wooden sentry boxes next to them. Behind a tall wire mesh fence to the left was a factory complex as big as the sergeant's timber yard and sawmill in Bachwald. There was one large two-storey factory building with four chimneys against the river wall. Next to it was a two-storey office block, with many windows. Both buildings were made of brick and painted cream. There was little sign of weathering. A large yard ran across the front and right hand side of the property. There was a pair of chained and locked gates in the fence. The sergeant gently ran the nose of his lorry up to the gates and continued to accelerate. The gates held firm and Tessy's back wheels began to spin.

"Another time then," said the sergeant as he reversed and turned the truck to face back towards the town. They took the left fork at the church and were able to confirm the considerable size of the cemetery; they passed a large school, which had extensive playing fields to the side and rear. Otherwise the street was residential, with houses and cottages of various ages and designs along both sides. As they passed it, Terry pointed to the back entrance to the hotel. They met the main north-south road at the garage. The sergeant stopped the lorry for a moment.

"If you look through the dirty side windows of this repair garage you will see the outline of a lorry," he said. "We might need that before long. The big house will know we're on the move and be expecting us, but this little detour may well confuse them. Have you cooled down a bit because I want you to act sensibly?"

"Sergeant, I have not cooled down, but I will act sensibly as soon as you get us to that big bastard's big house, sir," Terry replied hotly.

They turned right and headed north over the bridge and up the incline to the lane on their right leading into the estate. After half a mile there was a track leading up to two old cottages, one of which had smoke curling out of its high pointed chimney; along side these were rows of glass houses, each full of green plants. There were no people about. Half a mile in front of them was an orchard of fruit trees almost empty of blossom and with many small apples and plums appearing. The road skirted south of these and faced a small wood to the north of which was the large house.

"This reminds me," said Terry, "at home we used to receive a weekly order for fruit from Lord and Lady Somebody. They lived in a big Hall three miles south of Stone. It had a long drive like this. Another greengrocer in Stone received the vegetable order but our shop always got the one for fruit. I don't know why that was. Anyway when I was nine I started delivering their order on my shop bicycle. You know the type, sergeant, with the small front wheel and a big basket and our shop name written on a metal plate hanging from the cross bar. It was my treat of the week, because I would have to deliver the fruit to the side kitchen door and the cook was a really nice woman.

Every week I was invited into the kitchen and if it was cold or raining, I'd get a cup of tea and a piece of cake; if it was warm and sunny, she'd have a glass of real lemonade and a sweet for me. One time, I must have been twelve or thirteen, the cook says that Lord and Lady What's-Her-Name are away and would I like a look around the house. So she shows me how the other half live. Bloody luxury there was. He only owned a few pot banks; I thought there must be a lot of money in making cups and saucers to afford a place like that. They had a big dining room with a table for fourteen people, a library, a gunroom, two lounges, a billiard room, a sitting room, a conservatory full of wild flowers and that was only on the ground floor. This place we are coming to is much the same size. This one looks newer. Mrs Rozen-Kranz said it was built a hundred years ago; the one near Stone was Elizabethan the cook told me."

"Did they have a butler?" the sergeant asked.

"No I don't think so sir, but this one does, because that chap coming down the steps towards us looks just like a butler to me. Unless von Lutken normally meets guests dressed in a stripped shirt under a leather apron."

The truck swung round on the gravel circle at the front of the house and before getting out of the cab, the sergeant spoke.

"Have a look up that side of the house, see the stables. There are two horses' heads popping out and neither looks like the carthorses we passed yesterday. The three nearest stables are certainly vehicle garages now. See the nose of a Mercedes Sport Roadster peaking out of one and I'd say that next pretty nose is a Sedan of some sort. Stay calm, I'll do the talking," the sergeant said nervously as he climbed down to meet the butler. He swung the Tommy gun over his shoulder, but Terry walked round the truck with his rifle pointing at the ground fifteen feet in front of himself.

"Good morning," said the butler politely, " what do you want?" His heavy accent sounded Polish or Russian.

"Mr von Lutken, is he in?" snapped Wilkes.

"No he is out."

"When will he return?"

"Please, speak clearly, my English is poor," the butler spoke confidently despite the show of arms. He was over sixty and his shaved head shone in the sun. On a chain hanging from his belt was a bunch of large keys partly hidden in the front pouch pocket of his apron.

"Mr von Lutken comes back when?" shouted the sergeant. The butler shrugged a 'don't know', so the sergeant continued. "Where is he, what is he doing?" As if by reply a shotgun sounded in the distance. Terry looked towards the orchard, confused about the direction the sound had travelled, but Wilkes visibly ducked down. A second shot rang out, this time Terry was certain it came from the woods behind the house and possibly a mile away. The butler smiled.

"Hunting," he said. "He is shooting dinner."

"Bollocks," the sweating sergeant replied and turned to Terry. "Do we hang around or come back later?"

Terry ignored him and slowly lifted the rifle until the barrel was pointing at the butler's nose.

"Lead us to the gunroom, please," he said quietly. The butler now looked alarmed.

"No. You wait for Mr von Lutken."

Terry smiled at him and noisily switched the rifle safety catch off. The butler evidently was aware of the significance of this noise.

"No gunroom," he muttered. "I am only a servant." Terry appeared to pull the rifle away from the butler's face, but then suddenly rammed it forward into his teeth. The barrel hit the left front upper tooth with such force that it snapped it at the gum and broke the top lip, so that a spurt of blood shot on to the rifle sights.

"Take us to the gun store or I will push this down your throat," Terry said sharply. The butler, now ashen with fright, turned and led the two soldiers up the steps and into the cool shadowy house. The wood panelling was hung with paintings of formal German gentlemen all with walrus moustaches. They walked on a fine brown and green carpet, passed doors leading to a dining room, sunny lounge, and dark pantry. There was a wide staircase with ornately carved banisters in the centre of the house and near it was a door that the butler opened. The room was long and narrow and led to a tall window. The left and right walls were covered with shelving full of books. There was a reading table and two comfortable cushioned chairs. The butler closed the door behind them, his lip bleeding profusely and Terry's rifle barrel dripping six inches from his cheek. To the left of the door was a tall glass fronted cabinet inside which were three double barrel shot guns standing to attention. There was an empty space next to the last one. Terry spoke calmly to the butler. "Open it."

"No keys. I am a servant. Do not hurt me please."

It soon became obvious that the sergeant had not seen the keys in the butler's pouch for he un-slung the Tommy gun and used its butt to smash the glass in the cabinet. He removed the three shotguns and pulled open the two low drawers at the foot of the cabinet. The first one contained a number of boxes of shotgun cartridges and low calibre bullets. The bottom drawer held gun cleaning material and tools. To the right of the door was a narrow four-drawer chest with a small bronze statue of a pheasant on top of it. The top draw had a polished brass keyhole in it. Terry indicated this with the rifle.

"Open that with one of the keys in your pocket." The butler hesitated for only a second before finding a key that fitted. Wilkes opened the top draw in which was a shining wooden box; inside this was a dark grey automatic pistol laying to the left and an empty indentation for a matching pistol to the right. Above these were a silencer and a cleaning rod and two unloaded ammunition clips.

"Very nice, it says inside the lid here, Walther made them," Wilkes said. "Shame one is missing."

"Sir if I may I would like that lot," Terry interrupted.

The sergeant pushed the bronze pheasant to the floor and placed the gun box on top of the chest of drawers. He opened the second drawer. This one contained a black leather gun box with an enamel swastika in the centre. The box held one black lugar pistol and some tools. The third drawer revealed a pair of very old matching duelling pistols in a carved wooden case. The bottom drawer held a plain wooden box with a small oblong metal inscription plate which showed that it had been the property of Colonel Wilfred Scott-Porter of the Welsh Guards in 1915. It contained a simple British Army issue Webbley revolver. The sergeant loaded the butler's outstretched arms with the four gun boxes and ten cartons of cartridges and one of bullets. He filled his own arms with the Tommy gun and the three shotguns. With Terry guiding the butler with his rifle barrel they walked back through the house to the hot and sultry Tessy.

As the two soldiers started to drive away the sergeant shouted over the engine noise to the butler.

"Tell von Lutken he must bring his remaining shotgun to the Hotel Alte Poste, immediately".

The butler made no sign of having understood what was said, but just stared sadly at the rear of the truck as it trundled away. The shotguns and gun boxes were behind the two seats on the floor of the cab. Terry laid his rifle against his door and turned to retrieve the wooden box containing the single automatic pistol.

"You did say I could keep this one, didn't you, sir?" he asked the sergeant.

"You've earned it by that display of controlled violence, I'd say. The others are of far greater value and I'll put them in the kitty. Take one of the shotguns and some cartridges; who knows von Lutken may offer to teach you how to shoot dinner. What's that say on the inside of that gun box?"

Terry had opened the box and was loading one of the two magazine clips with bullets from the carton. Stuck to the underside of the box lid was a document written in old Gothic script, which Terry tried to decipher.

"From the few bits that I can guess at, sir, I'd say this pair of guns were presented to Officer von Lutken, by his regiment, on the day of his marriage in 1912. One for each of the happy couple; she's dead now, by the way."

"Perhaps her one of the pair was buried with her. That pistol is very light in weight and calibre; you'd be better off with the Webbley."

"No this little thing will be fine, sir. I'm going to have two practice shots at those marsh reeds by the river, so hold tight."

With that he fired twice, the empty cases pinging into the truck door and bouncing into the road. Terry seemed pleased with the action and put the automatic into his right-hand tunic pocket. He replaced the gun case behind the sergeant's seat and lifted his rifle onto his lap, its bloodied barrel sticking out of the truck. They drove quickly and directly back to the hotel where Arthur greeted them from the top step.

"All bin quiet here, sir, but I heard a couple of shots a while ago, coming from where you was."

"Yes," said the sergeant, "bloody Tom Mix here decided to have a practice shoot at some grass and missed. We are expecting some reaction from von bloody Lutken so keep your eyes peeled and the Tommy gun ready. Look behind the seats and move the shotguns and three gun cases under the tarpaulin. Terry has just taken one case and a shotgun up to his room. Did he take a couple of cartons of ammo? Good. He and I are going to take a walk round the square. We'll be in eye contact with you but if anything starts to happen, hold your fire until we're behind you. Terry has the keys to the back door so we'll make our way round there and join you here; that is if any trouble starts. With or without Terry, we leave at two thirty, so be ready."

Terry re-appeared on the steps and handed the sergeant a letter and a postcard.

"Sir, can you stick that letter in an envelope and post it for me, please. It's to my Mum and Dad and I've just written their address on the back. On the postcard is my shopping list, I hope it's OK, sir?"

Wilkes placed the letter into his tunic breast pocket and read the list. "My name is Sergeant Wilkes not Jesus - miracles I do not perform. Envelopes, coffee, more cash, matches, will be here on Thursday. Torch and batteries you should have in your kit, but we'll assume they forgot to give you them, so Thursday, too. Lice soap and sugar, no bloody chance. Photographs of the King and Monty will take one week, as will a Union Jack. There is no German flag anymore - they are to use ours or nothing. Book on fertiliser mixing, now I was wondering what colour cover you had in mind, but I'll make the request and doubt anyone will do anything about it. Government of Occupation letterheads can only be issued to officers of rank of Captain and above and who can read and write. I know what you want them for but we haven't got access to any. What we'll do is get some Altewiese Town Council letterheads from the town hall and you sign at the bottom, Corporal T Hall for the Government of Occupation British Zone. The piece of paper will prove worthless but will carry some weight locally for a time. Now let's get over to the police station and see what his lordship is telling our loyal constables. Whichever building we go into one of us must wait at the door so Arthur here can see him. Arthur gets to feeling lonely if he can't see one of us, don't you son?"

They all smiled nervously and Wilkes and Terry walked quickly across the square to the police station. On the way Terry asked to be allowed to go inside and have the sergeant stand at the threshold. The station door was closed, but unlocked; inside was a gloomy room with a high counter slicing it in half. There were dusty posters on the walls, one with a cartoon of aggressive British soldiers strangling babies. There was no one on duty in the police station, but a telephone was ringing on a desk behind the counter. Terry jumped onto the counter with a clatter of boots and rifle; he swung himself over and picked up the telephone receiver. He said nothing but listened for a few moments to a shouted German barrage, none of which he understood. Finally there was a pause and Terry spoke into the mouthpiece.

"Hair Lutken come on see here bitter, schnell," which was Terry's total German vocabulary, all having been learned at the cinema in Stone during the past four years. The phone went dead and Terry replaced the receiver; traced the wiring to a socket in the rear wall and tore the wiring from it. The two now headed to the bank opposite, tried the large doors and peered through the windows. There was no one inside and they could not gain entry. They decided to try later; in fact Terry was not to go inside the bank until December and Wilkes never did.

The town hall was next door and its double doors were propped wide open. This time Terry stood just inside the doors but in full view of Arthur who was standing on the top step of their hotel. It was obvious to the sergeant that the desks and chairs that would normally be to the rear of the building had all been dragged forward into the entrance hall in order to enjoy the light from the windows and open doors. There were six such desks but only one was occupied now. A young female secretary sat at a typewriter, her eyes bulging with fright at the sight of the stocky armed and threatening soldier. The sergeant noted that there were papers scattered on three other desks which possibly indicated that the occupiers had left hastily leaving the secretary to face his menace all alone. The sergeant smiled at her, walked towards her slowly and put out his right hand. They shook hands. The sergeant continued smiling despite the distinct smell of fresh urine. He did not look below her desk for fear of embarrassing the young lady. To the right of the typewriter was a pile of town hall letterheads; he took them and indicated to the girl that he wanted more. She stood and crabbed her way to the next desk, keeping her face to the sergeant all the time. She gave him a few more copies, but did not move again.

Wilkes looked around the entrance office and then peered into the rear rooms but they were too dark to identify anything. As he was making his way back to Terry by the door, he spotted a small wall cupboard which he correctly guessed contained numerous keys. He called the girl over to him and pointing at the keys and then going to the door and pointing at the Party Offices, managed to make her understand. She shook her head and said, "Nein."

With the sheets of paper tucked into the sergeant's tunic the two soldiers made their way to the still swastika emblazoned party office. The sergeant tried the doors and found them locked. He waved at Arthur to attract his attention and showed him the Tommy gun; he stepped away from the door and then fired eight rounds at its lock. The noise was deafening in the quiet square; startled birds flew quickly away and curtains swung closed. Wilkes then kicked the door open and indicated that Terry should enter. Inside was a long wide corridor with four doors to the left and one to the right. The first one on the left was furnished with desks and chairs and rows of filing cabinets. It was lit from the windows overlooking the square and Terry could see posters and photographs on the walls all bearing swastikas or images of Hitler. The remaining rooms to the left were too dark to enter but appeared cold and empty. The door to the right led into a large meeting chamber with five rows of tiered bench seating around the three walls and alongside the door a raised canopied chair. The light from the windows was augmented by light streaming in from a glass dome in the roof. At the far end of the room was a very large print of Hitler in full military uniform and to either side of the canopied chair were red and black flags each sporting bold swastikas. Terry looked again at the benches and estimated that they had seating capacity for five hundred people. That the small town of Altewiese required seating for five hundred local party members on a regular basis was not comforting for Terry, neither was the lack of dust.

They both walked up to the post office building but this too proved to be locked and there was no apparent activity inside. As they moved back to the hotel and Arthur, they spotted movement in Meyer's Gasthof bar but the regulars were always scurrying around so they paid scant attention to them.

"Have you seen the manageress, Mrs Rozen-Kranz?" Terry asked Arthur when they reached him.

"No, I've seen no one in the hotel, nor heard anyone."

"If you need a shit go now," the sergeant said. "Then I'll go and we'll be off."

"I'm staying Sergeant Wilkes," said Terry.

"Von Lutken has not reacted to our gun taking. He might be waiting for one of us to be left alone. He might then collect a few comrades and come looking for a fight. Three of us all heavily armed are a big deterrent, but one young lad would not be. I would not be happy leaving you here alone."

"Sergeant Wilkes, you will be routinely visiting me again on Thursday. I want to stay here, at least until then; it's only two days from today. I have the Tommy gun, rifle, shotgun and pistol. If it gets too hot I'm going to camp in the cellar; there's plenty of food, drink and oil lamp paraffin down there. When you get here on Thursday, if I'm not on this step, call for me down the cellar stairs. I don't know why, sir, but I do not feel afraid; angry and irritated by them, but not frightened of what they might try."

"Not frightened is close to not breathing, Terry."

"Please, sir, trust me; give me another chance to prove that I can control myself and these bastards."

Tessy rolled across the square with Wilkes at the wheel and Arthur pointing a shotgun out of its glassless window. Terry watched them from the hotel steps. When the truck was out of sight he breathed deeply, wondered how big a fool he had been and returned to his green leather swivel chair. He placed the smelly Tommy gun on the table in the position he had chosen for it that morning. The rifle and loaded shotgun he put against the wall just inside the door of the dark office. When he found her, he would have Paula unlock the cellar door. He closed one half of the front doors, bolting it securely to its floor catch. He reasoned that if attacked through the door, they would only be able to enter one at a time. He would spray the door with machine gun rapid fire while making his way to the office. He would, from the office door, give two blasts of his shotgun and retreat to the cellar. From there he would shoot at anything that tried to follow him down the stairs. Therefore he made the next part of his preparations the transfer of all his ammunition to the cellar. He needed to find Paula urgently and equally as urgently he needed to visit the lavatory - he hoped he had not caught Wilkes's bowel complaint.

He could not find Mrs Rozen-Kranz in the kitchen or her room. The rear door was locked and both her keys were in the locks. He called her, but received no reply. He went into the lavatory and sat in the darker of the two cubicles, he had purposely left the lavatory and cubicle doors open. While he sat there and before he was ready to stand, he heard the muffled sound of a vehicle engine. It did not sound like Tessy, a noise he now knew well. It was a car engine and the car was approaching quickly. He heard the squeal of brakes as it stopped in front of the hotel. Terry only then realised the ridiculousness of his situation. He was mid way through a shit, his Tommy gun lay on the table by the front door, his rifle and newly acquired shotgun were in the office next door, the cellar door was locked and a car load of enemy were even now entering the hotel in search of him, and there was no toilet paper. He heard one set of metal studded boots on the reception floor, which then stopped.

A loud angry German voice shouted, "Tommy, shit house Tommy." Terry wondered how whoever it was knew that he was in the lavatory. He pulled up his long pants and battledress trousers, fastening them only at the waistband. He peeped around the lavatory door and could make out the silhouette of one large figure set against the backlight of the open door. As Terry's eyes became accustomed to the light he could see that the man was not carrying a weapon but was looking now towards the table where the Tommy gun lay. As the figure began to move towards it Terry decided to attract its attention; he walked smartly out of the lavatory to the gap between the reception counter and the office, saying at the same time, "Who are you? What do you want?"

The figure was tall, but thin and over sixty years of age; he was dressed in a hunting jacket and plus four trousers all in matching green velvet. Around the waist of the jacket was a light brown leather belt and to its right was attached a small covered holster. The holster cover was fastened. On his head he wore a Tyrolean style hat. He walked towards Terry in a threatening confident manner and when close to him, Terry could see that he had a bushy, white, walrus moustache, his eyes were wide with anger and his lower lip twitched, before he said in broken English, "You shit house, Tommy. Who stole my guns?"

"Who are you?" asked Terry in a composed manner, although his stomach was starting to knot with rage.

"Helmut von Lutken," the man said proudly and then put his face very close to that of Terry; when he spoke again it was in a screamed German and spittle splashed onto Terry's face. Terry had no idea what was being shouted at him and when von Lutken poked a finger into his chest, he refused to give ground. Von Lutken stopped to catch his breath; he took one step back and Terry took one step forwards to re-establish the forehead-to-forehead confrontation. Before von Lutken could resume his tirade, Terry spoke calmly.

"Hair von Lutken, you are under arrest for crimes against humanity, for your use of slave labour at your factory here in Altewiese."

Von Lutken looked puzzled and again stepped back.

"What did you say, shit house corporal?" he said, more quietly this time.

From the half landing of the staircase Paula translated into German what Terry had said. Von Lutken looked up to her, startled. Terry kept staring directly at him; he then spurted a short barrage of German. On finishing, Paula said in English, "He thinks you are a part of a female's anatomy, he wants to speak to a British officer not a worthless Corporal."

Terry continued to stare at von Lutken and spoke more loudly now and with growing vehemence.

"Tell him he is also under arrest for the capital crime of carrying a weapon and that if he does not give that gun to me I will shoot him."

On hearing the translation, von Lutken laughed loudly and falsely.

"You are a weak shit house Tommy. I have killed a British Colonel, I will not listen to a scum corporal, get an officer for me."

"You are under arrest. Give me your gun and sit over there," Terry said pointing at the rows of chairs. Paula repeated the words in German. Von Lutken stepped back and swiftly slapped Terry hard across the face with his open hand and then turned and walked out of the front door.

Terry stood stunned for a moment and then started after the German. The following three seconds were to be remembered by Terry in slow motion detail. He saw every colour and movement as though magnified; the sounds echoed and reverberated inside his head and he knew that he did not breath, nor did his heart beat during that brief moment. When half way to the door Terry put his right hand in to his tunic pocket; without his brain's instruction his fingers gripped the handle of the automatic pistol that hid there; his thumb pushed the safety catch to 'off'; his hand and the gun left his pocket and slowly arched up; his right arm became rigid and straight.

Terry was now on the top step, pistol pointing directly at the back of the German's head. Von Lutken stopped on the bottom step and gracefully swung his body in a half turn, but his head came completely round to face Terry. The gun was six inches from his nose and he sneered and spat at Terry. The movement caused von Lutken's head to tilt backwards slightly. Very, very slowly, Terry's right index finger squeezed the trigger of the little pistol. Terry saw a red third eye appear on the bridge of von Lutken's nose; he heard a crackling sound, like wood being snapped; he saw the Tyrolean hat leave the German's head and fly backwards towards the roof of the parked car; the hat contained hair and pieces of bone and grey porridge. There was a dull thunderous bang. Von Lutken's body fell gently to the floor, his head hitting the running board of the black four-door sedan behind him. Terry felt the soft recoil of the pistol through his hand. Then the three seconds were over.

Terry next noticed how sunny and warm it was, the morning breeze had gone. He saw a swollen and blood caked lip in the tall car. He signalled with the pistol for the butler to leave the car and walk around it to the hotel side. He felt that Paula was watching him from inside the hotel but did not see her smiling. Without looking Terry could see the whole square and saw men in the distant bar stare in disbelief and fear. He spoke slowly and distinctly to the butler.

"Put Mr von Lutken's body on the back seat of the car. Drive it to the Catholic Church and give the body to the priest. Wash the outside of the car and the back seat and carpets. Return the car to this spot in two hours. Do you understand what I have told you to do?"

"Yes, sir." The butler gave a stunted salute and opened the rear door of the car. Terry put the pistol back into his tunic pocket and helped the butler push and pull the body into the car. Terry unbuckled the light brown gun belt with its holster and took it from around the dead man's waist. When he had finished he saw blood and brain on his trouser fronts. The car sped quickly away. Terry unfastened the holster and took out of it the matching pair to the pistol he had used; it had no bullets in its magazine.

"Corporal, please come into the hotel."

It was Paula calling from the top step. As he passed through the door the big woman came close to him and whispered shyly.

"You need to change your trousers and underwear. You have messed them. Do not be ashamed this can happen to the bravest of men."

Terry smiled, the mess had been there for some time, but he did not bother to explain what had happened in the lavatory. He collected the Tommy gun from the table, told Paula to lock and bolt the front door and retired to his room to strip, wash and change. It was while standing in front of the washbasin that he began to feel uneasy. His bottom half was uncovered and he felt vulnerable. He quickly dried himself and put on his standard army trousers but this did not help his nervousness. It was the room, it felt insecure; the large window, the largeness of the room, all worried him. He went to the wardrobe and pulled out the green metal ammunition box containing the paper money. He put into it five hands full of one-mark coins and a box of cartridges. He carried this with difficulty down the stairs. He could not see Paula so put the box inside the office. The two guns were still there and he stood staring at the darkness. He was startled to hear the front door being unlocked but from the outside. He swung his Tommy gun from his shoulder and held it ready to fire; he crouched low behind the reception counter.

Paula came through the door speaking German to people behind her. She opened both doors; a woman entered followed by the schoolmaster and Kurt Muller. Paula pointed at the rows of chairs and they all smiled politely and sat down on the front row. Paula walked towards the foot of the stairs and called loudly.

"Corporal we have our first visitors."

Terry could see that the three seated people were unarmed and sitting passively; he could see through the open doors that no one else was approaching the hotel. He stood up.

"Mrs Rozen-Kranz, what is happening?"

Mrs Rozen-Kranz jumped one foot in to the air; the shock on her face as she landed could have indicated that she may need to do even more clothes washing. She composed herself quickly, although her ample bosom was pounding rapidly.

"Corporal, a number of townsfolk have asked to see you. These are the first three, but I understand from the baker that more will follow. They want to be of assistance to you. I believe that they all disliked von Lutken sufficiently to not mourn his sudden loss. I am particularly certain that these ones here now have skills to offer. May I bring Mr and Mrs Schrader to your interview table?"

Terry was confused and unsure; he wanted to concentrate on building a fortification in the cellar. He did not feel that his nerves could control a conversation, but Paula was already showing Mr Schrader to the table. He joined them, but Paula did not sit down.

"This is the schoolmaster, Mr Manfred Schrader. I must go and boil some washing."

"Mrs Rozen-Kranz, please unlock the door to the cellar and light four oil lamps and leave them at the top of the cellar stairs." She nodded and walked away.

"Hello, what do you want?" asked Terry sternly.

"My wife and I speak impeccable English. We are both well educated and she is a trained administrator. I believe we can help you supervise the town of Altewiese until there are educational authorities re-established and we can return to our preferred teaching profession, that is. We have exhausted our meagre savings and hoped that you might employ one or both of us and reward us monetarily. We were not part of von Lutken's inner circle and therefore should pose no threat to you."

"Are you hungry?" The question stunned the schoolmaster, so Terry continued. "You see I am suddenly feeling very hungry and thought it would be nice if you and your wife could join me for dinner at five o'clock." Terry looked at his watch, and added "in one hour?"

"Both my wife and I are extremely hungry and we would be delighted to join you. If I remain here and assist you with any translating you may need would you object to my wife returning home in order to change her attire and refresh her person. We did not leave the house this morning with the intention of dining out."

"Does that other man speak English, do you know?" Terry pointed at Kurt Muller.

"I believe that he does not speak English," Manfred Schrader answered.

"Then you stay and ask your wife to be back here by five o'clock and bring Mr Muller over here." Paula returned to the reception-interview area and Terry turned to her.

"I would like you to prepare dinner for three people, for five o'clock. Mr and Mrs Schrader will be joining me. We will eat at this table."

Terry had been watching the mayor enter and sit behind Kurt and at the door were standing the two constables. Terry picked up the Tommy gun and waved it in their general direction. They both looked frightened and rushed to seats near to the mayor. Terry glanced at Paula, she was frowning.

"Am I not to join you at dinner?" she asked.

"No, Mrs Rozen-Kranz, not tonight, but directly after the Schrader couple leave I will wish to talk to you alone on a most important subject. I want to put to you my plans and ask you to help me implement them."

She smiled and Terry felt he had salvaged a tricky situation; he wondered to himself what plans he had that they could discuss. He was feeling disoriented since the shooting and now gangs of unfriendly people were wanting to talk to him. He sat back in the chair and listened to the echoes of the gunshot and then thought about the hotel office to his left and felt happier.

Kurt Muller, the ex-policeman sat in front of Terry and spoke quietly to Mr Schrader who translated. Kurt stared continuously at Terry during the whole conversation. Terry, on the other hand, moved his eyes about the room and fidgeted. He kept on hearing the sound of bones cracking and splintering when he should have been listening to Mr Schrader's excellent English. He was holding the grip of the Tommy gun so tightly that his fingers eventually became numb. He could not concentrate and in any case he knew he had to employ Kurt, but wasn't sure why.

"I was born in Frankfurt. I am twenty-nine years of age. After attending university in Dresden I joined the police force and was placed on an officer-training course. I transferred from there to police headquarters in Berlin six years ago. I have worked primarily in administration and recruitment. I attained the rank equivalent to that of a British Chief Inspector. In July last year I was wounded in a bombing raid and sustained shoulder and arm injuries. I took the opportunity to leave Berlin which was getting extremely uncomfortable and managed to get convalescence duties here in Altewiese. My friends in Berlin arranged for my files to go missing so even after I had recovered I managed to remain here. I should have taken over the local police station as senior officer but von Lutken had the regional police authority treat me as a convalescent.

As the war was obviously drawing to a close I thought it best to stay quiet and cause no unrest among the parochial local establishment. I am not married, but have been seeing one of the girls here in town for the last four months. I hope that very soon, either the American or British Governments of Occupation will start to recruit policemen from the German population. I would immediately apply for I believe my experience would be invaluable at headquarters' level. I enjoyed a good salary and have saved sufficient money to see me through to next year. I am applying to help you here in Altewiese, because I want to try and prevent the town from falling into anarchy or to communism and I think you, Corporal, offer the best chance for us of doing that."

Terry asked him what branch of the police service had he worked for, but when Kurt answered "Staatpolizei" and Mr Schrader translated it as Secret State Police force, Terry was not listening; he was again staring at the wall of the office and the edge of the reception counter. There was silence for a moment and then Terry jumped to attention.

"I will give you one hundred and fifteen marks each week to command the towns police force. You answer only to me and have authority to hire or fire anyone in your constabulary. There are only two current constables, both or either of which you can discard. We should attempt to have ten trusted and hard working policemen as soon as possible. You can pay constables one hundred marks and senior constables one hundred and five marks per week. The duties of your police force will alter as time goes by, but initially it will be to control the local population, help to start the factories again, manage the distribution of displaced persons and the destruction of Nazism in all its forms. You have no jurisdiction over British personnel. You can ask me for money to cover any expenses and if I have any available I will share it with you. Do you accept this position?"

"With pleasure sir, and I assure you of my support and loyalty as long as your wish is for the good health and well being of my countrymen here in Altewiese. Thank you. Do you have any orders for me at this time?"

"Yes," said Terry with a sly smile, "But first I want Mr Schrader to go to those people over there and tell the two constables what has happened and have them join their new boss here at this table. Tell Mayor Hasch that his appointment was for ten o'clock this morning; he is six hours late. He will be punished; he is to report to me here at ten o'clock tomorrow morning and if he is late again, I will shoot him. The other people there, tell them my visiting times are seven to eleven each day except Sunday. They must return tomorrow morning. When that is done, Mr Schrader, report to me."

The two policemen were soon standing sheepishly with Kurt. Terry stood up, slung the Tommy gun over his shoulder, rubbed his cramped hand and while waiting for the return of Mr Schrader, walked to the office and pulled his green ammunition box back to the table and then bought the shotgun and rifle to the table too. He had decided, while not listening to Kurt, what he had to do next. He was going to station himself by the reception counter and watch the table and his workforce at the same time. He called loudly for Mrs Rozen-Kranz and when she, the three policemen and Schrader were assembled in front of him he issued his instructions.

"Mrs Rozen-Kranz, where is the nearest single bed that is not in use?"

"Room number six, corporal," she answered.

"Give the key to Mr Muller and he and one of the constables will bring the bed here and put it in the office, I want the pillow end to be in the far left corner. They should then bring a washbasin stand and a low chest of drawers to the office; the drawers should be left close to the rear of the door. Would Mr Schrader and the other constable kindly remove from the office, the desk and one of the armchairs and leave them somewhere out here. Mrs Rozen-Kranz, you fetch the oil lamps from the top of the cellar stairs and place them in the office and would you make up the bed later. Then will you take Mr Schrader to room number one and transfer all my remaining belongings to the office. Tell the other policeman to begin removing the boxes of old invoices from the left of the fireplace to wherever you have decided to store them. It is my intention to use the office as my bedroom and to ensure it is well defended. Now please do as I have asked."

That evening's dinner was delayed to five-thirty. The three diners sat nervously at the dining table and even when their conversation started, it would halt abruptly each time Paula came to serve or remove dishes. Terry noticed that there appeared to be a significant age difference between the Schrader couple. Manfred looked to be in his early sixties, with grey receding hair cut short and high above his large ears. He had a stern white face with a deep furrowed forehead but no laughter lines by his eyes. He wore a dark blue business suit, drab brown tie and white shirt with a high starched collar. Terry saw, while they were eating, that the shirt cuffs were frayed and had been poorly repaired. When Manfred spoke it was in a deep resonant voice. He spoke slowly and with an educated English accent. Terry knew that he was German but would not have been surprised if he had claimed to be a BBC radio newsreader, his diction being so clear and accurate.

In contrast Ingrid was much younger and had a faint smile on her lips almost permanently although her eyes were puppy dog sad. She wore a plain green dress under a jolly patterned cardigan. Except for a wedding ring she wore no jewellery. Her hair was light brown and cut neatly short. Terry considered her too thin. She had a flat chest but an attractive face; she seemed quiet and kindly and he felt comfortable sitting at the table and eating in her company. On the other hand he found Manfred's tall barrel-chested, physique almost as disconcerting as his strong domineering Teutonic character. Terry felt as though he were an errant schoolboy in the presence of a feared headmaster and in a way he was correct.

They would eat hot potato soup followed by a small helping of chicken with boiled potatoes; there was to be no dessert or coffee - Paula was evidently still annoyed. On the table was a jug of beer which only Terry sampled. At one point Manfred spoke to Paula in German and she quickly returned with a glass of water which she laid before him. Paula was not particularly friendly to any of the three sitting at the table and displayed no awe for the imposing schoolmaster.

Terry began by telling the Schraders about his home and childhood, but did not mention his school days. He told them what he had been ordered to do here in Altewiese and how he was confused as to how to implement his instructions. He pointed at his Tommy gun and asked them to try and ignore it but that he had been ordered to keep it close to him. He told Ingrid that he was probably as nervous about the gun as she was. She made no comment. By his right hand was a pile of six-picture postcards, a freshly sharpened pencil and a small India rubber eraser that had been found in the desk. Both Manfred and Ingrid had regularly stared at the postcards. On finishing his main dish, Terry pushed his plate to one side and pointed at the cards and lifted the pencil.

"I found these cards in the office and I thought they might come in handy. I'm not very good at remembering names and German names will be a nightmare for me. I imagine I will be meeting a lot of people over the next few months some of whom I may want to employ. I have already appointed four and will soon get muddled and confused. What I was thinking of doing was writing on the blank side of these cards a few basic details about the main people I have contact with and notes on all the people I employ on behalf of the Government of Occupation. I'm sure someone will invent a form for that soon but in the meantime I'm going to use these. I'll write the detail in pencil because I suspect I might make some spelling mistakes and maybe some of the things I will be told may eventually prove to be inaccurate and I'll need to change the details. The cards are not official; they are just a way of helping me remember who is who and who does what. I'm not sure how much detail I need to record for each person or in which order to write it. There isn't much room on the card anyway, so I'm bound to keep it simple. Would you mind if I tried it out on you two? Mr Schrader, I'll ask you first a few questions and you can spell the answers for me and suggest new or different items I should or should not include. I'll start with the surname and write that in large letters because I'm going to file them in surname order. Surname, please?"

"Schrader."

"First names?"

"Manfred and Klein."

"Birth date and place, please?"

Manfred leaned forward in a condescending manner.

"8th March, 1892, I am therefore fifty three years of age, and was born in Berlin. Let me give you some of my history and you can choose which pieces you wish to record. I was educated in Berlin and between 1912 and 1914 I studied languages at your Cambridge University. In 1914, I was imprisoned by your Government and released in 1918. My crime was being German."

"You were in an internment camp, where?"

"North Wales, near to Wrexham, it was uncomfortable, unhealthy and wasteful. I returned to Germany as soon as the war ended but could not find employment or further educational opportunities. Eventually, late in 1921, after roaming the country looking for a position, I was appointed as an English teacher in a school in Munich. I continued to study languages and to write articles on the subject for various educational magazines. Then in 1930 I was awarded a post as professor of languages at Manchester University and again resided in your country. I taught there until 1933, at which time I returned to Germany to take up a commercial position with I G Fabens in Frankfurt. I served in the planning and project division and my work mainly consisted of translating technical and scientific documents, articles and patents for example. Late in 1939 we removed to Hamburg where I found a placement at a private adult educational facility, as controller of foreign language teaching. In 1943 we moved here to Altewiese in order to avoid the bombing. Here, I am... I was, the senior schoolmaster, headmaster you would call it, of our town school. You seem to have completely filled your postcard, Corporal"

"No not quite. I have one or two more questions, which I think I should ask everybody I interview. Have you been a member of the Nazi party?"

"Yes," said Manfred curtly.

"Have you ever been a member of the SS, SD, SA, or Gestapo?" Terry enquired calmly.

"No."

"Your history explains how you have developed such a good English accent. Please, look at the card. If there is anything wrong, fact or spelling, go ahead and change it."

Terry slid the card across the tablecloth to Manfred and took a new one from the pile. He stared at Ingrid and realised that since he had met her she had only spoken a greeting and to give her name. He wondered if she did actually speak English well, or at all. She had smiled and nodded politely while Terry had been speaking.

"You do speak English, don't you?" he asked.

"Yes," she replied.

"Can we carry out the same exercise with you telling me your name, birth details and history and such?"

"Yes," she replied.

Terry saw that she had become even tenser and her little smile had almost disappeared, but he persevered.

"Name?"

"Schrader," she spoke quietly.

"First name?"

"Ingrid."

"Date and place of birth, please."

"11th October, 1912."

Although this was all she said, Terry had heard her speak in a cultured clear English showing no sign of a German accent. Ingrid looked at her husband for support or assistance, he looked at her and his hard eyes suddenly became sad. He took a deep breath and then nodded to her in a gesture indicating that she should continue. She looked about the room to confirm that Paula was not there.

"I was raised and educated in Wilmslow, Cheshire. Although I have not returned there for many years, I believe you may detect that I bear an upper class Cheshire accent."

Terry did not look up as he wrote his pencil notes, but simply asked her to continue.

"I attended Manchester University and studied modern languages. As some times happens at universities, I fell in love with and married my teacher. In 1933, Manfred and I moved to Frankfurt and I too found employment with I G Fabens, in their personnel department. Before you ask, I will tell you that, at that time, I became a member of the Nazi party, but have had no connection with the SS, or Gestapo, or any similar organisation. Then, in 1939 we thought it best to move away from Frankfurt and we chose to relocate to Hamburg. I had a German passport and nationality, but many people in Frankfurt knew that I was from England and that would have made things difficult, uncomfortable and in the long run dangerous for both of us. Manfred's experience of internment had not been pleasant.

We changed our names, our old one's would be of no interest to you Corporal, and they would unnecessarily complicate your record card."

"My wife speaks fluent German," Manfred interrupted, "she can speak with an educated Frankfurt, or natural Berlin accent and vocabulary, so we felt that her Britishness would not be detected."

"I decided it would be sensible to stay at home and become a housewife. We took the opportunity to start a family. In 1940 we had a little boy. He was killed in a bombing raid in 1943."

"I'm sorry," said Terry.

"Don't be," Manfred interrupted again. "You personally were not responsible or to blame," he snapped.

"Please Manfred, not now. Within a few months of arriving here, we managed to arrange employment for me as a primary schoolteacher. The school was closed in March. Everyone was preparing to evacuate should the Russians cross the river Elbe. The school board in Luneburg had been disbanded in February so we were receiving no directives or salaries. Since then we have been living off our savings, but soon will need to begin to sell some of our belongings in order to feed ourselves. We are both quite anxious to find employment with you; with the new government. Could I suggest how I may be of assistance to you?"

Terry nodded.

"My position in the personnel department at I G Fabens included the maintenance of the personnel files. We kept record cards for every employee, whether temporary worker or director. The cards were larger and more complex than your system there, but we were able to sort all the companies' employees, either by name in alphabetical order, job specification, age, nationality and," here Ingrid hesitated again, but then went on, "religion. I could create a simplified version of that system for you. We can both translate for you and Manfred is known by most of the population of Altewiese and is respected. Of course we would both be happy to be reinstated as school teachers, but assume that it may take a few weeks to re-establish the education authorities."

"Education does not have a priority at the moment," Terry explained. "I would guess that it will be some months before we see any investment in it. But, I could definitely use your skills here, now." He turned to Manfred.

" Would you accept the position of translator and organiser, working for me here in Altewiese? It's a temporary job, well I hope it is only temporary and I'll pay you one hundred marks and five free meals each week, like the one we just ate. I don't know exactly how I'll use your organising skills but we can see what happens."

"Yes, I would accept that proposition, thank you." Manfred said without smiling. Terry turned to Ingrid.

"And would you Ingrid accept the position of translator and administrator with me with a weekly salary of one hundred marks and five meals? I would expect you to do forty-five working hours, spread over six days, sometimes on Sunday and possibly not at the same times as Mr Schrader."

"Yes," answered Ingrid, "and could I suggest that I keep a ledger recording all of your payments and personnel agreements. I could also act as a Cashier; I would make the payments, if you can learn to trust me, that is. Although, you have sufficient information about me to cause me damage if I was to be found to be dishonest in any way."

"Now this is beginning to make me feel less worried." Terry smiled. He'd been tense since the shooting and his stomach felt knotted; he had been surprised that he could eat his meal. He extracted two hundred marks in notes and coins from his tunic pocket and made two piles of them, sliding one to each of his table companions. "That is your first week's pay in advance. If you have any expenses doing the jobs you must reclaim them from me. No, reclaim them from Ingrid, who will record them. I'll authorise any expenses in advance and tell you, Ingrid, about them; I'll give you a note or just tell you. There is no tax to pay, either to the national or local government, because there are no national or local governments. We start work together at seven o'clock tomorrow morning, if that's OK with you both. Ingrid you make a desk on the lower tier of that reception counter. You will need to stand up to get people to sign things. You'll have a box of money to protect, so perhaps you should keep to the middle of the counter. Other administrators we may need can have positions on either side of you.

Mr Schrader, we will work at this table. You could sit on that side, facing the window and any interviewees could sit directly opposite me. What do you think? When Ingrid has designed her personnel forms, you could fill them out in English and make any notes you or I consider might be useful. Yes, I'm beginning to see how this might work."

Terry's excitement did not appear to be shared by his two new assistants, but Manfred addressed him in a formal manner.

"Corporal, we will both be present at seven o'clock tomorrow and we will both work diligently and honestly for you. We will do this as much for the money and food you have offered as for the people of Altewiese. Without the authority and organisation you are bringing to us I fear our community would disintegrate into chaos. As for working for you personally I have no inhibitions or worries because this evening, by your manner and politeness, you have shown us that you are civil and concerned. I am sorry there had to be a shooting this afternoon but I do not believe the consequences of it will be as severe as you may have imagined. Mr von Lutken was liked by only five or six people of the town and admired by none. I think you would have found that his activities during the last five years with regard to the use of prison labour, was a cause of great regret to us all; his greed far out weighing his sense of fair play.

I noted that you have given the position of senior police officer to Mr Kurt Muller. He is a recent addition to our community and I have had little to do with him personally. His experience of policing and his lack of friends in the town, would, I suggest, make him eminently suited to the position of authority you have given him; may I congratulate you on your swift perception. Discovering a replacement mayor may prove a much more demanding task. If you would excuse me, I will find Mrs Rozen-Kranz and thank her for her culinary efforts under trying circumstances and then we will bid you good evening."

Manfred rose, slid his chair seat beneath the table and walked to the rear of the hotel. Ingrid's smile widened when he was out of sight.

"Manfred has always considered that he could do a better job than Mr Hasch. He will be dropping hints to you all the time. Do whatever you consider right but my husband is at heart a kindly and understanding person, despite the strict exterior, and would consider all of the town's people equally. He has no favourites and owes no favours. No one else in Altewiese is aware that I was born in the United Kingdom, I beg you to keep our secret. We must leave now. Thank you for the meal and the work."

She rose as Manfred returned. They gave their farewells and departed. Paula re-locked the door behind them and wedged two chairs against the door handles. She faced Terry.

"Coffee for two, sir?" she asked.

Terry went to the office and felt pleased with the result of his move. There were two oil lamps burning at each end of the mantle piece and they created a good light in the small office space. Without them the area of his bed would be completely dark; an intruder would be unable to see were the sleeper actually was. He wedged open the small quarter light above the door and considered this would give a safe airflow even with the door shut and both lamps burning.

In the corner of the room, at the foot of the bed, Terry had placed the rifle and shotgun with the ammunition boxes. His shirts and underwear Paula had neatly folded into the chest of drawers; his battle dress trousers were on a coat hanger and still felt damp from their recent washing. To the right of the fireplace stood the washbasin stand. The shelves behind and level with the basin had been cleared; here he found his flannel, towel, hairbrush and shaving kit laid out with precise neatness. The recently converted bedroom had the appearance of a prison cell and Terry reasoned that what was hard to get out of could be equally difficult to get into. Paula was standing next to him and he took a mug of milky coffee from her.

"Tomorrow morning remind me to get a shop door bell fixed to the inside of this door. You know the type that rings when the door is opened in order to attract the shopkeeper's attention. And, I promise that before I enter the lavatory room I will call your name, to make sure you are not in there."

They both smiled and returned to the recent dining table on which was an unlabelled bottle of clear liquid and two tiny glasses. Paula filled both of the glasses.

"Schnapps, it is our national drink. It is very strong. You can sip it or gulp all of it in one go. It calms the nerves, relaxes tension and helps you sleep which I believe is exactly what you need right now."

They both finished the whole glass in one gulp and Terry felt as though he had been poisoned, but tried to smile and speak and failed to do either. Eventually he spoke.

"Very nice, an acquired taste, I would say. Mrs Rozen-Kranz..." She interrupted him.

"Corporal, when we are alone or in friendly company, why don't you call me Paula. Out of respect for your position here, I would prefer to always call you Corporal."

"Paula, that may not be too easy for me, because of your age and things, I regard you like I would my mother and I would never use her name." He smiled widely. "But I can't call you mother, either, so Paula it will be. Can I tell you what I think I must do next, here in Altewiese, having found some English speakers? I must create a hospital for Displaced Persons. Yes you are, in a way, correct, there are many more important things to do for the present population of the town. But, in the rest of Germany the problem of DP's is out of control. There are one million in the north of the country. Many thousands more are arriving every day, my senior officers will be delivering my first batch of twelve refugees on Thursday.

Yes, Thursday and we can expect twenty or thirty more next week. What I want to do is share this problem with you. I need your help and advice. We will need to force the people in the town to take one or two DPs each and house and feed them. They will not be happy about that, especially as the refugees are in a dirty and pitiful state. I was thinking that if the poor refugees could be washed and re-clothed and checked medically, they might look more attractive to the local people. Would you Paula, create for me in this building a Displaced Persons and Prisoner of War Reception Centre and Hospital? You don't look very happy about my suggestion. Let me tell you how I imagine this place may work. The refugees or ex-prisoners arrive at those seats over there; I interview and record their details. Eventually, using that information, I and Mr Schrader decide where best to place the people and arrange for that to happen.

Once I have their information I hand them to you. You wash them and re-clothe them where necessary. Infested clothes will need to be burnt. Infested people will need to be shaved and washed in lice soap. You then need to have them examined medically and I don't know how we are going to do this without a doctor. Any people who are ill will be kept here and nursed. People who are well may not immediately be found homes and will be accommodated here. Families could share a room and strangers will have to share. I must try to avoid over crowding. Everyone, including our staff, will need to be fed. I have offered Mr and Mrs Schrader five meals per week as part of their wages for working here. I think anyone you employ should be offered a meal on each day they work in your centre.

You will need a large number of staff - nurses, cooks, cleaners, people washers and clothes burners and more. You will need staff on duty day and night. We may find suitable staff among the refugees as well as in the town. You will need to buy food and bedding and medicines and employ a store man to organise and protect the cellar. You can have as much of my money as you want but if things get hard to find I will ensure you are given priority. Mrs Schrader will be the cashier and I will instruct her to give you what you want. When she runs out of money, it will be my job to find some more. You can make your office behind the bar; use the roller front desk if you want to. In a few weeks, when we have a routine and I feel safer, I may well move my billet to another building and then you can use the office again. You should have a title - Manageress or Controller or Matron, whatever you think would be best. Paula you are laughing at me, what have I said that is funny?"

"Nothing at all," she said and held his left hand in both of her own. "I am laughing because I am happy. Your enthusiasm is so much like that of my Peter when he had a new idea. The task you have given me will take all of my time; it will keep me occupied for I have recently been spending too much time with my memories. There will be many difficulties and some of your suggestions will need to be modified, but what you want will happen. I would be delighted to create a Refugee Centre in this hotel. I doubt that I shall sleep tonight; I will be making notes and planning and imagining. Tomorrow morning at six thirty, your new Director of the Altewiese Displaced Persons and Prisoner of War Reception Centre and Hospital, will bring you another fine breakfast. She hopes that she may always be allowed to wash the Corporal's underpants, too."

They both laughed loudly and Terry believed that for a second he could see Paula's happiness and not the Tyrolean hat full of death.

CHAPTER FOUR

WEDNESDAY 23RD JUNE

Terry believed he had not slept at all during the night. The room had been pitch black and he had stared at the slightly less dark of the small vent window above the door. It was hot and humid in the office and he had ended the night naked, lying on top of the blanket Paula had provided. The door was locked and he had left the key, half turned in the keyhole. He had pushed the chest of drawers behind the door and stood the loaded shotgun against the shelving at the head of his narrow bed. On the shelf directly above the pillow he had placed both the Tommy gun and one of his newly acquired automatic pistols. At first it had been the pistol he had fired that day, but early in the night he had re-lit one of the oil lamps and put the unfired gun on the shelf. The used one he placed into its box and put this in the bottom drawer of the chest.

He had listened to the creaks and the night noises of the silent hotel. Once he thought he could make out the scrape of wood as a window was slid open; it could have been a hot night for Paula, too. He had often heard the afternoon bang of the pistol echo through the reception area and along the corridor. Terry had discovered that in the darkness he could design the plan of action he would take in the morning and the order in which he would give his commands. Then the noise of the Tyrolean hat falling on a car roof would distract him and when he tried to remember the great ideas he had created, they had vanished. He had lost five master plans that would have made everything work smoothly but in the morning all his brain would tell him was that he was drained; he felt tired and confused again.

In the darkness he could not read his cheap wristwatch, but as the small vent turned to grey he realised it was morning and that it was Wednesday and that Wilkes was not coming to Altewiese that day. He heard a door open and close gently and saw the flash of a soft light, shadow the vent glass. Then muffled kitchen noises; the pumping of water into a metal bucket; the clink of dishes. His good friend Paula was already preparing for her day. He looked but did not see his nakedness. He rose and stumbled around the room to find his long underpants. He lit both of the oil lamps and removed the chest of drawers from behind the door. He opened it and warily peeked around it. He could see in the brightening morning light that there was no enemy in sight, but still he collected his Tommy gun before he walked bare footed to the kitchen.

"Good morning," he said to the rear of a large, pink, woollen dressing gown. "Who is first for the toilet? In my home my Mum demands priority."

"Then," said the dressing gown, "I had better go first too. You can watch the bucket of water warm on the stove. That is a striking uniform and the gun looks very comfortable hanging from your shoulder. Don't be offended, I was trying to make a British joke and, in any case, I have already become very well acquainted with those long underpants." She smiled and walked passed him carrying a full bucket of sloshing water.

By one minute to seven o'clock Terry was sitting on the green leather chair, clean, shaved and well fed. He had draped his tunic jacket over the back of the chair and had rolled his shirtsleeves above his elbows. His collar button was unfastened. He had removed his belt from his army trousers and replaced it with the late Mr von Lutken's belt and holster. He had cleaned yesterday's active pistol and it now sat quietly in the holster. On the table in front of him, arranged neatly from left to right were - a green metal ammunition box, a small stack of town hall letterheads, a pile of postcards, a piece of paper on which he had written in pencil 'Dear Mum and Dad' and 'market day is Saturday', a short stub of pencil and a recently cleaned and oiled Tommy gun. In his breast pocket was a key to the office which he had locked, and inside the office on the bed that Paula had already made up lay his rifle and the shotgun. Paula stood near the front door and stared at Terry.

"I wonder what this morning will bring us," she said. "I will stay by your side in case you need me to translate. Who knows who may not turn up. Shall I open the door now, Corporal?"

"Yes please Paula and then you can be Director Rozen-Kranz."

Terry felt hot and tired, but in some strange way neither fearful nor apprehensive. She dragged the two chairs from the doors, unlocked and opened both of them. A stream of people entered quietly and in single file. They nodded to Terry and acknowledged Paula with German good mornings. Terry had leant forward and laid his hand on top of the Tommy gun but as everyone was acting politely and civilly he relaxed a little. The first to approach the table was Mr Schrader, who bowed slightly from the neck and put out his hand for shaking.

"Good morning Corporal, I hope the excitement of yesterday did not inflict upon you a sleepless night."

Terry was slightly flustered and stood up clumsily to shake the schoolmaster's hand.

"No, I slept OK. Good morning, please sit here to my left."

Then Paula was standing before Terry, she was smiling broadly.

"You have succeeded in recruiting some very good English speakers so I will busy myself behind the bar area preparing a Director's office. If you need me, or anything else, call. Congratulations Corporal."

Terry saw the cheerful grin on her face and imagined she made the word 'Corporal' sound like 'son'. Then came Mrs Schrader, dressed in a bright flowery summer dress, making her look even younger than she had the previous night.

"Corporal, good morning, what do you wish me to do?"

She had spoken with a slight false German accent. Something she was to continue to do until their final meeting, which was many months away.

"Ingrid, I would like to call you Ingrid if I may," began Terry, but he heard Mr Schrader say a strong 'yes'.

Terry ignored him and stood up and put out his hand to Ingrid.

"Ingrid, welcome to your new job. Please take this metal box which is full of marks over to your position at the reception counter. It is now your responsibility. Mrs Rozen-Kranz will need most of that money over the next few days. You record what she takes and why but there is no need to check with me first. She will also tell you of her management tasks and whenever possible you may help her, but I am your boss; she will shortly be employing her own staff."

"As Director of the centre," Ingrid stated. Manfred coughed noisily and Terry simply nodded enthusiastically.

"You are carrying a bundle of white paper; should you need more supplies - ink, pens and things like that, see if any can be purchased locally. Mr Schrader, I see that you are well prepared with lined paper and pen, thank you. During the morning, when you have the chance, perhaps you could fill out forms for yourself and Ingrid, Mrs Rozen-Kranz and Kurt and his two constables marking clearly the weekly pay and, where appropriate meals. You know what we have already agreed. The forms can then be given to Ingrid." Mr Schrader looked at Terry disdainfully.

"The forms were completed last night and Mrs Schrader is in possession of them already."

Terry was certain that he saw Ingrid wink her left eye at him as she turned away but it may just have been the sun catching her face.

Kurt Muller, dressed in a smart blue civilian suit, gave his greetings and asked what were the priorities for the day. As they shook hands Terry noticed the butler sitting on one of the chairs among the other waiting people. He had a white gauze pad taped to his top lip and it was obvious he had had difficulty shaving. Terry felt concerned that this man, who had recently undergone dentistry and unemployment at his hand, should be here.

"Good morning Inspector," he said. "What does the butler want?"

Mr Schrader called the man across and, although he had proven that he could speak some English, Mr Schrader interpreted.

"Sir," said the butler nervously, "my name is Otto Vramp. Yesterday you told me to clean the car and bring it back to you immediately. I was here at four p.m. but you sent everyone away. I was frightened to leave the car without your knowledge, so I took it back to the house. I came here this morning at six o'clock. The car is parked outside the hotel. You can see the outline of the roof of it through the window. Please sir, do not punish me, I swear that I returned as you ordered yesterday. I am sorry if I have offended you."

Terry was shocked at the elderly man's pleading. He could not recall having asked him to return but it had been a traumatic moment when they had last met. He felt embarrassed at the man's need to beg and irritated at Mr Schrader's obvious delight at his having to do so.

"Is this man German, Mr Schrader?"

Schrader had begun to fill out a form for Otto Vramp, and while writing, replied.

"He is a national of the German State that existed six weeks ago. He is from the town of Old Stein. That is in a part of Germany that has been claimed by Poland and Russia in the past. He will speak Polish and better Russian than his terrible German."

"Mr Vramp," said Terry, "I thank you for returning this morning. It was my decision not to speak to you last night. How long have you lived in Altewiese?"

"Ten years, sir."

"How long were you employed by mister….. by your previous employer?"

"Ten years, sir, always as his butler and driver."

"Have you ever been a member of the Nazi party?"

"Yes, sir."

"Have you ever been a member of the SS, or Gestapo?"

"No, sir."

"Where do you live, sleep?"

"My home is a room in the basement of the big house, sir."

Terry looked hard at Kurt Muller and then spoke to Otto Vramp.

"I want you to continue to live at the house for the time being. I want you to make sure the house is secure and that no one steals from it. Every day at eleven o'clock I want you to come here in the car and ask me if there's any driving I would like you to do. Sometimes there will be none and you can return to the house. Other times I might want to visit Brick, or local farmers and you will drive me. On behalf of the Government of Occupation I am employing you as a driver at a weekly wage of one hundred marks. Have you any questions?"

"Sir, that is very kind of you. Do you want me here on Sundays as well as weekdays and, sir, there are only twenty gallons of petrol remaining?"

Terry was confused for a moment and Schrader whispered to him in a confidential manner.

"The five gallon drum of diesel which is causing Mrs Rozen-Kranz much unnecessary inconvenience over behind the bar could, I suggest, be exchanged for ten gallons of petrol. This servant, butler, would be well aware of how to transact such a piece of commerce. You have overpaid him."

"Yes, I want you here at eleven every morning," Terry said to Vramp. "Would you please take the drum of diesel from behind the bar and exchange it for petrol. Return to me here at fifteen hundred hours this afternoon, thank you Mr Vramp."

The older man nodded his head and fled from the hotel. Terry looked again at Kurt Muller.

"I am sorry for that interruption. I see that your previous constabulary is still here; is that your choice?"

Kurt glanced at the two uniformed policemen sitting patiently in the second row of chairs; their hands crossed on their laps.

"Yes, for the moment. They have their uses and are surprisingly obedient and docile. I propose to add only one other man from the town. He is sitting next to them in the grey suit. He will be in uniform next time you meet him; there are spare uniforms at the station. His name is Ralf Engelbart; he is thirty-three years old, served on the Eastern front and there lost four toes to the cold. He is fit, healthy and has no work, his trade having been a mechanic or engineer at the fertiliser factory. I have known him for six months and believe him to be an honest hardworking man."

Kurt was watching Mr Schrader write as he translated.

"He was a member of the Nazi Party, but not the SS. He has lived in Altewiese for three years and was born in Dresden. You asked for a stronger force than I have now assembled and I suspect that the next recruits will be selected from either returning military personnel or from refugees. Mr Schrader will remind you of my needs if a likely candidate presents himself to you over the coming months."

Terry felt full of confidence in Kurt Muller; he was obviously competent and reliable; he had a strong forceful manner. He was fearful that if Kurt found the chance to move on he would not be able to persuade him to stay in a small town like Altewiese.

"Kurt there is so much we have to do to ensure the present population and the many more about to arrive are fed and comfortable. Speak to Paula and understand what her tasks are, you may be able to help. Can you organise a method of distributing information and proclamations to all the people of the town and district, please? I want everyone to be told again that they are not allowed to carry weapons. Can you repeat to them that Hitler and National Socialism is dead. I would like you to organise that the flags and photographs in the party offices are destroyed. The offices can be left unlocked. I would like you to find me an alternative builder to Mr Kahler."

At this point Kurt raised his hand to interrupt Terry.

"I think you will find that the emblem on the face of the party office is being hidden, even now. I will have the flags and photographs burnt immediately, but please remember few people will carry out that order willingly. Would you be happy to burn your famous flag? It will be done, but perhaps quietly and without display?"

Terry considered these wise words.

"I agree. Just make those things disappear without any fuss. Can you tell everyone that if my superior officers visit Altewiese and they find swastikas and flags and pictures of the Nazi leaders, they will be very angry with me and could arrest town's people. These things should go away. What was I saying? Yes, about the builders. I am glad Mr Kahler is doing as I instructed but I am still angry with him for not doing the work at the time I told him to. If you can find an alternative person with the skill I would be much happier. What I want is for five large signs to be painted and erected. The paint may be hard to find so I have no instruction as to the colours. Sign number one I would like to be in place by eleven o'clock tomorrow morning and this is very important. I want the hotel sign on this building to be overpainted with the words, in English, 'Altewiese Displaced Persons and POW Reception Centre and Hospital' and in small letters below 'Director Mrs P Rozen-Kranz'".

Again Kurt raised his hand to interject.

"Corporal whatever you require will be done, but could I suggest a minor change in the name of this establishment. Would it not be kinder to drop the words 'and POW'? Prisoners returning to the town will move to their own homes and family immediately. They can be processed here, or wherever you choose to set up your office. They are unlikely to need hospital treatment because they will have been helped to recover by your medical people before they are sent back here. What do you think?" Kurt smiled weakly.

"You are correct again. I hope to move from that office soon and our processing and recording could, or might move with me. Mr Schrader you are good with words in all languages. Which is less degrading, 'refugee' or 'displaced person'?" Schrader looked with pity at Terry.

"Both are equally offensive and insufferable," he said. "I cannot understand why you do not simply call the operation 'Altewiese Hospital and Reception Centre'."

Terry did not like Schrader's conceited attitude and told Kurt to drop only the 'and POW'.

"The next priority signs, which can be done by some day next week, are two town name plates. I want one alongside the road at the tops of the hills to north and south. I want a large 'Altewiese' in capital letters and in smaller letters below there should be 'British Zone Germany' and 'Corporal Hall'."

The smile on Terry's face dissuaded Kurt from proposing any alternatives. Schrader was pleased that Mr Hasch, the mayor, had not been included on the place name signs.

"Finally," Terry went on, "I want two large signs produced, one fixed to the front of the big house that was formerly owned by Mr von Lutken; the other to be fixed to posts planted in the field near the entrance to the estate; facing the main road. Both of these signs to read in German and English, 'Altewiese Hall Farmers Co-operative'."

Both Kurt and Schrader began to fidget alarmingly and both began to speak at once. As Terry could only understand Mr Schrader, it was him he listened to.

"We have fought communism and the Bolsheviks and did not expect you British to impose their tyranny on us. 'Altewiese' I can understand; the egotistical use of your name 'Hall' is almost acceptable; 'farmers', yes; but 'co-operative' - no never."

Schrader did not let Terry answer but spoke rapid and demonstrative German to Kurt. The busy reception area fell silent in response to the schoolmaster's tirade. Terry was slightly stunned by the reaction. He felt the first threads of knotting in his stomach. He saw Ingrid leave her place behind the reception counter and head cautiously towards them. Paula was staring at him with a concerned expression. The dozen or so people sitting waiting patient-like in their rows started to shuffle and grimace. Instinctively now his right hand calmly unbuckled the holster and extracted the pistol.

Terry, surprised at the gun's sudden appearance, checked the ammunition clip and slid the recoil mechanism backwards and forwards. There was complete silence.

"Mr Schrader, translate these words loudly to Kurt. If I want to use the word 'co-operative', I will...If I want to tattoo the word 'co-operative' on your arse, I will...The farmers who will each own part of Altewiese Hall Estate will be independent, but will co-operate with each other...They may live in different parts of the big house, but will own their own fields...They will sell their own produce as individuals or as a group if they so wish...They will spend their profit as they wish, but will jointly maintain the big house...I am sure you know that the word for big house in English is 'hall'; by an unforeseen coincidence it is also the name of my family...But, if I want to change the name of Altewiese to Terry Hall Burg, I will."

Kurt spoke to Mr Schrader who did not translate his words but showed agreement and subservience and sat down as though instructed to do so. Kurt then addressed some words to Terry and the people in the room relaxed. Ingrid nodded and Paula smiled at Terry.

"Inspector Muller has asked that you forgive us all for my mistranslation and our misunderstanding of your words," said Mr Schrader. "We will use a German word for co-operative that implies no political connotations. We all apologise and there is no need to hold your gun. We are well aware of our predicament and position. You did not give Kurt a priority timing for the Altewiese Hall signage."

Terry replaced the pistol into its holster and dramatised the fastening of the buckle. He sat down and indicated that Kurt should sit also.

"The signs should have been erected by, let us say, the 10th July. Now to another subject; let it be known that stealing from this Reception Centre and its garden is a serious crime; in extreme circumstances it may prove a capital crime. I want you to arrange for night-time patrols of the Town Square and the rear of the hotel, Reception Centre. Have your constable carry a hand bell and when necessary he can attract your and my attention by ringing it."

Terry turned over a postcard so that the two men at the table with him could clearly see the black and white photograph of Altewiese. He pointed to it.

"I want everyone to know that the Saturday market will resume this week. There will be a demand for many goods. Tell the farmers and townsfolk that we will be paying high prices for single beds with clean mattresses and bed linen, old clothes - but they must be clean and recently washed - the clothes to include ladies, gentlemen's and children's underclothes, coats, shoes, hats and caps. Soap, particularly lice soap, will be much sort after, as will barbering tools. The money that will be paid for these items will create a large demand for food. You should encourage farmers and gardeners and hoarders to bring plenty of foodstuff to market, they will get good prices. I will inspect the market and the stallholder with the best display of food produce will receive a prize from me. I suggest twenty cigarettes would be a suitable prize don't you Kurt?"

"I would think that an excellent inducement. Do you want a constable on duty here, now?" Kurt asked.

"No, but if you could pop in every hour or so, I would be grateful. Paula is recruiting staff and may need the news spread; see if you can help her. I am very concerned about our lack of doctors."

Kurt thought for a moment.

"I may be able to help there but it would be difficult to organise the paperwork and documentation. Remember I was in administration and lists of doctors passed through my hands frequently. If I could locate a doctor he would need travel documents to get here and that may not be easy."

Terry looked smug.

"I can obtain travel papers; it may take a few days, but how on earth can you communicate with people outside our district?" Kurt hesitated in embarrassment and replied cautiously.

"We have managed to set up a secret postal service between the villages on this road using bicycles and carts and walkers. It is centred on Bachwald and from there we can reach Luneburg and now even Hamburg. We use a little of the space on the timber trucks that run your sergeant's planks to the city. It is organised by the policemen and is used only for the most important correspondence. Perhaps I should not have told you this. If your sergeant discovers what is possible he will want us to charge for the service and make him a partner. I assure you it is not used for any political purposes and the correspondence can cause no harm to the British. It is mostly the transmission of news and enquiries about relatives. That is how I think I might find a doctor for us; the system where you know a relative of a relative who knows someone else." Kurt was looking worried, but Terry tried to reassure him.

"Inspector Muller, you find us a doctor who is willing to work here and I'll find his travel documents. And, I do not need to know how you found him. Thank you, I think you should be going. We are getting very busy aren't we?"

Kurt rose and left the hotel with his three constables following dutifully behind him.

Terry surveyed the scene in front of him. It was busy and active. At the bar counter Paula was talking to young women and making notes. Occasionally one of the ladies would smile and walk briskly to the rear of the hotel, evidently employed to carry out some task.

Some would appear upset and leave by the front doors. There was a line of women queuing from the bar around the tables against the far wall and out into the street. Ingrid was busy filing Paula's notes and sometimes issuing money to the chosen women who, with shopping baskets in hand, would scurry from the hotel.

There were ten men sitting in the waiting room chairs, each looking intently at either Terry or Mr Schrader, hoping to catch their attention and be called next. Terry recognised the mayor and his two colleagues, the priest and the pastor, who were no longer talking together - also Mr Kahler, the builder from the meeting of two days ago. The others he did not know.

Terry asked Schrader whom they should meet next and he chose the priest. Mr Schrader's translation of the priest's words was liberally sprinkled with his own observations and comments, a habit he was to continue at future interviews. Terry did not object as the schoolmaster's comments proved helpful, saved time, were sometimes entertaining and could normally be separated from the actual words being translated. Terry felt confident that he was receiving a fair translation and that Schrader was not inventing a new interpretation of the words being said to him. Even so, he was sorry that he hadn't chosen Ingrid to sit to his left and wondered how that could be arranged without being too obvious. For the moment though, Mr Schrader was working on his behalf with the priest.

"The good Father Podendorf has asked what you want him to do with the body of von Lutken, who he says you sinfully murdered yesterday. Von Lutken was a great patron of the local Catholic Church and the dear Father has fewer than thirty fellow Catholics in town, so will be concerned about his living."

"Bury it," suggested Terry.

"This he will do on Thursday afternoon. He wonders what religion you espouse to."

"Church of England."

"The Father was not impressed by that reply. He wishes to know which authority, either secular or heavenly, will punish you for the cold-blooded act of assassination you perpetrated on the innocent and unarmed von Lutken. I would venture that an apt riposte would be to advise the sweet priest to 'go to the devil', or even your terribly descriptive vernacular 'fuck off', would suffice."

"Fuck off."

"I imagine we lost a little of the feeling in my translation, for the priest now requires the name of your commanding officer."

"Field Marshal Bernard Law Montgomery."

"Now that appears to have had more effect than the short epithet we uttered earlier. He will correspond with his diocesan masters and attempt to have the wrath of his God descend on your being. I would not bother yourself on that score Corporal as the good father has been calling on his almighty to blight the host of Mr Kahler for some years, evidently without success. The Father, having been enamoured by the private regions of Mrs Kahler, has wanted her inattentive spouse to expire, I suppose."

"Tell the priest to bury the body without military honour or pompous ceremony. No flags, unless they are inside the coffin. He is not to incite any members of the community to react or comment. He may discuss the matter with Mrs Kahler only."

Terry saw Schrader smile and as he said the words 'Frau Kahler', the priest blushed and stumbled away from the table.

Schrader's next choice was the pastor, Pfarrer Lehmann, who had a short conversation in German with the schoolmaster.

"This is Mr Lehmann, the popular and highly respected vicar or pastor of our Lutheran Church. He speaks a few words of English, but not sufficient to enter into direct conversation with you; he apologises for his lack of confidence. He wishes to enquire if there is any way that he may be of assistance to the new Government of his community. You may have observed, Corporal, that Mr Lehmann has an extremely athletic appearance; he is an avid bicyclist. At his seminary he rode in amateur speed trials. In pursuit of maintaining his fitness he regularly visits all of the outlying farms. Could I venture to council his use as intermediary between yourself and the distant population?"

"Yes. Repeat the messages I gave to Kurt about the market on Saturday and everything. Tell him about what Mrs Rozen-Kranz is setting up. See if he can get some of the locals to be charitable and offer homes to their poor countrymen."

"The pastor says he would be delighted to help and will bicycle this very day with the town's news. Knowing now that you are of the Protestant persuasion, he wishes to enquire whether you will be attending his Sunday service."

"Tell him, no thanks. To be honest, I'm not much of a churchgoer and the things that have happened during this war have knocked my faith in the just and fair God."

"I did not exactly repeat to him your words. Pastor Lehmann would have been overly eager to convert you back to the divine ways he himself follows; from personal experience that can be a tedious, if not tortuous, ordeal. Unless you indicate otherwise, I will dismiss him now and call up our cherished mayor."

Mr Hasch sat and stared dolefully at Mr Schrader as they spoke together for some seconds. Despite understanding nothing of what was being said, Terry could discern from Schrader's manner and inflection that the schoolmaster had no sympathy or liking for the mayor.

"Mayor Hasch wishes to express his sorrow at not having accepted your invitation to visit you yesterday. He considers that any excuse he could give is dead and will shortly be buried. He states, weakly, that he has performed his duties as mayor of Altewiese for four years. He claims to have worked diligently, professionally and with due respect to the politics decreed at that time. He admits to being a member of the Nazi Party, but not of any other party affiliated service. The cretin wants to continue in his present post and work for the good of the people Altewiese. In my opinion this man is a lackey with neither the imagination nor intellect to do other than to follow orders."

"You are a good mayor and who of your staff are equally as good?" Terry asked calmly.

"Mr Hasch is highly complimentary towards his Treasurer, but less so for the Planning Officer. He does not acknowledge the lowly position held by the young lady secretary; the pompous man is aware though, that she, unlike he, receives no reward for her efforts. Your description of his work as 'good' has relaxed him somewhat, but perplexed me completely."

"In which case Mr Schrader," Terry said with a sly grin, "you may now, on my behalf, write on two of these town hall letterheads, the resignation of the present mayor and the town hall treasurer, dated today at nine o'clock. Having done so, please have the two gentlemen sign their resignations and we can have the letters filed in the town records." (Footnote: copies of these documents are still on file at the town archives). Schrader smiled.

"It would please me greatly to have them hesitate over the appending of their signatures. Should there be such an occurrence may I ask you to play with your shiny pistol?"

Mr Schrader took his time over the dismissal of the two town hall officials and even escorted them to the front door personally. He returned to the table with the planning officer and after talking to him, addressed Terry.

"This is Mr Ulrich Tiedemann, the incumbent Town Planning Office. He is fifty-five years of age and originates from Hamburg. He has worked for various departments of the Luneburg Regional Government for twenty-five years and here in Altewiese for eight. He has never been a member of the Party and consequently of none of its other branches. He suggests that his lack of advancement within local government was a result of his unusual political views. He claims not to be a communist, but to be a liberal thinker. To be frank, Corporal, this is the first opportunity I have had of conversing with this reclusive person. He has an educated Northern German accent, is married with three grown-up children and inhabits a cottage at the edge of the town. I am surprised to volunteer that this private man could be of some use to us."

"Mr Tiedemann," Terry spoke quietly and conspiratorially, "were you invited to dinner by von Lutken?"

"No sir, never," he replied.

"Are you Jewish?"

"No sir, but if I was, I would not wish to admit that fact in this town today."

Terry had watched Schrader closely as he made this translation and his swift response confirmed to Terry its accuracy.

"Are there many non-Nazi folk in this town?"

"I do not know as I have always thought it best, safer, to keep my political views to myself. If one was to extrapolate forward from the elections here nine years ago; discount the Jewish voter then, for there are none now; assume that the recorded membership of the local party cell was accurate. Then on the 1st of January this year there were possibly one thousand six hundred and twenty-three residents, two hundred and eighty children under sixteen, of which one hundred and seventy-eight attended Mr Schrader's school. - I can confirm the accuracy of this number and am impressed by this man's apparent ability - He says there was a party membership of nine hundred and ten, but I believe less than half of those were still resident at the start of this year. And, at that time his estimation of the voting pattern of those residents eligible to vote would be one thousand one hundred Nazi, fifty underground communist and one hundred silent liberals. He says that some communists are known to have agitated and caused some disruption in their effort to advertise what was occurring, particularly at the fertiliser plant. The silent liberals did nothing and share the guilt with the more active and therefore more honest National Socialists."

"It may be necessary to find people who were not members of the Nazi party and give them higher political and commercial positions than they are capable of handling. We will need to find assistants or deputies who are skilled and knowledgeable, but with tainted politics, who will actually do the work. That's how I see it, anyway. Here we have Mr Tiedemann, who, if he's telling the truth and if your opinion is correct, is competent and not a Nazi. That is a piece of luck for me. I want you to write a letter on one of those town letterheads; address it to Mr Tiedemann appointing him Deputy Town Mayor, Treasurer and Planning Officer at a weekly salary of one hundred marks. He is to have one secretarial staff member immediately although we can discuss the employment of rubbish collectors and road maintenance people over the next few weeks.

While you are writing tell him that I want him to bring to me here at ten o'clock tomorrow morning, copies of any district and town plans. I want one of von Lutken's estate and can he mark on the town map any of von Lutken's properties. I want him to tell me which houses are unoccupied, regardless of who owns them. Who are the other local landowners? Where is the electricity generator and water pumping station and things like that? Now Mr Schrader, write another town letter appointing me, Corporal Terence Hall, as Mayor of Altewiese as of nine o'clock today." (Footnote: copies of these documents are on file in the town archives).

"Deputy Mayor Tiedemann points out, with respect, that the town treasury is empty."

"Make a note for Ingrid asking her to lend the town council some money. He can collect a small rental from the market stallholders on Saturday and we will have to find a way of taxing anyone who appears to have too much money. Make a note to find out what cash von Lutken had in his house."

Mr Tiedemann was delighted with his new position and sped from the hotel enthusiastically. Terry dealt with the remaining visitors quickly. The apologetic builder, Mr Kahler, was dismissed unforgiven. A seventy-year-old Great War veteran, enquiring to be employed as a police officer, was sent to Kurt Muller. An aged man claimed to have been the gatekeeper of the fertiliser factory until 1939 when the SS took over. He was told that if he could find the keys to the gates, office and factory and bring them to Terry at eleven o'clock on Monday, he would be re-appointed. He never returned. The garage proprietor, Mr Reck, introduced himself. And, the manager of the creamery wanted to invite Terry to visit the site and help to re-establish production. Terry made an appointment to meet the man at four that afternoon at the door to the creamery.

When he had left, Paula had one of her new staff bring three mugs of weak tea to the table, for Terry, Schrader and herself. She excitedly reported to Terry that many of her old staff had agreed to return. Her most important find had followed her enrolment of the town's sixty year old mid-wife as a nurse; she found that this lady's delivery training had followed years of experience in hospitals treating wounded and sick Great War soldiers. She had coped with depressed, lice ridden, wounded or diseased patients and her knowledge would be invaluable for the Altewiese Displaced Persons Reception Centre and Hospital. They gave a toast in tea to the new venture. Terry felt satisfied that he had made a good start at control and management of the town and the systems for the reception of the DPs. He wanted to have the approval of Sergeant Wilkes tomorrow. He felt he now needed to let his first batch of orders and appointments settle down and begin to operate successfully, although he had hundreds more ideas swimming around in his head.

Otto the driver collected him at three o'clock that afternoon as arranged and proudly claimed to have changed the diesel into eleven gallons of petrol. Terry had him drive them south out of town up the long hill towards Hanover. They passed two military trucks heading in the opposite direction and a little later a line of ten German half-tracks, each flying a small British flag, growled passed. Terry saluted as they sped by and wanted very much to let their drivers know that they were now in his territory and under his protection.

Having reached the brow of the hill they entered thick woodland; the road surface was poor, with large chunks of the carriageway edge having slipped away. They slowed as they came across the odd unmade lane to left or right and peered along them, but noted only deserted and semi-demolished cottages. It was three miles before the woodland began to break up and small farms appeared; they observed few people, but most houses had wispy smoke curling from their chimneys. Terry spoke only a few words to Otto and had time to take in the scenes as they travelled cautiously along the broken road. He decided that it was as though every day was a Sunday both out here in the countryside and in the town they had only recently left behind.

Since the war had ended the economy and life of this part of Germany had descended into a week of Sundays. People stayed at home or did not go far from them. Little work was being done on farms or commercially so no one had a job to go to. The people were eating one Sunday meal each day and watched, with terror, as their larders emptied. Otto pulled the car to the roadside and pointed to a battered wooden sign; it marked the end of the Luneburg Region and Terry indicated that he should turn the car round and head back to Altewiese. He was sure that in the coming months he would have plenty of time to explore further and perhaps make contact with the next town's British leader.

As they drove north they met an officer's staff car, but it was only occupied by the driver. Two private trucks heavily laden with boxes or crates encased in tarpaulin and rope rolled south towards Hanover. At the brow of the hill leading down to the bridge, Terry asked Otto to stop; he got out of the car and surveyed the town from this new direction. Otto extracted a pair of binoculars from the dashboard and handed them to Terry. Far to their right, along the tree line, Terry could see a water tower with a small, square, flat roofed building slightly behind it. From this a line of hedge showed that a lane or track fell down the incline of the hill to the rear of the cemetery he had spotted yesterday. Half a mile in front of them, to the right of the main road, were many newly built houses; there were two rows of them running alongside and behind the agricultural merchant's yard. The first cottage on the left of the road, with the neat garden and nearly new paintwork would be that of the newly appointed Deputy Mayor of Altewiese.

Over in the fields to the left was a large farm with two houses and a barn and other smaller outbuildings. Using the binoculars, Terry traced the track running further up the river and could just identify a lone cyclist moving quickly along it. The track disappeared into woodland, but there was a strong confirmation in the deeply rutted track of more farms beyond. Down stream of the town, Terry could also see that the riverside road became a track on passing the fertiliser factory; this track wound its way close to the riverbank and only disappeared from sight after two or three miles. Terry called to Otto and pointing and speaking slowly, asked where the track went to.

"Fifteen, sixteen kilometres to a town," Otto replied, "then five kilometres to a town and the river Elbe - then the Russians. The track is not in good condition and is not suitable for cars or lorries. There are many small farms leading from the track. The farmers use horses and carts, or legs, to reach Altewiese. They have cattle in the fields and pigs in the woods. It is the same if you follow the track to the west, but that one leads to nowhere. There is a dead end after ten kilometres, then only trees. There are many birds and still some deer in the woods. The hunting was very famous before 1940. The trees are good and old and make fine furniture, but only a small amount was cut each year, so as to protect the hunting. In the woods, in special places, there are small lodges where night hunters can rest. Few people know where these lodges are, but young courting couples seem to be able to find them very easily. Three years ago the police found a group of communists in one of the lodges; they were having an illegal political meeting. There was shooting and the soldiers from the factory went out to the scene and shot all of the communists. They found evidence that escaped workers were being hidden in the lodge. The families of the local communists were arrested and taken away. The only communists that remain, if there are any, would be very secret. Me, I am not a communist. I fought in the 1914 War in the same regiment as von Lutken; we fought against the Russians.

Yes, I speak Russian, but my family language is Polish; I am a German citizen. Sometimes I would speak to the Russian and Polish workers we used on the farm; they were surprised that I could speak to them and they would beg me to help them. I couldn't help them although I was sorry at the harsh treatment they suffered. Sometimes the guards were Polish and they treated the prisoners worse than the soldiers. It was a very bad time and I am glad it is over for the prisoners. Am I angry that you shot von Lutken? I'm sorry he is dead; he was my boss, a very strict boss, but sometimes he was kind. May I have your permission to attend his funeral tomorrow? Thank you, sir. You are the big boss now. I hope I can remain at the big house for that is the only home I now know. My family are in the hands of the Russians and I fear for them. If I stay at the big house, you want to know what I would do? I would like to have five acres of the woodland, just above the house. There I would grow pigs and mushrooms and build little houses for the pigs to live in during winter. I would like to own a gun again and sometimes shoot a bird for my dinner. I would like to own a dog."

Terry felt touched by the man's simple desires and by the respect he was showing, despite the altercation and violence of yesterday.

"Otto, work hard for me and protect me and I have it in my power to grant you what you want. The dog may be the most difficult thing."

Terry was shocked at the power he now possessed and more than a little frightened by it.

"Drive me to the hotel, the Displaced Persons Centre and we can collect Ingrid and visit the creamery."

Terry, returned to the back seat of the car and laid the Tommy gun on the seat beside him and then said to the back of his driver's head, "please".

Ingrid was delighted to be away from the still bustling Reception Centre, or her husband. She chatted to Terry as they drove slowly along the riverside road to the creamery gates.

"Yes Corporal," she said, still maintaining her German accent for Otto's sake, "there is a smell from the river this year. The sewage pipes run from the houses and square, underground to the marsh over there, where the tall reeds are, see? The raw sewage is deposited in the river. We have not had much rain this summer so the river is low and slow. Usually there is much water from the town, mixed with the sewage, but since we have no longer got any piped water, the amount is too small. I think the pumping station runs on petrol and there is no petrol available.

That is Mr Richard Gerdes at the gate. The creamery is owned.... was owned by von Lutken and Mr Gerdes was the manager."

Once the car was parked Ingrid and Terry followed Mr Gerdes into the creamery yard. The manager was a short stocky man of fifty-five or sixty, wearing a leather apron over his jacket and trousers. To Terry he sounded a jovial jolly man who was showing no sadness at the recent loss of the creamery owner. Ingrid's translations were quick and un-embellished, although she showed great interest in what was being said. Mr Gerdes gave them a brief tour of the buildings set around the edge of the cobbled yard. They saw horseless stables with two rubber tyred carts outside; there was a milk reception bay in which three shiny metal tanks stood in the shadowy gloom of the unlit building. They saw a cheese making room containing two long vats, presses, metal moulds and rows of wooden storage shelves, on some of which lay a few sacks of salt. Next to this room was a small cheese-smoking house, with a tall thin chimney. There was a buttery with a number of mechanically spinning churns and packing tables. In the warehouse were rows of metal milk churns of various sizes and a cream separation tank sat silently in one corner.

"As you can see," explained Mr Gerdes, "this was a fully operational creamery. We delivered milk daily to the shops in Brick and Worpswede. In winter the local cows have to eat hay and stored grass so the milk they give is poor; it is then that we only sell milk. But, when the cows are in our meadows they give good rich milk and we can make butter and delicious cream and cheese. Altewiese is famous for its cheese. There is a hard white strong cheese and also a smoked variety. The smoking room uses wood chipping from the timber yard, so everything is authentically 'local'. In December last year the army took two hundred cows from the fields to feed to the troops near to Luxembourg. Since then the farmers of Altewiese have hidden their herds and been reluctant to bring milk to the creamery for fear that their cows may be taken.

Von Lutken, the creamery's owner, has cattle in the field and wood far down stream and the milk has been distributed through the creamery. I have made some cheese for sale in town. I have a sample for you and Mrs Schrader. I did not bother smoking any. I know that the sergeant in Bachwald trades food and wood as far as Hamburg. Would it be possible for him to buy my cheese and sell it in the city? If I could get enough money to re-employ four or five of my old staff and encourage the farmers to bring their milk to me, we could start the business again. In 1936 we employed thirty people here. Our cheese was famous in Hamburg, Hanover and even in Berlin. We have sufficient poor quality salt to make one ton of cheese. The rennet we can get from a calf's stomach and the milk is out there somewhere inside the cows. For heating we can use wood from the forest. We still have a small stock of wrapping paper and churns and cartons. I have some money saved and can afford to re-start production.

My problem is distribution. Our horses were taken to feed to the factory workers. We have no lorries or fuel. We can find no transport company to help us. Can you ask the sergeant when he is next here? I have twenty pounds of cheese ready if he wants to try to sell it in Hamburg or Luneburg."

Terry was excited by the opportunity to contribute to the food supply of the British zone and the unit's profit contribution would please the sergeant he was sure.

"Mr Gerdes, if you use your finances to re-open the creamery, I will give you a letter of ownership for fifty percent of the creamery. The balance to be owned by the town council and any profit they earn will be spent on town amenities. The mayor will be a director of the creamery. I am certain that the local unit of the British Army will be happy to assist in the sale and distribution of the cheese and butter. Their involvement will be very confidential and unofficial. I saw some horses recently on the estate. I will get one for you and you can begin your deliveries to Brick again. Send ten pounds of your cheese to me early tomorrow and we'll have it taken to Hamburg and priced. The remaining stock could be offered for sale at the market on Saturday."

Mr Gerdes shook Terry's hand frantically.

"Who is the mayor now?"

"I am," said Terry proudly.

"But don't you want a share of the profit of the creamery?" asked Mr Gerdes slyly.

"No, I want half of your profits to go to the town."

That evening Terry ate dinner with Paula at the interview table. The food had been prepared and served by a cheerful woman of twenty-three who lived in a house close to the hotel and had worked for Paula for over a year. Paula monopolised the conversation with her plans and ideas for the hospital. She thought they would be able to handle the twenty-four guests Terry had indicated might arrive each week. A full compliment of staff would be on hand to meet the first consignment tomorrow. She noted that Ingrid's money boxes were getting low. She had to pay high prices to encourage people to sell her their food supplies but the stock now in the cellar could cater for a full house for one week. With the extra money arriving with the sergeant the next day, they could attack the Saturday market and build up food stocks and bed numbers. If lice soap was to be impossible to find, the nurse had suggested washing infected persons in a solution of paraffin lamp oil. The oil would soon run out though as it would be needed to light the corridors and kitchen all night. There would be staff on duty for twenty-four hours each day from Thursday night. Terry would need to know who was on night duty and to be able to trust them, in order to sleep soundly.

Having had one glass of schnapps as a nightcap he locked himself in his office fortress and slept, unguarded and soundly, for nine peaceful hours.

CHAPTER FIVE

ANNA-MARIE AND THE DOCTOR

Between seven and eleven o'clock that Thursday morning only five people visited Terry and Mr Schrader. Ulrich Tiedemann bought five large maps of the town and district, one endorsed in different coloured ink to show empty houses (twenty), von Lutken's properties (many), and homes with only one occupant (thirty). The school had been marked with the notes, in English, 'six classrooms, say eighty people, water pump and lavatories in working order'. The map of the district had the borders of the town council authority outlined in red and von Lutken's estate in green. Other farms had their owner's name marked against the main farm building. (Footnote: these maps are still on file at the town archives).

Terry spent some time studying the maps, but could not find any additional information that he required. The Deputy Mayor then asked for permission to leave as he had found the keys to the water pumping station and wanted to examine the machinery immediately. Mr Gerdes delivered fifteen pounds of cheese, saying that he had discovered a little more stock since their meeting yesterday; he again shook Terry's hand warmly and rushed off to find an old reliable colleague.

Pfarrer Lehmann reported that he had visited many outlying homes and given them news and blessings. He said there was great interest in the Saturday market but even greater uncertainty as to the future of Altewiese and Germany. The rumour that the town would soon be given to the Russians was rife and was causing fear and consternation. Only one of his parishioners had admitted to being a communist and was eagerly awaiting the arrival of the Russians and his immediate advancement. The pastor planned to attend the funeral that afternoon and was happy to represent the new mayor and the town council of Altewiese. He left after talking with Paula for some time.

Mr Kahler, the builder, asked if the redecoration of the fascia of the Party Offices was to Terry's liking. He much regretted not having been given the job of painting and erecting the new sign above the hotel door but hoped he could be of service soon and the next work he did for the Government of Occupation would be for free. Terry made a note that he would allocate the next very large and expensive building project to Mr Kahler's firm.

The owner of the grocery shop next to the hotel wanted permission to re-open for business on the following Monday. He planned to buy some produce at the Saturday market and add that to his existing meagre stock. He also wanted permission to visit his old wholesaler in Bachwald to discover if any new produce was likely to become available soon. Terry told him he could open his shop whenever he felt like and to travel to Bachwald. As the man was insistent, Terry had Mr Schrader write a travel authority for him, using a town hall letterhead.

Throughout the morning the new police constable, Ralf Engelbart, had stood in his bright, but ill fitting uniform at the hotel door. He had asked various visitors what they wanted and had supervised the painting of the DP Reception Centre name over that of the Alte Poste Hotel. The new sign was in bright orange on a jet-black background. Mr Schrader considered it would be a distraction and therefore a hazard to low flying aircraft but conceded that almost all the words had been spelt correctly; a speedy re-positioning of the 'e' and 'r' of Centre followed.

The last visitor to the table was Kurt Muller dressed in a dark grey suit with a police service badge pinned to the breast pocket of the jacket. He said that none of the uniforms at the station fitted him and in any case he had been a plain clothed officer for many years and was happy to remain in a civilian suit. Like the pastor, he reported that the people had shown interest in the coming market and saw it as a sign of a return to a kind of normality. The general reaction to the banning of the National Socialist Party was muted, the death of Adolf Hitler having been seen as the end for the party. The fear of a Russian take over was strong and he proposed to send one of his men to patrol the lane to the east of the factory as a token gesture to calm the town's folk's anxiety. Terry asked that a watch be kept on that lane for any unauthorised refugees that might try to enter the town. Should any be found he must be immediately informed.

With no one else to interview and thirty minutes to wait before the arrival of Tessy, Terry wrote a brief note to his parents. Kurt talked at length with Ingrid and Schrader interrupted Paula's busy morning. Otto arrived and having parked the car in front of the grocer's shop, stood just inside the hotel door watching Terry intently.

As the two-ton truck eased its way across the square towards the hotel, Terry sensed a growing tension among his newly appointed staff. On looking from the top step of the hotel at the lorry, he assumed it was as a result of the re-appearance of Hardaker in the passenger seat, or maybe because the truck now had a closed canopy over the rear portion. Wilkes and Hardaker jumped from the truck and immediately pointed at the new hotel sign and the space above the Party Offices that no longer bore an emblem. The sergeant slapped Terry on the shoulder as they made their way to the interview table, while Hardaker untied the ropes at the back of the canopy and unloaded three wooden crates and began to help passengers climb down.

"Well bugger me, there's bin a few changes here recently," Wilkes said loudly while surveying the whole reception area. The cook carried a jug of beer and three glasses to the table and curtsied humorously to the two soldiers.

"Where did my new corporal get that pretty young waitress from? And where did he find that fine new belt and holster?"

"Good morning Sergeant Wilkes, sir." Terry said proudly. "The waitress was employed by Mrs Rozen-Kranz. The belt and holster and a second automatic pistol are all presents from Mr von Lutken."

"Generous sod isn't he. Where is he now?"

"He is to be buried this afternoon, sir."

"Died did he?"

"Yes sir, permanently," Terry smiled. "He accidentally ran onto one of his own bullets. The local priest seemed to get a bit upset but most of the other locals appear to be happy about his leaving, sir."

"Did you pull the trigger?"

"Yes sir. He was armed and refused to give me his gun."

"He had a lot of friends and influence I remember. Where have they all gone?

"Don't know sir. The ones that didn't like him have helped me sort out some things in town. We've turned this place into..."

"Hang on a minute," interrupted the sergeant testily, "who are your sudden allies among this load of bastards?"

"Well sir, I'd like to introduce you to some of them."

Terry signalled to each person to come forward and meet the sergeant. Most offered their hands but Wilkes just scowled back at them in hatred.

"Firstly, Mrs Rozen-Kranz, who you have already met. She is now the Director of the Altewiese Displaced Persons Reception Centre and Hospital. This is Mr and Mrs Schrader - they both speak excellent English and are helping me with administration and organisation. This is Kurt Muller, the policeman von Lutken didn't like - he is my new police inspector. The man with no tooth, we met before, he now drives for me."

"That's all of them?"

"No sir. I've sacked the town council and appointed a new Deputy Mayor: the man I have chosen is the only non-party member I have been able to find. And there are the staff that Paula and Kurt have taken on." Terry was feeling anxious at the sergeant's persistent negative manner.

"I thought you would be pleased with what I've done, sir."

Wilkes came close to Terry and spoke quietly, but forcefully.

"Lutken owned half this town and was powerful enough to control who did or did not speak to us. Now you have found three or four people who appear to have replaced him and his power. Who are they? Be careful….. out of the fire into the frying pan, is what may have happened. Watch these bastards. Sack some of them soon and see what reaction you get. Where are you sleeping, is it safe?"

Terry was bitterly disappointed at the sergeant's attitude and response to the transformation he had created in just two days. He showed him his office bedroom and how he secured it at night. Wilkes was happy with the situation of the billet.

"OK, Corporal that looks good. Let's get your town's new inhabitants introduced."

A man and two young boys were, at Hardaker's Tommy gun gestures, placing three small wooden crates by the table. Terry signalled to Mr Schrader to come near and be prepared to translate if necessary.

"The bigger of the shits," began Wilkes, "is claiming to be a twenty-two year old artillery gunner, regular army, POW for the last ten months. Says he lives on one of your farms and is a dairyman. These two young thugs are both under eighteen. Hitler Youth training and called up for service in a minor SS infantry unit only nine months ago. Both look and are snide pieces of shit. They both claim to be from farming families around here."

Terry turned to Mr Schrader.

"Have forms filled out for these three and get Otto to take them to their homes and report back to us with confirmation that their families recognised and accepted them. Tell Kurt I want a watch kept on the two youngest."

"Yes sir," Schrader said and led the three ex-POWs to Ingrid at the reception counter. Hardaker had been directing a line of bedraggled, weary and sad refugees to the rows of chairs to the right of the room. The hotel staff watched, aghast and silent as the wretches sat as ordered, and whose eyes were fixed in a sad stare at the floor in shame at their condition and situation.

"That little lot," Wilkes explained, "is this weeks consignment of humanity for you."

As he went on Terry noticed that Hardaker was standing close to Kurt and was curling his lip at him. Kurt was ignoring him and staring ahead at Ingrid. The last refugee to enter was a short dirty old hag that Terry thought he recognised. As she passed Kurt she appeared to look at his face and then scream. She ran to the far corner of the room near to the bar and knelt on the floor praying and crying. The nurse went to her and began to speak to her and lift her gently. Kurt did not see the incident clearly and shrugged his shoulders in disinterest.

"As I was saying," went on Wilkes, "there are fifteen of the poor buggers. That one causing the trouble was sent to you special, at the request of your mate Christine. Her name's Anna-Marie something. He says you know her but Christine has bin on the piss again so don't worry if you don't recognise her. The others came to us on Tuesday and we haven't been able to do much for them. There's a family of three, mother and two sons - all the rest seem to be loners. They are in a terrible mess and we'll soon see whether the super efficient Altewiese DP Centre can cope.

Now let's sit down here and have a drop of beer and I can give you the real bad news. You get fifty more next week. No reaction from our Corporal? Well that's a change. We are to get one thousand for my patch over the next five weeks. Yes, one bloody thousand. Apparently the flood crossing over the Elbe is deeper than the river itself. Next bad news is your shopping list - I didn't get much of it. In the crates there, you will find a dozen envelopes and one bar of soap, a framed photograph of Monty, two boxes of matches, your cigarette ration for three weeks, four fairly recent copies of The Daily Express, two letters from your Mum, a torch and batteries, courtesy of Arthur and a one pound bag of sugar from me, 'cos I'm embarrassed at not getting the other stuff you wanted. I'm going to visit Hamburg this weekend again, so what else do you want?"

"Where's the tin of extra cash, sir?" Terry asked disappointedly.

"We ran out. I can't guarantee there will be any next week either, although I'll try hard. What we do get I'll share between us all, but remember Christine has over two hundred DPs now."

"Please try to get the things from my first list sir. Then I'd like paraffin, movement documents to get a doctor that Kurt knows out of Hamburg, and more money."

"Kurt knows a doctor in Hamburg willing to travel to Altewiese, does he? That's unusual, but I'll get some papers and travel warrants this Saturday. I'll have them here on Tuesday. How does your smart Mr Kurt hope to get the documents back to his doctor friend?"

"Sir, he says he uses a courier service between police stations."

"Very good. Clever bastard is Kurt. Yes I know how it works and every so often I check on what goes through their Bachwald 'post-office'. It's useful for me to have access to the service from time to time, so I let it run. If your man Kurt can get you a real doctor who knows the difference between a stethoscope and a howitzer, I might like him to find me one.

Now for that crate there - it contains fifty copies of a German newspaper printed on Monday in Luneburg. It's an independent newspaper according to our officers, which means it isn't. It has some local news and stuff about what the Russians are up to. There are some translations of Monty's ramblings and a few recipes telling you how to cook a three course chicken dinner using only one damaged potato. The shocker is on pages two to five - pictures from the death camps and reports from eyewitnesses. We are to pin copies of those pages on notice boards, in churches and bars. Churchill wants all these bastards to know what they have done, but Terry some of the photographs can't be real, they are too horrific. Don't read the paper before a meal or you won't be able to eat. The other crate has the mixture of different medicines I promised you. The chemist or the phantom doctor can sort them out for you. I'm glad I didn't bring any extra ammunition for you; you only use one bullet a week I guess. You look comfortable here but have you spotted any opportunities to increase our unit's collective wealth?"

"I think so, sir. Those packets contain a local cheese which we can buy. That's a sample so you can find a selling price for it in the city. Then we'll know how much to pay for it. Apparently it's a popular cheese in Hamburg. If you agree and there's a market for it, I can get the creamery to produce a regular quantity. You tell me how much and I'll have it made. I'm going to find them a horse and they will re-start the daily milk delivery to Brick. I haven't had a chance yet to check on the timber yard or the factory. The grocer next door wants to visit his wholesaler in Bachwald and get some new produce so he can open his shop again. If you find anything suitable we could sell it to him. I've organised a trial Saturday market."

"That's good Corporal. You must have a lot of cattle hidden in the woods around here. Tell the farmers to keep them out of sight of the road. There's more traffic using this route for some reason and we've heard of a lot more looting for food. It could get bloody bad this winter. I would not bet on the milk float horse getting much older."

"They're having a hell of a time calming down that old lady sir. What was that screaming all about?"

"She threw a fit when she saw Hardaker the first time too. He gave her one of his sandwiches before she would let him lift her into the lorry. Some of these people have real bad injuries inside their heads. I'm off to the lavatory, that is if you haven't had it moved."

Wilkes smiled at Terry and slowly walked through to the toilets, glaring wildly at everyone he encountered. Terry went over to Hardaker with a glass of beer. Hardaker had been standing in the doorway casually watching Tessy and the people inside the hotel; he was still grinning. Kurt had moved away, but the new constable was still standing, dwarfed, next to him.

"Hello Hardaker, you OK?" asked Terry.

"Sure am Mr 'all," he answered, emptying the glass in one long slurp.

"I moved the bed like you said Hardaker, but then decided to sleep in that office over there."

"No windows and only one door, it's like a prison cell, but that's where I would 'ave chosen to be if I'd 'ave been 'ere. That lady pissed 'erself all over the floor. She was so scared of that man in the grey suit. She knows 'im. She knows 'im to be bad. I don't know who he is but he smells very rotten. Do you know, he's the only person in this room who isn't shit scared of me. That old lady could smell 'im. You still got the schoolteacher close, I see. That's not a good idea. The two young POW's are good lads at heart, but they've got one heavy load of hatred on their shoulders; that's all that's wrong with them. The little old man with the busted lip what you gave 'im, he smells nice and clean to me; I'd make 'im my friend if I was 'ere.

You done real well, Mr 'all; you got things organised good. You've only made two mistakes as far as I can see - the schoolmaster and the grey suit. Arthur sends 'is love. Don didn't, but he only loves fanny. Wilkes was real worried about you being 'ere all alone, but I told 'im you'd shoot the top bastard and this morning we learn from Don what you gone and done was shoot the top bastard. Wilkes was pissed off 'cos I was right. You ask me, you goin' to shoot one or two more before very long. I can see it in your eyes."

"Do I smell bad, Hardaker?" Terry asked.

"You smell like an officer, which is bloody awful, but you'd be a good mate if I needed one. So you just 'eed what I says about them two and watch them closely. That poxy little gun in that holster ain't worth shit, keep Tommy Gun close by all the time."

"Thanks, I'll be careful, I promise. What do you think of these poor refugees?"

"They're sad; mostly old people and young ladies and kids. None of this load will do you any 'arm. Not unless you get close enough to get a dose of VD. See the woman in the middle of the back row. She keeps her 'ead down all the time, but I've seen her eyes. They are the lightest blue I 'ave ever seen and bright and shiny. She might be a kind person." Wilkes was returning to the door, inspecting odd things on the way.

"Corporal what's the routine you've got running here?"

Terry pointed to the people in the chairs and replied.

"This is the reception area, the waiting room, each man is interviewed by Mr Schrader and Ingrid Schrader does women and children. The records are in English and we use them to help us find suitable homes for them. Next the women and children go upstairs for a bath and are shaved and washed in paraffin if they are lousy. The men wait until last. Next we have found a nurse who examines the person and advises us if they find an illness of the body. They are given clean, second hand clothes and their old stuff is burned. They have a good meal and are allowed to sleep here for a day or two by which time Kurt and I should have found homes for them to be sent to. The really sick ones will stay here, like in hospital. Once we get that doctor we should be able to handle fifty or so every week. I reckon I could absorb two hundred and fifty into the town if I get the cash to keep the system going, that is, sir."

"I heard you, Corporal. I'll do my best. Now here are some more directives and orders from our masters. Read them, burn them and forget them - they are all a load of bollocks. If you have no objection, I will take a walk with Hardaker and visit the Meyer Café. I fancy a glass of red wine and Hardaker wants a pint or two, don't you? If we have a discourteous reception, like last time, we might get angry and noisy. Mr Meyer a friend of yours, Corporal? No, then you won't mind if we get a little rough. Then we'll hang around for a bit, but I want to be away early as I'm going up to the city first thing tomorrow. Hardaker, load the cheese into our Tessy and we'll then have our walk."

Later Terry learned that Hardaker drank two pints of warm beer and the sergeant was given a full bottle of good French red wine to take away with him, all on the house. No violence was offered and the other customers exited on the British soldiers' entry. After Tessy had disappeared Terry checked the progress in the processing of the refugees. It was slow and steady. He had to tell Ingrid that it would be Tuesday before more cash funds would arrive. He asked her to reduce the allocation of money and if necessary sign a few IOUs. He asked Schrader and Kurt to join him at the table with the interview records of the DPs and to suggest and decide on the dispersal of the people.

Terry spent most of the meeting listening to the two speak in German and was not surprised that after thirty minutes all had been settled. On the Friday morning Kurt's constables would escort each refugee to his or her new home and ensure the happy compliance of the home providers. He again ate his evening meal with Paula and heard of the pitiful stories being related by some of the victims of the Russian violence. During the meal he kept on staring at the still closed crate of German newspapers.

Early the next morning he learned from a distraught Paula that Anna-Marie Becker, the opera singer from Berlin, had died in her sleep during the night. The nurse suggested that she had suffered a heart attack; others said that she had died of a broken heart. Terry felt uneasy about the death and at the first opportunity asked Ingrid to walk to the cinema steps with him. With the chance to speak to her without the overpowering presence of her husband nearby, he said to her, "I want you to find out where Inspector Muller lives."

"In the house directly opposite the entry to the rear of the hotel," she answered immediately.

"Ingrid, I am asking you this in total confidence, can you find out where Kurt spent last night?"

"Sure I know already," she replied momentarily dropping her German accent, "he was in the police station until eight o'clock. He had his evening meal at his home between eight and nine and he was in his bed by a little after nine. He woke this morning at six-thirty."

"Bloody hell," exclaimed Terry, "how do you know all that?"

"Because I cooked the meal for him and I was in bed with him from nine last night to six this morning. We have become lovers. Manfred has not been a husband to me since our son died. He is absolutely loyal to our marriage and our faith but has agreed to my living with Kurt for two nights each week. He doesn't wish for other people to know of my adultery but in a small town like this such secrets cannot be secure for very long. Kurt is unaware that I was bought up in England. He loves me very much I think. Manfred and Kurt are not friendly towards each other but have agreed to be professional and respectful when together in public. It is a sad coincidence that both have been forced to work in close proximity. Soon I hope that Kurt will find employment with a police force in a big city. When that happens I might move with him. I have promised you honesty and now you have all of my secrets; I hope you will respect my confidence if not my morals."

"Thank you Ingrid. You have nothing to fear from me. I hope you achieve the happiness you deserve."

Something did bother him though; she had spoken a few words with her rarely used Cheshire accent but Terry was sure he had heard one word roll with an Irish lilt. He didn't know if it was important or not.

"I have a difficult job to do now. When we return to the Reception Centre you must tell the people what I want them to do. Otto, with the car, will be here soon and I have told Kurt he can help with the distribution of the DPs who are well enough to move today. In addition I want him and the policemen to distribute a German language newspaper. I want copies pinned to the walls of the town hall and bar, churches and any shops that are open. There are fifty copies, so they can give them to many people; give the priest and pastor extra copies. I haven't seen the papers; they are in the crate by the interview table. Tell them to give me one copy."

The knowledge of the existence of the German newspaper created much interest among the people in the centre. Otto and the new policeman, Ralf, raced each other to open the crate and Ralf was the first to wave the top copy in triumph. Only Ingrid stood back as a queue formed to receive the newspaper; she knew from Terry's concern that it would hold bad news. Quickly the avid readers fell silent and moved away to the corners of the room, or out into the square. Ingrid had to repeat the orders for the distribution of the papers and gave Terry his copy herself.

The pictures of skeletons and ovens were horrific. The place names, mostly in Poland, meant nothing, but one name did, Bergen-Belsen, a town thirty kilometres from Altewiese. There was to be a trial in Nuremberg. Many leading Nazis were already in prison; well-known names like Goering, Hess and Ribbentrop, but some that few claimed to have heard of, Kaltenbrunner, Frank and Streicher. Then there were more pictures, each with its short terse description written below. War Crimes, that was a term that the defeated had expected to hear, but not the words 'Crimes Against Humanity'.

There were six refugees well enough to be driven to their new homes that day, the remainder were in bedrooms, or sitting quietly by the tables at the edge of the room. Terry noticed that the blue-eyed lady that Hardaker had admired was one of them. He asked Ingrid for her file and said he would like to talk to her, with Ingrid translating. The record card read: name Fredda Marnitz-Schule, born Leipzig, 20th April 1925, widow (?), millinery shop assistant, Berlin since 1942. Arrived Luneburg British Zone 12th June 1945, arrived Altewiese 23rd June 1945. Health: suspected VD, but refused examination, left forearm recently broken and poorly reset, lice, malnutrition.

Fredda sat with her eyes firmly fixed on her two hands clasped tightly to her lap. She was completely bald, having been recently shaved and bathed in paraffin. She wore a threadbare fabric long sleeved factory dress buttoned up the front and three sizes too big for her thin, bony frame. Terry had noticed that she now had men's' ankle socks and a pair of black ladies boots. She had been given a green headscarf, but this hung loosely from a dress pocket. Her face was white with black rings around deep sunken eyes; she wore no make up. Terry had guessed she would be thirty, or older and recalculated her age twice in order to confirm that she was only twenty. Ingrid told Terry that she would talk gently to Fredda for a while and see if she would respond to yet another interview. Terry felt that Ingrid had scolded him for intruding on this young lady's silent sadness; he wished he had read his Daily Express and not tried to interfere in a business about which he knew nothing. Ingrid spoke quietly to Fredda for sometime before a response was forthcoming and even then it was only a few words. Ingrid turned to Terry.

"Corporal it is much too soon to understand what is in this young person's memory. She has been badly mistreated by Russian soldiers; she is lost and believes her family is dead or in Russian death camps. Her strongest wish is to die. Our nurse has given her sulphur tablets from your medical box. She is a savage example of the cruelty of war. The men who did this to her will not appear in the courts of Nuremberg. Fredda momentarily looked at you and despite everything she has stunningly attractive pale blue eyes. What a dreadful shame she is in this awful mess. What do you want me to ask her Corporal?"

"Nothing," Terry said with deep sadness. "Just tell her that I will protect her from now on. Take her to her chair and find Paula for me, please."

Paula arrived breathless from the staircase and dropped herself into the chair next to Terry.

"I've been running around since five o'clock, without a break. First we find poor Mrs Becker is dead, and then one of the other old ladies throws a tantrum and smashes a washbasin and jug. We have run out of clean clothes. The woman with the two boys is very sick and Nurse is worried about her. One of the old men insists on showing me his private thing. You issue the horror comic and shock everybody into lethargy; cook is in tears in the kitchen over the pictures. I've told her it is only propaganda, the thin people are American actors and the dead ones are military corpses, but she won't listen. You know I lived in Bergen and did not see any of that stuff. It is propaganda isn't it Corporal, you know?"

Terry looked sadly at Paula and watched a tear fall rapidly down her cheek, her lips tremble and he said the worst possible thing.

"Carl Peter saw."

Terry knew he was not hard and unfeeling, just thoughtless sometimes, but he did not know how to mend what he had said. He lifted his Tommy gun and left the Reception Centre and walked across the square, through the lane to the river road and to the bridge. It began to rain - a warm drizzly summer rain when the sun still shines. He was pleased that it was raining and he let the light droplets sting his cheeks and mix with the salty tears that no one could see. He knew now that he would not fear the revenge of a defeated enemy but the sadness of the constant queue of despair and tragedy that he would have to face each day. He understood what Christine had said to him only four days ago. He understood why Christine would find solace and a hiding place in a whisky bottle. Perhaps, like Don, he should let the more experienced Germans take care of the sadness and sickness that was to pass through their town.

Terry crossed the bridge and took the long walk to the stables near to the left side of the quiet and boarded big house. There was no one about but the horses had only recently been placed in the stables. He found a large black and white carthorse, still bridled. With a piece of rope he led the large docile animal back to the road, over the bridge and to the creamery. He presented the horse to the beaming creamery manager. It was now late evening and he was late for his meal. He ate alone in a room full of sad people. He read a British newspaper but only the parts about home. He re-read the letters from his mother which she'd written two weeks before and was happy that his Dad had found an extra crate of apples at the wholesalers.

The Saturday market was a sombre affair. Among themselves the Germans whispered and pointed at the newspaper articles and pictures; when Terry approached, the papers were quickly hidden and all talking stopped. He had given Paula all but twenty of his cigarette ration to barter for the most important items she needed for the Centre. His task now was to find the food stall with the largest display. There were many sellers - a woman with a pile of bedding, another with a table covered with children's clothes, an old man with boxes of shiny, worn carpentry tools and another with green felt curtains draped over his shoulders. There were many farmers wives with baskets of green beans and cabbages and carrots. One woman had tomatoes and lettuces - Terry suspected that they came from the estate's glasshouses. The creamery manager had a table covered with small slices of cheese and a large tub of butter. There were three stalls displaying meat, mostly sausages, cured pork and smoked bacon and the occasional wild bird and rabbit. Terry examined the rabbits and was relieved to see no shot holes and blood; they had, he assumed, been trapped. The largest and most impressive stall was that of the baker; he had cream cakes and loaves of various shapes and sizes and shades of brown. The baker received his twenty cigarettes from Terry with much gratitude and bowing.

Terry told Ingrid to persuade the people she had paid salaries to, to arrive early at the market. He wanted their money to begin to circulate and create some trade. The square was half full of sellers and their wares, but there were not many buyers. Paula had two women with her and was actively negotiating and carrying goods back to the Centre; her cigarettes being eagerly sort. Some of the successful stallholders eventually became buyers and towards midday other women and children appeared cautiously in the market place. Terry recognised very few of the people and was the object of guarded curiosity. The only ones brave enough to address him were children who had shed the grip of their mother or grandparent's hands. He smiled at them and if close enough handed them a fifty-pfenning coin. He wore his battle dress uniform and beret and had the Tommy gun over his shoulder.

He entered Meyer's bar as the market was drawing to a close; it would have been twelve-thirty. There was a large jovial woman behind the shadowy bar who he took to be Mrs Meyer. In German she asked loudly what he wanted, he assumed. Terry laid four fifty pfennig pieces on the bar and spoke in English.

"One beer please."

While she poured him a glass of beer from a jug, he cast his eye casually over the other customers. He saw the rear of Mr Hasch disappear out of the door. Ernst Fromming, the older policeman, was at a window table eating cheese and bread, Meyer the bar owner opposite him. Mr Kahler, the builder, was at the far end of the bar and acknowledged Terry's existence with a nod of the head. Soon stallholders entered the bar noisily but became silent on seeing Terry. It was some time before Terry noticed the German newspaper pinned to the wall behind the open front door. It was pinned to show only the front and rear pages. Terry did not alter this design and felt that the paper had spoiled the Saturday market; its distribution could have waited until Monday. He regretted his error. He finished the beer and said good-bye to the bar in general.

As he crossed the emptying square he heard the noise of chatter start up in the bar. Back at the Centre he dismissed Ingrid and Mr Schrader until Monday at eight o'clock. He told Paula to arrange for a late breakfast for him on Sunday morning and ate alone again that Saturday evening. Before retiring to his cell, he walked up the stairs to the first floor and found the nurse tending to the sick lady, the two boys silent and ashen on the bed next to her.

"Marnitz-Schule?" he asked.

The nurse put up three fingers. He knocked gently on the door of room number three and entered. An old lady sat in bed slowly wringing her hands; at the window stood Fredda. She turned suddenly and with fear stared at Terry. He spoke softly.

"Sorry. Good-night Fredda Marnitz-Schule." He left the room, closing the door carefully behind himself.

Sharp at eleven o'clock on Sunday morning, Otto and the black Mercedes sedan pulled up to the right of the hotel steps. Terry, without his tunic, but with the Tommy gun, climbed into the rear of the car. He had with him a map of the town and the coloured plan of von Lutken's estate.

"Good morning Otto Vramp," he said happily.

"Morgan Corporal; today we go where?"

"Otto, first you will show me the five acres of woodland you desire so much."

Terry and Otto spent most of that Sunday walking about the land, gardens and glasshouses of the von Lutken estate. They had a bread and cheese lunch at one of the cottages next to the greenhouses. The old couple living there were happy to entertain them once they had been able to mark on Terry's map the garden of the cottage and the two acres of field behind it. The area they understood might be assigned to them as their own.

Late in the afternoon Otto gave Terry a guided tour of the big house. While there, Terry had insisted that Otto move his belongings from the damp cellar bedroom to the comfort and light of the number two bedroom on the first floor. Terry had spent some time in von Lutken's vast room and study. There he had dreamed and enjoyed the splendour and considered the advantages it held over his current office cell.

As they drove back to the town Terry suddenly asked Otto to drive up to the water tower. He would be late for his evening meal, but did not care. Otto parked the car at the rear of the pumping house beneath the first trees of the vast wood that covered the top of hill behind them. There was a stout lock on the door of the pumping station with wet oil around its keyhole. The water tower stood to the left and was not very much higher than the station. Otto had taken the binoculars from the dashboard of the car and now was vigorously pointing to the sheer ladder that gave access to the top of the tower. On top they were only twenty feet above the car roof, but the view was magnificent. The sun was about to set far to their left and it cast a golden glow over the buildings of the town a mile away down the hill. The nearest building to them was the school with its overgrown football pitch and toppling goal posts. They could see the back of the factory warehouse; to the right of the cemetery, the stubby spire of the Catholic Church and the tops of the town square buildings.

In the far distance in front of them they could see the roof of the big house which they had recently vacated and the glint of the sun on the glasshouse roofs. Terry could see very little to the west as the sun was low and shone directly into the lenses of the binoculars. But to the east the view was crisp and clear. He could see the river glinting as it sauntered away and the double track of the lane as it wandered in rhythm with the riverbank. Terry was surprised to see four people far away on that lane. He sat down on the tin roof of the water tower so as to steady his arms on a low rail that ran around the rim of the roof. Otto, obviously bored and annoyed at not being given a chance to share the view through the binoculars, climbed down the ladder and wandered into the wood.

Terry watched the four figures become more distinct as they got closer. The first person was pushing a bicycle and from his shape and uniform could be none other than Senior Constable Fromming. Behind him was a tall heavily set man wearing a long black leather coat and a black trilby hat; Terry could not see his face, hidden under the brim. Third in the single file of men was a short, older man with brilliant white hair; he wore a suit and tie and carried a small brown suitcase. Lastly was a tall man in a green army coat; he wore a patterned cap and was constantly turning to look behind at the lane they had walked. This man carried a large black canvas bag. Terry concentrated on their torsos, anxious to see evidence of weapons; he could see none. He pondered for a while, as to what the scene meant. Finally he decided that Fromming must have been on patrol in the lane and encountered three refugees who he now was escorting to the police station. He considered that Fromming was a fool to be leading the group; he should have been trailing them to deter escape. Though one elderly, unarmed policeman would not have been difficult to evade, he thought. He watched the four men as they passed the factory and was surprised that Fromming chose to take the left fork at the church on to the road passed the school and the rear of the DP Centre. He lost sight of them then as the dusk was descending quickly.

He climbed from the tower and found Otto sleeping at the wheel of the sedan. He also found his Tommy gun resting peacefully on the back seat of the car in exactly the position he had left it. He felt angry with himself for forgetting to protect it but pleased that his growing trust in Otto had been strengthened. He did not mention the sighting of the policeman and the three men. Otto bid him goodnight and dropped him at the front door of the Centre. Terry entered and was greeted by an angry and scowling Paula and a saddened nurse. The woman with the two boys had died and Terry's expensive dinner had spoiled; the former of internal bleeding, the latter of over cooking. Terry asked what had they done with the two young boys and could they make up a sandwich. The boys had been transferred to another room where two elderly women were holding them close and singing them to sleep. Paula said that a sandwich and a cream cake would shortly be served to him at the interview table and would he care to wash first as he appeared to be somewhat dirty. They had planned to have a much-reduced staff on that Sunday and Terry was not surprised that his regular jovial waitress did not serve him with the sandwich and cake. He was surprised that the Sunday waitress should turn out to be a very bald, timid waitress with crystal clear blue eyes. Terry smiled broadly at her.

"Thank you Fredda Marnitz-Schule."

"Thank you sir," she replied.

"You speak English?" Terry said in astonishment.

" No," she said meekly, "like in school only."

There was the faintest of redness high on her cheeks and she turned and ran from the room. Paula entered and sat opposite Terry.

"What did you say to Fredda to frighten her away like that? No, don't worry, she is still not well yet. The improvement started last night when some gallant gentleman showed her the courtesy of wishing her a goodnight. Most of the men she has encountered over the last two months would have beaten her senseless and raped her. This morning she took a bath and has had four more since. She wanted to look her best for you I suppose. When the nurse asked if she would be your waitress tonight she began to cry with happiness. Then you decided not to come home on time and the meal spoiled and she cried in disappointment. Why have you stopped eating the sandwich? No, no I made the sandwich, she only served it. I promise to check that she washes her hands thoroughly after visiting the lavatory. Corporal you are a very fussy young man."

On the Monday morning Paula announced that Fredda had been appointed as a cleaner and relief waitress for the Centre. Neither Kurt nor Fromming delivered or mentioned the three refugees Terry had seen from the water tower. Terry also decided not to tell anyone of his observations. Mr Schrader suggested that interview hours could be shortened to eight to eleven and Terry agreed.

Ulrich Tiedemann, the deputy mayor, believed he had a plan that would restore piped water to the town. It involved removing a steam-powered threshing machine from a nearby farm and placing it under a temporary roof next to the engine room of the water tower. The firebox would require constant feeding with finely chopped wood but he could harness a belt drive from the steam engine to the water pump and fill the reservoir at the top of the tower regularly. Otto drove all of the remaining refugees to their new homes with the exception of Fredda who was given a permanent room on the top floor of the Centre.

There were twelve visitors that day, all women and all with very similar questions; where were the British or Americans holding their husbands, sons or brothers? When would they be released? Could Terry help find them? Terry told Schrader to make notes and he would ask the sergeant to circulate the request around the system in Luneburg. Women who had family in the Russian Zone did not ask for Terry's help. Kurt said he had persuaded the ancient pharmacist to assist in sorting and adding to the hospital's medicine chest. Terry had walked in the afternoon along the river road to the bridge and stood there for some while. He noted that there were more people about; women walking children or carrying shopping bags; trucks and the occasional car drove over the bridge, some stopping next to him, wrongly assuming he was part of a road block check point. It had rained heavily during the morning and now the air was clear and the river flowed more quickly. He stared to the west at the lane and river as they both disappeared into the wood. He promised that next Sunday he would have Otto take him to the end of that lane, through the woods with the hunting lodges, to a dead end he could not understand.

By Tuesday morning Paula had everything ready for the next batch of DPs. Terry had warned her that they might need to handle fifty that week in two batches. At the market she had purchased four single beds and placed each into a room already having a double bed, this way she had said six people could sleep in comfort in each room. A large but holed and rusty water tank had been found and placed in the middle of the access yard to the rear of the Centre; this would be used as the firebox, incinerator, for the lousy clothes. A good quantity of old clothes had been bought and the cellar was well stocked. The staff was eager and motivated. Fredda kept exclusively to the top floor, where she had swept and re-swept the tiny rooms ready for the new arrivals. She visited the ground floor only twice each day; at those times she delivered dishes of food to Terry and if he had any, to his guests. She would carry her own food and drink from the kitchen to her room on the top floor and always ate alone.

When the sergeant drove Tessy and Arthur into the square there were five hospital staff waiting on the top step for him. Kurt had one of the junior constables assist in the unloading of the truck and later stand guard over it. Wilkes swept passed Terry with only the flimsiest of salutes. He returned from the lavatory showing much relief.

"Sorry about that Corporal," he said as he sat at the side of the interview table. "Almost didn't bloody make it that time. That stupid sod Arthur insisted we stop at the top of the hill and admire the new Altewiese, British Zone, and Corporal Big Head Sod Hall signpost. What's that all about?"

Terry felt annoyed at the stinging jibe from the sergeant who he considered to be full of bull shit and snapped back.

"I am the chief of police, mayor and since I killed von Lutken, the unopposed ruler of this town. Oh and I forgot to say sir, sir."

"Temper, temper young man. Your orders were to do just as you have done and if you want to advertise your name to every passing officer or kraut bastard, that's OK by me. Arthur, stand the two POWs next to the window there and show the DPs to that waiting room arrangement. The Corporal's staff will take over then. How was your weekend, quiet?"

"Yes Sergeant, sort of. I had a good look at the big house and that might be where I'll billet when I'm certain of everything here. We lost two of the DPs. The woman who had the two little boys with her and Anna-Marie Becker."

"Lost, as in dead?" asked the sergeant. "I don't like Anna-Marie dying so soon.... suspicious, you sure she died of her own accord?"

"No sir, but I am sure Kurt Muller was not involved."

"Be careful, watch for things; maybe you're not in danger here but something is going on. Some of your Germans are being too damned helpful and nice. Whatever it is may well create a profit opportunity for us. We passed the milk cart heading back from Brick just now. The milk churns may have been empty but the boxes of oats were not. Don't let the manager of the creamery get away without paying you..... us, his dues.

Right, these two bastards against the window, they're both Hitler Youth trained, both claim to have family in Altewiese and are both younger than you. This town appears to have donated its boy children to Hitler. There are thirty DPs as well. It was a tight squeeze getting them on board Tessy and the journey can't have been too comfortable for them. Sorry there are thirty when I said less but to make it up to you I've bought you some presents. Nice of Uncle Bloody Wilkes, isn't it? Arthur is currently supervising the unloading of ten gallons of paraffin; a metal ammo box containing mostly coins, but some large denomination paper money too; a crate in which you'll find a flag, a colour picture of the King, some more newspapers, five tins of sardines, a bottle of Scotch and two pound weight of carbolic soap.

Here I have a bundle of papers for you. Two letters from your Mum, two movement authorities and travel warrants, all blank as to start and finish point. They are very valuable, use them wisely and to our unit's benefit in the long run. Two letters from Major 'I Never Wank' Connolly. Read them and use them as you see fit, but make sure the ink doesn't stain your arse. Finally here's some money for your creamery; we got six marks a pound for that cheese so we should pay four marks a pound for it. Do you agree that's fair? Good. To tell the truth I was cheated when I sold it in Hamburg this last weekend. It's popular and well known and I'll get seven marks next time, for sure.

Now for some local news; there will be a lot more heavy traffic on this road over the next three weeks. Mostly military, British and German - moving men, sleepers, gravel, rails and things. They are trying to repair the railway line from Luneburg to Hanover. It runs about ten miles west of here so it won't be much use to us. With luck no nosey bastards will need to stop here but warn Kurt and his merry men to keep the through traffic, moving through. Have you had any unofficial refugees showing up?"

"No sir," replied Terry confidently.

"We've seen more, so keep an eye open for them. The desperate sods may steal one of your precious cows. We need all of the cheese you can produce. Now what have you got for me?"

Terry took a deep breath and plunged in.

"Can you get some strong VD medicine?"

"You got a dose?" the sergeant asked in amazement.

"No, but I know someone who does and I'd like to help her."

"OK, I'll see what I can get for your friend and in the meantime when you are with her, wear a sheath and gloves and goggles and to be sure we can find you again, brightly coloured wellingtons."

"Thank you sir," Terry said smiling. "I have another letter for my parents. I need more ammo boxes of money. I can take another thirty DPs on Thursday. Get me more German newspapers with the horror stories. Here's a list of POWs sought by people in town, see if they can be sent home soon. And answer me a simple question sir; what does the co-op mean to you?" The sergeant looked puzzled but was happy to play Terry's silly games.

"It's a shop that is owned by its customers who get divvy. Am I right?"

"Yes sir."

"Good. And, another thing, get the keys to that factory and the bank, oh and the warehouse on the other side of the road to the factory. On Thursday we should have a look round 'em and see what possibilities there are. Have you used any of the requisition forms I gave you?"

"No sir. I haven't needed to yet. All I am using I have borrowed from von Lutken"

Wilkes thought for a moment.

"Mr Lutken must have family who will want to read his last will and testament. The priest will be able to contact them through the catholic grapevine. Even if none of the family shows up, the Catholic

Church will try and get their hands on the land and money. Be prepared to issue forms, but lots of them, duplicate them and forget to sign or date them. In a few years time it will take a regiment of lawyers to sort out the mess you could cause and you will be snug behind a market stall in Hanley. That's what paperwork is best for: confetti, confusion and constipation."

The sergeant and Arthur sat at the interview table while Terry called people to them and Mr Schrader translated. Firstly Kurt Muller who was instructed to warn the population in general and farmers in particular of the growing threat of theft as a result of the higher volume of traffic that was likely to occur over the next three weeks. Terry gave one travel permit and warrant to him and asked him to speed the arrival of a doctor as many more sick refugees were about to arrive. He asked Kurt to find the keys to the factory and bank.

Then Mr Gerdes was called. He was given the price that the soldiers would pay for his cheese. He grumbled that he had expected more, but accepted and said that the truck should stop at the creamery each time it was leaving Altewiese and fresh cheese could be purchased. There was thirty pounds ready today he added. The sergeant remarked that the creamery manager was in possession of a secret formula as cheese took a day to produce and months to mature, yet he seemed to have overcome those time difficulties. The stock he had built up and hidden must be getting ripe by now; it was a buyer's market. The sergeant then smiled at the grinning Mr Gerdes and said he would collect the thirty pounds of cheese at thirteen hours thirty.

The priest, Father Podendorf, insisted on addressing the sergeant, but before he could begin Wilkes had Mr Schrader tell him that it was a disgrace to the Catholic Church that a young, active priest should be wasting his time in a small town like Altewiese. There were enormous amounts of work and ministry to do in the devastated cities and in the DP camps. The aged Father in Bachwald could protect the small flock of the area. Sergeant Wilkes said that he would ensure that the Bishop in Hamburg knew of the disgrace. Father Podendorf would soon be transferred to a camp east of the Elbe where he was needed. He then told the priest to go away and examine his own conscience and to extract a digit for his anal passage.

Terry showed the sergeant the maps that Deputy Mayor Tiedemann had prepared. The three soldiers then drove to the estate and quickly Terry told Wilkes and Arthur of his ideas and plans. They both seemed impressed. They dropped Terry at the Creamery, collected the cheese and drove north to Brick.

On the Wednesday Terry received reports from Paula and Mr Schrader regarding yesterday's intake of displaced persons. A total of thirty consisting of: one mother with a baby boy of six months and one son of three years; one mother with two daughters, six and eight; six boys aged between seven and ten with no family in attendance; five girls between eight and twelve years, with no family; ten women aged between thirty and fifty-eight, with skills ranging from housekeeper to school teacher, but no medical or nursing experience; three men all over fifty, one a builder and two labourers. Of the thirty, none admitted to having ever belonged to the Nazi party. All were dirty and twenty were lice ridden. All were malnourished and the mother and baby and her son were suffering from starvation. Of the females, half admitted to suffering from some kind of genital infection. All of the thirty came from the Mecklenburg region of North East Germany and had fled towards Hamburg to avoid the depravation and terror of the Russian occupation. All of them had been found accommodation in the Centre that night and Kurt had begun to distribute the fittest to families in the town that morning. The nurse believed eight were seriously ill and should remain in the Hospital for at least three days. She wanted to retain a further ten for one more night. Mr Schrader and Kurt had decided where all thirty would be placed eventually and none were going to be employed by the Centre. Paula pointed out that the hospital would not be empty on Thursday and that if more than twenty-two DPs arrived they would have an accommodation problem.

On the Thursday they had an accommodation problem. Wilkes arrived with Arthur and no POWs. Tessy discharged thirty-three DPs onto the square. There were only four children, and eight men, which proved to be a statistical improvement, although two of the men were over seventy years old. Wilkes explained that the lack of male workers was not causing him too much aggravation in Bachwald. The women were working well; even moving heavy logs and managing to operate complicated machines. The release of prisoners of war was proceeding very slowly. Major Connolly had told him that he could not comprehend the logic of holding a million regular army troops, with their weapons and tanks stored close to the POW camps; he said it was dangerous, but that Monty had ordered it so it must be sensible.

Wilkes bought no more tins of money and he delivered to Terry two letters from Stone and a packet of German language leaflets giving news of the latest proclamation and rules. Kurt had found the keys to the factory and its warehouse so Wilkes and Terry spent most of the mid-morning exploring them. The inside of the factory smelled of cow shit, but they saw none; the inside of the warehouse smelled of human shit and they found an open latrine had been dug across the back wall on the inside of the building. In the gloom they used their torches to examine the empty eerie warehouse but left when the stench became too overpowering. There were not many sound pieces of furniture remaining in the factory offices and the smell from the factory, mixed with the memory of the stink of the warehouse, made them extremely uncomfortable. As they re-examined the factory they could find no stores of any kind, neither bags of chemicals and fertiliser, nor tools and oil in the workshop. The boiler houses at the rear had wood burning fireboxes and they assumed that the ash was mixed into the fertiliser. There were four large mixing vats, with enormous paddle-wheel blades in them, driven by a series of leather belts linked to a piston wheel near the boiler house. Neither man had seen inside a fertiliser factory before and had no idea what they were looking at.

They returned to the Centre and found Arthur drinking beer. Terry asked him to help hang the photographs on the walls; King George behind Terry's green leather chair and Montgomery on the wall to the other side of the room. Terry asked Kurt to find a flagpole and have the Union Flag flown from the top of the town hall roof. Wilkes re-emerged from the lavatory and Terry asked him about Christine's mate.

"Did he come back off leave sir?"

"No," replied the sergeant sadly, "Connolly says he's in a sick ward in Ipswich and won't be coming back. The poor bastard was in a mess here, but when he got home he found his wife had been shagging the postman and didn't want him any more. He tried to top himself but was too shaken to even do that properly. Our Major has found a replacement who I will collect on Sunday. God knows which type he'll be. Did you notice, Corporal, that our unit is made up of young, know sod all, done sod all, straight out of training, recruits, or long service, long record of naughtiness, longing to get home, shits like me? The good guys are being shipped to Japan and the bad ones assigned to governing Germany and Italy. So what chance of Germany and Italy becoming a shit heap by this winter? I reckon we have three, maybe four months to create as much profit and comfort for ourselves before this place moves towards starvation and anarchy. We have our own election coming up soon; Churchill will win and he'll say bugger the Germans, let them rot and he'll be cheered by the civilians for saying it. But, where does that leave us poor sods; in the middle of the latrine, with only a Tommy gun to cover our arses.

The creamery is good, but see if the super intelligent Schrader and Muller can find a way for us to make some jewellery out of that factory. If not get that sawmill to make some planks. I'm up in Hamburg again this weekend to see a lady friend and will do some shopping. Shit, I almost forgot, I put this in my tunic pocket, so I wouldn't forget. It's a file of magic medicine called 'penny shilling' and a needle thing for injecting it into the bum. It clears most VD really quickly. It's scarce as hen's teeth, so she better be worth it. I still have the rest of your list and will try my best for you. There is another edition of the German newspaper coming out on Monday so I'll have that for you too."

After Tessy's crew had collected and paid for more cheese from the creamery and chugged over the brow of the hill to the north, Terry asked Mr Schrader to show him around the school. It was identical to the one Terry had attended in Stone three years, and an aeon, ago. The individual wooden desks with stained inkwells, faded grey blackboards, toilets with no seats, just the thin cold porcelain rim of the bowl. The playground was dusty and weeds had begun to play at its edges; the sports field of long grass and the fallen goal posts that Terry had seen on Sunday. Von Lutken had owned the farmland to the rear of the school and Mr Schrader agreed that families living in the school could share the fields and farm them, growing vegetables or raising animals. Mr Schrader then raised a point.

"With the school employed as accommodation for smallholders, where would the school for the smallholder's children be located?"

"I was thinking you might want to examine the Party Offices. The large meeting room would make a great assembly hall. The smaller offices could be classrooms. I don't think the building would work for accommodation. I'm not saying we need to do these things yet, but you just think about it."

The schoolmaster looked doubtful but agreed to at least consider the idea. They returned via the rear entrance to the Centre and Terry was pleased to see Paula's potato peeling chair in place beneath her bedroom window. There were clothes lines suspended at all angles and in all directions across the access alley draped with bed linen and washed underclothes. Further round the alley, opposite the rear of the tailor's shop, was a smoking metal water tank sending cremated lice and shitty clothes towards heaven.

Terry returned to his desk while the last of the refugees were being interviewed by Ingrid. Mr Schrader was about to join her when Kurt Muller marched smartly into the Centre, followed by a short grey haired gentleman and announced loudly: "Here is Herr

Doctor." Terry watched the man as he sat on the chair in front of the table. Schrader spoke to Kurt for a minute.

"This is Doctor Roland Dressler," he told Terry. "He has just this minute materialised from the appalling conditions of Hamburg, with the assistance of the documentation you were so kind to procure."

"That was quick," said Terry, "I only gave Kurt the papers on Tuesday."

"Our Mr Muller understood that you required the urgent manifestation of a medical doctor and Mr Muller is nothing if he is not efficient and obedient."

Terry stood and shook hands with the doctor and stared with amazement at the little man's brilliant white hair. It was far whiter close to than it had appeared through binoculars from the roof of the water tower. His shabby suit and off centre tie were the same, as too was the small brown suitcase he carried.

"Kurt will allow this gentleman to share his lodgings," Schrader went on. "for the proximity to the hospital would be eminently convenient. Kurt wonders whether you would be willing to donate the keys to the rear door to the doctor, better to afford him swift access to his patients?"

Terry continued to stare at the little man and wondered where he had been for the last four days and what had become of the travel documents. He decided to say nothing on the subject for the time being. The doctor leaned slightly forward and coughed and then spoke in a quiet cultured tone and in English with the slightest hint of an American accent.

"I speak a little English and will understand you if you speak slowly, please."

"Good," said Terry, snapped out of his thoughts of policeman Fromming and three travellers.

"Excellent. What sort of doctor are you?"

"I am a medical doctor. My speciality was anthropology and I am also a Professor in that field. I fear that my academic expertise is of little use now, but Mr Muller tells me of the need for treatment of displaced persons and townsfolk. I am very happy to assist and am even happier to be away from dreadful cities."

"As you are a skilled man I can afford to pay you one hundred marks each week but there will also be a free meal on each day you work at the Centre. We will find you a house near by and you will be able to open a surgery for the people of the town. For the treatment you give them, you must charge them according to their ability to pay. We have medicines here which you can identify. Mr Schrader will arrange for Kurt to accompany you to the chemist shop on the square. You must take whatever medicines you need for this hospital. If you meet any resistance I will add my weight to your demands."

Terry tapped the Tommy gun lying in front of him. He then placed before the doctor the packet of penicillin and hypodermic needle he had received from Wilkes.

"This medicine is for Fredda Marnitz-Schule. Please examine her soon and if you agree administer the medicine to her."

Mr Schrader repeated some of Terry's words to ensure the doctor had understood clearly.

"Doctor Dressler, please start your work immediately and ask Paula, Mrs Rozen-Kranz, for any assistance or help you need," he instructed. "If you require food and drink after your long journey today, she will provide it. Mr Schrader here, will accompany you for a while and ask you questions for our record system. Tomorrow evening at six o'clock I want you to join me here at this table for dinner. As it will be an informal affair I think we will be able to manage without the help of translators. Mr Schrader, please give Kurt my thanks for the excellent achievement of finding a doctor for us so quickly. I am sure that our people in Bachwald and Bad Farven are in equal need of medically trained personnel; if he can find any we will be most grateful.

Next, I am not ordering that we should have another market on Saturday. If one happens naturally, that is fine, but on the following Saturday there must be one. I will again have a cigarette prize and more cash will be made available for Mrs Rozen-Kranz to spend. Doctor you should tell her what you need and with Mr Muller's help she might find some of the things in one of the houses in town. I was thinking of things like dentistry equipment and bandages and old medicines. Kurt, I want to gain entry to that house next to the chemist's shop, opposite Meyer's bar. If you can't find the keys please have one of your men accompany me tomorrow morning bringing with him an iron bar or large hammer, neither of which will I consider to be a weapon in this instance. Thank you, now all of you do as I have asked."

Terry slept poorly that Thursday night. Twice he got out of bed to check that the office door was locked and the chest of drawers was firmly in place behind the door. He heard babies crying and old men weeping. There was a sudden muffled scream which could have been an owl in the woods or someone awakened from a nightmare. The creaking of the hotel floorboards never stopped and he heard a sash window being closed quite close by.

After eleven o'clock the next morning and accompanied by Constable Engelbart and a large sledgehammer, Terry walked to the house opposite Meyer's bar. There were two steps from the lane up to the heavy dark wooden door in the middle of which was a small brass plate with a name engraved on it. They entered through the splintered and broken heavy dark wooden door and, using his torch, Terry explored each room on the two floors of the fine Victorian town house. There was furniture under white sheets and carpets in most rooms. The house had windows hung with heavy curtains and overlooking the river and reed beds. Later he was to learn that the house was owned by the bank and was for the use of the bank manager. Constable Engelbart spent most of the afternoon securing the front door and boarding the ground floor windows. Terry decided that there were too many windows for him to feel happy in the house. He knew he was no longer happy in the hotel office and was now even more convinced that his next billet would be near to Otto.

That evening Terry sat at the table reading the record card of Doctor Roland Dressler. The table was set for two and up-side-down wineglasses were included. At six thirty the doctor rushed to the table, apologising for his lateness. Paula served their meal and poured the warm white wine. She gave them an apple each for dessert. Coffee followed, accompanied by one shot each of schnapps. Later in the evening as the two sat relaxed by the table, the doctor smoked two valuable cigarettes. Terry collected the bottle of whisky from his bedroom. The doctor enjoyed his five glasses while Terry only sipped his very small single measure. The doctor was very quiet at the start of the meal and never spoke when Paula or anyone else was near. To Terry's early questions he gave uncertain hesitant one-word answers. Eventually Terry found a subject that set the doctor off on a long exhortation. Once started it was hard to get him to stop for breath and Terry had only to prompt with short questions to restart the flow. By the second whisky the doctor was happy to fill in the details of his life and work. Terry noticed with some amusement that what he was saying differed greatly from Manfred Schrader's notes. The subject that opened the doctor's floodgate was Fredda Marnitz-Schule.

"You gave Fredda an injection yesterday, how did she react?" Terry asked.

Doctor Dressler stared at Terry for some moments.

"There was no adverse reaction to the penicillin. It will be a few days before we know if it is helping to cure her physical sickness. I will be giving her a further injection tomorrow and again on Monday. It is very fine penicillin, produced in America, and we could make good use of many more packets. I can only hope your interest and concern for Fredda is out of kindness. For some years we doctors in Germany have not been restricted in our confidentiality and we have no Hippocratic oath to bind us. I will therefore tell you of my findings and details of my discussions with Fredda. It may help you understand her.

Because I am an old white haired doctor and have had experience of working with women like Fredda I was able to examine her thoroughly and to talk to her about her injuries. She would not allow the nurse to be present and I have found that to be a normal reaction. She is dreadfully ashamed. She is also terribly ill. She has syphilitic lesions in her womb, anal passage and throat. The work she restricts herself to here ensures she does not touch other patients although it is unlikely that she would pass the syphilis to others, except by direct bodily contact to the lesions. No, Corporal, I do not think that if she spat on your food you would contract the disease. If your magic penicillin manages to destroy the syphilis she will still bare physical scars. She should never have children; she may incur blindness later in her life. She is married and her husband is unaware of her condition. She believes her husband to be alive, although I personally doubt it. She was married seven months ago in Berlin. Her husband was in the regular army and following the wedding he was posted to Poland. There he was wounded and sent to a German military hospital in Gorzow, northwest Poland. She received a letter from him four months ago and he said that he had stood on a mine and had serious leg and abdominal injuries. She has not heard from him since.

She left Berlin and headed towards Gorzow, but was unable to get there as the Russian advance had swept over the border. It is my understanding that when the Russians capture fit German soldiers they have them sent to Russia to work on their farms. When they capture military hospitals they murder all the useless sick. I doubt that Fredda's husband has survived. Fredda decided to walk from the east to the western front and seek shelter in the British or American zones. Four times she was taken by a Russian soldier and raped and mistreated. On the last occasion she tried too hard to defend herself and suffered a broken arm. After the soldier had finished with her he took her to a Russian military hospital. She mistook this to be a kindness. In fact she was presented to a ward of fifty sick Russian soldiers. They raped her individually and in groups. It is likely that most of the patients were suffering from various stages of syphilis and knew that they were passing the disease to her. She lost consciousness during the ordeal and woke the next day buried in a refuse tip and midden. She found some rags and amazingly found the strength to walk to the British Zone. She has refused your British doctor's offers of examination and they were possibly too busy to insist. The mental scars she will carry will be very deep. She was not a Nazi, she was innocent, undoubtedly beautiful and in the wrong place at the wrong time, and those were her crimes.

The horrors of war will be forgotten in twenty years from now. They will remember the glory, the bravery of the fighting men, once a year some of you will remember the dead. It will happen, Corporal, I have seen it happen with the Great War of 1914. By 1934 we celebrated the fame and glory and had forgotten the mud, gas, rats, lice, rape, blinding chemicals and idiocy of phosphorous burns. Twenty years from now they will see war movies where no blood is shown on the screen. Fredda, if she survives, will remember the truth. Will she survive? With patience, kindness, love, tender care, then possibly, but I would only give her a fifty-fifty chance. I know of no medicine that can cure the injury to her heart and mind.

No I did not fight in the Great War, I was too old even then. I am sixty-one years old now. I was born in Berlin to a prosperous family. It does not say Berlin on Schrader's notes; but then again my real name is not Dressler. I had a fine education and passed my medical examination as a Doctor of Medicine. Because my family was rich, I continued to study and by 1909 I had become a Doctor of Anthropology. I travelled widely and spent three of the war years in the United States. In 1917 I fled to Mexico, but even there found time to make field trips and even followed in the steps of your Charles Darwin and visited the Galapagos Islands off South America. I wrote a number of papers in both German and English and for a time my work was thought to be highly original and exciting.

I had this idea regarding the evolution of man. I proposed that at one period in our evolution we had been swimming monkeys, or apes. I wrote that at the end of the last ice age the sea level of the world's oceans had gradually risen as the ice melted. The rising sea inundated forests near to the seashore. Many forest dwelling animals were forced to move inland, but some species of tree swinging ape stayed put. They adapted to the new environment. Their normal predator enemies had gone in land, so they were unopposed. They lived in high trees and the water level would have risen to only a few feet above the ground. Even so the ape learned to swim. It found new food sources in molluscs and fish. The process would have taken many tens of thousands of years and during that time the bodies of the ape would have changed significantly. Its back feet would have become more webbed, but his front feet needed long fingers to manipulate the tools it developed to open mollusc shells and to hang in the trees. Salt water would hurt the eyes of our ape, so eventually, through selection, it changed a sweat gland near the eye into a tear duct. The fresh water of this duct washed salt from the eye each time it blinked.

Do you know, Corporal, humans are the only creatures with a tear duct? Body hair causes drag when swimming. The apes that swam fastest and longest and found most food were those with less hair. It did not matter about the hair on top of the head, or under the arms, or between the legs, because that hair was not in the way of the flow of the water. The relatively small amount of hair on men's legs and chest today lies in the direction of the flow of water. Look at a dog or horse and you will see that their hair lies in many different directions. Did you know that at the moment of birth a human baby can instinctively swim? It can close the back of the nose and throat to prevent drowning. At some point in our evolution it must have been necessary for babies to swim at birth. Apes naturally walk on four legs; their backs are rounded. Swimming apes have to arch their backs to keep their head above water. When the water levels eventually receded those swimming apes found that their arched back made it easy to walk on their hind legs. The advantage this gave in speed of movement and having two free hands to carry tools and weapons was astounding. Soon it would use these advantages to overpower its enemies in the animal and bird kingdom. It would become numerous and need to develop skills in communication and in inventing tools.

I am sorry, Corporal, I am boring you? Let me tell you about my life not that of long dead apes. In 1922, I came back to Berlin and joined the staff of a University. I was lucky for that was a difficult time in Europe. In 1933, I was approached by a Government official and asked to develop an idea they had regarding different racial groupings. I was not a political person at that time but soon saw that being a member of the National Socialist Party would give me great advantages in my work and career. I joined the Party and received the study commission. It was a statistical study and the numbers were numbers; how those numbers have been interpreted is a great worry to me. I was given access to a large population of adult males of various races and groups and I measured them. I would take measurements of different parts of their anatomy, nose length, cranial capacity, height, arm, leg and body length and things like that. I would take one thousand men in each grouping all between the ages of twenty-five and thirty-five and measure them. For Aryan Germans I was given SS troops, for Jews, Gypsies, Poles, Russians, I was allowed to visit labour camps. I published my results and was alarmed at how they were misread and misused.

On average Jewish men have longer noses than the other groups. German men are taller and have greater cranial capacity than the Polish and the Polish more than Ukrainians. The shortest men were from eastern Russian. These factors are created from historic migration. The short Chinese and Mongolian people have bred with people in the east and passed to them their shortness. The Polish people have had much less of this influence and we Germans none. These facts have no bearing on the humanity of each group, or intelligence, or kindness, or abilities. Unfortunately the statistics were used to show unjustified inferiority. A tall English man with a small nose is not superior to a short Englishman with a big nose, but that sort of interpretation was given to my findings.

As time went by I saw horrific evidence of the misuse of my statistics. The so-called inferior groups were imprisoned and used as labour, yes, slaves. I saw rational, immensely well-educated and respected German doctors use these trapped people like you would use mice in an experiment. The results of the experiments are valid and will be used to better our knowledge and future, but how they were provided and developed was barbaric. I have seen over the last four years the conditions in the labour camps deteriorate; the inmates were made to suffer for no sensible reason. Yes, I was just there to take measurements. No, Corporal, I did not report what I had seen. Who could I tell? Who would believe me? I sat and watched it happen and hate myself for doing nothing, for saying nothing.

Yes, laboratory experiments were carried out on human beings. Today our knowledge of X-rays to see the bones of the body is much improved. The problems of over-exposure, burning and infertility will have been solved. To obtain that improvement many innocent men and women were burned by x-rays. After exposing Russian men to the radiation, Russian women were made to obtain samples of their sperm so that the effect of the levels of exposure on the fertility of those men could be measured. Exposed women had eggs removed surgically from their wombs. After the operation the women were allowed to die because to tend them was more costly than to obtain replacements. No, I was not involved in the experiments. I am an anthropologist not a butcher."

The Doctor sat sullen and forlorn while Terry poured the fourth deep whisky. It was dusk and the fading light made faces and expressions difficult to discern.

"Doctor Dressler, when you arrived here in Altewiese, who was the man walking in front of you, dressed in a black hat and coat?" Terry asked as casually as he could manage. From the doctor's voice it was clear that he appreciated the change of subject.

"That man was our guide. He collected us from the canal at Uelzen and led us here, mostly on foot. He had some refreshment when he got to the house and then started back."

"Who was the man behind you as you walked?"

"We called him Willi Schmitt, which is a joke. He only stayed at the house with me for one night. During Monday night the Policeman Fromming took him to the west somewhere. We are all using false names now but by coincidence I know the real name of Willi. He did not remember but we had met briefly four years ago in one of the camps. He was then a middle rank officer in the SS. His real name is Eichmann. Like me he is of no importance to the British and Americans. No one has ever heard of us but our involvement with the camps means we are hunted and hated. The SS system finds a way for us to leave Germany and start a new life in another country. Me, now, I am in your hands. I have confessed much and you could arrest me and I would be sent to prison. Do you know I would prefer your justice to shoot me and end my nightmare?"

It was then that the Doctor began to cry. Firstly there were sad, soft sobs, and then they grew louder until he was crying, head in hands, dripping tears from his wrists. Terry poured the final whisky of the night for him and spoke to the inhibriated, weeping man

"Drink this it will make you feel better. Doctor, what nightmares disturb your sleep?"

"Sleep? What sleep, Corporal? I have not slept for eighteen months. Sometimes I nap, but within minutes the scene of terror comes flooding back and I have to wake to stop the pictures. I have lied to you and that was stupid of me. I was happy telling you everything, but I told you nothing.

I met a propaganda official at one of the camps; he knew of my earlier work on evolution and the swimming ape. He cleverly seduced me into his evil. I mentioned that in some parts of the world women still give birth to their babies while standing or crouching in water. Both the mother and baby feel less strain and tension than during a bed birth and this links to my conjecture of a swimming ape. He suggested that for that link to be substantiated, the ideal temperature for the water would be that similar to the coastal waters of the tropics - that is cool to tepid. He said that he could arrange with the camp commandant for an experiment to be performed to indicate the validity of this claim. If nothing else we would learn the best temperature for the water, in water births.

We were at Ravensbrueck where Doctor Rascher had done much work on body heat and the revival of very cold bodies. Twenty pregnant women were selected for me; all due to deliver in the second half of January, it was 1944. They included a French resistance terrorist, a French Jewess, six Hungarian Jews, the rest were Polish and Russian partisans. We had two deep tanks prepared; the water temperature on the first day was thirty degrees centigrade in both tanks. Once we had observed two births we reduced the temperature by three degrees. This continued until the last pair would be immersed in freezing water at zero degrees. At the higher temperatures the mothers and babies became quickly exhausted; great strain was put on the babies' hearts. The most comfortable temperature was, as expected, in the cool range of fifteen to nine degrees. At three degrees both of the babies died.

I wanted to stop the experiment then, but the guards and other doctors persuaded me to continue with the last two women; one was Russian, the other a Rumanian gypsy. We waited two days and both entered labour on the same evening. They were placed naked into the freezing water and they screamed. After one hour the Russian woman suddenly fell quiet; she was dead. The gypsy continued to plead with us to take her from the water. She would yell and scream and after two more hours her body began to turn blue. When she tried to stand the two SS guards would push her shoulders back under the water. After four hours of torture the baby's head started to appear and at that moment the mother expired. As she died one of the guards began to laugh and to fondle her breasts. The scene was unimaginably horrific. I stood in the cold night air and shook with fear, rage, guilt and self-loathing. That night I returned to my barrack room intent in taking my own life. In the morning I was still alive; a coward whose hair had turned pure white during that tormented night. The camp officers thought my reaction odd and tried to ease my disgust by telling me that all of the women and babies used in the experiment during those three weeks had been gassed and incinerated. The gypsy had died more quickly than most, they said.

The propaganda ministry was to circulate to maternity clinics the results of the grotesque experiments using my name. I did not do any work or writing for them after that dreadful day when I watched the gypsy freeze to death. I fled to a large hospital in Leipzig and changed my name and tended the sick and worked twenty-four hours a day. My colleagues were amazed at my ability to work without sleep; only I knew that the work prevented me from sleeping and seeing those women again. When the Russian army approached Leipzig I volunteered to stay at the hospital with those too sick to move. I was hailed as a hero and my photograph used by the Ministry of Propaganda. They were stupid, what I wanted was a Russian bullet, not a medal.

Someone recognised my photograph and thought it best that I join the exodus of SS and Gestapo personnel. This was not out of kindness; they did not want me to relate my story to the Russians. If they knew that I had spoken to you tonight like this, they would kill us both. Fromming would be told to do it; his real boss is a fanatic, a ruthless evil fiend whose only priority is the security of the SS Brotherhood and their escape route. I am willing to stay here and work for you and help the sick. You will come to no harm if you know nothing. Or, you can arrest me now and we both must leave immediately and seek the protection of one of your army camps. Me, they can shoot, but it would be unfair of me to put you in danger with my drunken ramblings. What do you want to do, Corporal?"

Terry was astounded by the doctor's revelations. He had to sit in judgement over this old man. A man who had been involved in barbaric evil, but who even so did not act like a madman. Terry had to be Judge and Jury in a case that called out to him for both compassion and loathing. The irony was that if Terry shot this doctor now, the man would probably thank him. To let him live would be a much worse punishment and while he lived he could help Paula and the hospital and Fredda. Terry thought he was composing the words he would have liked to say to the doctor but was shocked to hear himself speaking aloud.

"Doctor Dressler, I sentence you to life. You shall stay here in Altewiese and look after the sick and injured to the best of your ability. You will be removed from the close proximity of bad influences. You will live at the house opposite Meyer's bar, next to the pharmacy. You will be my friend because I know of your guilt and nightmares. You will give me information about activities that are a threat to me personally or to the British in general. If minor criminals pass through the town, I want to know about it. I may choose to take no action where I believe the activity is of no consequence. In return Doctor Dressler, I will protect you. Doctor Dressler, I think you have just fallen asleep. I wish you pleasant dreams, but fear you will not have them."

CHAPTER SIX

JULY

On Sunday 1st July Otto drove Terry west from the town on the double dirt track that was the lane to the farms and woods with their hunters' shelters. They travelled slowly in the slightly sprung sedan and splashed into potholes full of overnight rain. After two miles they were completely out of sight of Altewiese and the main north-south road. There were black and white cows in the fields. They passed three large fields of young wheat and in front of one farmhouse lay a vast area of vegetables. The woods came down to the north bank of the river but on this side they lay one mile away to the south. There were many more farmhouses and cottages than Terry had imagined and each of them had activity about them - chimney smoke, herdsmen and women moving cattle and children playing in the yards. Kurt had informed Terry that many of the newcomers had been found accommodation and work at these westerly farms.

They drove for about ten miles and only then did the river valley appear to end. There was a large farmhouse with barns and outbuildings, surrounded on three sides by the dense woodland. As they neared the farm they saw many pigs in the fields and among the trees. A young man approached the car as they pulled to a halt in the smelly farmyard. He had been one of the POWs who had passed through the Centre during the previous week. Otto's poor English and German meant that little conversation passed between the men but he was friendly and invited them into the house. The man's mother prepared acorn coffee and sausage sandwiches for them. Another older lady entered ushering two young boys to greet Terry. They were shy and sad and Terry recognised them as the two recently orphaned DPs.

Later Otto and Terry were given a guided tour of the considerable farm facility. Of great interest were the smoking sheds where bacon and sausages were hung over a fire of wood chips. Terry could just understand that the young farmer wanted to increase production and sell his surplus to the sergeant for transporting to Hamburg. Terry signalled his agreement with an enthusiastic 'thumbs up'. Behind the farm was a steep climb through a wooded area thick with trees and brambles and Terry noticed a narrow track trodden through it. He started to follow the track despite the protests of the young farmer. After two hundred steep yards the wood abruptly ended and before him Terry looked down a shallow embankment to railway lines. The rails appeared rusty and weeds and brambles had spread to the nearest sleepers. Terry felt sure this was the soon to be reopened Luneburg to Hanover railway. The muddy track he was now standing on ended at the first rails. Whoever was using it turned either north or south and followed the rail lines. Terry wondered how many times Fromming may have passed this way.

Otto and Terry visited each of the farms on their return journey and were always received with politeness and respect. The displaced persons that they could recognise were grateful and insisted on shaking Terry's hand warmly and often with tears of relief and joy. The beauty and peace of this narrow valley contrasted starkly with their so recent experiences of horror and devastation.

On Monday morning 2nd July Mr Meyer of the bar and guest house asked for permission to open his establishment for five days each week, from ten in the morning to six at night, instead of the three days he had been opening since April. He wished to remain closed on Sundays and Mondays as these were his slowest days and traditionally he had never opened on Mondays. Terry agreed, although he had not known the bar was closed on any day of the week and did not much care anyway.

On Tuesday 3rd July Sergeant Wilkes gave to Terry a fine gold pocket watch and chain. That was his share of the unit's profit for the half month he had been part of the enterprise. Terry was amazed and pleased. He was less pleased by the delivery of twenty more DPs and ten young Hitler Youth trained ex-prisoners of war. Six were the sons of local families and four had distant relations in the area and nowhere else to go. Father Podendorf left Altewiese but did not say farewell to Terry, the sergeant or anyone at the Centre. He was collected by a large black limousine and whisked away north. He would soon be responsible for the souls of one hundred and fifty thousand Polish, Russian and German displaced persons in a camp on the west bank of the river near Lubeck.

On Thursday 5th Wilkes delivered a further nine young POWs and Terry was forced to consider the consequences of having two dozen, military trained, disillusioned, unskilled, Nazi educated boys of seventeen and eighteen idle in Altewiese. There was no school so the existing teenagers of the town had little to do and, together with the ex-Hitler Youth, would form a potent mixture of trouble. Terry had Mr Schrader, Kurt and Ralf discuss the problem and an exciting possible solution was to be tried. Constable Ralf, who had been a soccer player of note in his school days, was to add to his titles, 'Youth Leader' and 'Referee'.

Teams of twelve young people were to be formed. Immediately three such teams, but more as time and success allowed. The teams were to be selected by Ralf so as to mix the fit and unfit, military and school trained, younger and older youth. Each team would have a local tree as a name and emblem. A football tournament would be played on Saturdays and Sundays and paid work for the following week would be allocated according to winners and losers. The losing team to be paid one hundred marks to clean and cover the latrines in the factory warehouse; the winning team to be paid one hundred and twenty marks to mow and mark the lines on the football pitch. A constant workload for at least one of the teams would be chopping wood and feeding the fire of the water pump boiler, which was soon to be operational.

Each team was to nominate one linesman and eleven players, with Ralf as referee. Although the teams would commence with only male team members, over time girls would be recruited and added, and some were to play in matches. Election to, or ejection from a team was at Ralf's discretion only. The teams, which soon formed into bonded loyal gangs, became indispensable to the community taking on tasks that others were less likely to do - road and lane repairing, chopping and selling fire wood, clearing the smelly reed beds, repairing and strengthening the river bank and painting the town.

On Monday 9th at six thirty-five, Terry sat at the table waiting for his overdue breakfast. Paula rushed to him carrying a tray of toast, jam and a coffee pot and apologised for its late arrival.

"Good morning Corporal. Sorry for the slight delay, but Fredda is not well this morning. No nothing physically serious, just her monthly problem. What monthly problem? You have learned a great deal in the last few weeks but I see that we still have much to teach you about life. Once each month it is normal for Fredda to be tense and have a nagging stomach ache, unfortunately she does not bleed and that is not normal; she should mess her underclothes. Fredda believes this lack of mess means that she will never be able to have children and she gets very depressed. Where is she? Just on the next floor cleaning the bathroom before the rush."

Terry ran up the stairs and strode purposefully down the corridor to the open bathroom door. An oil lamp hanging from the ceiling lit Fredda and she looked pale and afraid; her head fell to her chest in a pose reminiscent of her first arrival. She backed to the bath, her calves touching its cold ceramic side. Terry walked right up to her and folded his arms around her in a tight hug; her head pressed firmly against his shirtfront. She felt tense and bony, but after one full minute her shoulders relaxed slightly and she began to tremble.

Terry heard her soft weeping. He was trying to remember why he was holding her like that.

As a small boy he could recall once having cut his hand while peeling an apple with a sharp knife. He had cried out and his mother had wordlessly come to him and held him tightly just as he was now doing to Fredda. For many minutes his mother had engulfed him in her arms and then silently released him. The hurt and fear had vanished; there remained only a slowing drip of blood and the sweet taste of the apple. Terry then remembered another time when he was older, perhaps ten or eleven, when he had fallen down the shop's cellar stairs. He had grazed both knees and elbows and had a painful back. His mother had flown down the stairs, lifted him to his feet and held him tightly in that wonderful embrace. After ten minutes the hurt had disappeared and only the drying grazes remained. He must have instinctively wanted to hold Fredda and remove her pain. Her sobbing stopped and he let her go and looked into her upturned pale blue eyes. He was astounded by her beauty - the sad eyes, perfect nose, lips parted a fraction in the gentlest of smiles. His stomach ached and his head buzzed. He did not want to see her body, he still feared the disease she may carry, but he craved to look at that simple sweet face forever. He stepped back from her and quietly whispered, "Good morning Fredda Marnitz-Schule", and left the bathroom wondering if he has taken the ache from her stomach and absorbed it into his own.

Paula was sitting staring at the oiled Tommy gun and as Terry approached she looked scornfully at him.

"What are those stains on the front of your clean shirt?" Terry stared at Paula and saw jealousy in the set of her lips.

"They are only Fredda's tears. Nothing important, Paula."

On Tuesday 10th one of the three ex-POWs delivered turned out to be the former under-manager of the sawmill. His wife and family were delighted to welcome him home but Terry was also extremely pleased. He had Kurt organise the full re-opening of the timber yard and sawmill. The second carthorse from the estate was donated to the yard and hauled logs from the surrounding woods. The first planks were taken to Hamburg in the last week of the month.

On Wednesday 11th at approximately eleven-thirty, Otto ran urgently into the Centre and called excitedly but unintelligibly to Terry. The words 'Russians' and 'officers' were sufficient to send Terry to the door and the others to cover. Two British Army staff cars, both carrying a General's insignia, were speeding round the square and on Terry's appearance at the top of the DP Centre's steps, they headed for and parked facing him. Terry returned his Tommy gun to his shoulder as a British Tank Corps major stepped from the front passenger seat of the left-hand car. A Tank Corps captain emerged from the second car. From the rears of both cars then appeared four Russian officers of various ranks but Terry noticed some red braid on one of the extremely wide hats. Terry saluted smartly and wondered if he was correctly dressed, but felt that only the belt and holster would concern the unexpected inspection.

"Stand at ease Corporal," said the tired major, "I'm Major Thompson and this is Captain Matthews. We are both 7th Armoured Division and those jolly chaps that have entered your Displaced Persons Reception Centre and Hospital are very impolite and damned annoying Russian officers and our very unwelcome guests."

"Corporal Terence Hall, sir. Staffordshire Light Infantry, now Governor's Office British Zone Germany. I'm responsible for the town of Altewiese, sirs".

"Jolly good," said the major. "How many of you are stationed here?"

"I am alone, sir. My sergeant is at Bachwald and my commanding officer is in Hamburg; that is Major Connolly, sir."

"Seen any of our Russians around here before Corporal?"

"No sir." Terry looked for Otto and noticed that he was following closely behind the Russians as they inspected the Centre. "I can't say I have ever seen a proper Russian ever, sir."

"Well aren't you the lucky one," the Captain said sarcastically. "Major Thompson here speaks some Russian and in my car one of the Russians speaks some English but I do wish he would shut up for a minute or two. We have to escort this pretty foursome to a meeting in Frankfurt. They did not want to drive or fly directly there. The cheeky blighters are having a good spy at our positions and activities and making us drive them too. You haven't got any Germans in uniform working for you round here have you?"

"No sir."

"Thank the Lord for that. We picked these Russians up at the Elbe crossing east of Luneburg at six this morning and they have insisted on stopping every time they see a work gang in green uniforms. It will take two more days to reach Frankfurt at this rate and I don't think my nerves and eardrums can take much more of a battering. Is there anything in there they should not see?" The Captain looked worried.

"No sir. The people are mostly victims of Russian violence; they may get a bit upset at the sight of those uniforms."

"I'll go and get them," said the Major. "If they ever come out, they may want to talk to you. Be polite, avoid politics and say as little as possible, that's a good chap."

"Running a good show here by the looks of it," the Captain said surveying the empty square,

"Keeping the Nazi bastards quiet. I like the road signs we passed too. Who is the little old chap with one tooth, sneaking about there?"

"He's my driver sir. Very loyal, he'll be watching that our visitors don't nick anything; present company excepted of course. I'd offer you all a drink sir but we only have acorn coffee and no sugar or milk."

"No, don't bother yourself Corporal, we want to get under way as soon as heavenly possible. The one who speaks English is a cocky bastard, but the General is very wise and watchful and we've only recently noticed that he makes copious notes of anything said, so we have to be on our guard all of the damned time. We have been reduced to small talk on the subject of cricket which is a game I hate. Watch it, they're heading for us. Take care old boy."

The most junior of the Russian officers was the translator and he and the General came close to Terry, who saluted.

"Corporal Hall sir, can I help you?"

"The General is a very great man," began the young Russian, "his tanks have killed many Germans. He wants to know who is in charge of this town?"

"I am sir. I am alone here."

"Are you a Communist Corporal Hall?"

"No sir, I'm C of E."

"But you believe that commune farming is the best way to farm. The big sign says Co-operative Hall Farm. Your farm Hall, is a co-operative, is it not?"

"Yes sir, it is. The landowner here died recently and I have split the land up among the needy of the town and his workers. It was much quicker and easier to get the land under cultivation."

"The General now wants to know Corporal Co-operative Hall, why you have pictures of your King and Field Marshal Montgomery, but not Churchill?"

Terry had not noticed this error; it was an oversight and he could not think of an excuse that would not sound silly.

"King George is my King and Field Marshal Montgomery is the greatest General of the War. Mr Churchill is a great leader but he's a politician and politicians don't count sir."

Major Thompson leaned close to Terry.

"You are too young to vote this month, thank God."

"The General very much likes your town and how every one hides from you. He likes the flag on the top of that building. He likes you Corporal and you may ask him a question."

"Take care old boy," repeated the Captain.

"Sir," Terry hesitated, then snapped, "why do you let your Russian soldiers abuse the civilian population in your zone of Germany?"

"Abuse, what is abuse?" the Russian translation officer asked.

"Rape, murder, maim, enslave, old people and young girls."

"Oops," murmured the Captain.

"Who told you we did that?" was the General's angry reply.

"Sir, the women your soldiers raped told me."

The General exploded into loud Russian; the translator had difficulty, but then spoke.

"The pig lying Germans are all lying pigs. It is not true; it is exaggerated. You come and look for yourself. Our towns are like this town, only much better. Everyone is happy. You come and we will show you and we will explain what we do and why we do it. Why we treat the German pigs like pigs. You should be told why. You should be told what they did to our people." The General went on more quietly.

"The General likes you Corporal," said the translator, "he says the Russian army is full of brave, wise Corporals like you and that is why the Russian army is the best army in the World. He says the Russian army does not have officers who say nothing and play cricket and bridge and diplomacy. That too, is why the Russian army is the best in the World. The General will send you an invitation to visit him in Russian Germany, Corporal Co-operative Hall. We must go now and we all thank you."

Terry saluted and they all rejoined their cars. The British captain stood at the door of his car.

"Damned good show Corporal Hall. I'll write to Major Connolly and say you are doing a fine job here. We're off to play cricket for the next two hundred miles, wish us luck old man. Purgatory can't be as bad as this."

The two staff cars sped out of the square and Terry breathed with relief. He and Otto were to spend the remainder of the day explaining to various townspeople that the hand-over of Altewiese to the Russians had not been discussed and would seem to be unlikely. Otto explained to Terry that the Russians had spoken in a dialect when close to the British Officers.

"They really believe you are a communist or at least a Socialist and have made a note to make contact with you again soon. The Co-operative sign was not such a good idea after all, I think."

On Tuesday 17th Wilkes had a long chat with Terry.

"As you know yesterday I was up in Hamburg and I make time to call on the major, which is the official reason I'm there. It must have been about fifteen thirty and he's all smiles and full of news and theories on how the Government of Occupation is performing. He's so full of himself that the weak little shit signs a stack of blank requisition forms, which happen to include, mixed in like, five travel passes and asks me is that enough. Then all of a sudden he stands up, comes round the desk and puts his arm round me. Bloody hell; I start to think he fancies me. Anyway, he says he has some private matters to discuss with me; he must have felt me tense up and get ready to punch his faggot nose, 'cos he adds that they are military matters of a delicate nature. So now I think maybe he has clap and wants to know where the clap doctor is in Hamburg. Then, I think, shit, he's found out about our trading business and wants a cut or something worse. He says he doesn't want to discuss the matter in his office so he invites me for a drink. I thought a weak kneed shit like him would only drink tea, but I'm thirsty and fascinated to see how long he would be allowed to have me in the Officers' Mess. It being late afternoon there wouldn't be many officers about, but come five o'clock they'd soon see a smelly sergeant chucked into the street. Officers Mess far sir, I ask. No he says, he will take me to his club; to his bloody club no less. Been open two weeks, owned by a vehemently anti-Nazi friend of his. Well I'm not sure what colour a vehemently anti-Nazi is, but if he's got a nice bar, that's all right with me.

He has me drive his American Jeep the forty minutes it takes to get to the club. It's a big posh manor house thing set in a big garden behind a tall brick wall. I don't see no damage to it. It must be the only building in Hamburg that hasn't taken a bomb or tank shell or two. An old impressive place it is. The front hall is all carved wood and paintings of big fat German businessmen. A bloody doorman wants to take my coat, I tell him to sod off and get his own. We go into this lounge bar. This is smart, let me tell you, all red leather comfy chairs, dark wood panelling, tall windows draped with nice thick curtains and a long heavy looking polished wood bar counter.

There are no other customers, just this bored old fart of a barman wiping glasses. As we go up to him I notice for the first time this big mirror behind the bar, no problem you think. Well, in front of the mirror and on the bar, nor anywhere else as far as I could see, was there any booze. No bottles, beer pumps, nothing; below the mirror there's a long row of cupboard doors, but all closed. The Major's striding up to the bar, all swagger and bluff and I think he has no choice but to order us two cups of bloody tea. The major turns to me, indicates the barman and asks me what I would like to drink. Well, I don't know what the choice is, but being in a bit of a stroppy mood I decide to ask for something he definitely will not have; I says to the barman that I would very much like a pint of best Burton ale.

This barman looks at me as though I've just crawled out of a dog turd, but I'm happy 'cos he's obviously buggered. I upset him, all right; off he goes, stomping out of the bar in a right huff. Don't he speak English sir, I ask the major. Oh yes, he replies all hoity-toity, he is Austrian, but he worked at the Savoy in London for a number of years. Hoping to find out what sort of liquid is available, I ask the major what he's drinking. The sly bastard says he is going to order his usual. Do you drink beer, I ask him. No he says, it gives him indigestion - which to you and me, means that it makes him fart. Do you like a drop of Scotch, I ask, trying again. No, he says, that makes his chest all blotchy. I look at him and think he wouldn't be able to find many blotches on that sparrow chest.

It was at that very moment that the barman marches back into the room carrying a silver tray, up high near his shoulder, and on it is a pint glass containing a dark golden liquid. It turns out to be the nicest drop of best Burton I've had in years. Shuts me up proper. While I taste this lovely nectar the barman opens one of the cupboards and takes out a bottle. Pours a long, long, long shot of it into a brandy glass, but the shit chose the wrong glass, 'cos its not brandy - a very fine vintage Cognac, the Major calls it. He also explains that the club members prefer not to have alcohol on show as it is quite ostentatious. German and Russian guests may be offended by a wanton display of items they themselves could not find or afford. Well, I don't know what Ostend Asians like to drink, but my pint was bloody brilliant.

He leads me out of the room through some tall French windows on to a terrace overlooking a long lawn surrounded by trees and bushes but only a few flowers. We sit down on nice wooden seats either side of a small white painted metal table and he starts to talk to me in a hushed voice, although there is no one around as far as I could see. He starts by saying that Field Marshal Montgomery is moving the Governor's Office to a palace near Osnabrook and the Major believes it would be in his own best interest to move our HQ there too in order to stay near the Field Marshal. He tells me it is his ambition to be retired from the army with the rank of full Colonel and to achieve that he needs to be where the action is and in regular eye contact with Montgomery and his staff.

The arse-licking bugger I think to myself. That explains why the Major moved his office from a house in Luneburg, early June it was, to that poky bedroom he has in Hamburg. Monty had moved the 21st Army Group Headquarters the week before from Luneburg to near Hamburg. Then I start to get worried; my visits to the Major, while he is in Hamburg, will give ample opportunity to generate some profit. I doubt whether there are many Germans in a palace outside

Osnabrook willing to exchange their gold watches for a few wooden planks. The port of Hamburg has great potential for import and export trade in the future, which is a line I had been thinking about for a week or two. There's not a port in Osnabrook.

So I say to the Major, all-casual and gently like, that Hamburg is very useful to our purpose, there being lots of commercial activity around the city, which allows my local Germans to trade and sell their food produce, which practice I like to supervise and control, but I wouldn't have time to do that and report to him in Osnabrook, which would be the priority of course. I am about to give him a load more bullshit reasons for his remaining in Hamburg and possibly not receiving a promotion to Colonel, when I look into his eyes. This little chicken shit is giving me the evil eye. He's staring at me all hard like while he has a sneaky grin on his lips. There's a silence for a second or two then he says, and I'll try to repeat his words accurately, that he knows exactly what I and our unit are up to, he knows all the details regarding planks and food and jewellery, he even knows the denier of the silk stockings we handled last week. My bloody heart stopped. I start to consider what it will be like to be a private again.

Then he changes; he puts his face close to mine and tells me he too has become involved in one or two business deals recently, one of which has the prospect of providing him with a relatively comfortable future. The business deals are both centred in or near Hamburg and that is why he is not sure whether it is best for him to remain here or move to be near the Field Marshal. I say it depends whether the difference in retirement pay between a major and a colonel is greater than any potential remuneration that may accrue from any local business activities. I thought that was a good answer considering I was under some pressure at that time. He is bloody delighted; he says that this is his view also; it is the size of the reward for staying here that matters.

Ever the one to grasp at the passing opportunity I ask him if there is any way I could be of assistance. He says certainly there is. The Major sits back now and becomes more relaxed; mind his brandy glass is almost empty. He tells me that it was me who suggested to him the importance of transport to the smooth running of the Occupied Zones. On first arriving in Hamburg he had observed that the lack of private haulage companies was critical. At the same time he had, by chance, found a farm a few miles east of the city that had ten thousand, repeat ten thousand, Wehmacht lorries, all parked in neat rows. He said he has managed to get hold of a few and to find some diesel for them. He gave them to a German friend who has now created a very successful haulage business. Bloody generous of you I think. Field Marshal Montgomery's orders do not include any support for transport this year, so the major has had to keep a very low profile for this programme. He goes on to say that he wishes to repeat the experiment elsewhere in his patch. He wants us to get some of our local entrepreneurs to start haulage companies and he will provide two or three lorries each month, for four months. The lorries will be delivered with spares and a small weekly ration of diesel. He insists genuine German owned companies that are moving goods for profit must use them. Then he says slowly...... 'outwardly owned by Germans'. I don't ask him to explain; I just say yes sir, I understand.

Now he gets all conspiratorial again, leaning forward and pointing his thin white finger at me. He tells me that when the particular model of Benz lorry he has chosen to use exclusively is delivered, we will notice that it would be very simple to move the steering wheel from the left to the right hand side of the cab. We must not do this and that was an order. The lorries must be seen to be working in the north of Germany. We are to ensure they are repainted in bright noticeable colours and have company names painted on them that will attract the attention of English speakers. Also, for each lorry that is delivered to our parish, the HQ records will show that we have received two. We will get the diesel rations for two, but there will only be one lorry. He says that it will not be a difficult task to amend the haulage company records accordingly. No, not difficult, I say. So, now I see his game. We boys get a slice of the action in a number of small haulage companies we help to set up; we get free lorries and spares; we get ample fuel for them too. Good. The Major gets our haulage company as legitimate cover for his other activities, which include the modification and export to England of an equal number of lorries to the number we'll be seeing.

The bastard then gives me a lecture on greed; the bloody hypocrite. I reckon the Hamburg haulage company he's already running must be doing the same 'one-for-me-one-for-you' routine. The demand he's getting from England is probably so big he needs extra through put. I think he's making a pretty packet out of this scam to risk involving us and the chance we may blow his cover, but say la vie. Then the bugger goes and destroys my belief in human nature; for Major meek and mild, wouldn't say boo to a goose, saying his prayers each night Connolly looks at me hard and guess what he says. He says that we are to remember that it is in all of our interests to be strictly confidential in handling this matter; he would not want to investigate plank trading by army personnel, nor misuse by those personnel of military property and time; the movement of stockings and jewellery in particular would be a quite serious crime. The bastard is threatening me, blackmailing me; I consider calling his bluff, but what the hell, our part in the deal looks easy, risk free and profitable. I say to him not to worry and that we all know the rules. You know what he says then? He says he knows we aren't greedy, that is why he has chosen to involve us in this philanthropic enterprise to assist the German people to feed themselves this winter. This Major is proving to be a very cool sod and that's for sure.

So, Corporal, in one week's time you will receive two nearly new German lorries with a reasonable amount of diesel. Find some lorry drivers; set up a private company with you as a silent, but controlling partner; get some planks, vegetables, sausages and cheese on them and send them to me for redirection to our colleagues in Hamburg. Got it? Good. Check out the garage owner and if you think you can trust him a little, ask him to create the company. If he turns out to be a good partner... good. If not then we'll dump him and find someone else."

On Thursday 19th two more young POWs arrived, but only four DPs. Two of the latter turned out to be sisters from Berlin. Both ladies were in their fifties and were large, flamboyant and noisy. They had extensive wobbly chests with cleavages to match the Cheddar Gorge. They had run a bar and guesthouse; bedrooms were probably rented by the hour and the bar had all night entertainment, more nipples than tipples. For once Mr Schrader and Kurt were hard pressed to find suitable employment and accommodation for the Sisters Hoffman.

On Tuesday 24th Wilkes had news and briefing notes from Major Connolly. Apparently there was to be a big meeting near Berlin, in Potsdam, with the Prime Minister, Stalin and Truman. While Britain and America had wanted to have one united Germany controlled by the allies through a council, Stalin and the French did not. They wanted four German states: Russian, American, British and French. Travel to the Russian Zone would be very difficult, if not impossible. Berlin would be split into four also, with one road and one rail access route through the Russian Zone. All British troops were now back on our side of the Elbe, the last ones having left Magdeburg on the 4th. In addition to over one million DPs, there were three hundred thousand Russian and Polish displaced persons still in the British Zone and the Russians did not seem too eager to have them back. There were still one million, eight hundred thousand Prisoners of War in camps in the British Zone following the arrival of a large batch from Norway. This lot was eating more food than could be supplied. The harvest was now a priority.

A problem about to add to the difficulties was only just filtering through; the Russians had given to the Polish Government that part of Germany east of the Oder-Neise Line and the Poles were evicting all the German population and replacing it with Polish DPs. Many of the evicted Germans would be making for the Elbe and crossing to the west bank. Food shortage was going to be a big problem. Relaxation on the movement of food was to be allowed; more trains and lorries were to be employed; diesel and petrol would be more freely available for civilian use. Altewiese Reck Spedition Europe, the haulage company part owned by Hans Reck, the garage proprietor, would receive priority diesel supplies because of the large volume of food and building material it was handling. Major Connolly believed that this company had received early recognition due to its use of the company initials on its lorry sides: ARSE.

On Friday 27th Doctor Dressler again had dinner with Terry at the interview table of the Centre. He reported that the general health of the community was good. There was no evidence of the import of serious disease by DPs and sufficient food was remaining in the local market place to ensure everyone was well fed. Medicines were in short supply and much more penicillin was required. He had set up a dentistry clinic at his house and Kurt was busily trying to find a qualified dentist to take over Dressler's amateur ministrations. The return of town water was moving effluent quickly from the town drains; the smell and number of rats had reduced considerably. The town was full and the arrival of more DPs would lead to overcrowding. The town should also endeavour to find a second doctor as the work load was very heavy, even for a man who was happy to work twenty-four hours each day.

Doctor Dressler mentioned that he understood that the flow of the lower class criminals through the SS Brotherhood pipeline through Altewiese had reduced to a trickle. On the other hand the activities of the National Socialist Party was on the increase. The party had changed its name but some of the old membership was regularly meeting again. The senior members were men that Terry had upset and included Mr Hasch the ex-mayor and Mr Kahler the builder. Von Lutken's puppets may be looking for revenge. Terry was considerably concerned about this threat. He asked Dressler to find out when and where they held their meetings and who the main activists were. He was to have Otto prepare for an early transfer of Terry's kit from the Centre to von Lutken's rooms in the big house.

On Sunday 29th July Terry had Otto drive him to Brick for lunch with Don. They arrived at eleven-thirty and Terry joined Don for cocktails at the stroke of noon. A number of beers followed. Late lunch was preceded by a bottle of warm Champagne. Lunch was accompanied by white wine. A red wine was opened to assist in the digestion of the heavy Altewiese cheese. Terry and Don's table companions, two young ladies who giggled continuously, refused the red wine and had to remove their dresses as forfeit. By the third round of brandy both young ladies were naked, Don was asleep and Terry was kneeling on the lavatory floor praying that the toilet bowl would not demand the removal of the whole of his stomach. At five o'clock Otto dragged Terry's unconscious body to the car, drove him to the big house and put him in von Lutken's cold bed.

On Monday 30th July, Kurt, via Paula's translation, asked permission of a very subdued Terry, for the dismissal from office of Constable Fromming. Kurt believed Fromming had been involved in the illegal movement of German people into and out of Altewiese; while the people were not of any consequence, Fromming's actions were not acceptable. Terry immediately agreed. Kurt also added that while endeavouring to find a dentist and second doctor, he had widened his search to include a bank manager and bank firm willing to re-open in Altewiese. The economy of the town was vigorous enough to warrant a bank and possibly a Wednesday market. Kurt also suggested that the activities of Mr Hasch and Mr and Mrs Meyer of the bar and guesthouse, were becoming suspicious and he agreed to keep a watch on them and any of von Lutken's old Nazi friends.

During the afternoon Terry lay on his bed in the darkened office and Fredda bought him glasses of water and sat and held his hand as his stomach continued to perform somersaults. He fell into and out of sleep, but was sure that he could hear the fall of teardrops on to the wooden floor. Later she would talk of the grand shop in Berlin where she had worked and of her wedding day and of the happiness she once had. She spoke of her husband and of his imminent return, on crutches certainly, but smiling the smile that would melt every woman's heart. Terry was happy to listen and dose and dream of the day soon when he would feel healthy again. At midnight he asked Fredda to leave the office and go to her room; he said goodnight to her, but forgot to thank her for the time she had spent with him. He locked the door and slid the chest of drawers across it. During the previous night he had been defenceless and completely in Otto's care. He had awoken in von Lutken's room with the Tommy gun propped against the ornate fireplace. He had vomited into the ornate fireplace and realised that he must move soon to the big house and its relaxed protection.

On Tuesday 31st, Wilkes gave Terry the shock news that Churchill had lost the General Election. The new Prime Minister was Clement Attlee; both men agreed that a Socialist Government should make their lives easier, but were not sure how or why.

CHAPTER SEVEN

MEYER'S BAR AND GUESTHOUSE

Sergeant Wilkes's first Tuesday visit in August was to be the prelude to an eventful and disturbing week for Terry. Wilkes jumped down from the large German truck, its orange ARSE shining brightly along its side panels. Arthur unloaded a few crates and boxes and drove the truck and its remaining cargo to various delivery points around the square. Later he would collect planks from the timber yard and cheese, vegetables and sausages from the creamery before returning to the DP Centre to retrieve the sergeant.

"Look what I've found," the sergeant held in front of Terry a small oil painting in a plain yellow frame; the whole thing measuring approximately two by two feet. The painting itself was a colourful abstract and bore a small, black, squiggled signature.

"It looked colourful to me and the bloke who sold it to me kept saying in English the words 'good' and 'valuable', so I believed him. Was I done Terry? What do you think it's worth?"

"I don't know," Terry said as he held the painting and examined the signature closely.

"Don't know, I thought you told me you knew about art and paintings and this sort of stuff?"

"At school I read some books about art and artists and the lives of some famous painters, but I don't know anything about how much paintings are worth. It's a real oil painting, though."

"Oh, that's bloody great", the sergeant said in exasperation.

"What did you pay for it sir?" asked Terry.

"Six sodding planks and that's a good quality watch in our language, possibly twenty quid."

Terry smiled.

"I would say it's worth more than that. I've heard of the artist. See this signature, if it's genuine, the painting could sell for quite a bit."

"French arty farty is he?" the sergeant asked, now relieved of the disgrace of a trading error.

"No, he's Spanish, Pablo Picasso".

"Shit, a Spaniard, I hoped a French man, a proper artist, would have done it. I thought the colours were nice; do you like it?"

"Yes, definitely, sir."

"Would you take it in place of a gold watch at our next share out?" the sergeant enquired tentatively.

"Yes."

"Good, then you can have it now and I'll make a note in my pocket book."

"Sergeant, this is a really nice oil painting, but if you get offered any old looking ones with cavaliers, or historic scenes, they might be much more valuable."

"OK, I'll watch out for that sort of thing, but size is the problem as I see it. This one would fit into a big suitcase, but a really large one will be hard to transport home without attracting attention, or involving people we don't know well, or can trust."

Terry put the painting on a shelf in his room and, re-locking the door behind him, returned to Wilkes. They sat and drank tea, Terry having explained that the supply of beer had run out and that he would like it added to the next shopping list.

"Well," said Wilkes, "here are two nice watches, a pearl necklace and four diamond rings; add that to the Pick Arsehole Spanish painting and you can see we had a good July. Your enterprises here in Altewiese are doing very nicely. Well-done young man. I had no POWs for you and the next big batch of DPs is due next week, so you'll be happy to know we bought you no troubles today. There's lots of paperwork though, so you'd better have the shits or you won't get through it all. Monty has been writing again; here's the English one for you and in that crate are some German copies for your people. There's another addition of the horror comic in German in the same crate. The people in Bachwald are becoming immune to the death camp stories; I reckon we're doing a bit of over kill on the subject, but orders is orders.

Connolly has four more lorries for us so two will be added to ARSE and the other two to Christine's SHIT fleet. You asked me to look out for some trailers for our lorries and I might have found a few - one flat bed with four wheels and three tankers with six wheels each. Yes, that's good isn't it? I have made contact with a man in Bremerhaven who has dealings with the oil refinery and he may be willing to over supply us with our diesel and petrol ration. Connolly has agreed to our hauling the fuel direct and not via the military fuel dump in Hamburg. I'll need to make a visit to the port area and find some merchants willing to buy some of our planks and foodstuff. Shouldn't be too difficult, but we'll see. What the tankers do mean is that we might be able to get some of the cheap oil refinery waste for your fertiliser factory. Set Muller to work on finding some chemical type people who know what the technical names are and give me a shopping list. I never see that old fart Schrader in the Centre anymore; what you done to him?"

"Sergeant Wilkes you know well that you have overloaded us with DPs recently. We had to open the school as a residence and farm and Schrader spends most of his time managing the project. Four mornings every week he holds a three-hour class for the Tree Teams. Gives them maths and English lessons - two teams at a time. Ingrid Schrader is here with me and is my main translator now. I prefer it that way. Mr Schrader got on my nerves a bit. I'm getting worried by an increase in rumours about von Lutken's Nazi friends. I may need to ask for Hardaker to spend a couple of nights with me, if that's OK sir?"

"No problem. Sort it out quickly; be violent if you need to be, but don't wait for them to act first. We haven't got too much time left to maximise our profits. I didn't tell you did I? I got my demob number.... thanks; the betting is it will get called by February at the latest - sooner if the bloody Japanese would cave in. If you still don't fear the odd SS officer passing through, you can continue to ignore them, but don't let any cocky local bastards interfere with you. Find out who they are and Hardaker and you can chop their bollocks off. You don't give me so many letters for your Mum and Dad, why? Don't forget to write, that's bullshit; you got plenty of fucking time. Which reminds me, how is your girlfriend.... her VD cleared up yet?"

TO THE POPULATION OF THE BRITISH ZONE IN GERMANY
Written 25th July 1945 Distribution 6th August 1945

1. Three months have now passed since Germany surrendered and your country passed to the control of the Allied Nations. The Allies are proceeding to the complete disarmament and demilitarization of Germany and to the final destruction of the Nazi Party and its affiliated organizations. These aims will be carried through to the end.

2. During this time the British Zone has been under Military Government. Members of the German armed forces have been sorted out by trades and occupations; many thousands have been discharged to work on the land and in other spheres, and this will continue. There is every prospect of a good harvest, and you must see that it is gathered in. My officers have been active in their endeavours to arrange that the German population have adequate food and housing and are kept free from disease. The first stage in the rehabilitation of Germany is under way.

3. I am now going to proceed with the second stage of the Allied policy. In this stage it is my intention that you shall have freedom to

get down to your own way of life: subject only to the provisions of military security and necessity. I will help you eradicate idleness, boredom, and fear of the future. Instead, I want to give you an objective, and hope for the future.

4. I will relax by stages the present restrictions on the freedom of the Press. It is Allied policy, subject to the necessity for maintaining military security, to encourage the formation of free trade unions in Germany. It is also Allied policy to encourage the formation in Germany of democratic political parties, which may form the basis of an ordered and peaceful German society in the future. We aim at the restoration of local self-government throughout Germany on democratic principles. And it is our intention that Nazis removed from office shall be replaced by persons who, by their political and moral qualities, can assist in developing genuinely democratic institutions in Germany. It is our purpose also to reorganise the judicial system in accordance with the principles of democracy, of justice under the law and equal rights for all citizens without distinction of race, nationality or religion. You may hold public meetings and discussions; I am anxious that you should talk over your problems among yourselves, and generally set on foot measures to help yourselves.

5. Your children are at present lacking juvenile organizations and facilities for education. I intend to encourage the forming of such organizations, on a voluntary basis, for the purpose of religious, cultural, health or recreational activities. Educational facilities will be provided at a relatively early date.

6. I have relaxed the rules about fraternization. Members of the British Forces are now allowed to engage in conversation with the German people in the streets and in public places; this will enable us to have contact with you and to understand your problems the more easily.

7. The coming winter will be a difficult time; there is much to mend and put right and time is short. We are faced with the probability of a shortage of food, a shortage of coal, insufficient accommodation and inadequate services of transportation and distribution. It is well that you should realize this now. I will do all I can to get the population of the British Zone through the coming winter. But you, the German people, must plan for these contingencies now; you must work to help yourselves.

8. I will continue to see that you are all kept informed by radio, and by the newspapers, of how we are progressing; I will give you German news as well as foreign news.

9. I expect the co-operation of you all in the second stage of the Allied policy

Signed Field Marshal B L Montgomery
Governor British Zone of Germany

(Footnote: extracted verbatim from 'The Memoirs of Field-Marshal The Viscount Montgomery of Alamein, KG '- 1958).

Neither this message nor the newspaper with its death camp scenes created the furore that the ones in June had. Terry waited in the Centre after Wilkes and Arthur had departed in the almost fully laden lorry. Otto fidgeted about in a silent sulk.

"What's the matter Otto?" Terry asked.

Otto signalled that they should leave the Centre and sit inside the parked sedan. It was raining heavily and the sky was dark and menacing. It was to continue with cloud, rain and high winds throughout the next ten days. The wheat fields to the west of Altewiese were to become sodden and damaged. The poor weather through Northern Germany was to reduce the harvest yield critically and city starvation became certain. Otto turned in his driving seat and addressed Terry in his poor and difficult accent.

"Please Corporal, can I take you to the big house. I have something very important to tell you?"

Terry said it was OK and Otto drove through the lashing rain to the estate; he did not speak during the short journey and appeared tense and nervy. Terry noticed with concern that on the front seat next to Otto lay a Germany-English dictionary.

He followed Otto into the big house and up to von Lutken's room.

"Please Corporal leave your tunic and gun here. If you think you need to, put a pistol in your trouser pocket, but you are in no danger here, I assure you."

He then led the way to the gunroom door of their first meeting. Inside this time Terry found four sleeping places constructed from quilts and blankets in each corner of the room. There were four people standing silently and Otto led Terry to the tall window and turned to face the four, so that the dull light illuminated the strangers' features. Otto began to explain.

"Corporal, these four displaced persons arrived at the Centre sixteen days ago. After two days Inspector Muller asked me to find them accommodation in the big house for a little while. Although I do not know the people they all come from my home region near Old Stein in German Poland. Muller knew this. We speak the same language and I have spent a lot of time talking with them. I have come to trust them and want to ask you to employ them here in the big house. You will need staff when you move here soon. Firstly I will introduce the old man.... Igor, the others call him Grand Pa, although he is not related; they picked him up along the way. He is sixty-six years old and lived in Old Stein all his life. He was the foreman in charge of maintenance at the grand church in the centre of town. It was the church where Copernicus worked hundreds of years ago. Igor is very skilled; if you give him a hammer and a screwdriver, he will fix anything. If he spoke English he would never need to learn the word 'impossible'. He is a quiet, simple man and would be comfortable in my old lodgings in the basement. Given the tools we have stored down there he would make an excellent maintenance man.

The woman is forty and her name is Olga; she and her two children here next to her, are from a village six miles south of Old Stein. Members of the SS Totenkopf Group killed her husband. She has been badly hurt by Russian soldiers. The Germans of Old Stein and that region are victims of all sides. She is an excellent cook. Her beetroot and spice soup and potato dumplings are delicious. She can make good meals from simple inexpensive ingredients. Her daughter, Lara, is seventeen and the Russians have cruelly mistreated her. She is a good house cleaner. If you tell her to polish the floor you must remember to tell her when to stop, or she will polish all night and all week. She is a very pretty girl. Well to my old eyes she is. OK, you say she is plain, but in that plainness is warmth. Her younger brother is called Stephan; he is only just fifteen. He has seen many horrors done to his mother and sister and eight months ago the Russians forced him to abuse his sister. Yes, he only now has one eye. Sixteen weeks ago he tried to blind himself, but passed out when he had pushed a bread knife into one eye. He thought that if he were blind he would no longer see what he had already seen. He is now immensely loyal and protective of his mother and sister and Grand Pa. Over the last ten days he has seen happiness and health return to the three here in the big house and as a result he has shown me great respect and loyalty. He can sleep for only two or three hours and even then it must be in daylight. He would make a fine night watchman. Yes, even with one eye, Corporal. Give him one of the hand fire bells from the front porch and he would wake the dead with his noise and bravery. These three could share a small bedroom on the top floor of the house; there would be no problem, for Stephan would be on patrol while the ladies slept. They would not eat too much and would deserve only the smallest of wages. With me as your butler and driver and these as my staff, you would have a great team. What do you think sir?"

"I agree entirely." Otto stood stunned and silent, so Terry continued, "I will now shake each of them by the hand and welcome them to our new home."

Otto spoke in Polish, through his tears, to each as Terry stepped up to them. The old man Igor cried. The mother cried. Lara boldly kissed Terry full on the lips and said in English, "Thank you". Stephan had a stern and unsmiling expression and let Terry stand for a moment with an outstretched hand. He did not move to respond even after Otto repeated the Polish words to him. Then Terry's instinct switched on and he came near to the young man and slowly placed his arms around his shoulders and drew him close. Stephan's tense strong yet bony shoulders began to shake and his hands slowly crept around Terry's waist. He silently sobbed into Terry's tunic shirt. After ten minutes they let go of each other and shook hands in a formal manner. Terry did not notice that the little boy was only three years younger than himself.

Otto now took Terry back to the next floor. The corridor that turned left at the head of the staircase led only to Otto's bedroom and von Lutken's bedroom, study and bathroom. Otto pointed out that if a strong door was placed at the entrance to this corridor and only Terry and Otto had keys to it, then with Stephan on patrol, Terry would be secure. Only the windows would give easy access to attackers. Here Otto suggested steel bars at all windows of any room leading off this corridor. Igor could do the work in four days. Terry said, "Do it". Otto nodded, but then spoke again in a sad and urgent voice.

"Corporal, I have brought you to the house to hear of a big problem we have. Last week I had these ideas for the defence of your apartments. I asked the builder, Mr Kahler, to come to the house and quote a price for the work. He refused to come. He said the estate is now a communist commune and he hates Bolsheviks. He said he hated the co-operative, but you, Corporal, he hated most. I think it would be wise to move here to the big house now, today. Kahler and his Nazi friends are dangerous men."

"Thank you for telling me this Otto," said Terry. "I will come soon. When I do I will need to bring a housekeeper that I can trust. Paula or Fredda, who do you suggest?"

"Not Paula."

On the drive back to the town, Terry had asked Otto to stop while he had a pee. He was happy to add to the wetness of the hedge grove, but was shocked to see blood in his urine. He had not noticed this before, but thought that the dark lavatories at the Centre gave little chance of observation or good aim. He slept poorly that night and at midnight decided he would visit the ever awake Doctor Dressler at his home. Dressed and armed Terry walked around the edge of the square in the cloud-covered darkness of the moonless night. He knocked at the Doctor's door, but received no reply. It was then that he saw a light through the ill-fitting curtains of the first floor of Meyer's Guesthouse. There were two windows next to each other showing light.

Terry quietly stepped into the narrow alley that ran between the side of the Doctor's house and the pharmacy and watched the doors to the bar. After five minutes Doctor Dressler emerged from the door, a little unsteadily, and with him was Mr Kahler. They said goodnight to Mr and Mrs Meyer who were standing inside the bar. The Doctor crossed the street and let himself into his house and Kahler walked off cautiously towards the riverside road. Terry waited until the guest house lights had all been extinguished and then knocked on the Doctor's door. This time it was answered almost immediately.

"Oh, Corporal you are out late, you quite startled me. Come in, what is the trouble?"

"Good evening Doctor Dressler. I am peeing blood."

"Yes, a lot of people in the town are doing the same. It's a mild kidney infection. I have tried to identify the cause of the outbreak and have arrived at two conclusions. A parasite has bred in the water tower tank during its period of inactivity and has yet to be flushed from the system. Or, secondly, someone has maliciously added a poison to the water supply. I would suggest one remedy for both alternatives; have the young workers' teams attend the water tower twenty-four hours each day for two weeks. They should ensure constant pumping and we could open some taps in town to flush the water pipes thoroughly. For you personally, I would recommend you drink lots of clean water from the hand pump in the kitchen at the Centre. Your infection will disappear in two or three days. Would you like something stronger to drink now?"

"No thank you Doctor, but while I am here, have you seen anything suspicious happening in connection with von Lutken's old friends?" Terry tried to put the question as casually as he could.

"Yes," said the Doctor happily, "they invited me and I have joined their little party. There was a meeting tonight, as there is every Tuesday night, at Meyer' place over the road. He has an upstairs private room set up as a meeting place. They start at nine at night and finished a few minutes ago. You must have seen me leave, of course. They are calling themselves the National League, but they are devout National Socialists. During the meeting they have a small photograph of Hitler on the table; they all worship him. They are not as militant or as military as the SS Brotherhood, who pray to their God, Himmler, but they are all as crazy as each other.

I joined them to obtain details of the organisation and threat they may pose to you. None of the National League adherents like you.

The chairperson is Mrs Meyer. Yes, she is the most active and aggressive, which is no accident. She was known to taunt the slave labour used at the fertiliser plant. She is a complete Nazi; probably eats Mein Kampf for breakfast. She is advocating your early removal. She is strongly backed by Mr Kahler and to a lesser degree by all the other members that I know of. Who are they? Wait will you, I am coming to that. Mr Meyer, obviously, then there is Fromming, but he did not attend tonight. Mr Hasch and his son. They believe Constable Neelmeyer may join soon, but he is much too close to Kurt Muller to do that. They have made contact with other underground Nazi groups and could obtain arms quite easily, if they haven't already."

"You say the next meeting is in seven days time. Would you help to ensure that meeting takes place and is fully attended. We can get together here after and you can tell me what was said. Why do they want to remove me from the scene, I will certainly be replaced by another British soldier?" Terry asked.

"Corporal you killed their previous local leader, von Lutken; revenge is a strong motive I would suggest. But, they also feel that your co-operative farm is a communist plot, particularly now your countrymen have chosen a Socialist government in preference to Churchill. I also suspect that they are aware of your closeness to the SS members of our Altewiese society and they have a dislike of them."

Terry could understand the motive of revenge, but had no idea what the Doctor's other speculations meant. He knew he must move quickly and by next Tuesday he could have a smiling Hardaker in Altewiese and they could both attend a Nazi gathering. In the event he found a much sweeter alternative to Hardaker.

A few minutes before ten o'clock the next morning the noise of a speeding motorcycle disturbed the damp morning. The rider was a policeman from Bachwald and Ingrid and Paula both met him as he entered the Centre. He pointed to Terry with some conviction and urgency. Ingrid said that the policeman had a message for him but he did not speak English and the message in German made no sense. Paula ordered the Bachwald constable to sit at the interview table and repeat slowly to her the words of the verbal message. He was becoming excited and agitated, so Terry passed to him his own mug of milky tea. It was then that Paula spoke.

"This man carries a message from the sergeant. He may have forgotten the exact words of the message, but insists that he his repeating the exact translation of the sergeant words. The translator in Bachwald must have been drunk, or is a complete moron. He is using poor German, impolite and bad words and I will give you the words in English, but you must excuse me if they sound offensive." Paula coughed and then continued.

"The courier's message for you is that a major masturbator will visit you today for a sexual intercourse inspection and you must keep the womb happy. A most unfortunate selection of words."

Terry smiled.

"We should now all panic. My commanding officer is about to make a surprise visit to Altewiese. Get everyone busy, tidy the tables, and straighten the King's photograph. Find my tunic, put the kettle on."

Major Connolly quickly walked through the bedroom wards of the Centre and noted that there were a number of empty beds. He talked to Paula and asked general questions concerning the health of refugees at the time of their arrival in Altewiese. He was particularly interested in the prevalence of VD among the female DPs. He made his way to the interview table and sat in Terry's green leather chair. He signalled to Terry to sit opposite to him.

"Corporal Hall I have been delighted with the inspection; long overdue, I'm afraid, but no harm done as I have found that everything here is in spiffing order. Before I leave, which will be almost immediately, I would like to see one of your youth work teams. Wilkes told me about them and I wrote a report to HQ on the idea. I received a highly complementary reply and the Field Marshal has given his support to the Zone-wide implementation of the project. I'm afraid I neglected to mention your name in my initial report, but rest assured that my gratitude would count for much, as you will see. The main reason for my visit is a tiny bit confidential and tricky." The Major extracted a manila file from a neat leather briefcase.

"This is your file, expanded somewhat since our first meeting, what? Full of mainly good things, I'm pleased to say. I have received some good personal news; I am to be demobilised on 15th January next year. Thank you, yes good news indeed. I am to remain in my present post until that date and will retire with the rank of Lieutenant Colonel. Thank you again, Corporal. I plan to take my accrued leave prior to demob so will be quitting Germany, a few days after Christmas. A civilian from England will almost certainly, replace me. Now that is where your file has proved very interesting. Three or four months ago some of the things you were doing here were, shall we say, not politically correct. I am referring to the fixing of a single wage level for all grades of Germans employed and that damned co-operative farm. I wasn't best pleased I can tell you; it all smelled unsavoury and a touch Socialist. But, now we have a change of Government, it seems likely that the civilian who comes to replace me will be left wing and impressed by your thinking. Your record sheet will appear golden. I am at liberty to tell you that Sergeant Wilkes has received his demob number and could be back home before Christmas. If he saves his leave time he could be back in Nottingham by 10th December. No replacement will be assigned to this unit.

Now here comes the tricky question for you; I would be most happy to send a report to HQ suggesting your promotion to sergeant with a view to you replacing Wilkes in Bachwald on the 10th of December. I can see that makes you smile, but please, before you answer, I must inform you of one or two significant facts. Corporals Stein and Hardaker have also received their demob numbers and will be out of uniform by the end of the year. Army personnel will not replace them. Sometime next year we will be allocated some British police constables and low rank civil servants, unless we can show that we have found a suitable German replacement. You are signed on to 1st February 1947, am I correct? I would guess you would be in Bachwald or Luneburg until then by which time all civilian posts will have been filled by British or German civilians. You would have to run the show in this sector with the unit strength of three corporals and as many locals as you can vet and safely appoint and you will have a civilian CO. Not an easy task, what? All early reports indicate that the harvest this year will be poor; too much and too little rain at the wrong times, apparently. There will be some starvation and unrest among the population. Remember, if I recommend you for promotion and command of the Bachwald sector, you will get it. Our current CO never argues with anything I put forward, he is too busy playing golf. Corporal Hall what would you like me to do?"

"Promotion to sergeant and to take over from Sergeant Wilkes would be a honour, sir," Terry said, with no hesitation.

"Excellent, excellent. If you had said no I would have had to order you to do it and I so much prefer consensus. Now I would like to discuss with you some delicate, confidential matters. Before Sergeant Wilkes departs I want him to shut down any involvement he and his unit may have in local commerce. When you takeover and I leave, I want this area to be running on strictly military lines. You do understand what I am saying Corporal, don't you? Oh, jolly good show. You are due some leave I notice. May I suggest that you take the week you are owed for this year, plus a week from next year, and that you take the two weeks in November? You will be back before Wilkes departs and be in a position to make a good unbroken run for your new CO. Where would you choose to take your leave?

Staffordshire - an excellent idea; to be with your parents for a couple of weeks, commendable.

"Next, and here I must admit to being a touch less than my normal efficient self. One of the letters in your file I had not read - very remiss of me, dear boy. It was from a Captain Matthews, on behalf of a Major Thompson, both of the 7th Armoured. Apparently they were escorting a number of Russian VIPs to Frankfurt and popped in on you unannounced, just like me now in fact. They wrote that you were doing a fine job and handled the Russians with confidence and aplomb. The Russians were very impressed. Jolly good show, corporal, jolly good. Well, last week Field Marshal Montgomery received a letter from the Russian General you met, enclosing an invitation for you to pay a visit to his Headquarters in the Russian Zone. Monty is away ill or that letter would have resulted in an extreme response. Depending on Monty's mood, you would have been court marshalled or given a medal. By chance Monty's number one, or two, or three, some Major General, got hold of the letter and had the imagination to pass it to the intelligence boys. As a result of their enthusiasm, the Major General, in the guise of Field Marshal Montgomery, has accepted the invitation and you are to spend a couple of days with the Russians. No, I am afraid there is no choice and it is not my idea of having a good time either. I would think that with a Russian General's invitation and Monty's consent, you would be the safest soldier in Europe for those two days. But, it is strictly business; you will be on duty at all times. Do you like vodka? No, nor do I, I prefer Cognac, but don't ask for that over there; you'd be thought of as a degenerate. The day before you travel, one or two intelligence chappies will give you a briefing on what to look for - tank types, regiment names, positions of radar masts, that sort of thing. For two days immediately after your return our intelligence boys will grill you on what you heard and saw and probably even what you smelt. You will be amazed at what you saw and cannot remember seeing, but the intelligence interrogators will dig it all out of you."

The Major and Terry visited the water tower where a team of young men and women were sawing wood and feeding a boiler fire. They all looked fit and happy and unthreatening and the Major was again delighted. As the Major drove away from Altewiese, Terry wondered if the 'womb was happy'.

In the Centre Terry was met by Ingrid and Kurt, they both seemed anxious and asked to talk to him privately. They asked what the

Major had wanted. Terry was about to tell them of his forthcoming visit to the Russian Zone, but stopped.

"Mind your own business," he said sharply.

"No, sorry corporal," stammered Ingrid, "we were worried about the coincidence of his arrival and that of a factory engineer and a factory chemist. Kurt was going to introduce them to you as the British officer drove into the square. We thought he was searching for them, well not searching, but knew of their arrival and objected. The two men are very good at their jobs and could be put to work in a much bigger factory and we would lose their help at the fertiliser factory."

"Bring them here now and fetch Paula also," Terry commanded.

On their arrival he dismissed Ingrid and Kurt and asked Paula to assist him with the interview of the two men. They were both in their mid-thirties, were tall and fit, and wore dark green regular army coats over white shirts and black trousers. Neither admitted to being in the SS or being members of the Nazi party, but neither did they have any papers or documents. They said that prior to 1942 they had both worked for I G Fabens in various factories around Germany. They claimed to have given up their army uniforms in April and avoided being taken prisoner by first the Russians and then the Americans. A friend of a friend had heard that Kurt Muller was looking for the skills they both had and they had walked to Altewiese to offer their services. Terry felt suspicious and uneasy about their story, but could not think what he could do about it. He confided in Paula.

"We will let Kurt put these two men to work at the fertiliser factory but I am worried that they are not what they seem. Ask one of them to prepare a list of chemicals and powders and things that he needs to mix to create a good fertilizer. Have him write the list this afternoon. There are no books on the subject in town I hope and he will have to know the correct chemical names. Tomorrow I will give the list to the sergeant and he will have it checked. If the items are actually used in the production of fertiliser then the sergeant can try to find them. If the items are not correct, we may need to speak again to these two. I may ask you to do more translating in the future, particularly when it involves Kurt Muller. Thank you, Paula."

Later that day Kurt and Paula came to Terry and Paula handed him a short list of chemical names, each with a weight in kilos.

"This is the shopping list for the factory. As soon as your sergeant can find all of the ingredients they can begin production. Kurt also has some other news. He says that a Swiss-German Bank is planning to open branches in various parts of Germany. They have not yet received permission to open a head office in Frankfurt, but that is their aim. If you agree they will send a senior director here to Altewiese and begin business in September or October. The director will move to Frankfurt as soon as the head office there is open. He will leave a working branch here, of course. It will be very useful to have a senior man here even for a short time because he will have access to large amounts of Swiss and American money. We may be able to persuade him to invest in the fertiliser factory and expansion of the sawmill. Kurt seems very excited about the idea and believes it can only be good for Altewiese and the district. On a private matter he wishes to assure you of his loyalty to you and the town. His attachment to Ingrid should not be seen as a threat to you. She will translate accurately and in confidence and report nothing to Kurt. Personally Corporal I would be a little wary. I am happy to work for you on any matters that you would prefer this man not to know about. I am busy here but can find time for you. You are very important to me, you know that don't you?"

"Yes," said Terry, "ask Kurt what he knows of the re-emergence of the local Nazi party."

"He says that a very small group of von Lutken's old allies are trying to form a new political party, which is the National Socialists in another name. They appear to have very little support from the general population, most of whom are sick of politics. The group may fade away through boredom or try some direct action to attract attention to themselves. Kurt is keeping a watch on them for you. Of more concern to him is the growing popularity of the trade unions. An association based in Hamburg has contacted the sawmill workers. The trade unions could be a front for the infiltration of Communists into our society. He wants to know what is your view?"

"Tell Inspector Muller," said Terry sternly, "that free trade unions are not a threat to society. The Government of Occupation wishes to encourage free trade unions. If the membership of a trade union all wish to be communist, that is their choice; if they wish to be liberals, that also is OK. Only if they want to be Nazis or fascist will the trade union be banned. Remind the Inspector that our Government is now Labour, that is Socialist and supporters of trades unions so he must adjust his views accordingly."

Having translated Terry's words and seen Kurt leave somewhat crestfallen, Paula sat with Terry.

"It will take time to change all of the hearts of the German people. Hitler is dead, thank goodness, but we have had fifteen years of his oratory and propaganda. Men like Kurt hate Hitler for what he has done to Germany, but he still fears the Russians and their evil regime. Kurt uses his old police contacts to help the people of Altewiese recover from the defeat and regain pride. He supports you because he sees you help the Germans of Altewiese. You need more Kurts and less Frommings; no we Germans need more Kurts and less Frommings. His affair with Ingrid is of no consequence; he is no threat to you."

Wilkes and Arthur arrived at exactly eleven the next day. They had only one DP with them and Wilkes was eager to learn of the Major's visit. Terry related all that had been said and Wilkes confirmed that he had had a similar conversation. Terry told him of the arrival of a production manager and chemist at the fertiliser factory; he did not express his concerns about them but asked the sergeant if the shopping list of chemicals were available and suitable for a fertiliser factory.

"Yes, I'll have them checked. If this little cocktail turned out to be a good bomb mix we might look a little silly. See the thin young man Arthur put over there; see the reaction of some of your staff to him; well he was born and bred in this little town and by now some of the locals will have recognised him even though he may have changed a lot. Why did we only bring one person with us? Actually we left Bachwald with two; one says he wanted off in Brick and this one here. They're both German but other Germans fear or hate them - they are Jewish. My guess is they will stick around for a few days then wander off to somewhere else in the hopes of finding other Jews. He was telling me what happened to him, but I had to stop him 'cos it was horrible. You know there were once two hundred Jews in Altewiese; well I think he's all that's left of them. Your local population will show some strange emotions about him - shame, fear, dislike, but never pity I bet. Keep an eye on him, he may need protection. If he starts to tell you his story, tell him you have a bloody headache; you won't like it and definitely won't believe it.

Now, soon to be Sergeant Sod Hall, let's go and see what nice things we have on the lorry for you. Then Arthur and I will do the rounds of the local shops and producers and get some trading done.

When Wilkes and Arthur had driven away, Terry looked for Paula but could not find her so asked Ingrid to have the young man join them at the table. Sandwiches and tea were laid out and the man sat quietly with his brown cap clasped tightly on his lap.

"Do you want some tea with milk? Do you speak English?" Terry asked. He smiled and nodded for the tea, and spoke via Ingrid.

"I speak only a few words of English but my friend in Brick speaks English well. If I could have your permission to stay here tonight, I will walk to Brick tomorrow and join him. I am here to ask if any of my family have survived and returned to Altewiese. My name is Jacob Rosenthal; I was born here twenty years ago. My family were tailors; we owned the shop next to the synagogue, which is now a cinema. My uncle managed the bank and another one was a foreman at the factory. Are there any Jewish people living here now? No, I thought that might be the case. When I depart tomorrow I would like to leave my name and some brief details and should any of my family ever appear you can tell them of my existence."

Terry stared at the sad man who spoke quietly and modestly. His gaunt face was shallow and very white and his short-cropped hair was grey at the sides of his head. He wore a threadbare blue suit which was many sizes too big for his bent bony frame. He looked very like most of the DPs that had arrived over the last months; the only difference was to be found on his arm. He was watching Ingrid make notes and took from his pocket a folded piece of paper and gave it to her to copy from. He then rolled up his right sleeve and showed her the inside of his forearm. There were eight numbers tattooed there and he read them to her as she wrote. Four of the town's women edged their way into the Centre's open doors and pointed at Jacob and placed their hands to their mouths in fright, or shock. They left muttering and one was crying. He looked around the room and began to smile.

"Am I to sleep here tonight at the Alte Poste Hotel? Yes, then that is ironic for my overseers lived here while I worked at the factory. But, that was a lifetime ago when I was young and alive. In 1937 all of the Jews of Altewiese were taken to Bergen-Belsen labour camp. The people of the town jeered and spat at us as we walked up the road. At the camp all of the children under twelve were taken away; my young sister was one of them; we never saw them again. I was just twelve so was put with all the men. Each day we had to work in one of the factories and we received only a little food. I was not then too frightened for I was with my father and elder brother and we soon found our uncles in another hut. My grandfather had disappeared along with the other old men. Our main aim was to find my mother and older sister. We knew they were in the women's barracks and each day we strained our eyes to see them through the wire fence, but never did. Much later we learned that my sister had been put to work in the camp brothel and was transferred to another camp when she became ill; she was sixteen when we left Altewiese.

After ten months my uncle who had worked at the fertiliser factory was asked to select twenty prisoners to join him and return to Altewiese and the factory. He chose my father and brother and I, of course. He asked for his wife and my mother to be found but they never joined us here. I was very young and small and the factory owner said I was of no use to him and I was sent back to the camp. For the first time in my life I was alone among hundreds of people. I soon learned the rules of how to exist in a labour camp: never make eye contact with anyone, guard or prisoner; never speak to anyone you did not trust totally, and you could trust only your closest family; eat what food you were given quickly and steal extra food at every opportunity. Early every morning and evening we would stand in the big court yard, to be counted, whether it was snowing or raining or sunny. It was then that we saw the punishment for breaking the labour camp rules. I saw people shot for attempting to escape; I saw people kicked to death for speaking to an officer; I saw naked people whipped until they had no skin left on their body in order to give pleasure to one of the insane guards. I thought the place was a nightmare, but I was so very wrong.

After two years I was transferred to the fertiliser factory in Altewiese again. I thought it was at the request of my uncle, but when I arrived here I learned that he and my father had been sent to another camp, but no one knew where. My oldest brother was dead. One night some months before he had got out of the warehouse barracks and tried to make contact with an old school friend. The school friend gave him food, but when that boy's parents discovered that my brother was from the factory labour team they called the police. Those people were the Meyer's who ran the bar and guesthouse, they had plenty of food but would not help my brother. An officer shot my brother the next morning. For twelve hours each day we worked in the factory carrying bags of fertiliser or chemicals or cleaning floors or pulling great logs from the woods. There were many guards as this was a very comfortable post for them. We slept and ate in the warehouse. In there were open latrines. In winter the warehouse was cold, we had no bedding or blankets; in summer the smell from the latrine was unbearable. There were fifty prisoners and every day at least one was severely punished. Beatings and whippings were common and the victims always died from the wounds. From the factory I could see the school that I had attended so recently and on the road I saw people who had bought clothes from my father's shop; they were happy and fat and none of them would recognise me.

Six months after I arrived at the factory here, I was transferred to another factory near Frankfurt. The work and conditions were equally as hard, but the guards were much worse. There were SS officers but many of the ordinary guards were Polish or Russian SS. The male guards were vicious and tormentors, but the female guards were evil and beasts. I saw dreadful things then. During my first week there I was used sexually by two of the male guards, I think they were Ukrainian. I was so ashamed that I hid from the other prisoners and would not talk to any of them. One day I saw an old man at a work bench stumble through starvation; a woman guard rushed at him and hit him with her stick. He was so terrified that he shit himself; she forced him to undress and to lick his clothes clean. That night he died. He was my father. He had never recognised me in my short time there and I was too ashamed to greet him. In a way I am pleased he died not knowing that his son had seen how he had died.

About this time last year we had learned that the British and Americans were in France and moving towards us. The Russians were in the Ukraine. My fellow slaves stopped praying for a British bomb to destroy our factory and our barracks and our lives. By then we knew the difference between a labour camp and a death camp; in one you worked until you were dead and in the other you were dead. In the Fabens factory we thought we might be able to survive until the Allies arrived. The killings and beatings continued, but there was hope again. We could see and sense that the civilian factory managers and directors were getting anxious and worried. They did not want our slave labour anymore; they feared reprisals after the war was lost and many of them knew it was lost even then. Our treatment and food worsened. When a prisoner died in his bunk at night, the other prisoners in the bunk or close by would rush to get a piece of his clothing for themselves. Sometimes, by a miracle, the naked body would come to life in the morning and sheepishly the grave robbers would give him back his clothes. Not me, I stole to live; I had become evil and callous, but I was still alive.

One morning in August last year, all of the slave labour in our factory were loaded into railway cattle trucks and told that we were going to be resettled in Poland, in a town called Auschwitz. The old Rabbi among us told the women that we were going to a new and better factory to work, but in truth everyone knew we were being taken to a death camp. Some tried to hide in the Fabens factory, but dogs found them and savaged them to death. There was great sadness among those on the train; the disappointment was sickening for we heard that the Americans were less than one hundred miles from our deliverance. We travelled in the cattle trucks for one day and one night and it was noted that the train was always heading south, not east. We spent one night stationary in a siding near Munich.

The next morning we were unloaded and counted and marched to a barracks in a large camp. At roll call that evening an angry SS officer told us we were in Dachau and that the railway company had made a mistake, we should have been taken to Auschwitz. She was sorry for the inconvenience this had caused. We would stay in the barracks, except for roll calls each day, until transport could be arranged to take us to our correct destination. We would be well fed and she was sorry for the mistake. We Germans are characterised by foreigners for our organisational genius so when we, condemned slaves, arrived at the wrong death camp, they said sorry. They had planned to kill us in Poland and only in Poland would we therefore be killed. It was insane Germanic logic. While in Dachau I managed to steal a new striped uniform and better shoes. I wore a badge indicating that I was a German Jew which in my experience provoked the Russian and Polish guards but got a little sympathy from the German officers. The food and rest did us all good.

After twelve days we were again loaded into cattle trucks and we began a nightmare journey to hell. We received no food or water or lavatory facilities and when we arrived at Auschwitz, almost half of the people in my cattle truck were dead. The survivors were sitting on the stinking bodies. Some of us had started to drink blood and some had eaten parts of the dead. Auschwitz was the nearest thing to hell you will ever find on earth. Strangely there were fewer beatings; many of the guards seemed less cruel. If you were alive the food was sufficient. If you were unlucky enough to be alive you worked for the killing machine. It was a death factory - a mass production line of death. It was as though the plague was not little bugs, but people killing other people, for no reason. I was young, relatively fit and German speaking, although by then I had learned some Russian, Polish and French. The SS officer at the station platform selected me for work. Everyone else on that train was dead, or would be dead in six hours. They had loaded more than one thousand adults in Dachau. The numbers were unreal and no one will ever comprehend them. Deaths per day were counted in thousands; tens and hundreds did not matter. In years to come no one will believe what happened in Auschwitz, but I saw it. That is why I am telling everyone I meet of the factory of death, so they can tell others and maybe it will be remembered. The beatings and whippings that I had seen before were barbaric but carried out by individual sadists; here everyone alive helped to kill five or six thousand human beings every single day.

The vast majority of the guards tried not to hurt individuals, they just led them from the station to the shower blocks. Everyone selected to die would be stripped naked - men, women and children; and hundreds at a time would be herded into the shower rooms and gassed. That was the start of the production line. My first job was clearing the showers after the gas had blown away. The double doors would open and the last of the gas would escape. Towards the end, before the Russians arrived, there was a panic to kill everyone quickly and many labourers were forced into the showers before the gas had cleared - they died too. Our job was to load the warm bodies onto wooden trolleys and wheel them to the crematorium. When the shower doors opened there were piles of naked bodies covered in shit and vomit, some still twitching, some with eyes bleeding, dead mothers holding their hand over their dead babies mouths. The smell was incredible, but the site was unbelievable. At the crematorium labourers examined the mouths of the dead and extracted any gold teeth; we were told that this gold was sent to Himmler's bank in Switzerland. At the station other workers sorted the clothes and belongings of the soon to die and these were sent to Germany for recycling; the gold rings and jewellery were for Himmler's bank too.

In my last two months at Auschwitz I worked in the crematorium. A colleague and I threw the dead bodies into one of the ovens that burned all day, all week, all the years. The heat was intense and what little fat was in the bodies helped to burn them quickly. When there was a strong wind, the chimneys were able to suck up the fumes and smoke of one body every minute. The officers found these numbers important in judging the efficiency of their factory. On one of my shifts another German Jew partnered me and although it was forbidden, we were able to talk as we threw the lifeless humans into the fire. By a coincidence he came from Brick although I had not known him then. We became inseparable friends and helped each other survive the insanity and murder of the camp. The ash from the ovens was loaded into trucks and sent to farms for use as fertiliser. That is how we believed we would leave Auschwitz. We knew that after working for seven or eight months the labourers were sent to be gassed or were shot at the ovens and their bodies burned with the others. My friend, who had adopted the name of Peter Brucke, and I managed to avoid being selected for death.

In the last week of the camp's production we could hear the shelling from Russian guns and we were desperate to survive. The SS officers began to panic. They refused new supplies of victims and tried to kill all the witnesses, including the non-German guards. They ordered us to dismantle the ovens and barracks. Peter and I hid in the still warm rubble of one of the oven houses. We heard the shooting and shouting as the officers tried to clean the camp of evidence. When the Russians arrived we climbed from our hiding place and pretended to be French Jews. Being German was not sensible at that time. The Russian soldiers fed us and sent us to a hospital where we recovered. Peter and I have travelled together and survived together. We have returned to our family homes to search for our relatives. We both know that it would be a miracle to find anyone alive. The numbers that were murdered were so great that only a handful of Jews could have survived. Do you know that is what hurts me most; that we survived. I should be dead and burned and my ashes be on some Polish field. It is wrong that I am alive; I have cheated and stolen from the dead; I am as bad as the sadistic guards. I have no right to be alive when so many good innocent people perished. No I could not kill myself, but I would be happy for some German Nazi to shoot me now. Until that time I will tell of what I have seen and hope people will remember and believe. Peter has a dream that we will both travel to Palestine and join the Jewish community there. If he finds a way of fulfilling his dream I will accompany him, but it is only a dream I think."

Ingrid had managed to translate Jacob's words calmly and without hesitation, but as he at last fell silent she burst into floods of tears. Jacob took her hand and held it for a few moments. When she had recovered her composure, Terry asked her to continue.

"Jacob do you hate your fellow Germans for what they have done to you and your family?" he asked.

"Hate? Yes possibly, but I still feel numb, asleep, as though in a dream world. When I wake I will undoubtedly be insane, so it is best that I just follow Peter."

Terry had been staring at the door, but faced Jacob.

"Tomorrow I will drive you to Brick and you can introduce me to Peter," he said. "I might have some ideas for you to think about. You will introduce me to him, won't you?" Jacob nodded. "Please use the facilities here; there is a doctor and food and a change of clothes if you wish. Ingrid will help you."

With that said, Terry rose from his chair and with his Tommy gun over his arm he walked slowly and without knowing why found that he had arrived at the gates of the factory warehouse. He stood there for some time, staring through the wire fence at the double doors behind which could be anything, but was nothing. As he walked back to the square he looked through the window of Meyer's bar and saw the fat Mrs Meyer laughing with a customer who was the happy Mr Hasch, the ex-mayor of quiet sweet Altewiese. He returned to the Centre and his office bedroom where he prepared in detail for his visit to Brick. He re-read an article in the Daily Express which explained that refugee Jews were fleeing Europe and invading Greece and Cyprus in their effort to reach Palestine. Terry placed travel documents in a leather briefcase and one of von Lutken's pistols with its silencer attachment; he added paper money, cigarettes and a box of matches.

Otto drove the sedan and its two passengers to Brick at eleven o'clock the next day. Terry explained to a recently awoken Don that he had come to speak to the Jew, Peter Brucke. Don sleepily told him where he had billeted Peter and agreed that the next party day would be on Sunday of the following weekend. He offered Terry the use of the offices and young girls that were already there. Peter, having seen the arrival of the black sedan, was talking to Jacob as Terry left Don's offices. Otto remained in the car as Terry was introduced. Terry, Peter and Jacob then walked slowly to the main road and headed north. While walking no other person came near them. The few who were about avoided the three men. Peter did speak reasonably good English and told Terry some of his story. It followed a similar tragic, cruel and unbelievable path as that of Jacob's history yesterday. As Peter finished they had reached a gate to a large empty field of grass and Terry stopped them there.

"Peter can either of you drive a lorry?" Peter was surprised at the question and spoke to Jacob.

"I can drive a tractor, which must be pretty similar, but why do you ask?"

Terry ignored the question.

"Peter your hatred of your fellow Germans is much stronger than Jacob's, as is your desire to travel to a Jewish homeland in Palestine. I have a proposition for you. I have a difficult and nasty job for you both, but I will offer a fine reward for doing it. I want you to load six bodies on a truck, take it to a field like this one and burn the six bodies. Your qualifications for loading and burning dead bodies are impeccable. These bodies will be those of six fanatical Nazi Germans. These Nazis are a threat to me and I must remove them from Altewiese. If you wish you may shoot them but my intention is that I will use this silenced pistol. You carry the bodies from the trial and execution room to a lorry I will provide. There will be petrol in a can and wooden planks as kindling; these matches will light your last oven. When the ashes have been scattered over the field, you can use the truck to drive to Hamburg. Leave it at the station and hand the keys to any British soldier. This is a blank travel authorisation document which I can sign and endorse with your and Jacob's names. It will show that you can travel from Hamburg to Bari in Italy. This travel warrant will allow you both to use free rail travel from Hamburg to Bari by any route you wish. In Bari you must buy a steamship passage to Cyprus. I will give you two hundred German marks in notes, but these one hundred cigarettes will be more useful. From Cyprus you will have to find your own method of reaching your Promised Land.

If you agree to do this work for me we will meet in secret at the gates to the fertiliser factory warehouse in Altewiese at nineteen hundred hours on Tuesday. Jacob is aware of exactly where that is. If you do not wish to help me dispose of six bad Nazis then I only ask you to forget this conversation. Please, now explain to Jacob what I have said and as we walk back to the car you can consider your reply."

They walked slowly into Brick while Peter spoke quietly to Jacob in German. Finally Jacob nodded his head, but his face was drawn and sad. Peter smiled.

"Your offer of employment is gratefully accepted. Our involvement, like yours, will be forgotten on completion of the task. Neither of us know if we are full of revenge but the offer of travel assistance cannot be refused. Jacob will stay with me here until Tuesday. We will meet again at the warehouse although I feel that Jacob would have preferred somewhere else. Until nineteen hundred hours on Tuesday, we say goodbye."

Wilkes arrived on Thursday with the news of the Japanese surrender on the 14th, which had followed the dropping of two enormously powerful bombs. They celebrated with many whiskies. Wilkes was convinced now of his December return to Nottingham.

On the following Monday morning Terry issued a series of bewildering orders through Paula. She was confused but he declined to explain his reasoning. Hans Reck was told to have a lorry fully fuelled and loaded and parked at the gates of the fertiliser factory at eighteen-thirty the next day. Its load to be one five-gallon can of petrol and twenty wooden planks. Otto was told to be available at the Centre from six o'clock on the Wednesday morning with the sedan. Fredda was to immediately transfer her belongings to the big house and prepare to manage the staff there. Inspector Muller and Constable Engelbart were to travel to Bachwald on Tuesday afternoon with Sergeant Wilkes and to attend a police conference the next day. They would return on Thursday with the Sergeant. Neelmeyer was to be in charge of police matters until Kurt's return. Mr Kahler the builder was ordered to attend a meeting on Wednesday morning at the fertiliser factory. The new production manager and Terry would like to discuss renovation work to the offices and factory boiler house which would be completed without charge, as agreed last month. Doctor Dressler was to provide Terry with a private consultation early on the Tuesday morning, when he may be required to lance a boil. Ulrich Tiedemann was to hold a town planning conference on Friday which Terry would attend. He should request the participation of Pfarrer Lehmann, Mr Hasch, Kurt Muller, Doctor

Dressler and Mr Wessel the previous finance officer for the town. Part of the meeting would be to discuss the re-establishment of the Gloria Cinema as a synagogue.

For the Saturday night Terry wished to book two double rooms at Meyer's guesthouse for himself and Corporal Don from Brick. Dinner and breakfast for four persons would also be required. Meyer was not to charge for this service. Terry may wish to stay at the guesthouse on the Sunday night also, but the other guests would have by then departed. On the Saturday night at Meyer's bar Terry may want to arrange some exotic entertainment. He would like to discuss this with the sisters Hoffmann at nine o'clock on Wednesday at the interview table.

During Terry's meeting with Wilkes on that Tuesday he made a request.

"I want Muller and Engelbart out of town tonight and would like you, sir, to take them back to Bachwald with you. I've told them there will be a police conference on Wednesday, but I don't much care what you do with them as long as they aren't here tonight."

"OK, no problem," replied Wilkes. "You planning something big are you? I thought you were a bit edgy this morning. You sure you shouldn't have Hardaker here with you? Bit late now, but it could be arranged. No, well I did offer. The two Jews disappeared from Brick last night, Don tells me and they are not here I notice. Must have buggered off to the Promised Land. Don says he's coming down to stay with you at the big house in a couple of weeks. Make sure you have a barrow full of johnnies. I might just donate a fine bottle of Champagne to your party; I picked it up in Luneburg last week after a Victory in Japan party but I reckon you pair of wild fuckers will have more need of it than I will. Last time I was in Hamburg, I bought back some fresh fish. This time I'll see if I can find some oysters. Don won't need them, but you will; I've met the lady he has lined up for you. Christ what a looker and tits to die for. Come to think of it I just might have a meeting of our over friendly police forces. It will give me a chance to check out Mr Muller, the Berlin policeman. I'll send him back on one of Reck's lorries on Wednesday afternoon. I might ask our intelligence boys what they know of Muller; more than likely that isn't his real name though. Do you know I haven't had to shit more than once every day since I received my number; funny that isn't it?"

Paula served Terry his evening meal at six o'clock that night as Fredda had moved to the big house. He ate heartily and he chatted casually with Paula until six forty-five, at which time he lifted a leather briefcase from under the table and swung his Tommy gun over his shoulder and announced that he had a business meeting and would return in two hours. He left by the rear door and walked smartly passed the busy school and silent shuttered church to the factory warehouse. A brightly painted ARSE truck sat purring by the gate; at the wheel sat Peter smiling and in the passenger seat was the still sullen Jacob. There was no one else around. Terry climbed into the cab and squeezed onto the passenger seat with Jacob.

"I am sure I can drive this thing," said Peter excitedly. "I have started the engine and driven backwards and forwards a couple of times. The load is as you promised, except for the Nazis."

"Those we must go and collect from the court room," said Terry. "I forgot to mention that you will be required to act as doorkeepers. Do either of you know how to use a Tommy gun?"

"We can both learn very quickly."

"You should not need to pull the trigger but point it and wave it about. I also have a second pistol that one of you can brandish. For the sake of security I would prefer to use my silenced pistol. In the briefcase here are the papers I promised and the money and cigarettes. You can keep the briefcase. Please check that its contents are in order."

Terry handed the case to Peter and offered them both a cigarette. Having lit them he presented the box of matches to Jacob with some formality. The truck was facing the town and the two Jewish men smoked in silence and stared at the lowering sun. At ten minutes to eight the truck lurched forwards and Jacob took one last glance at the warehouse of his pained memory. Terry had Peter drive passed the river view windows of Meyer's guesthouse and pull over to the left of the river road and park. Led by Terry they walked up a delivery access lane to the rear of the silent bar and hotel. Terry knocked quietly and listened. He heard voices and shoes on a bare wooden floor. A key turned in the lock and a bolt was pulled. Terry kicked the door hard and it hit Mr Meyer in the chest and head causing him to shout in pain. Terry stepped passed him and faced a shocked Mrs Meyer staring at him. Terry shouted to the Tommy gun toting Peter.

"Tell them to take us to the meeting room upstairs. Tell them I will kill them if they try to resist. Tell Jacob to lock and bolt this door and follow us."

Peter spoke in a hard and commanding German and when Mrs Meyer began to object he pushed the barrel of the Tommy gun, with force, into her large stomach. For a moment she was winded but soon recovered to follow her shaking husband up the staircase to the next floor and into a small meeting room. The room was laid out with one heavy carved wooden chair facing three rows of four dining chairs. On the seat of the heavy chair lay a framed photograph of

Adolf Hitler. It was a signed copy but it was different to the last one Terry had seen. The two windows to the room which would overlook the lane and the doctor's house had closed curtains on them. There were three oil lamps burning and suspended at various points from the ceiling. Even so the rear of the room behind the last row of chairs was dim and shadowy. Terry told the two Meyer's to kneel facing the dark back wall and to put their hands behind them for tying.

"But we did not bring rope," Peter said.

"Just tell them to do as I have said."

While Peter spoke to the Meyer's and they grumblingly got down on their knees, Terry took his silenced pistol from his pocket and looked at Jacob. He offered the pistol to Jacob but he shook his head. Terry spoke in English but did not wait for a translation. "You are both charged with being members of an illegal organisation. You are both charged with plotting to do harm to a member of the British Army. You are both charged with supporting the use and mistreatment of slave labour in this town. You are both found guilty and sentenced to death."

With that he walked to the back of Mr Meyer, who was still straining to push his hand far behind him. Terry coolly placed the silencer barrel to the back of Mr Meyer's head and pulled the trigger. There was a loud 'phutt' as the bullet passed through his head, exiting through his left eye and hit the wooden panelled wall. Mr Meyer began to topple forwards and Terry pointed the pistol at the side of the open mouthed Mrs Meyer. She was making a silent scream as the bullet hit her right temple and came out of her left ear. She fell sideways in a blubbering heap. Jacob at last spoke.

"Jacob feels that he may be able to let his brother rest now," Peter said. "He thanks you and is sorry he did not have the strength to carry out the execution himself."

Terry went to the heavy chair and sat. He extracted the pistol's magazine clip and slid two replacement bullets in it. As he re-assembled the pistol he gave his orders.

"Peter, you and Jacob go to the bar door at the side of this place. Make sure it is unlocked. Visitors will arrive in twos. They may make their own way to this meeting room, in which case you follow quietly behind them. If they see you, use the guns to force them here. I want you both to drag these two bodies through that door and into the next room. During the next trial I want Jacob to wait and watch at the bar door. The visitors normally arrive at ten minute intervals, but if they don't he must warn us. Do these things now and quickly, please."

Terry sat calmly in the chair for twenty minutes before he heard footsteps and jolly laughter from the staircase. He heard a loud call for Mr Meyer and the door opened and two men entered. First to enter were Mr Hasch followed closely by his old assistant Mr Wessel; Terry could just make out the shadow of Peter and his Tommy gun stealthily following behind.

"Come in gentlemen, please take a seat."

Terry was pointing the pistol in the general direction of the first row of chairs. Both men walked cautiously and sat down. They looked even more shocked at the door was closed behind them by a thin dark man pointing a Tommy gun at them. Wessel began to speak in a high-pitched German until Terry rose and quietly said, "Shut up." He proceeded to walk behind the two men, pushing the second row of chairs gently away with his knee.

"Mr Hasch and Mr Wessel, you are both charged with being members of an illegal organisation. You are both charged with supporting the use of and using slave labour. You are both found guilty. You are both sentenced to death."

With that he shot both men in the back of their heads. Hasch lay in a widening pool of blood and was speaking clearly in German. Terry walked to him, listened for a while and then placed the pistol to the temple of Hasch's head and shot him a second time. Hasch fell silent. Terry and Peter dragged the two bodies to the next room. The trail of blood was soaking into the darkly lit red carpet. Peter rejoined Jacob near the bar door and Terry placed three more bullets into his pistol. He noticed that his hands were not shaking and that the silencer was very hot.

Nine minutes later Mr Kahler and, to Terry's surprise, Constable Neelmeyer entered the meeting room. Terry sat them in the newly righted chairs and following the previous trial routine shot them both.

"Go back to the front door," Terry said. "I was expecting one other visitor. Your bonfire will be a little larger than I had expected." Eight minutes passed before Terry heard raised voices in the bar and then shouting and a sharp scream. The door opened and Jacob entered walking backwards, his pistol pointing at the bleeding forehead of ex-Senior Constable Fromming. He was followed by Doctor Dressler and then Peter. The bodies of Neelmeyer and Kahler still lay in front of the heavy chair; their heads to one side, large pools of blood haloing them, and their eyes were open. Fromming saw the two corpses and made to push Jacob into Terry. Jacob tripped and fell on top of Kahler and Fromming stumbled forward on to one knee. Without warning Terry shot him in his right eye, from a distance of six inches.

"Mr Fromming you are guilty of being a member of an illegal organisation. You are guilty of supporting the use of slave labour. You are guilty of assisting wanted war criminals to escape arrest. You are sentenced to death. You are dead. Hello Doctor Dressler, thank you for your help, but as I told you this morning you need not have attended the meeting tonight."

The Doctor looked at the scene of carnage and spoke in a strong and powerful voice.

"Your business is not yet over. There is one more Nazi who deserves to die tonight. Would you do me the honour of executing me, now, this minute please?" Terry was shocked and objected.

"Doctor Dressler you are needed here to help the DPs. You were not a proper member of this group. You were my spy. You helped set up this trial. I can't shoot you."

"Then let one of your two Jewish friends do the deed. I have seen enough of them die, without once trying to help or save them. Tell them I was a camp doctor."

Dressler started to speak in a pleading German. Peter and Jacob listened and began to weep. Peter gave the Tommy gun to Terry.

"He is a cruel Nazi bastard, but even so I have not the courage to put him out of his misery. Perhaps he should be allowed to live and suffer the memories just as we two shall. Jacob and I will bring the lorry to the rear door and remove the bodies to our crematorium. I had hoped that tonight's actions would have somehow helped me live with the horrors, but they have only made things worse. Killing, killing and more killing. I will take the briefcase now. Thank you and good luck Corporal."

Jacob handed his pistol to Terry and the two companions left the death room. Terry was beginning to tremble and was taking deep breaths to calm his growing fear and anxiety. The doctor looked at him.

"For the sake of my sanity, shoot me." Terry shook his head; he had had enough of killing for one night. Dressler continued to plead.

"Shoot me or I will tell you things you do not want to know. I have done much worse things than I told you on our drunken night together. Shoot me. I have betrayed God, my county, humanity and even this pathetic little murdering Corporal. Shoot me. You killed Neelmeyer there and he has never done harm to anyone. He was not a member. Shoot me. Neelmeyer wanted to save you. He wanted to find out about this group and tell you. Shoot me, or I will go on. Neelmeyer already knew who your real enemies were. That is why I was ordered by her to persuade him to attend tonight. You shot your only true ally, you pitiful idiot. All of these deaths tonight were needless. She fooled you. Hitler is dead and so is his strength.

Himmler had all of the power in Germany after 1940. He still has that power. They will use you, and then kill you. You stupid fool, like me you have been used by her tonight. Shoot me."

Terry lifted the pistol and shot Doctor Dressler in the nose. As he fell backwards his lips curled into a bright smile and he gasped, "Thank you."

Terry walked out of the guesthouse and kept to the edge of the square where the rain was lightest and the darkness heaviest. He used his keys to open the door to the rear of the Centre and entered as quietly as he could manage. Paula called from her bedroom.

"A late night Corporal, would you like me to prepare some tea for you?" She opened her door and stood in a long white nightdress; she held an oil lamp in front of her. "You had better give me those clothes you are wearing," she said to him without further comment. Terry looked at his sleeves and tunic front and saw that they were stained with blood as also were the legs of his trousers. He stepped into her room and Paula closed the door behind him. He removed his uniform and damp shoes. His shirt and long underwear were also stained red. He took those off too. Paula stood in front of him with a large towel in her hand. Terry, naked, but without embarrassment made to take the towel from her, but she placed it and the lamp on a cabinet. She put her arms around him and held him tightly; just as she knew he had done for others. Terry could feel the warmth of her ample bosom and smell a delicate perfume in her hair. It was a cool night and he had been shivering since he had fired a bullet into Doctor Dressler's face. Now in Paula's motherly arms he felt warm and calm and the night's bloody images were fading from his eyes. Without surprise he realised that he had an erection placed hard against her stomach. Only then did he understand that the reaction had started as he shot Mrs Meyer. He knew this should worry him and that his present position was less than gentlemanly, but he did not care; he felt warm and alive. Paula gently pushed Terry to her bed and laid him down. She sat on the edge of the bed.

"You try to sleep now and if you have bad dreams, wake and I can hold you."

The light from the oil lamp was flickering and dim, but he could clearly see his thing pointing at the ceiling. He whispered, "What am I going to do with this?"

"I will take good care of that too," Paula said as she placed her warm hand around it. Soon Terry fell into a sound dreamless sleep.

Paula, dressed in her Centre Manager's suit, bought a steaming mug of tea to Terry as he awoke. He was startled at the light and at first did not recognise the room.

"Good morning my Corporal, milky tea for you," Paula said. "It is now five-thirty and you have a busy day. A nurse is on duty upstairs. You should quietly go to your room and find some clothes before the Centre starts to wake. Both of our reputations may be compromised if you are found in my room in that state." Terry still had an erection, although he hoped it was not the same one as when he had fallen asleep.

At six o'clock Terry sat at the interview table in replacement boots, trousers and military shirt. He began to eat his breakfast; he felt unusually hungry and the fried bacon and egg tasted especially good this morning. Paula opened the double doors and the reflection of the dawn spread throughout the reception area. She removed the oil lamp from his table but left one burning on the bar near the foot of the staircase. A car drove across the square and parked outside the window next to Terry. Otto entered a little breathlessly.

"Sorry Corporal, I am five minutes late. The damp had got into the engine and it took me a long time to start the car. It has stopped raining now, but we will have more today for sure. Good morning sir."

Terry told Otto to sit at the table and take something to eat and drink. A woman carrying a brush and mop hurried through the door, bowed towards Terry and Otto and moved on to the kitchen area. Alone again Terry spoke to his driver.

"I will move to the big house this morning. I knew you would be pleased. The door to my office over there is unlocked and there are two lamps alight. When you have finished your breakfast move all of my things to my new rooms in the house. Everything should fit into the car in one trip. Take good care of the oil painting. The guns and ammunition, which you know well, might be heavy. If it takes two trips, that's not a problem, but collect me here at ten and take me to the fertiliser factory. If anyone asks tell them I have a meeting there with the new management and the builder. We will need to take Ingrid with us to translate. After that meeting we should drop Ingrid back here and then visit Mr Schrader at the school. We can come back here to see what's going on, but I would like to be at the big house by three this afternoon. Have Olga prepare one of her special meals for me. You, Lara and I can eat together at five-thirty. One other thing, you can have the shotgun and cartridges in your room." Otto wiped his greasy lips, slurped the last dregs of his tea and rushed to the office bedroom.

At eight o'clock Ingrid entered and said good morning. She busied herself at the reception counter. At ten minutes before nine the colourful Hoffmann sisters made a spectacular entrance. They called greetings loudly to everyone they could or could not see. They were both in flowing pink dresses and their make-up would have required many hours of trowelling to apply. Ingrid guided them to the interview table where they both kissed and smothered Terry. He considered for a moment that he might be attractive to older women, but then decided that these two were capable of much more affection if you were one of their paying customers. They spoke simultaneously in high-pitched guttural German. Eventually Ingrid managed to get them to sit down and be relatively quiet, although even then one or other of them would interrupt if Ingrid paused for breath.

"They are here as commanded by your lordship. I will try to translate their exact words, but there may be some colourful phrases you could have difficulty with. They say that it is dull weather and everyone is dull because of it. Everyone is stupid; rain was always good for their business. It brings punters in without the need for the crude display of nipples. They wanted to ask you if they could re-open the cinema as they have been unable to find any other place to establish entertainment for the boring cattle of the town. The one on the left is the older of the sisters, although she denies it, her name is Heidi. The other one who is adamant that she is and looks two years younger, is Trudi. I would guess that these two characters are in their sixties; at their interview they both claimed to be exactly thirty-nine." Terry smiled at them.

"Business?"

They both smiled and said, "Business", in English and fell silent.

"Do they speak English?" Terry asked Ingrid.

"On their record sheet here, I wrote that they speak only a few words of English. I would be extremely embarrassed to tell you which words they are, but would suggest body parts and sexual action would be their total vocabulary."

"OK," said Terry, "tell them I have been informed by Mr and Mrs Meyer of the bar and guesthouse that they no longer wish to live in Altewiese. I have purchased the bar and guesthouse from the Meyers. I am willing to enter into a partnership with Heidi and Trudi Hoffmann. Each of them will buy one third of the business from me. I know they say they have no money. I do not require money. I want them to give me one third of the profits of the business, or one third of the sale price if they ever sell. They are to buy all of the stock for the business and to attract entertainment. I will be allowed to drink one bottle of schnapps every week and use one bedroom at any time, without paying. From time to time I may ask them to do a favour for me. One such favour will be required immediately they accept my proposition."

Ingrid spoke quietly to them and they listened intently, glancing occasionally at Terry. The sisters looked at each other, wordlessly nodded and then said in English, "Deal done." They both stood and shook Terry's hand vigorously. They sat again and spoke to Ingrid.

"They wish to know of the favour, but as you have seen they have both accepted your proposition."

"They must go immediately from here to the bar and guesthouse. They will find the bar door open. They must clean or burn any dirty carpeting. They must clean any mess they find in the meeting room on the first floor and repair some damage to the wood panelling. All this they must do now and never discuss with anyone what work they have needed to do. Ingrid, you can draw up a simple handwritten contract between these ladies and myself."

When Ingrid had finished translating his words, Terry continued.

"As to their earlier idea regarding the cinema, I am interested. They should find out who stole it from the Jews. Who claims to own it now. They must search among our DPs for a projectionist. You know of one Ingrid, good, tell them who it is. They will need to find a generator and fuel for it. I can obtain Military Government censored films in German. German language newsreels are available also. If they have any naughty films, they must not have any political contents. I will buy the cinema and if they can do the rest we can add it to our current deal."

As Ingrid finished this translation, Terry continued.

"May I make the first booking at the Hoffmann Sisters' Guesthouse? For Sunday week, two double rooms for one night. An evening meal of some quality will be required for four persons. The best Schnapps should be provided, although the guests will bring their own champagne. Book it all in the name of the Government of the British Zone of Germany, under the heading 'Altewiese Brick Conference'." Terry stood and shook the sisters' hands and they left in a loud shouting cloud of goodbyes.

As Otto drove Ingrid and Terry to the fertiliser factory, they saw the Hoffmann sisters dressed in drab brown overalls dragging a piece of carpet across the river road to a smoking fire near the river.

"I will be moving my billet to the big house over there today. Our daily meetings at the Centre will continue, but the timing will be nine 'til eleven for me. You do whatever hours you wish. You have not spoken of our interview with Jacob last week. Is that because you agree with the way you Germans treated him and his family?"

Ingrid was stunned. Tears welled in her eyes, but Terry was not looking at her. She stuttered in frustration.

"The things that happened were terrible, but what can I do about them now?" She had tried to say more, but was too shocked to find the correct words. Terry stared out of the car window at his side.

"Terrible? That is not the word I would use, but then again I am not in control of this segment of the SS Brotherhood. I am not having an affair with a Nazi policeman from Berlin. I did not work in the Fabens factory watching my personnel files reduce as Jewish workers perished as they were forced to eat their own shit."

Terry was surprised that he could hear himself shouting. He went on more quietly.

"I am amazed that you can generate such convincing tears. You are a beautiful woman and my mother always warned me against beautiful women. So I will do as my mother says and not trust you an inch. I know who you are and what forces you can use against me. I will be watching you, just as you watch me. Tell your evil friends that I propose to carry on ignoring their traffic in criminals. Tell them I will be of no threat to them as long as I feel no threat from them. I am out numbered by more than eight to one this time but I still carry fifty rounds in my Tommy gun. Please stop crying, the actress in you is not that convincing."

"I don't know what you are talking about. I can't tell you what is happening here. I became involved by accident. It is not me; I will not hurt you."

"Shut your fucking mouth, you evil lying tart," Terry snapped.

In the factory office a red faced but composed Ingrid sat next to Terry, opposite the two factory men. They had waited some minutes when the door opened and a young man of twenty entered. He was wearing dusty overalls and introduced himself as Bruno Kahler. Ingrid explained his presence after a few moments conversation.

"This is Mr Kahler, the son of the builder. His father is missing or he would have been here at the meeting as ordered. Bruno Kahler apologises for his father's absence but asks that he take his place. He recently returned from a POW camp and has been working with his father."

Terry was confused and had not expected to have actually had a meeting with builders this morning.

"Tell them that the Kahler firm owe me a favour for an earlier late arrival. Tell them that if the factory management need any work doing they should show it to this Mr Kahler, who will list it all and give me the list. We will then discuss the fee. I know that the Tree Teams have been working to tidy this place but have the two managers any reason to believe that we could not make fertiliser here again?" Ingrid translated then spoke to Terry.

"The factory manager, Mr Schmitt, says that all of the equipment is in working order. He could find labour easily from the unemployed in town. The boiler house needs some resealing and he would like some work to be done in the offices to improve his living accommodation. He will need capital to pay for materials and labour. But everything depends on the procurement of the necessary chemicals."

"Tell him we are trying to find a source for them now. Ask him which factory he managed before he came here?"

"Corporal, like for many people in Germany now, that is not an easy answer for him to give." Ingrid swallowed deeply and went on. "Both of these men controlled production of a factory in Poland. Jacob was not there, but many of his kind were. It is part of the tragedy we have to live with."

As they dropped Ingrid at the doors of the Centre, Paula ran to the car.

"We have a missing persons problem," she shouted. "We have no policemen on duty; Neelmeyer has not been seen. Worst of all Doctor Dressler is nowhere to be found. I have searched for him. We have some very sick people in the Centre. He could not have run away, could he, Corporal?"

Terry leaned out of the window and as Ingrid joined Paula he replied.

"Better ask Ingrid. Muller will be back very soon, so give the problem to him."

"Good morning to you Mr Manfred Schrader," said Terry jovially as he walked into a classroom of forty teenagers. Schrader and the whole class were silent for a few seconds and then he shook hands with Terry and spoke to the pupils in English.

"This is Corporal Hall, say good morning to him." The class jumbled their response. "Corporal Hall is visiting us today. Why is Corporal Hall visiting us today?"

"I am visiting you today to ask Mr Schrader a question." Schrader said some words of explanation in German and then said, "What question would Corporal Hall like to ask Mr Schrader?"

"Is Mr Schrader married to Mrs Schrader, or is she only his boss?"

"Indeed a searching and deep question and one I have been endeavouring to answer for some years; matrimony being a most difficult subject. Perhaps the ignorant Corporal would allow me to provide him with some out of school-hours tuition. At his convenience I could advise him of the facts of life."

As they drove back to the Centre Otto was forced to halt the car by a frantically waving Pfarrer Lehmann. He spoke excitedly to Terry through the car window, in a broken, barely understandable English.

"I have been visited by three wives. Their husbands did not return home last night. This is unusual and very worrying. Mr Hasch's son is very upset. He was to attend a meeting with his father last night, but chose to meet a lady."

"What a pity the young man did not choose to be with his father," Terry said sarcastically, "but how can I help?"

"There are no policemen."

Terry sighed.

"Father, Inspector Muller will return to Altewiese within one or two hours. He will then help you find the missing men. What meeting were they to have attended? Ask young Mr Hasch to tell me. I do hope it was not a Nazi meeting. You must find this information for me and tell me. I will arrest all of the people who attended a Nazi meeting. If they have run away because they are Nazis, I will inform the military police. This is very bad Father Lehmann."

Terry was laughing so much that his jaw began to ache. He was sitting at a small round dining table in the study next to von Lutken's bedroom. Otto, with tears of laughter dripping from his chin, was to his right with his back to the window and the falling cloudy sun. To Terry's left was the smiling Lara.

Olga and Fredda had served the meal at the table and kept it warm only by running from the kitchen, up the staircase and along the corridor. Terry had eaten spicy beetroot soup for the first time and found it delicious. A rabbit stew and potato dumplings had been accompanied by a bottle of fine French wine. Apple tart with cream and two glasses of schnapps were followed by Camp coffee and real Polish vodka. Otto had until then managed to translate for Lara, but now his English was unintelligible. The words 'Lara' and 'likes' and 'you' would not co-ordinate in his mouth. Terry was certain that the plain Lara liked him. On arrival she had again kissed him full on the lips. During the meal she had stared at him longingly. His every translated word had been met with her laughing approval. He had teased her about her short stubby nose and she had laughed. He commented on her unevenly trimmed short hair and she blushed at the complement. He had rubbed the cream from the tart onto her strong calloused hands and she had thanked him for his kindness. Otto had warned Terry over the second schnapps, to use a rubber protective that night as Lara had only recently finished the doctor's medication for a problem with her hole. Terry had called the meal his 'house warming party' and Otto had only cared to hear 'party'.

Terry was beginning to think that parties in Old Stein were more of an orgy.

He had been concerned with Fredda's comfort and was delighted at her apparent happiness. Stephan was even now patrolling the house with his hand bell. A practice session with the bell had preceded the meal and everyone was satisfied with its loudness and tone. Otto staggered to his feet and proposed yet another toast to young love; emptied his glass and left the room, first hitting his head on the door. Terry stared out of focus at the double vision of Lara next to him. He was planning to stand and say good night to the two of her, but his legs refused to work. His head fell forward onto the table spilling the remainder of his glass of vodka and he fell into a deep sleep.

When he awoke next morning, he was in a large comfortable bed. Fredda was opening the curtains and the dull rain sodden light hurt his eyes. She handed him a cup of cool tea; he sat up and drank it in one go. Fredda was walking around the bed with yet another cup of tea and he was happy at her thoughtfulness. She handed the cup to a naked Lara who was sitting at the other side of the bed. Fredda looked sad and disappointed and Terry was very pleased that she looked sad and disappointed. He ached to have a naked Fredda in his bed.

CHAPTER EIGHT

THE VISITOR

Terry was suffering from a terrible hangover. As Fredda's thin neat frame exited through the bedroom door, Terry swung his legs out of the tall bed and sat shivering in the warm humid morning. He noticed his nakedness and hunched forward. He reached for his wristwatch which lay on the bedside cabinet next to him. He knew from the dull cloudy sky outside that it was daytime and considered that his watch had stopped during the previous night's party. Ten minutes past nine and the little second hand was sweeping round to mock him.

"Oh, bloody hell no," Terry muttered. He never over slept and today of all days was not a convenient day to start. He should already be at the Centre judging the reaction to the eight missing citizens and Wilkes was due at eleven. His body ached and his digestive system churned and Lara stood two feet in front of him. She was still totally naked and a sweet smile shone on her protruding lips. He could smell her stale sweetness; Terry noticed that many of her bones showed through her pale skin. She had broad shoulders and full, wobbly breasts; her pink left nipple pointed down and over to the left; her rosy right nipple pointed up and to the right. She had a narrow waist and flat stomach. Her stubbled pubic area had recently been shaved; it now resembled the chin of an old man with a seven-day beard. Her hips were wide, but her thighs were very thin; he could see clearly through the gap between the tops of her legs. Terry considered that she did not match any of the female bodies he had seen in 'Parade' or in the dirty pictures he had glimpsed in Holland. He looked down at his shrivelled, wrinkled penis, which nestled between his thighs. He felt sick. He stared directly ahead at the gap topped by the seven-day beard. Lara, in appreciation, opened her legs wider and placed her fingers to either side of her female crevice and opened her self for him. He saw the brown shiny skin and ran to the toilet. He vomited violently and then turned quickly and was only just in time to catch the bowl with his diarrhoea.

After a while he stood and peered into the bowl and howled. The dark red fluidy mess and his burning arsehole convinced him that he had been poisoned or fed glass filings. Even now he was dying of internal bleeding. He heard Otto's voice in the bedroom.

"Otto, you murdering bastard," he shouted.

Otto ran into the toilet and stared in horror at the standing Terry, who pointed at the bowl and whimpered, "Look, blood." Otto laughed loudly.

"Not blood, its beetroot. Well beetroot, lots of vodka and a little coffee. You will be better soon."

Otto left the lavatory laughing and Terry called after him.

"We're late; get my things ready quickly. We must hurry."

Lara had now entered the lavatory and Terry's embarrassment grew as he stood there with three small pieces of the Daily Express in his hand. She was giggling and turned away from him and bent to pour a pitcher of boiling water into the bath; he saw her backbone protruding like a thin row of mountains. She was still naked and he saw that her buttocks were covered with small ugly scars. Terry thought the scars looked like someone had stubbed cigarettes out on her bottom.

Terry asked Kurt Muller, Ralf Engelbart and Ingrid to join him at the interview table.

"Are you aware that a number of our population disappeared yesterday?" he asked.

"Yes," said Kurt, "we have received a number of strange reports. Two nights ago there was a large fire in the woods between here and Brick. The dampness caused by the recent rains prevented a major forest fire, but the blaze must have been fierce. We examined the site yesterday evening on our return journey from our meeting in Brick. The charred remains of two or more bodies could be seen. We took the precaution of covering the site with soil. We have received a number of reports regarding missing persons. Our enquiries, so far, have not given us any indication as to why so many men would have decided to desert the town so suddenly. There is a suggestion that they were all members of a secret organisation and may have needed to visit another town. We have alerted the police in the area but think it best to wait and see if the men return soon. My personal problem resulting from this incident is the possible loss of one of my officers. Neelmeyer was friendly with the disgraced Fromming, who is also missing. As you know I have one young recruit in training, he is only seventeen but has seen military service. I propose to you that it would be easier to find two or three women suitable to act as constables.

You agree? Then I will pursue that line. The disappearance of Doctor Dressler is a great mystery and very worrying. He should not have disappeared. I will urgently try to find a replacement. Unless the Corporal knows whether Dressler is likely to return? No he is not. That is a great shame and an unfortunate mistake, but our life must go on. My assistant Ralf, here alongside us, now has six Tree

Teams, but is failing to find sufficient work to keep them fully occupied. We have a town-planning meeting scheduled for Friday, may I invite Ralf to join us. Additional to his other varied skills, Ralf is also a competent photographer and would like to take a number of photographs of you. We could have some placed in the town records to mark this moment of the town's history. Others Ralf would present to you for transmission to your parents.

Finally Mr Hasch the younger and possibly Mr Kahler the younger are extremely agitated with the disappearance of their fathers. If Mr Meyer the younger were to be discharged from his prisoner of war camp, we would have the nucleus of a disruptive element within our town. I assure you I will be very watchful of these men."

With that Kurt nodded politely and fell silent.

"I do not have any objection to Constable Engelbart taking my photograph, but ask that it be delayed for a week or so," Terry responded. "I am expecting to receive a third stripe for my sleeve. Thank you. I have moved my billet to the big house which will give added office space here for Mrs Rozen-Kranz. I would like Ingrid to move her files and moneyboxes to the police station. This will give even more room for the Centre's work. It will also mean that I will have telephone contact with her, using the system installed so painfully by slave labourers, some time ago. I understand it has been recently repaired and is once again in full working order. I will use Paula to translate any business for me while I am at the Centre but will be making more use of the police station and the study at the big house. I know there are four families sharing the cottages on the estate but excluding myself, there are only six people in the big house. Send some DPs for Otto, Fredda and I to interview. Farmers, foresters, that sort of thing; there are nine fields and a good deal of woodland to share out. I prefer to have my billet surrounded by grateful and therefore possibly loyal people. If you would excuse me now, for I have an urgent need to visit the lavatory."

Wilkes arrived five minutes after eleven o'clock with two ARSE trucks and Tessy. Hardaker was with him as he stormed into the Centre.

"Good morning to you all. Hello, Sergeant Hall, for you have been a sergeant since twenty hours on Tuesday."

Terry shook hands with both of the soldiers and wondered if the timing of his promotion exactly coincided with the death of the Meyers'. He shivered slightly.

"Congratulation Mr 'all," said Hardaker smiling as ever. "You done alright. Now I can dislike you 'cos you got rank. I want to know if you got any work for me 'ere today. Like you need to remove some smelly turds?"

"No," replied Terry, "everything is very quiet at the moment. Eight citizens have disappeared; one of them was our doctor unfortunately. The bar and guesthouse has changed hands and I think you will like the new owners. We'll check it out at lunch time."

"Hardaker, you go and control the unloading, while I have a few words with the sergeant," said Sergeant Wilkes. "Eight was a big number to remove on your own. I don't need to know the details, only to let you know that last night we received an ARSE truck from the stationmaster in Hamburg. Two Jew boys gave him the keys; they were both very smoky and anxious to catch any train heading south, or west. The loss of the doctor is a bit of a shock, but that's your problem.

We had some fine trading last week and one of the trucks is full of stuff. The market on Saturday should be very good. You may find some traders from Hanover and Hamburg will show up. Mostly trying to buy food. The reputation of the Altewiese market is spreading. In the short term that may reduce our profits, but after we are away from here, it will not matter to us. My date is 10th December, did you know? I'm not sure what's going on for I was told in Hamburg that none of us are being replaced. As you can see, Hardaker is leading in another batch of pity - forty of them, sorry. Some of these are in a real mess - your hospital beds will be full for sometime. I have a crate of medicines but must warn you that they are running short again. I have five tins of cash for you which I can see makes you much happier.

The other lorry is for ARSE and the tank trailers will be here next week. I gave a copy of the list of chemicals to a friend in the know, in Hamburg. His initial report was very confusing. The chemicals are indeed suitable for fertiliser production but are twenty years out of date. Your chemist must have been asleep for the last twenty years. There's a good chance we will be able to find all of the stuff you want. As part of my handover to you, I want you to make a few weekend trips to Hamburg and Bremerhaven with me. You can see how we find the chemicals and everything else. I have here for you a load of stripes for you to sew on your uniform. You'll need to do it quickly because on Monday you are to report to an intelligence unit in Luneburg. One day with them, then two nights in the Russian Zone, followed by two more days in Luneburg. Here are your official written orders and Russian travel passes and the invitation letter; they are for you and one civilian driver. It will be a busy week for you. Do you want me to have someone down here while you're away? No, good. I knew you would have things under control.

That Kurt Muller was very impressive this week. My policemen in Bachwald showed him a lot of respect. You will be surprised to learn that the other one, Engelbart, was equally as impressive. They are not using their real names but my very friendly constable suggests strongly that they are both Gestapo trained. Well, I remember that old lady singer was frightened of Muller so I got my man to ask around to see if anyone else recognises him. The two were given a guided tour of our timber factory and one of the workers thinks she knows who Muller is. We haven't got his real name, but he was pictured often in the Berlin newspapers; he was one of Himmler's closest aids. That doesn't make him a torturer or death camp madman, but it makes him important. This escape route they're running through Altewiese might be handling some proper bad bastards. While I'm in charge we're going to look the other way. It's safer and a lot less stressful. When it's your show, you can do what you please, but 'til then you just keep out of their way and don't provoke them."

Terry stared across the room at Ingrid who was packing her papers and files into wooden crates.

"Sergeant Wilkes, what do I call you now?"

"Wilkes is fine with me Terry."

The records of the meeting at the town hall held on that Friday 24th August 1945, show that it was attended by Kurt Muller the police inspector and his assistant, Ralf Engelbart, Ulrich Tiedemann the liberal deputy mayor, Bruno Kahler the young and suspicious builder replacing his still missing father, Pfarrer Lehmann the energetic pastor, Manfred Klein Schrader as secretary and translator and Sergeant Terence Hall representing the Government of Occupation and acting Mayor. Extracts from the minutes of the meeting include:

Item 4: Gloria Cinema. Mrs Trudi Hoffmann having purchased the cinema from the estate of the deceased Mr von Lutken, is granted permission to re-open the cinema for two nights each week, Wednesday and Saturday, for the projection of suitable films and newsreels and to charge a reasonable fee of any viewer. A town tax of five pfennig per paying customer to be due to the town hall finance office.

Item 5: All houses and cottages formally owned by Mr von Lutken are confiscated and immediately become the property of the town council. These to be rented to their current occupiers at a weekly rental of ten marks or such lower amount as can be afforded by the occupier.

Item 6: The name of Helmut Str to be changed to Hall Str.

Item 7: The name on Von Lutken Str to be changed to Koenig George VI Str.

Item 8: The market square to re-apply its original name of Marktplatz and all reference to its recent name to be obliterated from all town records. (Adolf Hitler Platz).

Item 9: The former bank at number four Marktplatz that had been recently used by a defunct political party to be converted into a school. Mr Manfred Schrader to be appointed as Principle of Education for the district. Younger children to receive education at the school on Kirchwender Str and older children at Marktplatz. Free and universal education to be made available to all children between the ages of eight and fourteen years and who are resident in the districts of Altewiese and Brick.

Item 10: Permission is granted to the company ACF (Agri-Chemie-Fabrik), to re-open the factory at the eastern end of Wiesse Weg, for the manufacture, processing and distribution of agricultural fertilisers and household paints. A property rental to be due to the town council on successful return to profitable business.

Item 11: Permission is granted to Hans Reck to increase the number of vehicles operating from the garage at 14 Hanover Str to: eight lorries, eight trailers, three passenger buses and four light vans or cars. Diesel and petrol tanks on site to be inspected by a member of the town council annually. A town tax of five pfenning is due on each ton of cargo or passenger carried by any company operating from this site.

Item 12: The town council will evaluate the re-start of electricity generation at the town generating station at the junction of Wiesse Weg and Kirchwender Str. A report and feasibility study to be presented to the next town council meeting.

Item 13: The large quantity of black paint currently in store at the defunct politic offices to be transferred to the Tree Teams managed by Senior Constable Engelbart. All wooden doors and window frames facing the town square to be painted by the teams. Further enquiries to be made about the procurement or production of white wash paint. This to be applied to the brick and plaster work of all buildings facing the town square by member of the Teams.

Item 14: A public lavatory to be built at a suitable point on Wiesse Weg and near to the entrance to the town square. Facilities for men and women to be available separately. The project to be designed and built by the Teams.

Item 15: The reed beds on the river to be thinned and a lake to be formed in their place. The Teams to proceed with this work after the next spell of dry weather.

On that same evening Terry had dinner in his study with Fredda and Otto. Terry took great care not to drink in concert with Otto. The meal was served professionally by Olga and Lara and Terry constantly refilled Fredda's glass. Terry was frustrated by Otto's difficulty with the translating of more than the simplest English or German. His questions about her feelings and dreams received answers about her husband and desire for children.

"She thinks her husband must be still alive. She wants you to ask the authorities in Hamburg to find him. His name is Ludwig Marnitz-Schule. He was a private in the artillery, 188th Regiment; he was wounded at Nerve, in September; he was in a hospital in Gorzow, when it was over-run by the Russians during last winter. No she will never have feelings for other men. Yes, she's comfortable here at the big house. She's very grateful to you for your many kindnesses and wishes she could repay you somehow. She is only unhappy that there are no good German speakers for her to talk to. I am afraid Olga, Lara and I tend to speak in Polish. She believes she would be of more use cleaning at the Displaced Persons' Centre and Hospital. Yes, if some German families came to live in the house she would be happier. No she is no longer in pain. The sickness that was eating her body has gone away. Every month she does not act like other women; by that I assume she does not bleed. She wonders if she has offended you, as you are staring at her so strongly. She has beautiful eyes Sergeant that I agree, but she is so short and thin and her chest is flat. She is dead inside her head and body; she will be of no use to you. I am sorry I spoke out of turn; I apologise. You are correct, it is none of my business. I am drunk and should not interfere with your desires. Lara wants your body and to make you happy; this woman wants only what is left of her dead husband's body. Sorry, yes I will leave now. Good night."

Terry did not remain angry. When alone with Fredda he held her hand and tried to make her understand what he was saying and feeling. She nodded thoughtfully and her misty blue eyes crossed. She emptied yet another glass of vodka and Terry realised she was drunk and would soon collapse. He lifted her quickly and was surprised at her lightness. He took her to his bathroom and pointed at the toilet. She hiccupped and nodded and Terry left her alone in the bathroom. He walked to the bedroom window and looked out on to the moonlit fields and trees that lay to this side of the house.

He thought of Fredda's perfect eyes and he wanted her to know how much he wanted her. He could not believe that the woman he loved could not understand a thing he said to her. He wondered if she would realise his feelings if he were to touch her physically. Would she respond with anger or pleasure? He was feeling quite drunk himself and staggered slightly as he turned from the window. Fredda had not emerged from the bathroom and he felt concerned for her. He knocked on the bathroom door and when he received no answer he called her name quietly and slowly entered. She was asleep on the floor near to the toilet bowl; her baggy cloth knickers were around her ankles and her dress revealed both of her thin white thighs. He removed her knickers and lifted her gently. He took her to his bed and laid her there with her head on his pillow. He leant forward and kissed her softly on the lips and said, "I want you so much." She opened one eye and flung her arms around him, pulling him on top of her. Terry thought he heard her say in English, "I love you", but it might have been 'Ludwig'. He stood and stared at her; she had her arms spread at her sides, her knees moved slightly apart. Terry unbuttoned her dress and removed it and her small bra. She lay naked in front of him; the only blemish on this perfect creature was her misshapen forearm. Her small breasts were firm and topped with dark pointed nipples. He caressed them and he heard her sigh. He ran his hand over her flat stomach and parted her legs. She lifted her knees and whimpered something. He opened her and stared at her and was consumed with desire for her. He undressed in the bathroom and washed himself. When he returned to the bedroom she had her head to one side and was quietly snoring. Terry climbed on the bed and knelt between her legs. He kissed her on the lips and then placed one of her nipples in his mouth and placed a finger inside her. She made no response, but continued to breath deeply in her sleep. He put himself inside her; he groaned with pleasure. He raped his sleeping beauty.

He was awake early the next morning and was dreadfully ashamed of what he had done. He had not put on a rubber protective. How was he going to face the unit's medical officer with a case of rampant syphilis? He ran to the lavatory and peed. He washed himself twice. He poured cologne over his limp penis; he hoped the stinging was an indication of cleansing. He washed, shaved and dressed. Fredda was still soundly asleep on her side with a thumb in her smiling mouth. He left her there and found Otto eating breakfast in the kitchen with Stephan. Terry said good morning to them both.
"You are correct again Otto. Fredda is not happy here and would prefer to be with her friends at the hospital. I cannot be cruel to her any more so I want you to transfer her back, this morning. We will manage without a housekeeper. I will be visiting the market today. I want you to ask the nurse if Fredda is fully recovered from her illnesses. We will need to buy some things for my trip next week.

Find out if Fredda is completely well, I don't want to be away if she is still poorly".

As the car gently drove along the estate track, Terry reread his orders and called to Otto.

"Do you want a trip to see the Russians? On Monday morning before six I want to be on our way to Bachwald. I plan to have a quick breakfast with Sergeant Wilkes. Then we go to Luneburg; I have the address here; we must report to it by nine o'clock. You can collect me from the same address on Saturday. On the Tuesday I am to drive to Schwerin, which is in the Russian Zone and spend two days as the guest of that Russian General who called to visit us last month. I will drive back to Luneburg on Thursday morning. The army may have arranged for a driver for me but if they have not would you like to drive me? I would understand if you refused. Yes, you would do it; that's good. Drop me at the Hoffmann bar and go back for Fredda. I must remember to get some of our local cheese to carry as gifts."

As the sedan slowly turned into Ulzener Street in Luneburg, Terry realised that it was the street Wilkes had pointed out to him on their drive south, so many weeks ago. He found house number 31 and checked his wristwatch. It was ten minutes to nine.

"Otto wait here. I will come back soon and tell you if you will be driving me tomorrow."

The suburban house stood in a well-maintained garden of lawn and short shrubs. The front door was open and in the first room on the right Terry found a young private typing slowly with two fingers; he looked up at Terry.

"Good morning sir, who are you looking for?"

"Captain Wright, Intelligence Corp; I am Sergeant Hall. I have an appointment with him at nine o'clock. This is the correct address isn't it?"

"Oh yes sir. Captain Wright will be here directly. Take a seat. Would you care for a cup of tea?"

"Yes please and one for my driver. Milk and sugar if you have any."

The private left the room and Terry could hear him pouring water into a metal kettle and moving crockery cups. Terry wandered nonchalantly to the desk and glanced at the paper in the typewriter. So far the typist had addressed the report to a Mr K Philby, Military Intelligence, Mayfair Office. The title read 'Results of Search for Body/Remains of HH'. As yet there was no text. Terry returned to the rickety dining chair by the wall. The private gave two cups of tea to Terry, both with dainty saucers, but no spoons. "Sorry Sergeant Hall I'm not allowed to leave the office area unattended so would you be so kind as to take a cup to your driver. We have no biscuits until tomorrow." Terry gave Otto his cup of tea.

"It might be a long wait; these buggers don't seem to be early risers. Sorry, no biscuits."

Otto failed to understand, but was grateful for the sugary tea. Terry returned to the office and sat in the chair.

"Been out here long Private?" he asked.

"Three weeks, sir. It's a bit boring typing all day. There's a toilet and washbasin in the next door on the right, if you need them. Captain Wright does not normally arrive on Mondays much before eleven. Over taxes himself at the nineteenth hole at golf on Sunday nights. I was conscripted in February and have spent most of the time typing. I was captain of all the sports teams at school and thought I might see some physical action. Bashing this damned typewriter is my exercise now. I am eighteen sir. You been out here long, sir?"

"Yes," said Terry, "since June."

He looked at the cottage garden scene on the wall calendar and noted the red pencil line passing through the dates had stopped at 26th August. Terry considered that the time had passed quickly, so much had happened. The last date he had written was 9th, on a letter to his parents. He visited the toilet and examined his penis; Otto had told him Fredda was clean, but he still worried that her dirty insides may still be active.

"Sergeant Hall, my profound apologies for keeping you waiting; urgent meeting, you know, top secret stuff." The Captain was tall, young at twenty-two, overweight and overly charming. "Follow me won't you, my office is on the next landing. Is that your car outside? 1929 Mercedes Sedan, lovely condition; I'd like to find a nice roadster to take back with me. Sit down; take your tunic top off."

The Captain unlocked a filing cabinet with a key he'd taken from his desk draw; he extracted a brown manila folder and sat at his desk. Before he could speak, Terry decided to sort out Otto.

"Excuse me sir, but I told my driver to wait and see if I was to need him tomorrow. I was wondering if you had laid on transport for my trip?"

"Trip? Just let me read these notes and find out what all this is about. I didn't get a chance on Friday. Bit of a flap on, you know. No I can safely say we have not yet arranged for your mode of transport for this week. Damn, we might have got one of our boys to drive you and have a look round while you were partying. Missed that one didn't we? We can find a civilian billet in town for your driver and I have plenty of chittys for petrol, you know. He won't be staying? Ok, here take these petrol coupons and get him to tank up.

You'll be staying tonight at, let me see, damn we haven't got that sorted yet either. You could find accommodation at Bad Farven? Why that's only half an hour away. Splendid. Go and tell your driver to collect you from here at five o'clock. You should be heading east out of Luneburg by six o'clock tomorrow morning, so warn him. Yes, you go ahead."

As he re-entered the Captain's office Terry could see that he was busily reading the notes in the file. An empty water glass and paper packet of headache pills were lying to one side of his desk.

"Come on in dear boy. Sit there. I've got the gist of the story now. On the face of it, it is all a simple drive, but behind the green is a very tricky bunker. You have absolutely nothing to fear; you can enjoy yourself you know. But, my commanding officer and the civilian chappies in London want from me chapter and verse about your trip. Apparently some Major General is involved on our side and the Russian General is closely connected to Marshall Stalin; distant cousin, or something like that. You should be back here by lunchtime on Thursday and you are due to return to your post on Saturday. That gives us less than two days to debrief you. That's not much time. I was hoping to get up to Hamburg this weekend too. Damn. I will be writing reports all next week and that plays havoc with my putting. The debriefing is the most important time for us both.

A colleague and I will fire lots of questions at you. You will say you don't know the answers; that's normal. After some time and effort you'll give us the answer and you'll be amazed. Everything you see your brain remembers. The problem is that most of us have difficulty finding where our damned brain stores the memories. Given enough time we could have you tell us what you ate at your fifth birthday party. A fruit trifle? Oh, how clever of you. Well, all you need to do is stare hard at everything you see when you're with the Russians. If you see something which you consider interesting stare at it and say to yourself what it is. You can't make notes, or draw pictures, or take a camera with you. Firstly it would be impolite and secondly they will get you pissed and search you thoroughly.

So now we come to what's interesting; we are going to look through a picture book or two and I'll show you what we in the Luneburg intelligence service would think is interesting - for example these photographs of different designs of tanks and armoured guns. We would like you to come back and say that you saw twenty of the tank number three in a field ten miles from the checkpoint. In this book are photographs and drawings of radar installations - we would like you to say that you saw one of these or two of those or whatever. As you travel along in your fine car, stare at things and say to yourself, there are two anti-aircraft guns in that field and we are one mile from the checkpoint and those tanks over there have a machine gun on the left of the big barrel. Regimental insignia are on these pages; try and remember which ones you see. They will be on lorries and tanks and buildings.

Now the next task is a little bit more subjective. The Russians will surround you with a selection of their trusted henchmen but you just might be able to talk to real soldiers and NCOs. Ask them how long they will be stationed at their current post and do they like it there. Imagine what you would say if someone asked you that. What would you say Sergeant?"

"I'm going to be in this area until January 1947 and I'm happy in the post, but would prefer to be in Staffordshire, sir."

"From that I would gather that your Generals are not planning to move your unit for one year at least and that conditions are comfortable. If you'd said that you're moving to Berlin next week and you aren't happy about it, I might think your Generals are going to attack Berlin and you are naturally frightened. Can you see what I am saying; get the ordinary soldiers to give you a comment. We in intelligence will analyse the replies. Don't worry too much about what you see in the civilian areas; we have quite enough information from the Displaced Persons' flood to be going on with you know.

Once you are in a military camp, start staring. Now, where is Field Marshal Montgomery at this very moment?"

"I don't know sir. Should I know where he is?" Terry was puzzled.

"Which intelligence officer briefed you?"

"Well you are sir. Captain Wright."

"Which tank regiment is based in Luneburg?" The captain was smiling as he asked.

"I don't know sir. If I thought you were going to ask I would have found out, sorry sir." Terry sounded exasperated.

"Sergeant Hall, the extent of your knowledge is perfect. The Russians will ask you the same questions and more. From your file I gather that you work with the civilian population, good show, and everything you know is of little military value. You can relax when you are with the Russians; you don't have to lie. If they get you badly drunk on their fowl vodka and you tell them how much cheese is produced each week at your local creamery, we will not be placed in danger of an immediate Russian attack. Don't even bother making up stories for them; if you don't know the answer, just say so and if you do give them an answer, you will not be compromising our position at all. You try to stare and listen and we'll see what news you can bring us on Thursday.

Incidentally Monty is in London meeting the Joint Chiefs of Staff and planning troop allocation and replacements and they can read that in The Times. The local tanks are from the 7th Armoured Division. Half the division are now in Berlin and this half were to be shipped to China but they have now been ordered to stand fast here for the foreseeable future. I was playing golf the other day with one of their officers and he was concerned at the amount of new equipment he's to receive next week. Still, that is only tittle-tattle and of no importance.

One of the notes in this file is odd, it simply says - ask the General if Himmler is dead. Well, Sergeant Hall, at the opportune moment, ask the General if Himmler is dead. Yes, that's correct we know he died in May. Did you know he died right here in this house? I was not here at the time, thank goodness. All the boys that were here have been discharged. We have had a bit of a flap again recently about it. The boffins in London want us to find his grave. We have no idea where he was buried. Only the chaps who buried him know where his body is and they have all been demobilized. We know his soul is in hell, but have no idea where Himmler's body is. Do you want me to show you where he was interrogated? Come on then, it's downstairs."

That night Otto and Terry spent the night in Bad Farven; Otto in the company of a DP who he had recognised as coming from Old Stein; Terry with Christine and Corporal John Ballantine. Christine drank heavily and was put to bed at seven o'clock in the evening. John Ballantine and Terry continued sipping beer until ten. John was eighteen and tall and lanky. He had been born in Selkirk, but bought up and educated in Maidstone. He was quiet and thoughtful and highly protective of Chris Stein.

"If we can cover Chris's illness for the next four months," he said, "he'll be demobbed and his family might take care of him. If he gets discharged before then, and his record shows alcoholism as the cause, he'll have a hell of a problem finding a job. During the morning Chris is brilliant with the refugees; they warm to him immediately and will do anything he says. He takes his first drink in the mid-afternoon and it's then he starts to sulk and get tearful. I've been coming on duty at thirteen hundred hours and running the show 'til mid-night. We have the radiotelephone and can call Wilkes if we need to. I've had to call him twice; Chris was very pissed and was trying to hang himself, both times. That is I needed to call twice this month; last month he was much better.

Yes we have a good doctor; he was part of one of our DP allocations in July. He had told all the previous camps he was a schoolteacher but after two weeks here he admitted he was a GP.

Bloody useful as it turned out; we had five cases of typhoid fever that week and didn't know it. We have set him up in a nice house in town and he's got plenty of nursing staff and actually sleeps with one of them. We try to make him happy so one of you other towns doesn't try to tempt him away. No we don't produce anything for Wilkes' kitty; he says our job is to take the brunt of the refugee problem and protect you entrepreneurs from visitors.

Yes I've been getting a share of the profit and I'm OK about it. It isn't a serious crime what we're doing and it does help the locals and DPs indirectly. No, I haven't seen any SS or Gestapo types coming through here. I don't know what I would do about them if I saw some. They would be dressed in black and be covered in scull and crossbone emblems, I suppose. I would probably ignore them. The real baddies will be on trial in Nuremberg in November, so any around here would be of no interest to the authorities. Have you seen any Sergeant Hall?"

"Yes one or two, but they were in civilian clothes and said they could translate for me and run our police and a factory, so I employed them. I still think they could be dangerous but they are efficient and are good at controlling people."

"What would you do if you found out they'd done really bad things? Torture, starvation and mass murder, what would you do then Sergeant?"

"Shoot them," Terry said forcefully.

"That's what Wilkes keeps saying, but I reckon its not that easy to kill someone, even if you know they're guilty of serious crimes. It's easy to say, but normal people don't go round shooting criminals in the street without trial and witnesses. No, you'd have to be a nutter like Hardaker to pull the trigger. Even Hardaker couldn't kill a woman; not even the camp guards we've read about. I agree with you, employ them and get the best out of them; we can't go on arresting all of them, there aren't enough courthouses in the world for that."

As the orders had instructed, Otto had the sedan arrive at the Elbe crossing at ten o'clock precisely. They had encountered light traffic travelling in the same direction all morning and had stopped one mile short of the Elbe for a picnic breakfast. At the western end of the bridge, the British soldiers on border guard duty had called an officer to confirm that the smart sedan with a young sergeant sitting regally in the back was genuine; the bald, one toothed smiling chauffeur had attracted comment also.

Terry had found the whole episode amusing and when finally signalled to pass the raised barrier had offered the nearest private a pfennig piece as a tip for his trouble. The metal bridge was two vehicles wide and small groups of DPs were scurrying towards them. Only the sedan headed east. At the Russian checkpoint the barrier was already raised and two helmeted soldiers waved them through and saluted smartly. The officer with them signalled to them to halt a few yards inside the border post. He approached the car and was smiling broadly; he removed his wide brimmed officer's cap and leant into Terry's open window.

"Welcome to the Russian Zone of Germany Sergeant Hall. We must follow formalities I'm afraid. Please show me your documents and invitation letter. May I also look at your left nipple?" The Russian officer's English was accented but educated and grammatically correct. Terry found his last request amusing and unbuttoned his tunic and shirt and pulled his vest to one side, so as to expose his left nipple to the officer.

"Yes, exactly as we knew," he said. "You have a small brown mole two inches above your left nipple."

"How did you know that? I can't say I've ever noticed it before," exclaimed Terry.

"We have to know many things in order to maintain our security and a little mole is not very important. May I join you in your fine German car for the trip to Schwerin? If you object, I will travel in front of you in that rather uncomfortable and windy open VW wagon with those two rather boring soldiers. Oh thank you, I would be delighted to sit at the back with you. Firstly I will sign some documents for the crossing keepers and instruct the driver of the escort wagon.

As the Russian officer walked from the car towards a tin roofed hut next to the crossing barrier, Terry quietly spoke to Otto.

"Are you nervous now?"

"A little, Sergeant Hall; my hands are very wet but it's a very warm morning isn't it?"

"Yes Otto, it is. Strange that they've not asked for your papers yet."

The Russian officer climbed into the car and placed a small leather briefcase on the seat between Terry and himself. He handed Terry the bundle of papers containing his invitation and passes.

"Does you driver speak German or English, Sergeant Hall?"

"Both," replied Terry.

"Driver pass me your documents and follow that wagon which has just pulled in front of us."

The car accelerated as the officer scanned Otto's papers with apparent disinterest. He handed them to Otto over the seat back and said some words in Russian. Otto said nothing. The officer then spoke in Polish and Otto replied. The officer then spoke to Terry.

"Your driver speaks German, English and Polish but would appear to have forgotten his Russian vocabulary. I'm pleased that you've chosen to use him rather than some poorly disguised intelligence agent. It's so much more polite of you to bring your regular driver from Altewiese. I am being very impolite though; I must immediately introduce myself. I have the rank equivalent to a Captain in your army. My name is Boris Gorbachev and I am attached to the personal staff of General Novgorod, your host. My work mostly concerns intelligence and political security matters. I hope to learn something new from you and to ensure that you do not see anything that we might call delicate. I presume you have received an intensive briefing. I am sorry to be so blunt but if we can get rid of the silly spy business first, we can both relax and enjoy ourselves for a couple of days. Who was your briefing officer over this last weekend?"

"Captain Wright, but it consisted of seven hours of him talking to me yesterday, sir."

"Captain Wright is not the most hardworking of your intelligence community. From his appointment to this case I would assume that his masters are not taking this trip very seriously. We shall see. Please rest assured that we are extremely happy to have a British sergeant visit us. Your British working class are the salt of the earth. Your officer class are snobs and wastrels."

"When I get back," Terry interrupted, "I will have to repeat to Captain Wright what you have said about him and his kind. He will have to report it all to his commanders."

"I know; would you like to have a bit of fun at his expense? During his ample free time, Captain Wright plays golf and wagers relatively large sums on his matches. There are two golf courses near to Luneburg and he has told everyone who regularly uses them that his Surrey based handicap is sixteen; in truth it is six. He pays his mess bills with his golf winnings as a result. He has told everyone in his home village in Surrey that he has played golf with Field Marshal Montgomery. In truth he played golf in a foursome playing behind the one in which the Field Marshal was playing. Captain Wright has a normal sized left testicle, but his right one is very small. He does not like the ribald words to your song, 'Colonel Bogey' therefore. I may find you some more tit-bits in our files on Captain Wright.

Mr Vramp, Mr Vramp in two minutes the wagon will pull over to the side of the road. Please park behind it. Sergeant Hall we are now in quiet countryside and we will not be overlooked by anyone. I would very much like to search you, the driver and the car. It is a necessary precaution; I hope you will forgive the rudeness. Are you carrying any weapons on your person or in the car?"

"In this side pocket of my door is a small automatic pistol and in the boot of the car you will find a Thompson machine gun slung from the back panel along with two clips of ammunition. Otto, being a German citizen, is not allowed to carry weapons."

"I will need to hold your guns until we return to the border crossing on Thursday. You will not need them here in our zone. No German would dare look at you, let alone shoot at you. I understand that security is not that strong in your British Zone, is that correct?"

Terry stared out of the window at the empty fields and destroyed houses. He saw a steady stream of ragged refugees walking west. There were no civilians in the villages they passed through; shop windows were smashed and doors hung from broken hinges. There were many Russian troops standing on corners and rows of tanks in ripe cornfields. The civilians they did pass were in work teams with armed Russian guards; the teams of thin and fatigued labourers were mostly made up of women; they were repairing bridges and roads or loading trucks with furniture and machinery.

"In my part of the British Zone," Terry said slowly and deliberately, "we have a much larger population than you have in this district and far fewer troops. Our programme of denazification is not yet complete. Many hardened Nazis have fled from your zone to ours. The small number of British troops who work with the civilian population tend to feel more threatened than you may do here. Our aim, unlike yours, is to give the innocent civilian population food and a decent amount of comfort. I carry a Tommy gun at all times, but I don't need a squadron of tanks like those over there."

The car had stopped and was being thoroughly searched. The packets of cheese had been unloaded and were attracting suspicious looks from the two Russian soldiers.

"The cheese is produced and smoked in the town I control. I thought it would make an interesting gift for the General."

"I am sure General Novgorod will be very pleased and flattered. Unfortunately it has a texture similar to plastic explosive, but certainly not the smell."

The Captain gave some orders in Russian and the car was repacked and the two-vehicle convoy set off again. After a few miles the Captain spoke.

"Let me give you some details of your itinerary. You will be staying in a military hotel at the edge of the lake in Schwerin during your two nights with us. We should arrive in time for a light lunch. This afternoon we will walk around the ruins of the city and you can see how we have started to rebuild the living quarters in some areas. Tonight we will attend a formal diner in the hotel dining room. You will be the guest of honour at the General's table. At the tables around you will be representatives of various regiments who are based in or near Schwerin. There will be very few officers in attendance - mostly sergeants and corporals. The General wishes to show his troops that they are as important to him as his officers. This is a politically correct attitude. The General is required to be politically correct at all times for his real name is Vissarionovich. He is a cousin of Marshal Stalin. We will have a late night and there will be entertainment and much drinking.

Tomorrow we will rise late; be prepared to leave for a short trip at midday. The General wishes to have you visit some of our military hospitals and to talk to some of the patients. You must ask them how the Germans in Poland and Russia treated our families in 1942 and 1943. You will learn of the horrors that befell our woman folk. There will be some women patients who we released from Ravensbrueck Camp in April, but who are still too unwell to travel; some will be Polish, but you may find French and Belgium's too. You may talk to them and hear their stories. When you have heard you will understand why our gallant and brave Russian soldiers have no respect for German women. Yes we act out of revenge but you must understand the horror that we have witnessed and then you will forgive our actions. All Germans share the guilt of the torture and murder of millions of Russian civilians, even the German women who did not hold a gun or whip. They must all be punished. I am sorry, I am getting carried away with myself. Tomorrow afternoon's interviews will not be pleasant but in the evening you are invited to dinner at our equivalent of your Sergeants' Mess. There will be a lot of drinking and entertainment. I will not be allowed to join you and we will need to find a sergeant who can speak English.

On Thursday at midday I will collect you and your driver at the hotel and we will travel back to the border together. We have found a nice hotel for Mr Vramp and a secure garage for this car. The General will only be with you tonight so you should be ready to ask him many difficult questions. He likes blunt honesty and vodka."

The hotel opposite a large blue lake had been partially repaired. The left wing remained scarred and blackened but the main building was much like any hotel in the English Lake District. The rooms had high ceilings, metal fireplaces and clean, starched sheets with rips at foot level. Toilets with stained bowls and bathrooms with stained baths were always at the furthest end of the long and draughty corridor. Terry's room had a fine view over the boatless lake and had a small unsound balcony. There was electricity and clean running water. In a bedside cabinet he found a jug of water, an unopened bottle of vodka and a pottery night pot. The staff of the hotel were all Polish or Russian.

Terry, Otto, Captain Gorbachev and two soldiers carrying rifles walked for two hours after the chicken sandwich and watery beer lunch. The colourful lakeside properties were all occupied by military and civilian Russians. Behind these properties there were many demolished buildings, many with huts created from debris and caves excavated from the rubble; the German inhabitants stared with wide sunken eyes at the ground as the visiting party passed. Away from the lake they came to a tall granite regional parliamentary hall which had survived the shelling and now was acting as the regional military headquarters. Large fluttering Russian flags flew from the roof and two light tanks stood with their backs to the wall on either side of the grand flight of steps to the wide wooden front doors. The Captain apologised for not showing Terry inside the building but mentioned military security and politeness. To the right of the hall was a bombed and flattened site, but then there was another unharmed granite building - smaller and less ornate than the parliament hall. The Captain explained that this had been an important museum and had been re-opened for the education of the German population. Inside the high doors the group found a vast colonnaded area; immediately to the left were ten tables each with two chairs; no one sat at them. Fixed to the walls around the whole of the extensive room were photographs pinned unevenly and with corners curling. In the centre of the room, lying directly beneath a once glazed dome, was a pile of women's shoes. The pile formed a ten-feet high pyramid. The captain led Terry and Otto around the room.

"This display was completed at the end of May and since then every surviving German in Schwerin and the surrounding district has been forced to visit this room and look at the photographs and read the descriptions below them. When each group of Germans enter they are interviewed at those tables and issued with new Russian documents. Follow me and we will walk around the wall as the Germans are then told to do. The photographs are all real - many are from German files we have captured, others have been taken by our war correspondents and soldiers who have been assigned the awful task of recording war crimes. These are pictures of some of the atrocities committed by the Germans. Yes, that is of twenty naked Polish teenage girls hanging by their necks by piano wire from a metal beam over a railway platform. Their feet are seven feet off the platform and passengers are having to run under the bodies to avoid the dripping mess. One must ask what form of mental disease was being suffered by the minds that ordered that? The next group of photographs were taken by the Deputy Governor of Poland in 1941 - a German who took small boys and girls of six or seven from the streets of Warsaw and did things to them. Yes, in this example, he stitched a small boy's penis to that little girl's forehead and probably laughed as he took the photograph. But, Sergeant Hall look at this picture - is that not even more revolting. Here, look what these SS troops are doing to that tragic pregnant Russian woman.

There are thousands of photographs, all of deeds perpetrated by different Germans. We are not looking at the work of one mad Marquis de Sade, but of tens of thousands of warped Germans. On this last wall are photographs from the death camps - many from the women's camp at Ravensbrueck which is only two hours from Schwerin. Those are the pictures taken by our troops as they liberated the camp. Some of those skeletons are British women. Yes, we found brave British prisoners in Ravensbrueck. Finally we make the local Germans stand in front of this pile of shoes and imagine what has happened to the women who once wore them. This is a small sample from the camp's warehouse where we also found stacks of suitcases, boxes and boxes of eyeglasses and piles of tooth amalgam, many with pieces of teeth attached. The gold tooth fillings had all been taken to Himmler by the time we arrived. Tens of thousands of women perished through starvation, disease and torture in Ravensbrueck Camp. This is not some distant corner of Poland or the Ukraine; we are in the holiday area two hours north of Berlin.

The Germans who visit this room claim they did not know this was happening. That is nonsense. If there was a prison camp of that size, with that much activity on the roads and railways of Stoke on Trent, would your family in Stone not be curious enough to ask what was happening? When they were told it was a camp for killing innocent women and babies, would your family be happy and ignore the camp? But the German civilian population either ignored it or supported what went on. They got nearly new and still warm shoes and paid only a few pfennigs for them and were content to forget whose feet had just left them. They are all guilty and all deserve punishment. Two of every one hundred Germans who visit this room leave and commit suicide within three days; perhaps there is a God after all. Come on Sergeant Hall we have seen enough for today; let us drink one beer before we clean up and prepare ourselves for the dinner. Mr Vramp you will be eating at your hotel tonight; be at our hotel with the car at eleven o'clock in the morning. Mr Vramp, I hope you can sleep well tonight and not be disturbed by the memory of the things you did to our innocent women."

The dining room was very grand with red carpets and large sparkling chandeliers. During the vodka only cocktails, Terry had been introduced to almost all of the other one hundred guests. The Russian sergeants and corporals seemed nervous and ill at ease but were polite and respectful of a visiting British sergeant. Terry felt very young and inexperienced among these many war veterans, some of whom were in their forties. As each conversation lasted for only three or four words, Terry was pleased that he did not have time to admit to his wartime grocery occupation.

When General Novgorod entered the room a loud cheer erupted and all of the guests pressed to shake his hand. He wore a red-banded officer's cap with an enormous brim which appeared to Terry to resemble an umbrella perched on the General's head. The room was laid with ten round tables each of ten seats. The General's table was in the middle of the room. Captain Gorbachev explained that at each table was one VIP - often a political officer or visiting civilian from Russia. There were one hundred Polish waitresses constantly filling glasses or lighting cigarettes. The fog of cigarette smoke was thickening in unison with the growing loudness of vodka-oiled conversation. Eventually a loud bell was rung and the guests hurried to their seats.

Captain Gorbachev flanked Terry to his right and General Novgorod was to his left. Also at the table were two colonels and five nervous Russian sergeants. In front of Terry lay shiny solid silver cutlery - two forks and two knives. Above these was a row of eight small and medium sized glasses. In the centre of the table were a huddle of bottles: six large beer bottles, six red wine bottles and ten vodka bottles. Terry stared at them and mentally divided the table party by the bottles and decided some of the people at the table had better have a very large alcohol capacity. The General greeted Terry warmly with hugs and wet kisses and insisted on calling him Co-operative Hall.

The first course of cold salmon steaks and bread was served quickly and everyone chose vodka to accompany it. Terry followed the lead to maintained unanimity. As the salmon was being consumed the General rose and gave a loud and demonstrative but thankfully short speech. The Captain explained that the General was welcoming the brave and victorious soldiers to have dinner with him. They should all feel at ease as no interfering officers were watching them tonight. There was a small cheer from one of the tables. The General then pointed to Terry and the Captain pushed him in the kidneys and told him to stand, face everyone and say 'good evening' many times. As Terry resumed his seat everyone was rising in a toast. The Captain's hand on his shoulder and the loudly repeated

'Co-operative Hall' indicated to Terry that he was the subject of the toast; he smiled meekly and nodded his thanks. The waitresses poured more vodka and beer. The next course consisted of blinis and caviar and vodka during which the Captain turned to Terry.

"It is now your turn to give a short speech. Thank the General for his kind invitation and say how proud you are to be in the company of soldiers of the finest army in the world. I will stand next to you and translate what you say into Russian. If you forget anything or say something silly, don't worry, because I will say what you should be saying anyway."

Terry's legs felt like jelly but he managed to speak for five minutes but could not recall a single word up to the point when he proposed a toast to General Novgorod. A noisy cheer rang out again and glasses of vodka were drunk in single gulps. The glasses were then thrown at the marble fireplace set into one of the dining room walls. Terry sat and tried a fork full of caviar; he thought it tasted of fishy shit and was pleased that the waitresses were removing this round of dishes and delivering plates of steaming beef and mashed potatoes. This Terry ate with relish and a glass of never emptying red wine. The General turned to Terry and addressed him through the Captain.

"Co-operative Hall, that was a very good speech you gave just then; my congratulations on your political wisdom and politeness. How are you enjoying your trip so far?"

"I am finding everything interesting. The museum in the town was a shock to my senses. Do you think all of the allies should set up a display like that in every town in Germany and have the German population visit and understand what has happened in their name, General, sir?"

"Yes they should. I will have that idea added to the agenda for the next Control Council meeting. Marshall Georgi Zhukov will be very impressed when I tell him a young British sergeant suggested it. Well done Co-operative Hall."

"Sir, I have read and heard much about General Zhukov; is he really as good a General as Field Marshall Montgomery?"

Terry had practised this question in his hotel bedroom. There was a stunned silence at the table as the Captain's Russian translation landed. The General smiled.

"My friend and commander Marshall Zhukov is the second best military commander of all time."

The silence deepened, even the cigarette smoke stopped circling.

"Napoleon, Wellington and Caesar were good, but your Field Marshall is better and is number three. Supreme among all of history's military leaders is our own Grand Marshall Joseph

Vissarionovich Djugashvili, 'Stalin'," the General was shouting and all at the table jumped to their feet and shouted and downed another glass of vodka. The lead was followed at the other tables and pandemonium ensued. Terry had joined in and was relaxing under the onslaught of beer, red wine and vodka. When a modicum of calm had returned to the table the General leaned close to Terry.

"Where is the Field Marshall at the moment. We seem to have lost track of him?"

"Sir, Field Marshall Montgomery is in London at a meeting of the Joint Chiefs of Staff; they are planning troop allocations and replacements."

"Yes that would make sense. Your senior officers need some planning. We are allies but they tell us nothing. When I visited you in that town, the two cricket playing idiots who were assigned to me as guides said they were packing up to leave for Hong Kong, but I hear that the 7th Armoured Division is still here in Europe."

Terry smiled and thought he sounded as though he was reading from a script.

"Half of the 7th Armoured Division is in Berlin and the remainder have been ordered to stand fast in the Luneburg area. They will be receiving new equipment next week, sir. Well that's what I was told to say sir. To be honest I haven't a clue what is going on."

The General laughed loudly.

"Thank you Co-operative Hall, honesty is always the best route to take, I have heard."

"General, I have been told that I will not be meeting you tomorrow, so would you mind if I told you of a gift that I have bought from Altewiese for you? The town which is where we first met is famous for its cheese and I have bought a quantity of it for you."

The Captain and the General talked for a moment and then the General gave an order to one of the colonels present at the table. The colonel rose and left the room to reappear some minutes later.

"Thank you very much for your kind gift and more so for the thought of giving him a gift. The General is genuinely pleased Sergeant," said Captain Gorbachev.

"General why did you change your name to Novgorod?"

Again a silence fell on all the guests at the table. The General smiled and slapped Terry hard on the back.

"Sergeant Inquisitive Co-operative Hall is courageous in his questions. I like brave men. My family name is that of our great leader. I did not want to receive unfair advantages in the army by letting others know of my closeness to my Uncle Joe. I took the name of the town I was in when I enlisted in the army as a private soldier. My achievements therefore are my own."

The Russians at the table clapped enthusiastically and Terry could feel that they all knew that the General's words had been bullshit. The General went on.

"How are you coping with the Nazi bastards in the town you control? I hear you had to execute eight of them. Only eight? I would have considered eighty more appropriate."

His lips were still smiling, but his eyebrow had risen in mock seriousness.

"My complements on the skill of your intelligence service, sir. My orders are to keep the German population alive and well. A small number of still active Nazis posed a threat to me personally. I had to take drastic action."

At that point one of the sergeants at the table rose to his feet and called nervously for silence to all in the room. The sergeant was saying thank you to the General for his kind invitation to the NCOs in the room. He gave a brief account of his own service under the command of the great General and thanked him for being an officer for his men and counting the common soldier equal to his officers in respect of food, comfort and conditions. Until that point Terry had considered that the sergeant was regurgitating a prepared and practised speech, but then he surprised him.

"I have just listened to a conversation between our great General and our welcome guest from the British army. The General considers Field Marshal Montgomery to be the third greatest General of all time; our own Marshal Zhukov as number two. I would like to propose a toast to the greatest of all generals, to Marshal Stalin."

The room resounded with the repeated toast and smashing of glasses and loud cheering. The General was evidently pleased with the speech and left his seat to hug and kiss the now relaxed sergeant. The next course consisted of steaming cauliflower covered in a creamy cheese sauce and accompanied by a glass or more of vodka. The General was drinking faster than anyone at the table and his animated gestures were knocking over bottles and his voice was getting louder and more slurred.

"I will need to visit the other tables after this excellent cauliflower," he said to Terry. "I have one more question for you. Do you believe that the representative of the Devil, Heinrich Himmler is actually dead?"

"Sir, I am in no position to know the truth in this matter. All the reports indicate that he committed suicide while being interrogated by our officers. I can see no reason why they should lie."

"Oh, but there are reasons why they should lie. If Churchill ordered them to lie they would do so. If Churchill wanted to get Himmler's gold for the Bank of England he would have him spirited away to Sweden and fabricate his death to stop the Americans and we Russians from sharing Himmler's wealth. Of all the men in the world I personally want to kill, only Himmler remains. If you find any information about him being alive, you must tell me. I will be eternally grateful and my gratitude is boundless. Is there any favour you want to ask of me now? Go on, if I can do it, it will be done."

Terry spoke firmly and without emotion.

"I want to know if one particular German soldier is still alive and if so can he be sent to me. Private Ludwig Marnitz-Schule of the 188th Artillery Regiment was seriously wounded in September in the fighting near Narva. The German military hospital where he was treated was in Gorzow and was captured by your armies during last winter. He had suffered major damage to his legs and lower body."

"Why do you want half a German soldier?"

"I have my own reasons sir. They will have no effect on Britain or Russia. It is personal."

"That is a very strange request and one that we had not foreseen. This colonel has the details and we shall see if we can find out where half a German is buried. We then must dig him up and send him to you. Shake my hand Sergeant Co-operative Hall and let us swear friendship between us forever."

The two hugged and toasted each other and the General, hatless and open collared, moved to the next table.

The colonel who was sitting opposite Terry now proposed a room wide toast. His speech ran, "Comrades, brothers, we have won a great victory over the evil that is Germany. We have seen six million of our fellow citizens die at the hands of the German barbarian. Our country has been devastated by war and the need to give everything we have to fight the enemy. We cannot bring back our dead families and colleagues but we can extract payment from the German horde. We have taken their men to work on our farms; we have taken the tools and machinery from their factories. The Germans living in the British and American Zones will be asked to pay us too. We will take their coal and gold. But even this is but a fraction of what we have spent to defeat the German pigs. Tomorrow and the day after and the day after that you each will go out into this pigsty of a country and remove anything that can be of value to our mother Russia. To the last blade of grass, you must not leave the animals a single item. The sergeant here, represents the common soldier of Britain and he, like us, should be repaid by the German swine. I would like to propose a toast in honour of our brave ally. Fill your glasses to the brim and drink to King George."

Terry stood and emptied his glass of vodka and repeated to himself the wisdom of slowing up on his vodka intake. He poured himself a glass of warm beer.

A terrified young German girl of thirteen was dragged into the room and held tightly by two Polish waitresses. The girl was forced, among loud cheering, to eat a piece of cheese. She was then released and she fled from the room. An older waitress made a noisy statement and the other girls served Terry's Altewiese cheese with slices of brown bread.

"Your kind gift to the General is to be shared by the whole company," the Captain said quietly. "A taster has confirmed that it is not poisoned, so now we can all try Altewiese cheese."

A civilian Russian from one of the outer tables rose and gave a highly politized speech which was listened to in silence and cheered unenthusiastically at the points indicated by the speaker. His toast was Mother Russia and her lifeblood vodka. Terry had no choice but to drink a full glass of vodka. He drank some beer as well, in spite.

A white fish course was accompanied by a toast to Britain and its lifeblood vodka. A sweet course consisting of what Terry took to be jelly laced with vodka was followed by a toast to the Communist Party and its lifeblood vodka. Coffee and vodka were used to toast all sergeants who drank vodka. Vodka was then used to toast all corporals who loved vodka. At this point the lights in the room were dimmed and a noisy brass band began to play Russian folk songs. Five very overweight Russian ladies began to sing and dance. Terry noticed that at the end of each song the ladies would remove a piece of their colourful clothing. At the point when they were singing the Volga Boat Song they were wearing only red baggy bloomers; their breasts were swaying as they rowed their imaginary boat between the tables. As they returned to the bandstand to remove their loose last remaining underwear, Terry had a sudden need to relieve his bladder. All of the guests were standing in the aisles, some on the tables and Terry saw a few asleep under the tables. He could see no easy way of getting out of the room. The Captain was at another table in conversation. Terry tried to stand and found that his legs refused any orders and insisted on staying put. He shuffled his chair close to the table and lifted the tablecloth to his stomach. He extracted his penis with difficulty, his fingers having joined the same revolt as his legs. He peed with mounting satisfaction and relief; his eyes closed in happiness as the whole guest list went wild in appreciation. Terry wondered if they had seen him peeing, but thought it more likely they had all caught sight of five very fat and hairy triangles.

Terry rearranged his trousers and poured himself another glass of beer. One of the colonels arrived next to him and knelt on the floor. In poor English he said that the General was about to leave and he had been sent to collect his hat. The colonel disappeared below the table only to reappear immediately with the Generals enormous cap. The colonel said good-bye to Terry and walked very unsteadily away. Terry noticed that as the colonel swayed along a liquid swelled and spilled from the inside of the cap. Terry moved to an empty seat at the next table and listened for the drowning cries of a pissed on Russian General. He fell asleep before that happened.

Terry was ill during the night and spent much time holding the sink in his bedroom. He was only faintly aware that someone was in the room with him for some of the time. He could recall being given a large glass of water and of being undressed. There were three bright flashes of light in his dreams which coincided with the feeling that his testicles were being pleasantly massaged. He awoke in the morning with a raging stomach ache and was forced through lack of time to use the chamber pot. The smell was dreadful and he feared that someone might call on him before he had time to dress and run to the distant bathroom. On reaching the bathroom door pot in hand, he found that it was locked and he could hear a man tunelessly singing in Russian and splashing water. Terry returned forlornly along the corridor but noticed by chance that one bedroom door was very slightly ajar. He knocked with his free hand and on receiving no reply, pushed the door open and peered inside. There was a Russian military uniform laid neatly on the bed and a large brown suitcase on the floor. He checked that there was no one in the corridor, entered the room and sped to the bedside cabinet. The bottle of vodka was half full, but the pot was empty; Terry exchanged his wreaking chamber pot for the clean one and ran swiftly back to his own bedroom.

He lay on his bed until ten o'clock and realised that the pains in his head and stomach had all eased considerably. He walked to the bathroom again and this time found it unoccupied. At a little after eleven he was in the hotel foyer talking to Otto. Terry, as always, was correctly dressed in tunic and trousers, with his black beret set neatly so as to not quite touch his right ear. His boots shone brightly and his belt webbing was brushed to perfection. Terry and Otto walked to the edge of the lake and discussed the previous night's adventure. Terry asked Otto to listen for any references to the General and his piss filled hat and to whether it was linked to Terry in any way. Terry admitted that he had missed breakfast but refused Otto's suggestion of a glass of vodka to settle his upset stomach. As they stood by the roadside Terry stared pointedly at the insignia on each of the many military vehicles that drove passed them. After thirty minutes he noticed the arrival at the hotel steps of the VW wagon and Captain Gorbachev. Terry walked quickly across the road and greeted the Captain with exaggerated enthusiasm.

"A very good morning to you Captain. Extremely fine weather we are having and no sign of rain."

"Good morning Sergeant Hall, could I ask you to speak a little slower and a lot quieter. My head is in a very sensitive condition, what with the vodka and the General's abusive shouting."

"Oh, what happened sir? I was very tired and must have fallen asleep quite early." Terry said with much less fervour.

"That stupid colonel sitting next to the General drank too much and urinated in the General's hat. He will wake up this morning with the rank of private. The General eventually calmed down but insisted we all join him at the hotel bar for five hours of singing and vodka. The General passed out at four-thirty this morning and we could then all retire to bed. The General said many, many times that he enjoyed your refreshing company and thanked you for the gift, which everyone enjoyed. The many political commissars who were present, both in and out of uniform, were impressed with the General's ability and wisdom in obtaining a British soldier to show off to his enlisted troops. Our first appointment this morning is at a military hospital one hour from here, but before we leave I must visit the lavatory; please excuse me."

The hospital was set in a wooded area overlooking a lake and had been designed to house one hundred patients with lung problems. As Terry stepped from the car onto the rough gravel forecourt he saw crowds of patients lying, or sitting on the un-mown lawn that ran to the water's edge. A doctor in a long white smock tentatively approached the party of visitors as they emerged from their two vehicles. He was Polish and after a lengthy conversation with the Captain, agreed to be their guide. The doctor out ranked the Captain, but the Captain's contacts had considerable influence. The doctor began his tour by pointing to the patients on the lawn.

"These," he said, "are patients who we will discharge over the next month; there are eighty-five of them. They are close to physical recovery although most have mental scars that will take a long time to heal. In the hospital building itself we have a further six hundred and twenty-two other patients. During the last month our rate of discharge has been higher than our intake by five patients per day. Forty percent of our patients are female, mostly Polish, but from many parts of Europe. The male population is mainly Russian.

We have less than twenty military wounded left with us now as we were required to give them priority treatment and get them fit enough to travel as quickly as possible.

The vast majority of people here are suffering from damage, disease and malnutrition associated with slave labour and death camp internment. We have a high proportion of female patients as a result of our proximity to the women's camp at Ravensbrueck, which is ten miles south of us. Our staff at the hospital is relatively small; we have two male doctors and twenty-six trained nurses. We have employed a number of auxiliary nurses from among the recovered patient list. There are no German patients or staff. We use fifty Germans, under guard, from the local village to clean the latrines and chamber pots and to wash linen. They also dig the graves for our dead. We are losing one patient per day this month, which is a vast improvement over the June figures.

The Captain wishes for you to speak to female civilians to learn at firsthand how the Germans treated them. I am a Doctor of Medicine and with limited resources am endeavouring to make these people's bodies well. We have no expertise here to treat the mind. You will meet women who have been so badly mistreated that their brains are at the point of collapse. Please be understanding if they do not wish to relate their experiences to you. Let us talk to these Polish girls on the lawn. The four of them have become good friends and I propose to send them back to Poland together next week. It is too early for the one with the heavily plastered legs, but she would not survive without the support of her friends, so she will travel with them."

The girl of twenty-two with her legs in plaster agreed to speak to Terry through Otto's translation; the Captain listened attentively.

"I am from Leszno in western Poland and was taken by the Germans in November 1939, to work as a housemaid for a German industrialist in Frankfurt. The conditions were poor and I received no pay, but the family did not mistreat me. After two years I met a Polish boy who was working as a gardener at a house in the same street. We stole time to be together. My master discovered our secret and my lover was sent to a labour camp in Austria. I have not heard of him since. I was punished by being locked in a dark coal shed for one week. I hated the family after that and in order to make me work harder than I wanted to, they had a friend in the Gestapo flog me. I was tied between two trees in the garden, stripped of all my clothes and whipped. The children thought it was fun and clapped and cheered. That night the master of the house forced me to do sexual things to him. I ran away. I was arrested two days later and sent to a labour camp near to Munich. In order to stay alive I volunteered to work in the brothel. In the camp one would die within six months; in the brothel one would die within nine months. I was there for twenty weeks, when I was transferred to Ravensbrueck.

There I was assigned to a large wooden hut with two hundred other women inmates. We received better food and conditions than the rest of the camp. I was used in medical experiments. A very famous German Surgeon was studying bone grafting. He removed pieces of bone from my legs and grafted them to the legs of other women. Later he grafted other women's bone on to my leg bones. I am alive today because the Surgeon insisted that we were fed correctly and kept clean and disease free; he wanted his experimental patients to be as natural as possible. This Polish Doctor with us now has tried to mend my legs; the grafts did not take and I have pieces of partially attached bone which pierce the skin and cause bleeding and sores. No, do not feel sorry for me, I survived.

I saw thousands of women die in agony in Ravensbrueck. I saw a German female doctor carry out a series of experiments on women - her name was Doctor Herta Oberheuser. She injected different substances into different girls and recorded the reactions. She used acid, air, water, urine and many other things. Some girls would scream in torment for weeks before they died. There were always two hundred of us in the hut; when someone died they were replaced. With that many women it was natural that some would be pregnant when they arrived at the camp. Experiments in childbirth techniques were tried. One German doctor, I think he was a professor, had babies born in water of different temperatures. The freezing temperatures caused acute pain to the mother and we could hear the victims screaming for many days; in the end all of the women and babies were killed.

An armaments manufacturer killed one of my friends in the camp. The company had designed poison bullets for a rifle and to test them they shot one hundred women in the calf muscle with bullets carrying different amounts of poison. There were seven civilian bullet designers present at the test. You ask if my legs will repair themselves? I hope so, but I have seen many of the women from the bone graft experiments die; we called ourselves the Rabbit Girls. Before the Nazis existed these experiments would have been carried out on rabbits. I lasted twelve months in that place, which is a miracle, so every day I live now is a bonus; I just want to see my mother and father one more time. I have many more stories to tell you, but you do not look very well. Too much vodka last night, I think?"

"I chose this girl to speak to you for as you can see she has accepted what happened and is now looking forward," said the Polish doctor. "I think her ability to talk about what she saw and suffered has helped her cope with the enormity of the situation she witnessed. The doctors who carried out those experiments were not mad professors; they were highly respected physicians and surgeons. The results they published will be used to improve medicine and medical treatment in the future. But, at what a cost was the information obtained. Over there are two women holding hands. Do you see the way that they both look blankly ahead? They are both French and were tortured before they arrived at the camp. They helped each other survive, but now will only speak to each other; they refuse all contact with anyone else. They were both dreadfully thin and had contracted typhus when the Russian army delivered them to us. We have made their bodies well, but I do not know how to break into the world they share with each other. We shall send them back to France next week if we can find any transport. Please follow me into the hospital and let us see what hell on earth has produced."

The hospital was critically over full; many single beds were occupied by two people and the ward and corridor floors were covered with patients on makeshift mattress beds. The smell in the wards on that warm breezeless day was unbelievably obnoxious. The Doctor pointed at a row of beds and mattresses and said that the ten men and women there had all survived gangrene experiments, but were now slowly rotting from their wounds. Terry declined to speak to any of them and rushed on to a balcony to breathe again. As they entered each new ward the cause of the patients' suffering became more horrific and the scenes of utter desperation more unbearable. The visitors returned to the car and wagon and Terry spoke to the Doctor.

"I cannot thank you for what you have shown us and I do not want to keep you from your enormous task any more. I am leaving for Luneburg tomorrow. I have space in this car for three extra passengers. Can I take any of the people on the lawn with me?"

Captain Gorbachev and the Doctor had a short discussion and then the Captain said, "We may have difficulty getting the paperwork that quickly."

"Sir, with the greatest of respect may I suggest you fuck the paperwork and let me take three of these poor sods home."

"Sergeant Hall, I understand your anger. I will use the General's name and obtain the necessary documents by early tomorrow. The Doctor thinks it should be possible to take the two French ladies and he will add a Belgium girl who is somewhere over there. She too is reclusive and is unlikely to speak to you. I will cable your Captain Wright and ask him to clear the three women through your border post. I will ask him to have a French ambulance meet you in Luneburg. He will probably do nothing and play golf. I wish he could play golf on this lawn for a few hours."

They visited other hospitals nearer to Schwerin but the shock of the first one had dulled their appreciation of the later ones. At one military hospital Terry talked to wounded Russian soldiers and asked them how the Germans had treated the civilian population in Russia. The answers were gruesome but somehow Terry was becoming immune to the nightmare stories. He knew exactly what he now wanted to do.

"Captain can we meet some of the Germans who did these things and ask them why? Perhaps I would prefer to ask them 'how' they could have done these things to other human beings."

"You have met men and women in Altewiese who have been involved. You employ them still. We have prisons for Germans accused of committing serious crimes against the Russian people, but the majority of the prisoners are now executed. Those with lesser guilt have been sent to work in Russia as punishment. The ones that remain around here are those that will deny all knowledge of what has happened in their name. You should ask Inspector Muller to find you torturers to interview. You are in shock I can see. Let us return to the hotel and you can get two hours rest. I will collect you at seven this evening and deliver you to the Sergeant's Mess. I will be in civilian clothes and as your interpreter will be allowed to accompany you. The object of the evening is to forget the atrocities and live for tonight - well, until the vodka puts you to sleep again. The Sergeant's Mess parties are renowned for their excesses; do you object to nudity and sexy things? No, then you should find the whole thing entertaining."

As they drove back to the hotel Terry spoke to the Captain.

"Sir, the Regular German Army, Air Force and Navy were made up of troops like me. They did bad things like the bombing of civilian targets, but they were soldiers fighting a war. The really bad ones who did the things we have seen today, they were not regular army. They were SS, the Gestapo and the camp guards. All of these evildoers were under the command of Himmler. He built up and controlled all of the evil - labour camps, death camps, experiments, civilian killings, torture, the whole thing. In the end he had SS Regiments fighting alongside regular army regiments. He had millions of men under his personal command. All of them happy to do any evil he could imagine. Last night General Novgorod asked me if I believed Himmler was dead. That was strange because I was instructed to ask the General the same question. Sir, no one seems to doubt that Hitler is dead, so why is there a question about the death of Himmler?"

"In the end Himmler was more powerful than Hitler. Everyone thought that Himmler was totally loyal to Hitler, but that was not true. Himmler had been communicating with your government for over one year - either via the Red Cross representative in Sweden or through the King of Sweden. He made direct contact with Eisenhower in March. He offered to end the war in the west if the Americans and British would join him and continue to fight against we Russians. Of course no sane person would work with Himmler, but he had the power to overthrow Hitler and knew it. In April Hitler issued an arrest order against Himmler, denouncing him as a traitor. Only a very few fanatical Nazis would have dared to arrest Himmler. Hitler appointed Admiral Donitz as his successor. We know that Himmler visited Donitz in May, in the town of Flensburg, which is on the border with Denmark. A British and a Russian agent saw him there on the 12th of May. We know that he spent that night, fifty miles away along the Baltic coast, near Lubeck. He owns a house there and his mistress and their two children were occupying it; her name is Hedwig Potthast. One mile from the house is an airfield on which was Himmler's private plane. Squadron Leader Werner Baumbach was in charge of flying SS and Nazi leaders out of Germany throughout March and April. He travelled to Lubeck on the 12th. Himmler, Baumbach and the plane had disappeared on the morning of the 13th.

It would have taken ninety minutes to fly to Sweden. The war was already over, so your RAF was not patrolling the air route over the Baltic. Himmler's closest assistant, Walter Schellenburg, had left Flensburg for Sweden on the 8th of May. On the 21st, Himmler's private secretary, Mrs Schienke, and Schellenberg's secretary, both escaped from our house arrest in Berlin. Our agents spotted them both in Sweden on the 23rd. The British captured Heinrich Hitzinger on the afternoon of the 22nd, near Luneburg. He and his companions had been walking since the 10th, from near Flensburg. Hitzinger soon claims to be Himmler and commits suicide. He is buried before one of our war crime agents can get to Luneburg with Himmler's Berlin dental records. Your people cannot now find his grave.

Himmler had set up an elaborate escape network for SS and Gestapo officers; the routes led to Spain and South America and many tens of thousands of men and their families have taken it. Himmler had untold wealth in gold stored in Sweden and Switzerland. He had Germany's best pilot with him. He had a plane and a ninety-minute flight to safety in Sweden. Yet it is claimed that he decided to walk the eight hundred miles from Flensburg to his home in

Bavaria. To walk through your tank divisions and right passed your Headquarters in Luneburg. The General is not convinced that the man you arrested was Heinrich Himmler."

"He thinks that our Bank of England is trying to keep all of Himmler's gold?"

"That may have been a joke. The General likes pulling legs. If Himmler is alive and well in Sweden, or God knows where now, he has sufficient money to raise an army. If he were to choose the best ten-percent of his SS fanatics, he would have two hundred thousand, skilled, motivated, insane and loyal killers. He has knowledge of the very latest German weapons. Weapons that could include bombs like the ones the Americans dropped on the Japanese. Alive he poses a major threat to Russia and Communism. That is why we need to know for sure."

The party that night at the Sergeant's Mess was dissimilar to the General's party of the previous night in many ways. There were only thirty present at the beginning, of whom Terry thought he had been introduced to half already; there were only three speeches, but three times the number of toasts; Terry found this night's food bland and enjoyable. There was no wine, but more beer and the vodka was tastier. The evening's entertainment began during the first course and continued with hardly any interruption until everyone was asleep. Every attendee had to sing a song or tell a joke. Terry sang the hymn 'He Who Would Valiant Be'; his school song and the only one to which he could remember all of the words. He received a standing ovation and was extremely pleased, until he realised that every singer received a similar tribute. Jokers were inevitably booed and hissed, there evidently being a dearth of new Russian jokes. Captain Gorbachev sang tunefully and with expression in Russian - the homely lullaby bringing tears to the eyes of many hardened sergeants.

The meal was ended with competitions between the five tables. Terry was delighted to have come second in the peeing competition; his over full bladder helping to project a steady stream for a distance of ten feet, while standing still on the bar counter. Three men teams from each table competed in Russian, thigh breaking, dancing. There were the usual drinking games which Terry avoided. By early in the morning there were only fifteen sergeants standing - the remainder and the civilian Captain were asleep or had passed out. Terry was drunk enough to join in without the need of English. The oddest form of musical chairs was now performed. With three sergeant's playing music on mouth organs, the twelve remaining men were faced by eleven naked Polish waitresses; when the music stopped the sergeants had to grab one waitress and lodge his penis into any of her most available orifices. The Sergeant who failed to grab a waitress was eliminated. The majority of the Russians were strong and well practised and Terry was left with his dick in his hand at the end of the third round. The Polish waitresses appeared to enjoy the game and were angry if chosen to be removed from the file. The final successful couple continued the act until satisfied, accompanied by loud cheers and urgent pleas to allow others to join in.

By the end of the next drinking game only seven sergeants remained, but this included Terry. This group was led into the kitchen and through to a poorly lit store room in which were eight or nine terrified young German girls, each with their hands tied behind their backs and under the supervision of a number of glazed looking Polish waitresses. The Russian sergeants took one young girl each and proceeded to abuse, punch and kick them; they then raped them. Terry was presented with the thirteen-year-old girl who had been employed as a cheese taster the night before. She, like the other girls was naked, half-starved and shaking with terror. Terry stood watching the other men beating and performing with the other girls and was astounded that he had an erection. A Polish waitress came to him and took his trousers and underclothes from him. She slapped the German girl hard across her face and forced her to kneel in front of Terry and perform oral sex on him. This was Terry's first experience of oral sex and as he watched the various other couples in inventive positions he realised he was enjoying himself. The Polish waitress continued to kick the German girl in her kidneys to ensure her full co-operation.

Then Terry began to identify some even more degrading and worrying activities; a German girl was so severely kicked in the head by one of the sergeants that one of her eyes fell out of its socket and dangled on her chin. Many were being forced to drink urine and others were having various utensils poked into various parts of their bodies. Terry found his trousers and prepared to leave the room in which he could see that at least two of the German girls were now dead. As he left the room he could not help but snatch one last glimpse of the bloody orgy. One Russian sergeant with a bayonet was cutting pieces from a screaming German girl of nine or ten and was eating them. Terry knew that his stomach should be turning, but through alcohol, or fascination he found that he was still aroused by what he had seen and heard. He found the Captain asleep under one of the tables and woke him.

"Come on sir, it's time you got me back to the hotel. Things are getting a little out of hand here. Come on we have to find that wagon of yours."

Otto and the Captain were in his room when Terry awoke at eleven the next morning. They helped him wash and shave; dressed him and packed his gear. At the hotel doors Terry saw that the sedan had three women from the hospital in the back seat and squashed between them was a small figure with her head buried in her hands.

"Here are the papers for those three. I have written something on an official looking piece of paper which might get the little German girl through our checkpoint. I'll try to have you waved straight through without inspection. The German girl? Apparently you told one of the sergeants that you wanted to keep the girl you were coupling with in the storeroom. If you have changed your mind we can send her back to the brothel. No? OK we will give her to you. You really are too soft hearted with these evil Germans. I will not be riding with you as the car is full but one mile before the crossing we will halt and I will return your guns, that will also give us an opportunity to say our farewells. The early reports from the Sergeant's Mess would indicate that you did the British Army proud. Joining in is the key to acceptance by our rough sergeants and apparently they all like your attitude and smile. Well done, few have had such a glowing report. You were not sick, did not fall asleep and did not piss in a General's hat; all in all a good night for you."

"No sir, I did some daft things and my head aches badly this morning, but thank the sergeants and the waitresses for their kindness. I am supposed to be watching your tanks and equipment on the road back, but fear I may fall asleep. Would you be so kind as to write down what your forces are doing? No. Oh well it was worth asking."

As they drove Terry tried to stare at each vehicle he saw as Otto talked softly to the young German girl. After ten miles and to Terry's acute embarrassment, Otto whispered to him.

"The German girl is named Victoria and she is very grateful to you for saving her life last night. She says five of the eight young girls at the party were dead this morning, one having been eaten alive. Sergeant, I don't want to know what went on at the party, but it was very brave of you to get this girl out of there. The Belgium lady in the back must know some German and is comforting Victoria, but the two Frenchies are in their own world. I do not believe any of them will be any trouble, but just in case, the second of von Lutken's two pistols is hanging behind the dashboard on your side; it is loaded. One can never tell what these insane types might do."

Terry smiled at Otto and was amazed that what he had done during his sinful night time orgy was now being seen as heroic. His head ached and he wondered how soon it would be before the remorse he should be feeling would begin. A column of tanks was heading in their direction and their speed was down to a crawl. The car windows were open, but the heat and dust were uncomfortable. Then smells began to reach Terry's nose; they emanated from the back seat and Terry realised that at least one of his passengers was not potty trained. He was not enjoying today.

Terry shook the Captain's hand and thanked him for his help and patience.

"Sergeant Hall, it has been our pleasure to have you here with us. My orders were to show you why our troops have no respect for German women. I hope you now have some insight to the depth our revenge will need to fall, before we are satisfied. We checked on you in Altewiese before you came on this visit in order to impress you with our superior knowledge. The town is of little interest to us, although we may continue to keep an eye on it. You are aware that Inspector Muller was a Gestapo officer of course, but his boss is very dangerous."

"Yes sir, I know. I recently had harsh words with her, but apart from shooting her I do not know what to do." Terry spoke candidly with the Captain he had come to respect.

"You spoke harshly to her and you are still alive? Now that is a wondrous thing. My advice is to keep well away from her and advise your superiors that she is there in Altewiese. I would have thought her important enough to be put on trial at Nuremberg. I cannot imagine that we shall meet again so I will say good luck in whichever future you choose; read some Marx and think about Communism in a neutral light. Goodbye, Sergeant Co-operative Hall."

"Goodbye Captain Gorbachev, and thanks."

The smelly fly ridden car drove straight through the Russian checkpoint and crept slowly across the bridge, behind a queue of refugees. An inquisitive major came to the car window at the British side of the river and handed Terry a sealed envelope; he was about to ask questions and carry out a vehicle search when he caught a flavour of the car's interior scent. He stepped back and ordered the barrier to be lifted and Otto accelerated the car onto the Luneburg road. The envelope contained orders from Captain Wright; Terry was to deliver his three passengers to the military hospital in Luneburg and hand them to a Major Whittington who would have a French Medical officer with him. He then was to proceed to Bad Farven for the night, but report to Ulzener Street at eight o'clock sharp on

Friday. He would also be required to attend at that Intelligence Office on Saturday. Terry read the orders to Otto as they slowed to pass yet another group of refugees.

"What are we to do with Victoria?" asked Otto.

"She should be handed to one of the Displaced Persons Centres for processing and to get documentation, but I don't want her to report the happenings of last night to some nosey bastard. Does she have family in our Zone?"

"No Sergeant, she has no family anywhere. This kid is as lonely as you can get. If it were my decision I would hand her to Fredda for a while. They probably have a lot in common."

Terry was concerned about that remark, but assumed Otto had miss-chosen his words.

"Good idea Otto. We'll keep her with us and leave her in Bad Farven on Friday and Saturday. She is a nice looking little girl when you look at her properly."

Terry thoroughly enjoyed his Friday with Captain Wright and Colonel Musgrove in the front room of the house at 31a Ulzener Street. Musgrove was in civilian clothes and acted professionally and intelligently. He had bought with him a pretty twenty three-year-old stenographer. She had shapely legs and a plunging neckline to her flimsy summer dress. She, like Musgrove, had been flown from London the day before to manage Terry's debriefing. Terry wondered if the two had slept together last night and that the chance of illicit fornication was the real reason for their visit to Luneburg. Terry replied effortlessly to the barrage of questions and was genuinely amazed at the details he could recall. He volunteered no trivialities regarding his own experiences with a General's hat, pot full of shit, or a thirteen-year-old German girl, but most other things he vomited out faster than the stenographer could type.

At one point Captain Wright, who was proving to be an embarrassment with silly, pointless questions and comments, asked Terry about Captain Gorbachev.

"That certainly is not his name of course. I assume he asked you who your controlling intelligence officer was. And, of course when you told him it was me, he immediately recognised my name, didn't he?"

"Oh yes sir, he did," answered Terry, "but he wasn't very complimentary about you sir, so I'll skip that bit."

"No, no you must not," insisted Wright. "You go ahead and tell us what he said about me and my important work here."

"He said that you were not the most hardworking of our intelligence community. If you were on the case, then our bosses didn't think it was very important. He said you play golf for money and lie about your handicap. You say it is sixteen and in fact it is six. He said you keep telling people that you have played golf with Monty, but you only were in a following four-some."

The Colonel sniggered at this comment and had obviously heard of Wright's golf heroics. Terry went on.

"Captain Gorbachev was showing off to me I think, because he also said you don't like to sing the words to 'Colonel Bogey'. "

"Why," asked the Colonel, "would Gorbachev have the impression that Captain Wright did not like that song?"

"He said sir, that Captain Wright had a normal sized left testicle, but that his right one was very small."

The stenographer dropped her typing machine and began to giggle uncontrollably. Wright had a fuming red face and spluttered, "Damned cheek of the fellow".

"We must run a security inspection on our medical filing," the Colonel said. "We all may be hiding some weird secrets in there. The golf-scoring thing is hard to fathom. Captain you must have dropped a right bollock and told someone. Oh, I am sorry dear chap, an unfortunate choice of words there. Have you recovered, Susan, my dear?"

As Terry had expected, the Colonel showed particular interest in any mention of Heinrich Himmler. The Captain kept saying that they were in the very room that Himmler had died and wasn't that a coincidence. The Colonel ignored him and simply asked Terry to repeat again exactly what Gorbachev had said. He also showed great interest in Schwerin and the district around it saying that he had once spent a happy holiday in the German Lake District. His three-member audience met the details of the horror museum and Terry's meetings with victims with gloomy silence. Terry spent an hour flipping through the picture books and pointed to tanks, vehicles and insignia he had seen.

At six-thirty that evening the Colonel said they were pleased with Terry's speed of recall and the volume of information he had gathered would take some days to evaluate. He suggested to the Captain that there would be little value in the Sergeant coming back the next day and the Captain readily agreed. As the young lady gleefully packed her typing machine into a leather case, the Colonel warned Terry to tell no one of his adventure, except in the sketchiest of ways. He then took Terry by the shoulder and walked outside with him alone.

"You got drunk twice with them. Did you do anything illegal with girls or boys or animals by any chance?"

"No sir, certainly not, sir," protested Terry.

"You said there were flashes of light in one of your drunken dreams. They may have taken photographs of you in compromising positions while you were unconscious. Be aware that if they ever try to blackmail you, you should immediately contact our office in London. We may be able to turn their blackmail to our advantage. You mentioned the infamous woman in Altewiese that Gorbachev warned you about. You say her name is Ingrid Schrader, although that name is certainly of no use to us. Could you get a photograph of her and send it to me?"

CHAPTER NINE

THE BANK MANAGER

Terry had found his Saturday night with Don and his two lady companions less than entertaining. Don had proved to have a limited range of conversation and none of it was of great interest to Terry. The young ladies spoke English poorly and had chatted to each other in a high pitched, irritating drone. One of the girls had grudgingly agreed to sleep with Terry in his guesthouse bedroom but had been unimpressed with the décor or bedding; she had slept soundly and did not wake when Terry prepared to leave for his Sunday morning breakfast.

The entertainment provided by the sisters Hoffman had been disappointing too, consisting of a two-piece band and three female singers. The German songs enlivened the two young lady companions, but proved boring to Terry. The three singers were extreme in their differences - a thin plain teenager with a deep voice and tight black dress stood next to a tall and glamorous, blond wigged, rouged cheeked and scarlet-lipped soprano. The third member of the trio was obese to the extent of appearing perfectly spherical in her flowing ball gown which contained enough material to curtain a small hotel; she sang in a pitch, so high that Terry felt obliged to protect his wineglass by holding it firmly. The night of German cabaret songs was bought to a less than rousing finale by each lady removing her dress to display their flat manly chests and bulging manly g-strings. Even then Terry was not quite convinced of the fat man's masculinity, having seen women in the 'Parade' magazine with smaller breasts and larger pubic bulges.

At breakfast Terry ate as Don recounted the details of the conquest he had made in bed with his lady friend. At an interlude in Don's saga, Terry managed to get a word in.

"Don when Wilkes leaves in December either you or I should move to Bachwald. Would you like to try your ardour on the young ladies of a different town?"

"Yes I definitely would. To be honest I'm bored with Brick and the people are so passive and civilised that I don't think we need anyone stationed there anyway. What are you considering you will do when you take over?"

"If I stay right here? You and Arthur control things from Bachwald and John Ballantine holds on in Bad Farven. I will insist we get a new set of radiotelephones for each of us. Either you or Arthur patrol the villages to the north and south of Bachwald during the week and on every-other Friday I'll drive to Hamburg visiting each of you en route. I may return on the Sunday or Monday morning, but either way we would be able to meet again on that return trip. I don't know where our civilian masters will choose to billet but would guess it would be Hamburg.

We can keep our little business ventures running for as long as possible, but shouldn't try to expand. Greed could prove our undoing. We'll continue to buy cheese and planks but only transport them to our customers using the ARSE or SHIT lorries. In Hamburg I'll make sure we are paid in the correct type of currency and divide the profits between the four of us. I'll also buy or obtain the luxuries we need for the factories or ourselves. I would like to have Wilkes arrange for a regular supply of fuel for the generators before he leaves. He says he has found the chemicals we need for the fertiliser factory in Altewiese but we haven't received any of them yet. Would you be happy with that arrangement and with being with Arthur?" Don beamed a smile.

"Terry, I would be more than happy to move and agree we should take our reasonable profit and not take risks. These girls are boring and there is nothing else for me to do. I even find sex is boring, that's how fed up I am."

"It's your turn next month to provide the accommodation and food and wine. What if I bring the sexual partners?" Terry said haltingly. " Maybe it's time you experimented a bit?"

"That sounds great to me," Don was again happy. "But no men please. Those singers last night made sheep look more attractive."

The following week Terry agreed to be photographed. He posed on the steps of various buildings around the square carrying his Tommy gun in such a way that one set of his three stripes always faced the camera. At the town hall he insisted on a group photograph with the town officials being joined by the members of the now expanded police constabulary. At the Displaced Persons Centre and Hospital he again insisted on being joined by all of the staff. He placed Paula to his right and Ingrid to his left. He insisted that a second photograph be taken after he noticed that Ingrid had looked down to her feet at the crucial moment during the first pose. Seven days later Ralf had delivered a copy of all of the photographs to Terry. The unfocused and badly developed ones were discarded and the rest were distributed as follows:

- Ten of Terry alone, to his kit bag for delivery to his parents in Stone when on leave.

- One of Terry alone, to an envelope for posting this week to his parents with his weekly letter.
- The group photographs to the town hall archives, where they still remain.
- A DP Centre photograph to Paula.
- The re-taken photograph of the DP group to an envelope to be given to Sergeant Wilkes, for posting to a 'Mr Musgrove' in London.

Paula was not pleased with the Centre's photograph, not only was Ingrid looking at the floor, but she herself had been brushing her hair back and her arm had obscured her face.

Terry ate at least three lunches each week with Paula and never tired of her stories of the recoveries from illness or trauma of individual refugees, of her childhood and life; she loved showing him photographs of herself while at University and of her husband in smart SS uniforms. Occasionally she would subject him to motherly scolding for his waywardness with women. She felt he should have treated Fredda better; she questioned the wisdom of his private meetings in his 'study' with Victoria, especially as in her innocence she told her roommate, Fredda, many of the details. His bedding for one night only of some of the DPs might be seen as selfishness and lay himself open to disease. She wanted him to find a nice German girl, like Fredda, as a full time companion.

The rebukes were delivered kindly and often disguised and referred to obliquely. Terry, without anger, would defend himself, by saying that Victoria had experienced more of life in her thirteen years than many fifty-four year olds; that Fredda longed only for her dead husband; and that his masculine desires had to be sated and his treatment of the DPs was always gentle and rewarded. He agreed under Paula's pressure to have lunch with Fredda soon and to check again on his feelings for her. He rarely spoke to Paula of his fear of Ingrid and Kurt but when he did she would say that he could call on her for help and protection whenever he needed it.

"The office can quickly be returned to a fortress bedroom," she would say.

Paula organised a surprise party for Terry on the night following the arrival in Altewiese of the five hundredth displaced person; a small orchestra had been assembled from the refugees already absorbed into the town and others danced or sang for Terry. Paula had even arranged that he stay the night at Hoffmann's guesthouse and had installed Victoria in his bedroom for the night. Paula appeared totally happy with her work at the Centre and when Terry was there during each weekday morning she would conduct all of his translating.

One cold and wet weekend in early November Terry and Wilkes were in the sedan, with Otto driving. They were returning from Hamburg where they had had meetings with Acting Lieutenant Colonel Connolly, three wholesalers, a Medical Officer at the main military hospital and a brothel Madame, but not all at the same time. They were heading towards Luneburg.

"Connolly is getting nervy," said Wilkes. "Until he's gone you'd better keep the trading down to a minimum. I thought he might have handed the lorry scam to you, but the shit has closed that deal already. You have now met all six of the wholesalers through whom I buy and sell things. Connolly calls them black marketers as though that's a bad thing to be. You'll have noticed how important cigarettes have become - not for smoking, but as currency. I said that would happen didn't I? Unfortunately we only have one friendly soul in the NAAFI stores and when he goes in March you'll find it difficult to obtain the extra fags you'll need. We must have half a million marks in paper money in the boot of this car but its value is getting less by the day. You got a good idea of the value of a fag didn't you. Hamburg is bloody frightening isn't it? That old girl in the brothel last night said she could arrange the death of anyone in the city for ten fags and, do you know what, I believe her. What gets me is the crap we hear about seven hundred thousand German troops still working for us; did you see any evidence of them in that hellhole of a city? No, bloody right we didn't. The place stinks; there are piles of shit everywhere. The city dwellers are living in caves dug out of the rubble like in the Stone Age. The price we get for the cheese is three times what it was in July but they're running short of the cash to buy it. We had to take those two paintings you liked or we could have run into a problem with the wholesaler in Lubeck Street. Don't give that shit any more credit. All they keep offering us is posh French furniture; I don't give a toss how many cans Louis had, we can't carry a dining table in our kit bags when we go home.

On the other hand when it comes to buying things, we have to pay stupidly high prices. Those medicines were very expensive and the champagne Don ordered is a crazy price now. We're still getting our extra fuel for the lorries from the military dump. If you could get your hands on some more you'd get a fancy painting for each gallon from the civilians. There's still no coal in the city and it's freezing at night now. I reckon there'll be a lot of dead Germans by spring, what with the lack of food and warm shelter. Monty will have to find a way of hiding the news from everyone. You still getting the films and newsreels for your cinema? Good. I have a cinema opening in Bachwald at the end of the month. You're still adamant on staying in Altewiese after I'm in my beloved Nottingham, aren't you? Well it's your choice, but a change is as good as a rest, they say. Better the devils you know, I suppose. That hospital visit was a bit odd; what was it all about? No don't tell me, I don't want to know about another one of your women. You still fucking the refugees as they arrive? No, thank God for that. You will be in your mother's arms in two weeks - don't give her some horrible disease.

You never heard anymore about your trip to the Russian Zone did you? Strange that, I would have thought the pissed on General would have sent you a post card. Someone in Altewiese gave them chapter and verse on you and we've still not found out who. Connolly gave you your travel documents for your leave and a sealed envelope; what was in it? You have to visit an officer in London before you come back here. Well if you're not worried about it, I won't be. Remember Saturday 8th December, we are having a surprise leaving party for me at the cuckoo hotel in Bad Farven but you and Don are barred from bringing any fanny with you. And, I don't want any of the Hoffman Sisters' idea of entertainment. A nice meal and a few beers are what I would like to be surprised by. That fertiliser factory hasn't made anything yet; you should find out why. They received a big loan from the bank didn't they? I wonder how that bank will operate when the people loose their faith in hard currency; a tobacco kiosk would be more useful. The bank manager arrived from a branch in Sweden five weeks ago and you still haven't met him. That's odd because if I were him I would definitely have tried to meet you. Your reputation as being a bloody hard bastard with German officialdom should have scared him. He offered to buy our transport company from Mr Reck, which was also odd. I like the ARSE bus service, Terry. Daily to Luneburg station, stopping at each of our villages was neat, but the one to Hanover has created a lot of interest and trade.

The number of DPs we are to receive in December is still too many. We hardly have the space and food for what we've got already, let alone another one hundred and twenty. You got another twelve prisoners of war returned to you again last week - all youngsters from the Hitler Youth Regiments. The Meyer's son was among them, I noticed. Has he given any trouble, what with you being the prime suspect in his parent's sudden disappearance? No, good, but take care. Last time I stayed at the big house with you I saw that the cellars were full of food and stuff. You had plenty of fruit from your orchard packed up neatly and cheese and salted meat, well done, I think the food shortages this winter will be critical. You may need to share some of your stuff with the other lads before very long. I laughed at your cowboys and indians idea when you first told me about it, but you were absolutely right. Von

Lutken's three fancy riding horses being used by the police to watch over the cattle and pigs will be very necessary when starvation really strikes this country. Using policewomen to ride the horses was colourful. No, I still can't bring myself to recommend to you that you issue shotguns to three or four of your constabulary. I know the arguments for doing so, but it's too soon and too dangerous. By chance you have one of the strongest deterrents against city folk stealing from Altewiese - Inspector Evil Bugger Muller and his SS and Gestapo escape network. That Muller even has Hardaker shaking.

You still convinced that Mrs Schrader is the mastermind behind the whole thing? You are keeping away from her and her husband aren't you? Good. I have said this before to you, but I'll say it again, I like the set up you have at the big house. Otto and that family are unbelievably loyal to you. That little one eyed runt Stephan attacked Hardaker with the fire bell the last time we stopped at the house to drop off some personal items for you. The young woman thinks the sun shines out of your arse; I've seen the way she looks at you. So she's ugly - with the lights out she'll feel like any other woman and you'd be a damn sight safer. Yes, I know you can have any woman you want, so why not choose the pretty ones. Don't shout at me, I know you can have the best food and drink and women, but Terry slow down a bit. I know you are the Chief of Police, Judge, jury, tax collector, Mayor and unopposed ruler of Altewiese, I'm just saying take it easy, have a wank sometimes instead of raping some young lady. Stop shouting at me, I'm sorry, I didn't mean to say 'rape', I meant 'fuck'. It is none of my business that's correct. No, I'm not your Dad, which reminds me, I must chase my friend at the airfield and get you on a transport plane to the Midlands in ten days time."

Early on the following Saturday morning Terry stood by the driver's door of the car talking to Otto. The car was parked at the foot of the steps to the big house and the gravel and frost crunched below Terry's shiny black boots.

"I will repeat my orders again," he said deliberately and slowly. "You have our maintenance man Igor with you to help if you have any problems on the return journey and I have given you documents to clear all of you through any roadside checks. Show them to me. That's good. So you drive from here directly to the doctor in Hamburg we met the other day. He is expecting you and will have everything ready. You have lots of blankets and pillows on the back seat. You have food on board, but eat it before you get to the doctor. Return to exactly this spot as quickly as you can. I would hope you were back by three o'clock this afternoon. When you get here come alone to the study and I will either give you instructions or come down to the car myself. I am not sure which yet. Tell me again that you have cleaned and loaded the pistol and that it is in its straps under the dashboard. Good. You have the marks to give to the doctor if he delivers his side of the bargain. I am sure that is everything, so drive carefully and good luck Otto."

At twelve-thirty that Saturday morning an old car driven by one of Muller's latest recruits pulled up at the steps in front of the big house. Paula and Fredda got out and were warmly greeted by Terry. The three had lunch together in his study. A log fire burned brightly in the hearth and the room was warm and cosy. Olga and Lara served the food; Terry poured the drinks, sparingly. With Paula translating they talked of the work at the DP Centre and of Fredda's duties on the top floor. She currently had her bedroom to herself as the hospital was only half full. As they began to eat the cheese course Terry left the table and went to a writing desk; he returned with a number of small packages.

"The things I want to say to Fredda are personal and private and my lack of German words make everything so difficult. Please Paula, help me tell her my feelings. I have here some small gifts for you both as thanks for joining me at lunch today. The silk stocking may keep you a little warmer this winter. From the first time I saw Fredda I have thought of her as the most beautiful woman I have ever seen. My guts ached to hold her. I am truly in love with her. Tell her these things now. If she would agree to return here to the house and be with me I would do everything in my power to make her happy. I would learn to speak German properly. I would treat her with the greatest respect. I would keep myself only for her. I want to wake up in the mornings with that beauty in my arms and to look at her forever."

Paula and Fredda talked quietly for a while. Then Paula spoke.

"Fredda thanks you for the stockings and is extremely touched by the thought that you are in love with her. She wants you to know that before he disappeared, Doctor Dressler confirmed to her that she would be unable to have children. You may not think this is important today, but in the future you may find that you would regret having no family. Fredda has this regret already and she feels like she is only half a woman. Her love for her husband is total. If he were confirmed as dead then in time that love may subside, but until then she would be unable to love you. She likes you and has respect for you and that is why she cannot lie now, despite the consequences. You have the power to force her to live with you and to sleep with her. If that is what you want she will do it. She cannot love you for her heart is with her husband Ludwig."

Terry, full of sadness asked Paula to speak for him again.

"If I could obtain conclusive proof of her husband's death, would she live with me of her own free will? Would she try and see if she could learn to love me for what I am?"

"No Terry she does not want to live with you. You were correct. She will sleep with you and do as you command because you have the Tommy gun. She only wants to be with Ludwig, wherever he is. I am sorry but if you want me to stay with you tonight, I would be happy to do so. We could talk things over and perhaps think about a different future for you."

Terry heard the crunch of gravel under car tyres and walked to the window to look down on Otto leaving the Mercedes sedan. He went to Fredda and kissed her softly on the cheek.

"You are my true friend and I thank you," he said to Paula, "but I think I would prefer to spend this weekend alone. Tell Fredda that I will always love and want her. She is my idea of a perfect woman."

Otto entered the room.

"Everything was as planned. What do you want me to do sir?" Terry stared at him for a moment.

"Otto these two charming ladies would like you to drive them back to the Centre. If you would lead Fredda to the car, I will give my arm to Mrs Rozen-Kranz and follow you."

The ladies retrieved their coats and handbags and with shy smiles and thanks to Olga for her cooking, walked from the house. Otto opened the rear passenger door for Fredda. She stood quite still and then let out a trembling whimper. Terry and Paula, close behind her, could see a bundle wrapped in blankets lying on the rear seat. Propped on a large white pillow in the far corner of the seat was a smiling face. His arms were outstretched towards Fredda. As she fell into the car and held her husband she was crying bitterly. From the shape of the blankets it was clear that Ludwig had no legs and on the floor of the car was a glass bottle of golden liquid with a thin rubber tube running under the blankets. Otto had begun to cry. Paula turned to Terry.

"Where did you find him?"

"I asked a Russian General to look for him. I received a message three weeks ago via their agency in Luneburg saying that what was left of Private Ludwig Marnitz-Schule had been handed to the Americans at the end of May. The Russians only shoot wounded soldiers who might one day recover. I used our people to trace him and get him transferred to a clinic in Hamburg. He's been there for two weeks. I paid a doctor to do the best they could for him, but he's in a mess. He stepped on a land mine and it blew both of his legs off. They have repaired his back passage, but he has no genitalia. They have inserted a tube into his bladder. Ironic isn't it, he cannot make babies and Fredda cannot produce babies. Perhaps the two half people can create one happiness. Paula I would suggest you put him in Fredda's room at the hospital; he will always need lots of care and treatment. He is not expected to live to see next summer."

"Terry," Paula asked, "if Fredda had agreed to stay with you and learn to love you, what would you have done with Ludwig?"

"I'm not sure. I really am not sure."

Ten days later Terry walked into his parent's greengrocer's shop on the high street of the small town of Stone in Staffordshire. He was wearing a heavy military overcoat over his uniform for the late November day was cold and windy. He had a kit bag slung over his shoulder and a large brown suitcase in his gloved hand. His mother was serving a customer and glanced up from wrapping half a cabbage in newspaper to say, "I won't be a minute sir." She looked up again only when she heard his voice.

"Hello mum, do you want me to give you a hand?"

She threw the cabbage at the customer and flung herself into the out-stretched arms of her son.

"Sidney, Sidney come out here and look what we have," she called excitedly while she locked the shop door and turned the 'open' sign to 'closed'.

"Welcome home son," his father blurted as he hurried from the rear stock room and kissed Terry affectionately. They went to the kitchen and brewed tea while he told them of his town in Germany; he gave them photographs and explained what the buildings were. He showed them his stripes and they said how amazed they were at how much weight he had put on and how he looked so well. After an hour his father said he had better re-open the shop or people would think they had a death in the family. His mother touched his stripes and asked him why he hadn't found a nice girl friend, but that she was pleased he hadn't. She said how proud the family was that he had received promotion so quickly and of how important his job must be. She held him tight and then said that she must get something nice for their tea. She had saved some ration coupons and would see if the butcher had anything left. She put on her coat and hurried out of the shop.

Terry went to his room and found it full of clothes he didn't recognise. He returned to the shop.

"Whose are the clothes in my room Dad?"

"Oh they belong to the lodger, Alfred. He's a teacher and is trying to find somewhere to buy. He stays here during the week. We thought you wouldn't be back until Saturday, what with the bad weather in the Channel and the unreliable trains and things. You won't mind kipping on the sofa for a couple of nights will you? What with all the hardships you have in Germany, it will still be more comfortable. Alfred is paying us five shillings a week in advance."

"No that's OK Dad. The sofa will be just fine. I managed to find an aeroplane to bring me from Hamburg to Birmingham yesterday afternoon and I caught the train to Stoke station today. I hitched a lift on a Michelin lorry as it was coming out of the factory gate."

"How long are you staying? We told Alfred you'd be needing the room all of next week so he's got a place at the Roebuck."

"I have two weeks leave, like I said in my letters."

"Oh, I don't know if the Roebuck can put him up for two weeks," his father said frowning.

"No, don't worry, I was planning to spend a few days in London. See a show or something."

Terry, his mother and father and the lodger, Alfred, attended the evening meal. By the time they had finished their onion soup the conversation had switched from Germany and its problems to local education and trade unionism. Terry and Alfred walked to the local pub at eight o'clock and over two pints of Ind Coop mild chatted about things that were of absolutely no interest to Terry. A young woman came into the half full bar looking for her errant grandfather. She recognised Terry and complimented him on his uniform and stripes. He had dated her a year before and asked her now if she would like to go to the pictures with him. She declined, saying her husband would be angry if she did.

The following day Terry caught the bus to Newcastle-under-Lyme and visited two jewellery shops. At one he sold the pearl necklace and three diamond rings and at the other four gold watches. The transactions were completed without show of suspicion or receipts.

On that Friday evening, the tea table was attended by Uncle Fred and Aunt May who were proud of their nephew's stripes, but showed no interest in Germany or Altewiese. On Saturday night Terry and his parents dined with Uncle Tom and Aunty Hilda. Uncle Tom was proud of his own war record on the Somme and did not like Germans. Everyone agreed that the new season would be good for Stoke as Stanley Matthews had been demobbed from the Royal Airforce. On Monday Alfred joined their evening meal as he was staying on a room only basis at the Roebuck. He went to fetch Granny Hall from her cottage in Barleston, which everyone agreed was a very nice thing to do. Granny did not like talk about the war so Germany was not mentioned. On Tuesday evening they visited Aunty Sheila and Alfred kept her in fits of laughter with his stories of school children's pranks.

"Has there been much in the papers about the atrocities and concentration camps?" Terry asked his Dad. The room was stunned into silence and Terry took the opportunity to ask, "anything about the Russians mutilating and raping the German womenfolk?"

"That's quite enough of that sort of talk, our Terry," scolded his father, "not with your mother and Sheila in the room."

On the Wednesday morning Terry walked in civilian clothes west out of Stone along a narrow lane. He saw the empty fields but knew the cows were already in their wintering barns. Two cyclists passed him and said 'good morning' and rode on singing. He reached a village before midday and saw a school yard full of shouting skipping children. There was a pub next to the school and he went into the empty bar.

"A pint of bitter please," he asked the barman who was busily polishing the bar counter.

"Certainly squire," said the barman, "walked far have we?"

"From my home in Altewiese," Terry said absentmindedly.

"That's a dead hole if ever I saw one," the barman said. Terry was stunned for a moment and as a foaming tankard was placed in front of him, the barman added, "I was there before the war. Visited a fertiliser factory on behalf of the Red Cross. The conditions at the factory were pretty diabolical, but nothing compared to the camp near Bergen. What's it like now?"

Terry spent the next three hours talking to the barman, interrupted rarely by customers. They talked mostly about the total disinterest shown by everyone at home; about the plight of people overseas and about the shortness of the concentration level of anyone forced to listen to a traveller's tale.

"I went to many places with the Red Cross and when I got back my family and friends were polite and listened to what I said but I could see they were bored. Eventually I would rehearse a two-minute resume of my travels and repeat it, and then I would ask the listener how had their day been - that made me feel happy. From what you've told me of Altewiese and your job there, I would strongly suggest that you would not be happy coming back to a greengrocery after you've done your time. Me I kept on travelling - finding pub jobs at the seaside in summer and inland in winter. This place is quiet and that makes a change. *Labour in Vain* the pub is called and that is a very apt description of my way of living."

Terry walked smartly back to Stone. He had drunk four pints but felt clear headed and confident. That night they all sat at the dining table with the next door neighbours, Mr and Mrs Smith, and after showing them his photographs and giving them a two minute lecture on Germany's economic problems Terry announced "I'm going to London tomorrow so Alfred, you can have your room back. I'll be back in Germany next week and may not be back in time for the start of the next football season, so can you post me the match reports from the Evening Sentinel?"

Before the shop was open the next morning, Terry gave his mother a long and loving hug, a technique she knew he had learned from her and as she relaxed she felt warm and happy. He gave her fifty pounds in one pound notes and said he had collected some back pay and she must spend it on herself. He gave his father a gold wristwatch and remembered that only nine months before his father had given him a Woolworth's watch as he had left for the training camp. His father remembered that too and was sad and disappointed. He had meant to leave a note for Alfred tucked under his pillow but in the end found that he could not spell the word 'cuckoo'.

In London he chose a small hotel near Victoria Station that accepted young sergeants and did not charge extra for the use of a second blanket. On his first morning in the capital he visited Hatton Garden. There he easily found a jeweller happy to buy six loose diamonds and one large ruby. Terry was shocked to find that the ruby was worth six months pay. For two days, dressed in civilian clothes, he spent his time visiting art dealers in the middle of London. He was most fascinated by those on the grand main streets. He studied prices. Most of the big museums were still not open but some galleries at the Tate had been restocked and he spent a lot of time there. He thoroughly enjoyed his time with the art dealers; a few were snobby, but interesting; all of them were friendly and helpful. By that weekend he had a good idea of the value of the Picasso he had brought with him. On Monday he retraced his visits to the art dealers and asked them what they would pay him for it. There were two reactions to the painting - the most common one being, 'where did you steal it from and I'll give you ten pounds for it'. The other reaction was, 'that's very nice and is worth fifty pounds, but as you collected it for free in Europe, I'll give you ten pounds for it'. One shop owner in Bond Street threatened to call the police. He approached a middle aged Jewish dealer in an office on a lane off Bond Street.

"What do you think it's worth young man?" he said.

"I believe you could sell it at retail for ninety-nine pounds sir. Trade would be eighty pounds. You will offer me ten, because you think I stole it." The man smiled.

"Ninety-nine pounds would be the retail ticket price, that's correct. Only rich fools pay retail so it would sell for eight-five. I could sell it to a posh shop for sixty-five. I should pay you forty for it, but I will give you fifty pounds. I will tell you why I will pay you fifty for it - because I want you to bring me more paintings like this one. The painting was stolen once, that is likely. But the previous owner is now ash in some Polish field, so will not call the police. You traded your cigarette ration for it, so that makes you its legitimate owner. May I give you this book which is a study in modern art since 1900. Any artist mentioned in this book painted pictures I would like to buy. Do you think you could find some for me?"

"Yes sir, I think I could. I return to my posting in Germany in a few days and will endeavour to trade my cigarette ration for some more paintings. Thank you for the book. I will open a bank account with the fifty pounds. Please call me Paul."

Terry had dinner alone that night at the Savoy Grill and watched avidly the antics of the rich and titled as they displayed their wealth and had fun doing so. The next morning he called at the Mayfair address given to him by Colonel Musgrove and was shown to a seat in a waiting room not unlike that found at a dentist. The Colonel soon ushered him into a brightly lit private office and Terry sat in a high backed leather chair. Terry became nervous and tense.

"Thank you for coming to visit me today Sergeant Hall. I am very pleased that you decided to wear ordinary tatty civilian clothes, most inconspicuous."

"These are my best clothes sir," protested Terry shyly.

"Yes, yes indeed they are. I will only take a few minutes of your time for I'm sure you will want to get down to the girlie clubs in Soho. I am told there is a terrific comedian at the Windmill Theatre this week and the lady dancers do not wear a stitch. Most enjoyable, I'm sure. The photograph you sent me proved interesting for all the wrong reasons, where is it now? Here, look at the woman to your right - your note called her Ingrid Schrader. No one in this service has the slightest idea who she is. I have also shown it to some of our war crimes boys and they don't know of her either. But, and this is a big but, they did recognise the lady on your left. She is attempting to look away, but there is enough of her for them to be fairly sure of who she is. She is an SS Major from one of the worst concentration camps."

Terry stared at the shadowed face of Paula Rozen-Kranz and his stomach turned and cramped.

"The war crimes chappies would be happy to receive her at one of their centres, although she was not important enough to send a team to arrest her in person. To me that would mean that it is up to you what you do about her. Rumour has it that you are quite useful with a pistol; that would save us all a lot of time and trouble wouldn't it?"

"Are you sure that she was an SS officer sir?" Terry pleaded.

"My dear chap, one cannot be certain of anything these days, but the balance of probability would lie with her being a murderer and torturer. Captain Wright had made a note in the file about an Inspector Muller that you were interested in. I'm afraid our friend with the small testicle did nothing about your request and without a photograph I can't really help you."

Terry stared at the group photograph and saw a shadowy image of Muller standing to the rear, but he said nothing. The Colonel continued.

"In your file here is a copy of a letter sent by Field Marshal Montgomery to General Novgorod thanking him for the kind hospitality he showed to you during your trip to Schwerin. At the time you were over there things were getting a bit tense between the Allies. I can tell you now that we thought Uncle Joe might try to move on to Paris or even here to London. Yes, really, it was that serious. The bombs we dropped on the Japanese have quietened him down though. Ten bombs like those and we could do more damage to Mother Russia than the Germans did in two years with three million troops. So you go on back to Luneburg, or wherever it is you are and rest assured that the nasty Russian General will not be knocking on your door telling you stories about Captain Wright's genitalia. You look a little worried, are you all right?"

"Yes sir, it's nothing sir. Mrs Rozen-Kranz has been very kind to me and the news about her is a bit of a shock."

"Oh, don't concern yourself with that. If she's turned into a saint, then you just go and worship her. I am sure no action will be taken against her now. A lot of these killers are working for us. It is sad to say, but there were too many of them involved in the atrocities for us to cope with. The big cheeses are at the trials at Nuremberg and their hanging will have to stand in for the punishment of all the guilty. Sergeant you go back to your post and have a good think about it and then decide what you must do."

That night Terry attended the second show at the Windmill Theatre. It was fully booked except for a stage-side box for four. He paid for the box and watched the show alone. He had ordered a bottle of champagne and officers and their ladies sitting in other boxes toasted him from a distance. His opulence was attracting their attention. He was enjoying having their attention. He was glad he was not in his sergeant's uniform. The good jokes and fine array of nipples, mixed with the ordinary champagne, managed to relax the anger he had built against his friend Paula Rozen-Kranz.

Terry's journey back to Altewiese was difficult and took three days. He booked a ticket to Paris Gare St Lazaire and caught the train from Victoria Station early on Tuesday morning. It ran to Newhaven where a pitching and rolling ferry crossed the English Channel to the fishing port of Dieppe. He stepped from the ferry directly onto the Dieppe-Paris train. An expensive taxi ride across the French Capital to the Gare Du Nord was followed by a freezing overnight train journey to Brussels. From Brussels he took a slow train to Hamburg. Here he visited Colonel Connolly who telephoned Wilkes with a request for a car to be sent to collect Terry from the Hotel Astrid early the next morning. While in Hamburg Terry took the opportunity to visit two of the wholesalers that were having difficulty in finding gold watch currency. Terry showed them his book of twentieth century art and asked them to find paintings by the artists listed. He restricted the maximum size of canvas to that of his large brown suitcase. He refused a night of entertainment and retired to bed early.

At eight the next morning he was awoken by a jovial Otto. After a leisurely breakfast they drove in the sedan through the cold, wet and depressing city.

"Otto, have you any news for me?" Terry asked, once they were over the river bridges. "What has been happening while I was in England?"

"Sir," Otto shouted over his shoulder to Terry in the rear seat, "I have good news, bad news and a mystery for you. First the good news, the Russian agent in Luneburg who is my contact told me that they have released my uncle and his wife from prison. Yes sir, that is very good news. The agent said that I was no longer of any use to Russian intelligence and I was not to make contact with him again. He said they would kill me if I reported my spy work to the British authorities and in any case the British would shoot me as a spy. Without my family in their prison they cannot continue to blackmail me into helping them. My uncle and his wife will try to reach Altewiese, but that may take months."

"That is good news Otto. If they no longer want you to spy for them, it must mean that they have lost interest in Altewiese and me. They must have bigger things to spy on; the A Bomb I suppose. What will be disappointing though is that we will no longer have fun composing your reports to them. I enjoyed trying to write the most boring drivel possible. The one we sent them about the fall in milk production caused by finding three cows with five nipples was one of our best."

Otto chuckled and nodded in agreement.

"Or how about on the last morning of our visit to Schwerin when we agreed that you would tell Captain Gorbachev it was me who'd pissed in the General's hat. That was great. When he told you that he didn't like the colonel who had taken the blame, so wouldn't report my involvement, I knew we had a possible ally set up. I still think you chickened out by telling them about the mole on my chest. I would really have liked the Captain to have asked to see the scar on my right buttock..... So what's the bad news?"

"Ha, Sergeant Hall we may have a security problem. On the day you left, a friend of the Meyer family said that the recently returned son had disappeared just like his parents had some weeks before. A rumour started that you were involved again. Last Sunday young Mr Kahler the builder and Franz Hasch, the old mayor's son, did not attend church. That was unusual and Pastor Lehmann was causing a big fuss on Monday. Everyone realised that you could not be blamed this time. I went to see Inspector Muller and told him that I was very concerned about the three young men. If they were hiding and preparing to take violent action against you we must increase our security at the big house. I am sorry to report that Muller showed very little interest in my concern. He did say something odd, which I may have misunderstood. He said he knew that the three men had gone into hiding, but that from the field where they were, they would never hurt anyone ever again. You must speak to Muller and ask him what he meant."

"Yes Otto I'll do that, but I feel that there will be no urgency needed. The Inspector is a very dangerous man."

"Now I will tell you of the mystery Sergeant. Yesterday afternoon a policeman from Bachwald motorcycled to our police station with the message that you were in Hamburg. Muller telephoned me with the instructions to be on the road by five o'clock this morning. It was dark and raining as I left the house and as I reached the gate to the main road a man jumped out from the hedge and stopped me. I reached for the pistol, because I was so frightened. It was Mr Schrader dressed in a green military overcoat. I didn't recognise him until he spoke to me. He said that he and Mrs Schrader wanted to have a meeting with you tonight. I said you would be too tired after the journey from England. He was very insistent. He said the meeting could be in the car or at the house and would take one hour. I said that I would ask you, but could not promise anything. He said it was a matter of great importance to your safety sir. He said that he and his wife would be waiting in the shadows of the Creamery gates at eight o'clock tonight. He would be disappointed if I did not collect them or bring you to talk to them. I was impressed with Mr Schrader, for he spoke to me in faultless Polish."

"Then you must collect them at eight o'clock and bring them to the study."

"But sir, Ingrid Schrader is a very bad woman. She is dangerous. Shall I carry your Tommy gun and sit in the study with you?"

"No Otto that will not be necessary. You can sit in the corridor with the Tommy gun if you wish, but I no longer fear Ingrid. We can halt at Bad Farven for tea with Christine soon and later have a sandwich with Sergeant Wilkes. I will rest in bed this afternoon and be ready to listen closely to the Schrader's. How are Mrs Rozen-Kranz and Fredda?"

Otto glanced in his rear view mirror perched on the dashboard.

"I have not seen Mrs Rozen-Kranz for two weeks. I heard she was involved in discussions at the fertiliser factory and with the bank manager. Something to do with employing DPs, I was told. She spends a lot of time at the bank now. Fredda and Ludwig Marnitz-Schule are very happy. Everyone in town is pleased for them and many people appreciate your kindness to them. I went to visit him for he was very friendly during our trip from the hospital in Hamburg. He is grateful to you. I am sure that Fredda has not told him that you slept with her. In my opinion he will not live for more than a year; he is suffering great pain from his legs that are not there and is seriously ill inside too."

"Have you seen the bank manager?" Terry asked.

"No sir and few people have met him. The confusion is that there is a bank clerk at the bank counter who calls himself the Manager. The big boss man who no one meets is called the Director. You should meet him I think."

"Indeed I will Otto. Tomorrow would seem soon enough though."

Terry reported to Wilkes and over a hastily eaten lunch they discussed trading and the art book. Wilkes was excited about his demob. Hardaker was too.

"Terry I'll be leaving on the 22nd so you'd better find me some trouble before I go."

"Hardaker I have a feeling that you and I may have some shooting to do very soon. Your sense of smell was very accurate; it's a pity I ignored you."

Before Terry drove away, Wilkes said that he had totalled up the unit's bank balance and having deducted expenses for his farewell surprise party, he had divided the proceeds and wanted everyone to have their share now. Terry received a boxed four-stand diamond and sapphire necklace, a small cloth bag containing twelve unmounted diamonds, ten gold pocket watches and a painting by Miro. He was given a shoebox to give to Don.

In Brick Don opened the shoebox and was delighted with the selection of jewellery and watches it contained. He extracted a gold cigarette case and began to fill it with cigarettes from a packet on his desk.

"I thought you would be glad to be back off leave," he said. "We have moved onto another planet haven't we? I am really looking forward to my move to Bachwald. I made a quick reccy of the town last week and the possibilities that we can have ultra entertainment at our private parties are there, ready and waiting. You know that in October, Wilkes assigned all the children DPs who arrived without any parents to an orphanage he'd sorted in Bachwald? Well I took a look at it. There must be fifty girls there who look as ripe as young cherries; they are dying to be plucked; many of them, untouched by Russian members. There was one pretty blonde of twelve who could be mistaken for a seven-year-old. I want her for Christmas."

Terry stood with his back to the blazing log fire in the study and surveyed the round table and three chairs set in the middle of the dimly lit room. The teapot and three cups and saucers were on a tray in the centre of the table and on a chest of drawers to the side of the room were three glasses and a bottle of fine Cognac. He was wearing black highly polished shoes and his uniform trousers. His white linen shirt and cravat were not official uniform, but he felt more like von Lutken when wearing some of von Lutken's styles. On his trouser belt was the little leather holster inside of which was a recently oiled and loaded pistol. At ten minutes past eight that evening Otto followed Manfred and Ingrid Schrader into the study.

"I will keep Mr and Mrs Schrader's suitcases in the car sir," he said. "I will be outside in the corridor when you need me." He then went to the bedroom, collected the Tommy gun and with some display walked from the room and closed the door behind him.

"Good evening Mr Schrader and Ingrid. Please sit down at the table. Help yourselves to the tea. It is freshly made and hot. You must be cold having stood in the freezing wind that sweeps passed the Creamery. Perhaps a stronger drink would warm you more quickly. The Cognac is excellent but if you prefer Mr Schrader I can offer Schnapps. I am sorry Ingrid but my cellar contains no Pocheen."

Terry moved the bottle and glasses to the table and sat in the chair facing the fire and with his back to the door. The Schraders had removed their coats and Terry noted that they were both wearing more than one layer of outer clothing. He saw the hem of a second dress below the skirt Ingrid had on.

"Rather late to be starting a long journey, is it not?" Terry asked.

"Your observational prowess is commendable, my dear boy. We have been preparing for our excursion for some weeks but have found it necessary to commence rather hastily. Our schedule includes the use of Mr Reck's coach service to Hanover which departs from his garage at seven o'clock tomorrow morning. It is general knowledge in the town that we boarded the midday bus to Luneburg today, which indeed we did. We alighted from that conveyance some mile north of here. We want it to be known that we had vacated the area prior to your return from vacation. Our being here and talking to you would endanger our fragile future. For my part I believe it is a reckless risk we should not have taken. My dear wife insisted." Manfred Schrader nodded formally to his wife. Terry turned to her.

"Still so silent Ingrid. Have you decided which English accent you will use tonight? The German one is unnecessary, as we have no German witnesses of consequence. I find the posh Cheshire one snobby. The Irish one appeals though."

Ingrid spoke quietly in an educated Cheshire accent.

"I had to tell you of the danger you're in. We are running away, but I could not leave you without a warning."

"Now what I have to do," said Terry," is to decide which facts you are about to tell me are true and which are lies."

"We have never had the need to lie to you Sergeant," insisted Ingrid.

"You mean that the interview forms we completed together at our first meeting were correct in every detail?"

"Strangely," interrupted Mr Schrader, "they were. Your inexperience in interview techniques was contemptible. You should have perceived that there were interludes in our histories and enquired about them. Then we would have been untruthful."

"Ingrid you said you were born in England?" Terry snapped at her.

"I said I was raised and educated in Wilmslow, Cheshire, which is true. I was born in Cork. My father was active in the Irish independence movement and took part in the Easter Rebellion of 1916. He was arrested and your soldiers killed him. I was sent to live with a relative in Wilmslow. I was four years old. My hatred of the British started at that age. By the time I had reached University I had learned of the British atrocities done to our people. Less than seventy years before two million Irish men, women and children had been starved to death by British greed and ignorance. To the British, the Irish have always been worthless peasants. The evil you have done over centuries is damnable.

I told no one of my stomach wrenching hatred of the British, but I planned to one day return to Ireland and join the Republican movement. I met Manfred and we fell in love. I only then told him of my desire to hurt Britain. To my astonishment he confided to me that he too had a deep hatred of all things British. His unjustified internment and maltreatment during the Great War had wounded him."

"May I be impolite and intervene in my wife's confessions. I had related to you that I had found employment in 1921 as a teacher in Munich. I neglected to inform you that I lost that position two years later. Soon afterwards our Military Intelligence Bureau employed my services. The department is known in German as the Abwehr and was eventually, and during all of my association with it, headed by Admiral Canaris. He was the most astute and intelligent man I have had the pleasure to meet. He was not a Nazi and was sadly murdered by the Gestapo. I was trained in espionage in Bavaria and in 1930 was sent to Manchester University. Apart from my teaching assignments I travelled widely around the north of England. I visited military establishments and armament factories. On one occasion in Preston, I was left alone in the drawing office of a firm that built your army's latest tank. I purloined a copy of the design and specifications.

By 1933 we had the suspicion that my cover had been penetrated and I was ordered to return to Germany. By then I had married Ingrid and she had become aware of my double life. She supported me wholeheartedly and derived satisfaction from my efforts to undermine the security of Britain."

"As I told you," went on Ingrid after a nod from Manfred, "we worked in Frankfurt at the I G Fabens offices. Manfred travelled widely combining difficult translation work with the gathering of information for the Bureau. I did work in the Personnel department and it was there that I began to feel uneasy about the labour regulations and use of slave labour. Manfred mentioned this to his military commanders and as you are now aware everyone who should have felt guilty turned to face the other way. In 1939 we moved to Hamburg. Manfred said he had found a placement in an adult education facility, as controller of language teaching. That was absolutely true. The adults were trainee spies."

Mr Schrader again took up the story.

"The work was absorbing. I operated in numerous languages and had time to study their use and our teaching methods. Sadly the military control of the school slipped into the hands of the extremely political SS. I became aware of the atrocities and misguided morals of a substantial proportion of my fellow citizens. Some of the men and women I was endeavouring to educate were fanatical anti Semites. The illogicality of their arguments was monstrous. I came to realise that I was not assisting my country in its war with the despised British, but I was being used to further the aims of a government of evil gangsters. On the death of our boy, the ever considerate Admiral Canaris arranged for me to receive indefinite sick leave. As we told you we removed here to Altewiese."

"We believe that Manfred's work as a spy was legitimate," Ingrid said, "but to be associated with the killing machine was not. We have seen the newsreels and I have translated Jacob's experiences and we have come to hate Germany as much, if not more, than we hate Britain. We can no longer stay here and remain happy.

Before we go I need to tell you of the conspiracy of evil which exists and is growing in Altewiese. Manfred thinks that I should not, but that would be us turning to face the other way again. You are very close to Paula Rozen-Kranz and therefore you may choose to disbelieve what I am about to tell you. She is the head of the SS escape network for this district. She came here over eighteen months ago to establish safe accommodation for escaping criminals. You commandeered the hotel she was using, so she used Kurt's house for a time and now the factory offices are employed to house criminal travellers. She was married to a hero of the SS. When he was made Governor of the concentration camp at Bergen-Belsen, she worked for him."

"She told me she never saw inside the camp," Terry calmly stated.

"She and her husband lived in the camp. She was given a rank in the SS and supervised the women guards. She was known as the 'Bitch of Belsen'."

"But her son objected to the way prisoners were treated."

"Mrs Rozen-Kranz gave birth to a son nineteen years ago," said Manfred, "he died of diphtheria at the age of two."

"No that was her daughter some years earlier."

"Her daughter was still born. Did she show you photographs of her husband?"

"Yes many."

"And of her son?"

"No, none."

Ingrid spoke with sympathy.

"When her husband was given a regiment of 'Deaths Head' troops to command in battle, she moved from Belsen."

"Yes she told me she went to live near her parents in Munich."

"In Munich or near Munich?" asked Manfred.

"I think she said ten miles west of Munich."

"The village she moved to ten miles west of Munich is known as Dachau. She had the rank of SS Major and was in command of the women's camp. She was highly praised by the elite staff of the SS. She often dined with Himmler. She is a highly respected member of the inner circle of madmen. And, you don't believe us do you?" pleaded Ingrid loudly.

"Oh yes, I believe you." There was silence at Terry's blandly delivered remark. "Her henchman in Altewiese is Kurt Muller, who is your lover Ingrid."

"I will answer him my dear," said Manfred. "When Kurt Muller first arrived here I became concerned for our safety. I was known by the Gestapo to be a supporter of the disgraced Canaris. I knew who Muller was and realised his purpose. I requested Ingrid to ingratiate herself with him. Muller seduced my wife, but was less than professional in her bed. Paula Rozen-Kranz needed to know what was being said to you after you dismissed her translation services in favour of those provided by Ingrid. She asked Muller to interrogate Ingrid from his pillow. For my part I wanted to discover what level of tyranny was about to exist in our midst. I encouraged Ingrid to interrogate him in his post coital defencelessness. In the world of espionage this practice is not unusual. Ingrid was not hurt and I am not a jealous husband. When you transferred Ingrid to the police station and re-employed Paula, Kurt had no further need of Ingrid's bedtime stories and did not invite her to join him again. From her vantage point in the police station Ingrid could observe the development of the SS operation without the need to resort to exaggerating his masculinity for him. From my vantage point at the school, I have watched the movement of persons through the factory gate.

We have come to the conclusion that something spectacular will occur imminently, or is in our midst even now. We have recently come under suspicion. People who threaten the network are eliminated. You attract a modicum of their protection through your acquiescence or naiveté. They would not appreciate a horde of British troops in their lair investigating any mishap that you may have befallen. Kurt Muller and Ralf Engelbart enticed three probably innocent young men to the factory last Saturday night. The factory chimneys have disgorged acrid smelling fumes since. But then one of the two regular guests at the factory was commandant of Chelmno Camp and Crematorium. The taller of the two so called factory managers was Himmler's personal bodyguard for many years before transfer to disposal duties at Ravensbrueck."

"But," said Terry, "they were able to write a technical shopping list for the fertiliser."

"No, Paula would have written that list. She was a University graduate in chemistry many years ago. Kurt Muller, under his previous name was head of the Gestapo in Berlin. The opera singer Anna-Marie Becker recognised him. I believe her husband and manager were both Jewish and were arrested in Berlin. Anna-Marie spent weeks at the Gestapo headquarters pleading for their release and would have faced Muller on many occasions. Her death was certainly under the hands of Mrs Rozen-Kranz and her pillow."

"And Doctor Dressler," asked Terry quietly, "and Kahler, the Meyers and Fromming….. were their deaths arranged by Paula?"

"Yes Sergeant they were," Ingrid replied, "Dressler was to arrange for the killing to take place. He worked under threat from Paula. His death was not foreseen and no one but you knows why he died. The policeman Willi Neelmeyer was our friend and was trying to infiltrate both the SS controlled police and the Nazi Party enthusiasts. The old men in that room were dreamers and without von Lutken could not organise a children's party. They were an old man's drinking society, but Paula saw them as a threat to her security and the peace and quiet she wants for her hiding place called Altewiese. She must have suspected Neelmeyer also.

A woman of enormous influence and persuasion tricked you into killing eight innocent men. She hated von Lutken and would have eventually had him killed, but you did that for her too. She knew then that you could be manipulated into killing other of her enemies. We would certainly have been at the top of her list for you quite soon."

"Do you know what major development is likely to take place?" Terry asked, still showing no emotion.

"No," said Ingrid, "but, during the last four or five weeks there has been a great deal of feverish activity. Manfred noted that the two factory managers were buying suits and underclothes at last Saturday's market. The indication being that they are about to travel and will need new identities. Muller has handed virtually all of his police work to Engelbart so he too may be about to move on."

"Do you know anything of the bank director?"

"Nothing at all," said Mr Schrader, "which is remarkable. The increase in the SS activity coincided with his arrival, but that may be a coincidence. I have not met the man and therefore can offer no comment as to his civility, or true identity."

"What do you suggest I do Ingrid?"

"I don't know. You would need considerable reinforcement to tackle this powerful group. I am certain they have light weapons. I have given you the information concerning them because I hate them more than I despise you, a lone British soldier. But I can help you no further."

"Where are you going to take Ingrid, Mr Schrader, after you reach Hanover?"

"We plan to travel west from that destroyed city."

"Many miles in a westerly direction?" suggested Terry.

"A considerable number of miles in a westerly direction."

"Towards a new life," Ingrid sighed, "and another new name. I was born a Mary, in Cheshire I was Evelyn and here in Germany I've been Maria and Ingrid. Perhaps it's time to have Evelyn return. I think it sad that even my name is not a home."

Terry stood and loudly called for Otto. He entered with the Tommy gun raised and ready to fire. Ingrid and Manfred looked shocked and she whispered... "No."

"Otto, make sure you have a full tank of petrol. You and Igor will leave at three in the morning and take Mr and Mrs Schrader to the main railway station in Hanover. They wish to catch the first train out of the city. Then return here and before lunch we will drive around our peaceful town of Altewiese for a while. Mr Schrader, Ingrid, please use my bedroom for what is left of the night for you. The bathroom is also at your disposal. I will sleep in Lara's bed and will not be here to wish you a safe and comfortable journey. So may I say goodbye and thank you?"

At eleven o'clock the next morning Terry strode into the police station and asked to speak to Mrs Schrader. With some difficulty he was made to understand that Ingrid had not arrived at the station that morning. He walked across the square slowly and entered the DP Centre. He spoke to Paula.

"I wanted to have Ingrid do some translation work for me today, but I can't find her. Would you have a couple of hours to spare Paula?"

"Welcome back Sergeant. I hope you had an enjoyable holiday with your parents. I will send someone to Ingrid's house and to the school and check to see if she is ill. I am busy today and wanted to call on the factory and discuss their labour requirements, but that can wait. I do have to visit the bank at twelve-thirty and that is quite important."

"Now that is a lucky because those are the places I wanted to visit today. We can travel and work together. Let's get your coat and bag."

"Just give me five minutes to organise things here," Paula said, but Terry was striding towards her bedroom door at the end of the corridor. Inside her room Terry lifted a silver-framed photograph of her husband. He had noticed it before, but this time said to a startled Paula, "This uniform is different from the one in the other photographs. Your husband is wearing a sword and a wide sash. Are these things to do with the SS Regiment he commanded?"

"Sergeant, you have returned to us with a change in attitude and politeness. You barge into my private room and ask about a photograph, but have not enquired after Fredda and Ludwig, nor even Victoria."

"Mrs Rozen-Kranz, please forgive me. I need to clear up a confusion I have regarding the fertiliser factory and the matter is occupying my mind. You are right though; I will run upstairs and check on Fredda and Victoria."

Terry left the room quickly, but at the turn in the staircase he stopped and listened carefully. As he had assumed he heard the rear door of the hotel open and close gently. He found Fredda in her room sitting on a bed talking to Ludwig. He greeted them and as he asked in single word German and sign language about Ludwig's health, he looked from the window down into the back yard of the hotel and across the road to the house occupied by Kurt Muller. Paula soon appeared at the door of the house and ran towards the DP Centre. Kurt emerged seconds later and headed east along the road which leads to Ingrid's house and the school and eventually to the factory. On the landing Terry met Victoria carrying a covered chamber pot. He kissed her on the cheek and ruffled her hair playfully.

Before he descended the staircase he touched the leather holster at his waist and then bent foreword and adjusted the second pistol which nestled inside his right sock, its barrel wedged into the top of his boot. He checked that his trouser bottoms fell neatly and the concealed gun formed no bulge. He did not wear his overcoat despite the coldness of the frosty morning; he felt warm and excited. In the reception area he smiled at the photograph of Field Marshal Montgomery and saluted the photograph of the King. At the door he corrected the angle of his beret and nodded to Otto who opened the rear door of the car and bowed to Paula as she climbed in.

One of the two gates to the factory was open and they drove through and parked in front of the office doors. Through the windows it could be seen that oil lamps were burning on the first floor. Terry and Paula entered the building and mounted the wooded stairs. The two German managers were sitting along side each other at a table already laid for lunch.

"Good morning gentlemen," Terry said through Paula's translation. "I thought you would have been on the factory floor preparing for the production of fertiliser. No please do not rise; Mrs Rozen-Kranz can show me around the living quarters you have created."

Terry walked quickly through the rooms that had once been used as offices and a canteen. He returned to the two men.

"A very nice billet gentlemen. Four bedrooms and eight beds would seem a little excessive for just the two of you. And the kitchen is well stocked. I assume that you are therefore about to start production at any moment?"

The slightly shorter of the two men who Terry knew as Erwin and now suspected had been a commandant of a concentration camp, stood and replied.

"Sergeant.... an unexpected visit, but welcome. All but one chemical and bulking agent is now in our warehouse. As soon as the last ingredient is available the factory will commence production. The boilers and machinery are all in good working order and have been tested. Mrs Rozen-Kranz has been pressuring us to enrol the factory workers early and to have them fully trained before the arrival of the last chemical. Only this morning did my colleague and I come to the decision to accept her proposals although this will put a strain on our finances. Mrs Rozen-Kranz even there has been a wonderful supporter and has engaged on our behalf in negotiations with the Director of the bank."

"What bulking agents are you going to use?" Terry asked, now less confident in the perceived incompetence of the managers.

"We will have two fertiliser compounds produced here. The first one to be mixed will use wood ash as filler. We have obtained sawdust, bark and waste wood from the Timber Company and have sufficient to create one ton of ash. A nitrogen oxide is missing though; perhaps you could use your contacts in Hamburg to find two hundred pounds weight of it for us?"

"I understand you were in charge of a factory that produced large quantities of ash in Poland. Am I correct in believing that was near the town of Chelmno?" Terry asked, his hand moving slowly to rest on the holster.

"Your informer is accurate. The ash of the last factory I managed was used in an undiluted state as fertiliser. The ash naturally contained a form of bone meal, but even so was only of limited benefit. It helped to breakdown stubborn clay. The compound we will produce here will have great value in the increasing of crop yields and will contain a formula for defence against root pests."

"Do you intend to remain in Altewiese for a long time?" asked Terry.

Erwin cast his eyes at his colleague who had remained sitting at the table.

"No we were planning to see production start and appoint a competent manager and then move on. Your knowledge of my previous employment may mean we will have to reconsider our schedule. A more urgent departure may be necessary. We had planned to leave your quiet town on the last day of this year."

Terry was now confused. The man had more or less admitted to being a concentration camp commander, but had offered no threat. If he could start production, that would be useful to the town. When he left in four weeks time this man's crimes would be someone else's problem. He chose to press on but with much less venom than he had rehearsed.

"Your silent friend... what was his previous job?"

The second man rose to his feet, clicked his heels together and gave a small bow of the head.

"My name is Heinrich. I have worked in a number of police and military posts. Notably I was a bodyguard to the Reichfuhrer SS. I have carried out functions similar to those of my colleague, Erwin. I was stationed north of Berlin until the unfortunate arrival of the Russian Army. I, too, now find that my future would appear to be in your hands. Sergeant, what are you going to do?"

"Nothing. But, with or without nitrogen, I want this factory in production by Friday of next week. In January I want the agricultural agent in town to begin selling the fertiliser throughout Northern Germany. The factory is owned by the town council and it will be in need of funds next year."

Erwin raised a Teutonic eyebrow at this.

"The town council had to sell sixty percent of its shares in this fertiliser company to the bank in order to raise sufficient capital to commence operation. The bank is now the major stock holder."

"No one told me of this transaction. Did you know of it Mrs Rozen-Kranz? I gave this factory to the town. If I want it for myself I will take it, bank or no bank. I rule here unopposed. We must visit the Director of the bank and put him right. You two carry on and get this place running quickly. I will remember your employment record details but use the information only if you fail to produce saleable fertiliser in one week and are still in Altewiese in January. Good day to you."

As Terry turned to leave he left Paula translating his words but she was talking to them for far too long. He sat in the car and waited for her.

"You have the Tommy gun under your seat don't you Otto? Good. When Mrs Rozen-Kranz joins us hand it to me. Then drive to the bank. Park with one set of wheels on the first step. Then get the shotgun from the boot of the car and stand between the car and the bank doors and scare away anyone who tries to enter. If you have any trouble fire one of the cartridges and I'll come out and join you. People who I would not like to interrupt my meeting at the bank would be Muller or any of his police force and the two SS types who live in these offices. If I'm not back with you by one-thirty, you drive straight to Sergeant Wilkes in Bachwald and tell him I need Hardaker. Say 'Sergeant Hall needs Hardaker'. Oh, hello Paula, I thought you had got lost in the hotel they have created in the offices. We really must sit down and discuss the value of my lack of observation of your network with its fugitives passing under my nose and me receiving no reward for my carelessness."

Paula was shocked by the speed at which Otto had driven the car into the square and onto the bank steps. Terry did not wait for her but strode purposefully through the bank door and into the grand hall of its retail area. He realised that he had never before entered the building and was unsure where he would find the Director's office. Towards the rear of the hall was a wide and imposing staircase and at the top of it stood Kurt Muller. He was glaring at Terry and his fists were buried into his waistband. As Terry marched towards him and began to scale the steps he noticed with astonishment but no fear that tucked into Kurt's belt, just to the right of his buckle, was a black lugar pistol. Paula was hurrying to catch up with Terry.

"Sergeant, slow down, we have plenty of time. Our appointment with the Director is not until twelve-thirty."

Terry reached the landing and faced Kurt. Paula appeared between them and spoke German authoritatively to Kurt who nodded and walked smartly down the corridor to their left. She turned to Terry and spoke sharply.

"I am ordering you to stop and reconsider what you are doing. You have no idea of the danger you are in. I don't know how much that dreamer Schrader knew or guessed, nor how much they told you, but Sergeant you have entered a lion's den without invitation. My advice would be to take Victoria to your bed and do to her whatever is your latest perversion."

"Firstly, my dear Mrs Rozen-Kranz, you will never order me to do anything." Terry was angry. "Secondly I do not require an invitation to visit a lowly Bank Manager, I rule this sodding town, and thirdly Victoria does for me what a jealous fifty-four year old woman did for me eight weeks ago."

Paula stood silently for a moment and then smiled and began to laugh.

"Touché, my dear. Until that night I saw you as the son I had lost but I became confused and thought I was twenty and you were so like Peter."

"The son you had lost when he was two years old?"

"Yes, Carl Peter would have grown to look like his father and you have always reminded me of my husband before we were married. Sergeant Hall, I have asked the Bank Director for permission to meet him immediately. He likes me and therefore may agree. If he says no, we will wait. If you barge into his office they will kill you. The Director of this Bank is a very, very powerful man. He knows everything about you and wanted me to arrange for him to meet with you in one or two week's time. There is Kurt - he's waving us to join him; that must mean that we have our appointment now. Sergeant, please give that pistol and machinegun to Kurt without a fuss. Meet the Director, hear what he has to say and then decide on the heroics you will perform but remember you are in more danger than you could ever imagine; take care of that temper of yours."

They entered a small wood panelled office where a young man in a dark suit sat at an ornate table with gilded legs. He nodded and Kurt opened the tall double doors to the Director's office. The room they entered was wide and very long. Terry realised that the bank was considerably bigger than the other buildings in the square. The room was tall and had a carved wooden ceiling. It was lit by a series of electric lights, each over a painting, equally spaced along the length of the room; Terry counted six paintings on each wall. At the far end of the room was a large desk. On it stood two tall candlesticks with electric bulbs in the shape of candle flames. There were two piles of manila folders to the left of the desk and a man sat behind it.

Some yards behind him burned a log fire in an elaborate stone fireplace and above the mantle shelf hung an enormous painting. Its extravagantly carved frame reached the ceiling and was wider than the wide fireplace. The painting was of an armour-clad warrior on a white horse; they appeared to be life sized. The warrior carried a lance from which flapped a red, white and black ribbon. The horse wore chest armour and the scenery behind them was of forests and hills. The painting dominated the room. Terry glanced quickly to the smaller paintings on the side walls. To his left they were by Dutch Masters, with skating and household scenes; to the right were modern classics. Terry stopped and then walked casually to this wall and examined the first four painting in detail. This took some minutes and eventually Terry sensed that the man had left his desk and was standing at his shoulder. Paula was close and translated the words he spoke.

"Do you recognise any of these paintings, young man?"

"Yes sir," and immediately Terry wished he had not said 'sir'. "This one is by Paul Cézanne and is a scene from Provence. This is by the Spanish painter Picasso and this by the Italian, Modigliani, a very typical head shape. This one is a miniature by Salvador Dali - it almost certainly contains a double image, but I cannot see it yet."

"Which of these paintings do you like and which is the most valuable?"

"The Cézanne would receive the highest price at auction, but my personal favourite would be the Dali - its detail and colour and deception are magnificent."

"Excellent. That's exactly what I have been told. Please come and sit at the desk; we have some matters to discuss. Would you like a drink? Tea, perhaps, no?"

Terry sat on the only other chair in the room and Paula stood at his shoulder. She showed great respect for the man on the other side of the desk. Kurt Muller was standing to the left of the desk facing Terry. He held Terry's pistol in his left hand. He was holding it by its barrel in a non-threatening manner but his face and features showed fury. The Director was of medium height, clean-shaven and wore no eyeglasses. He was approximately forty-five years old and his unruly hair was unfashionably long. By contrast he was dressed in an immaculate dark grey business suit and black tie over a shining white shirt. He sat in a relaxed position with his hands resting on the arms of his grand chair. He smiled from thin narrow lips but his piercing blue eyes were deadly serious. His stare was menacing, but his voice was calm, quiet and slightly high pitched.

"We have not had the chance to meet before," he said. "My name is Heinrich von Wolf, I am the Director of the Banking and Finance Group of which this is one of their branches. Until recently I was in control of the Swedish element of the organisation. We are in transit to Frankfurt where our new headquarters building is being repaired. I wished to spend a few months at a branch office and have taken the opportunity to interview and recruit staff for the Head Office. I plan to move to Frankfurt by the 1st of January at the latest. It should have been earlier, but we had a small disagreement with the American authorities regarding my residence and its security. I am afraid that I have poached your Chief of Police but am consoled to learn that his deputy is an able man. Your translator has requested to stay in Altewiese, although I feel that English speakers will be in great demand in our business world."

Terry was about to interrupt and tell this Wolf that he, Terry, was the Chief of Police and Wolf could take Inspector Muller with pleasure but he didn't.

"Our Finance Group is International. We have three branch offices in Scandinavia, three in Switzerland and seven in Spain. There are offices in New York, Buenos Aires, Montevideo and Asuncion. We have only two offices operating in Germany at this time but many more are planned. Primarily we operate as a bank. We lend money to businesses. We have taken the information we gain from research into those businesses to purchase all or part of the stock ownership of promising companies. We also own shares in companies who borrow from us; it is a kind of security for our investment risk. As a result of these activities we now own, for example, a motor car assembly plant in South America, a European tyre factory, a vast acreage of cattle ranching, a Spanish travel and steamship company, a soft drinks manufacturer in America, a steel works in Sweden and many more things as varied and various as that. We are an extremely rich group and have large reserves of cash, gold and valuables at our disposal."

Here Director von Wolf stopped speaking in order for Terry to fully appreciate his importance and financial power. Terry took a deep breath and plunged in.

"Was the gold in your reserves extracted from the mouths of dead Jews?"

There was a silence. Kurt reversed his hold on Terry's pistol. Director von Wolf's eyes narrowed and the smile fell from his lips.

"We have at our disposal one hundred million Bank of England five pound notes, and a marginally smaller value in fifty dollar bills. We have six hundred tons of gold, obtained from various sources, including some seized from criminals in Europe. It is our plan to create a strong and healthy conglomeration of profitable companies through out the free world. Our resources will be used to strengthen our peoples' defence against the evil of communism and the Asian hordes. Our money will help defend Stone in Staffordshire as well as Altewiese in Schleswig Holstein. Do you know this painting behind me Terry Hall?"

"No sir."

"This is a fine painting of King Heinrich I. He was a King in Medieval Germany who defended his country against the invasion of the Barbarians; the filth that came to us from the east. He defeated that scum and helped to protect the spread of civilisation and Christianity. That is the ultimate aim of our Financial Group. The Directors and Guardians of our company are like the Knights of the Round Table created by King Heinrich I, only instead of swords and horses, we will fight using wealth and commodities. Control of money will win the next international war not A-bombs; you make a note of that young man. In a few years our money will buy politicians and ideas. The controllers of wealth will be the controllers of the world.

And so, I have a proposition for you Mr Hall that will make you unimaginably rich. The money you will earn can be used by you to buy any lifestyle you have ever dreamed of or could have envisaged. Women, fancy cars, holidays in the South of France, all these can be yours. You can buy a life of ease for your parents and a life of luxury for yourself. You will be working indirectly for our Financial Group and our fight against communism and the Russian threat to subjugate our people in Western Europe. You will be part of a strong and powerful team of privileged and professional men and women and you will receive protection from them. And, the job I want you to do is already in your dreams. I want you to become one of the worlds most respected art dealers.

For the next year you should remain here and complete your military service. You will have much spare time and I want you to use it to study art and art history. Mrs Rozen-Kranz will be here with you and will assist you and coach you in your studies. Mr Engelbart will ensure that you are not disturbed by any local trivialities. In February 1947 you will begin to travel Europe visiting art galleries and museums. We will arrange for you to meet artists. Our influence in Spain is considerable and Picasso, Miro and Dali will be delighted and honoured to accept our invitation to talk to you. Your only contact with us will be through your friend Paula. In 1948 we want you to open an art dealership and retail shop in Bond Street, London. You will buy and sell great works of art. We will deliver to you a regular supply of paintings from our stores. These you will sell and keep twenty-five percent of the sale price. You will pay one of our companies the balance. You will be the only London dealer with a steady flow of masterpieces. You will need to fabricate the recent history of many of the paintings, their provenance, but you should have no fear that ownership will be disputed.

Eventually you will expand your dealership and have shops in New York and Singapore and Monaco and Berlin and one day even in a free Moscow. You will own auction houses and be renowned as the most important art dealer of all time. I assure you that even by then you will have sold only a small fraction of our store of paintings. You will sell masterpieces to the King of England personally and may well receive a Knighthood from him. You are not eligible to be a Knight in the service of King Heinrich, as only those of pure blood and whose first language is German can be elected to that exalted position, but Sir Terry Hall sounds attractive I think. You may choose to change your name after you leave the army; you and Paula can invent a snobby British one. What we require in return for giving you the life you want is absolute loyalty to our organisation. You will divulge none of its secrets or aims to anyone on pain of immediate execution. I feel confident that you are a sensible and intelligent Englishman and will appreciate your responsibility and position. I can see a gleam of satisfaction in your eyes. What is your answer to my proposal?"

"I will become the world's most important art dealer sir."

"You will, you will. Is there a painting you would like to take with you now as confirmation of our contract and understanding? No, not that one, not even you could wrest Heinrich I from me. You should take the Cézanne and the Dali as you leave. Have you any questions?"

"Sir, where is Reichfuhrer Himmler?" Terry asked nonchalantly.

"He is dead Mr Hall. Your intelligence people witnessed his suicide." Director von Wolf still did not smile.

"They watched Heinrich Hitzinger die sir. To be honest I have no interest in Mr Himmler and am quite happy to forget all about him and concentrate on studying artists and their works. If you see him you should let him know that the Russians are not convinced of his death and nor are some intelligence people in London. The war is now over sir and we should concentrate on our futures. There were atrocities perpetrated by all sides and we waste our time blaming each other. The dead cannot return. Incidentally that pistol that Muller is holding - it is one of a matching pair. Its partner is resting inside my right sock which should be of concern to you. Lax of your security people, wasn't it? And, sir, it is the face of the Spanish poet, Garcia Lorca, hidden in the painting... typical of Dali."

On February 1st 1946 at three o'clock in the afternoon, Sergeant Terence Hall walked from a large black Mercedes sedan car into the Displaced Persons' Centre and Hospital in Altewiese, British Zone Germany. The reception area was unusually full of people. The staff of the Centre had all gathered there, as had many of the refugees who had passed through the Centre during the last seven months. Town hall officials and policemen were crowded onto the staircase that led to the hospital bedrooms and in the yard to the rear of the Centre a brass band and choir was hiding in preparation for a surprise fanfare and song. Jugs of beer and a large cake were laid on a table normally reserved for interviewing. The framed photograph of King George VI, which hung on the wall behind the leather chair at the table, had been tampered with. A photograph of Sergeant Hall had been pasted to the glass and obscured the King, and coloured paper streamers draped the frame. Terry stood stunned in the double doorway and listened in some embarrassment to the English words of

'Happy Birthday'. He looked at his photograph and smiled and said in an unheard whisper - "You really are the Chief of Police, Judge, jury, executioner, tax collector, Mayor, unopposed ruler and now the King of this bloody town."

CHAPTER TEN

THE OBITUARY

Under 'Lives in Brief' on the obituary page of The Times newspaper printed one day in April 2002, was:

Sir Paul Rose, art dealer and raconteur, was born February 1st, 1927. He died on April 10th, 2002, aged 75.

Owner of The Rose Dealership and founder and patron of The Rose Fellowship, The Rose Academy and The Rose Galleries. Renowned as the world's biggest fine art dealer with offices on four continents, Sir Paul Rose was a leading authority on oil paintings of the twentieth century. Little is known of his education and early life. He emerged at his first shop in Bond Street, London in the late 1940's. His reputation as a bon viveur, and wild party giver, saw him regularly in the company of film stars, artists and royalty. He was an advisor to Anthony Blunt, the Queen's art collection manager and was knighted in 1962. His reputation was sullied in 1964, when arrested but not charged with an assault on a minor. He moved to Monaco soon afterwards. From there he continued to run his art dealer-ships and created a number of charitable organisations aimed at developing young artistic talent. He travelled widely and had homes, at various times, in Spain, Thailand, Goa and Senegal. He returned to live in a retirement home in Guildford in 1998. He never married and leaves no known heirs.

Other titles published by Authors Online Ltd.

FICTION

By Peter Townsend

The Forties Man - ISBN 0-7552-0008-X - £9.95
Trevor must save Saltfleet from an unexploded bomb, with only a stuffed dog, some mismatched allies and the spirit of the Blitz to help him.

The Jet Stone – ISBN 0-7552-0003-9 - £11.95
Following the disappearance of two women in Whitby in the 1880s there is a frantic attempt to find them by two feuding cousins before it is too late.

The Flying Star – ISBN 0-7552-0005-5 - £8.95
Volunteers running a miniature railway are faced with a stark choice of having to commit a murder, or instead see their railway destined for the scrapheap.

By Wendy Anne Lake

Cinder Path – ISBN 0-7552-0017-9 - £8.95
Poignant family saga set in the heart of Lancashire. A sexually steamy story of jealousy, rejection, betrayal and loss. Will Vicky ever find the love she yearns for with Jim.

Inspired Urges – ISBN 0-7552-0019-5 - £12.95
A scintillating saga of rags to riches set on both sides of the Atlantic. Filled with deep sexual prowess and a dangerous ambition.

Sensual Rhythm of Perfect Melody – ISBN 0-7552-0010-1 - £11.95
Melody finds herself beautifully seduced by a tall stranger. In the midst of lust, she is asked what Mel is short for and thoughtlessly gasps out Melody. The consequences are more than far reaching as she descends into a life of an erotic dancer and sex object.

Labyrinth of Desire – ISBN 0-7552-0013-6 - £9.95
The sensual Evie Warrender trains alongside her idol, the handsome, eminent barrister, Bruce Manning. She is stunned one evening, when out of the blue, he leads her into the realms of exotic passion and an excitement she never knew existed

By Nick Wastnage

The Electronic Conspirator - ISBN 0-7552-0007-1 - £11.95

The most unlikely man pulls off the perfect electronic scam. He sets up five innocent, but desperate people, kills himself and escapes with the money: leaving behind a scorned ex-lover and a bitter ex-wife. His tranquillity is short-lived

---

By Tony Stowell

A Little Learning – ISBN 0-7552-0006-3 - £11.95

A work of fiction set in a secondary school that has some deadly accurate messages about the state of education today. A 'must' for all teachers and parents!

The Woolsack Conspiracy – ISBN 0-7552-0011-X - £11.95

A young man has his values turned upside down in this tense thriller, where terrorism meets rural tradition, and where romance and passion are never far from the surface.

By Desmond Tarrant

Power & Beauty – ISBN 0-7552-0015-2 - £12.95

Told with colour and humour, this outstanding novel is based on the truth. It ranges from RAF Bomber Command over Germany in 1944/45 and the heady days of the British Raj in India to international finance and romance - a real pleasure to read.

The Firebrand – ISBN 0-7552-0014-4 - £11.95

This major novel offers first class entertainment and craftsmanship with the latest understanding of what life is all about. It is a real page-turner, essential, vital reading today.

By Alan Taylor

One Day As A Tiger – ISBN 0-7552-0020-9 - £11.95

The last two turbulent decades of the British Raj in India is the exciting setting for an unusual saga of romance and colour imaginatively conceived by an author who lived there at the time.

By Sonia Y Lasser

The Deadly Conference – ISBN 0-7552-0021-7 - £9.95
Top, international scientists agree to gather at a conference eager to present their solutions for cheap and clean energy. Racing against time, the scientists are working around the clock to prove the feasibility of the suggested idea stolen from the big, secret computer program. Strange and bizarre things happen on the way to the conference, scheduled in a resort town in Northern Italy. But who is trying to stop them from achieving their goal?

By Simon Kalik

Blissful Assassination – ISBN 0-7552-0018-7 - £11.95
A thriller that will shock you with its goriness and arouse you with its sexual adventures

By Peter Hughes

Closing Time – ISBN 0-7552-0024-1 - £8.95
A compelling lightheartedness tumbles the reader through the sticky pages of 'Closing Time': Bad behaviour in bedsit land, bar-room philosophy and bodily functions are but some of the juicy centres of this delicious story-telling.

By Susan Shaw

Eleanor – ISBN 0-7552-0026-8 - £11.95
A novel of strong emotional turmoil regarding a woman's strife trying to overcome conventions so as to be equal to the men in her life, after the First World War.

NON-FICTION

By Evelyn Stewart

Totally Discombobulated –ISBN 0-7552-0012-8 - £14.95
A true, and sometimes tragic, family drama covering a period from 1940 through 1982. The story vividly follows the life of our author as she courageously walks through a seemingly unending cessation of spousal abuse, murder, incest and a legacy of turmoil.

By Annette Willoughby

Innocent in Africa - ISBN 0-7552-0009-8 - £14.95
An amusing and poignant story of a teacher from South London who, on an overnight impulse, joins her partner in The Mountain Kingdom of Lesotho.

By Keats Babel

Ant Musings – ISBN 0-7552-0022-5 - £12.95
In 1980s London, Bandit Matthews was a rebellious youngster with strong opinions and a passion for Ant Music. Twenty years later, nothing much had changed...

By Wendy Anne Lake

You've Been Wonderful To Your Father - ISBN 0-7552-0004-7 - £11.95
A heartrending, yet uplifting story of a stroke victim and the tender love of his family.

By Simon Lee

Spiritual Energy 0-7552-0023-3 - £11.95
An 'anti-materialistic, 21st Century Spiritual Metaphysics' which submits that The Mind and The Spirit are Real and Exist in their own right – they are not just 'froth made out of chemicals'! This book provides instead a complete analysis of both the component qualities, and the structure, of Spiritual Energy.

To order a copy of any of the above please fill out this form and post it to.
Authors OnLine Ltd
15-17 Maidenhead Street
Hertford SG14 1DW
England

theeditor@authorsonline.co.uk

Author	Title	ISBN	Price
		Total	
		P&P @ £1.95 per Book	
		Total Due	

Address for Delivery

_____

_____

_____

Post Code_____

Cheque enclosed £_____

www.authorsonline.co.uk